THE DROWNED OATH

Book II of *The Saint's Reckoning*

20251006

ISBN: 978-1-0697068-5-0

www.harwoodjones.com

The Kingdom of the Broken Isles

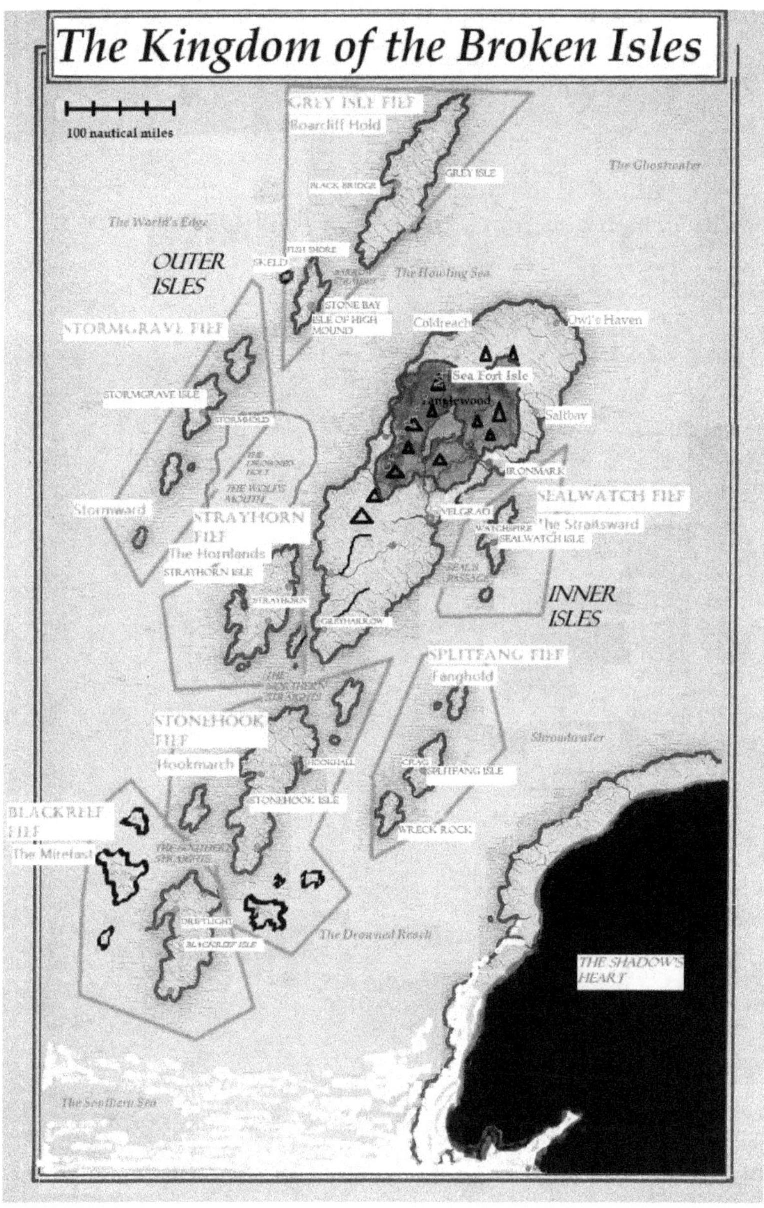

Table of Contents

Chapter I: The Tidecaller and the Witch

We fought in the mires.

We bled in the mires.

And we died.

I was young then—young enough to believe mud washed from steel as easily as from skin. Young enough to think God's light reached everywhere, even into the black hollows where air stank of rot and priests crossed themselves before speaking of what dwelt there.

The mires took us as the sea takes wrecks: slow, patient, without song. We went in as men—steel at our belts, oaths on our lips, banners bright as dawn over Velgrad's harbour. What came out wore the shape of men, and nothing more.

Twenty years have passed, and still I taste black water on my tongue.

The Mirefast war did not begin with swords. It began with ledgers.

South of Sea Fort Isle lay the Hookmarch—shipwrights and stone-cutters, men who knew hammer and chisel better than sword and shield. They bent knee to Mstislav because gold flows easier than blood. Their timber built Velgrad's oars; their quarries raised her walls. Bought fair, bought willing. They thought themselves merchants. We made them grave-diggers.

Beyond them lay the Mirefast: a scattered archipelago strewn across dark water like coins spilled from a dead man's purse. The Brackfolk lived there — dark-eyed as bog-pools, voices thin as wind through reeds. They ruled from manors built on stilts, from islands that vanished with tide, following marsh-priests who read futures in decay and spoke to gods whose names we dared not mouth.

I spat when they passed our markets. We all did. Something in their gaze made faith feel paper-thin.

Then Rogdai rose. Rogdai the Tidecaller.

He was broad for his people, shoulders thick as bound reeds, eyes narrow and measuring, as if the world were always smoke. Patience dwelt in him, more dangerous than any blade. They whispered he could summon fog from clear skies, call voices from beneath waves. Ships that strayed near his waters came back with crews babbling of shadows moving where no shadows should be.

He came as tide comes — silent, then sudden, then everywhere at once. Village by village, island by island, he bound the scattered Tide-Lords beneath his banner. Some with steel, others with promises of northern gold, still others with blood-oaths sworn under new moons.

At his side walked Dobrava. A priestess — abomination enough to make northern fathers cross themselves and spit. She prayed to waters with no saints. The waters answered.

I saw her once, when a Brackfolk vessel docked in Velgrad. She stood at the prow like a carved figurehead, robes the colour of deep water, hair grey as storm-clouds. Even from the quay, her gaze fixed me. As if she knew secrets I had forgotten about myself. The gulls fell silent. The tide seemed to wait on her leave.

Together they took the straits. First Greenvault, then Saltmere. Not heathen islets but lands that had flown Mstislav's banner, whose sons had marched in our ranks. Soon every merchant seeking passage bent to Rogdai's horn. Our granaries rotted while his ships bore southern wheat to northern ports. The Hookmarch bent quick. Gold knows no loyalty.

Fear smoked through Velgrad's streets. Priests thundered of heresy, and the Queen declared God's will revealed. When gold fails and trade turns sour, kings reach for swords.

Mstislav declared holy war.

I was nine years blooded then—trained from boyhood, sworn at thirteen kneeling in my father's blood. The Boarcliff had taught me the weight of a blade; the Straightsward, how men die. Or so I thought.

Bands gathered in Velgrad's courtyards. Veterans whose scars shone like medals. Oath-sworn who bore steel that had tasted victory. Shields painted with the Grey Hand that had never known defeat.

The outer isles fell quickly. Reeds and mud-brick could not stand against our iron. Their bows were keen, their blades curved and sharp, but they were fishermen conscripted, not soldiers. We cut through them like wolves among sheep. We planted banners, burned dead, took what we pleased.

But the Mirefast itself was different.

That place is not land as decent folk know it. Half-world, caught between earth and water, belonging to neither. Paths vanish when the tide turns. The air itself conspires—fog thick as wool swallowing men until their shouts sound distant when they stand close enough to touch.

Step wrong and you sink—not quick, like drowning, but slow, like nightmare. Black mud tugging at boots, knees, chest. Men I had known since boyhood vanished beside me, the mire closing smooth as silk. Only ripples. Only silence.

Our weapons betrayed us. Heavy swords dragged us under. Shields caught in reeds. We learned long knives, short spears. Learned moss-colours that meant solid ground, bird-calls that warned of deep water.

Rogdai never faced us in open field. He struck and vanished, a horn in the mist, arrows whispering out of fog, silence closing again. At dawn, sentries dead with throats split like second mouths. At dusk, comrades gone without a sound, only bootprints in mud.

The Brackfolk fought as their land fought—patient, cunning, treacherous as black water. They rose from pools we thought empty, struck with poison, sank away. They moved through waterways like ghosts, channels unseen to us.

We burned stilt-houses, shrines carved from bog-oak and hung with bone. Smoke rose in still air, visible for miles, but the people vanished deeper into their maze. And the more we burned, the less the world resembled anything made by God.

Even Mstislav felt it. He marched with us, banner high above sucking mud. But his laughter died, his eyes grew restless, his crown weighed heavy. The golden king bent toward black pools like a penitent.

In that place where God's light seemed far, honour learned to drown.

We learned to kill quietly. Strike before cries could rise. Leave no voice alive. We told ourselves it was war, necessity. But war was only the name.

We fought as Brackfolk fought. Ambush at dawn in thick mist. Torture for secrets of waterways. Kill them after, silent.

In learning their ways, we lost something else—the clean surface of the soul, the part that reflects light instead of swallowing it. The mire took that as surely as it took our dead.

At last we drove Rogdai to his stronghold—a manor on stilts above a lake of glassy black water. We ringed it like wolves around a stag. Arrows could have ended him. Fire could have consumed the hall. But Rogdai was not a rat to be smoked.

He emerged at dawn, walking the bridge alone. No armour but mail, no weapon but his father's sword. Behind him, smoke rose from the chimney—Dobrava still inside, waiting.

"Mstislav," he called. "You have taken my lands, burned my halls. Will you face me yourself, or hide behind oath-sworn like a merchant behind guards?"

The challenge carried strange weight—not defiance but acceptance. The certainty of a man who knows death has found him and chooses to meet it standing.

Mstislav stepped forward. He might have loosed arrows. Instead he drew his sword—the blade that carved his kingdom—and met Rogdai on muddy ground.

Steel rang in grey morning. Rogdai was skilled, but Mstislav was anointed. When it ended, Rogdai lay still, his sword fallen. The king bowed his head. There had been honour in the Tidecaller. He was a worthy foe.

But Dobrava—her ending was different.

They dragged her from the burning hall, robes torn, eyes blazing defiance. We had been too long in the swamps. Too long breathing rot and fear. The men who bound her were not those who had sailed from Velgrad. They had learned cruelty, found killing came easy when you ceased to see enemies as human.

I will not tell what we did. Her screams carried farther than any prayer. When it was finished, we declared evil vanquished. But evil does not die. It only changes hands. Her blood spread like poison. We drank deep.

We emerged from Mirefast mud-caked, hollow-eyed, banners flying. Priests sang that God had granted triumph. The Church proclaimed heretics defeated.

But when I closed my eyes, I heard her screams. Saw black water swallowing friends and foes alike.

Dobrava taught me the beast lived beneath my skin. The wolf-skin. It smiled with my lips, licked them with her blood. The king named me Volkolak in those reeds, and pride shone in his eyes.

I did not want to own it. Yet I wore it sixteen years. Mstislav made use of what the mire had unearthed. Men cheered when I cut paths through his enemies. They feared me, and fear was counted loyalty. Even the king loved me for it. Worst of all, I loved myself for it. I was unstoppable. Steel meant nothing. Walls meant nothing. The Volkolak made a weapon of my body.

But the part that might have prayed, that might have lifted its face to heaven—he drowned in the reeds. With every village burned, every throat cut, that self sank deeper until nothing remained but the cruel delight of killing.

And even that burned out.

A strange thing: the more I slaughtered, the less it filled me. When Mstislav's enemies were gone and he offered reward, I wanted nothing. Not gold, not land, not women. I wanted silence. I wanted death. The beast was fed, and I was hollow.

So I chose exile. Skeld's rocks and winds. No war, no crown, no praise. Only stillness, which I mistook for absolution. But stillness was only emptiness.

I swore never to return to that cursed place. Swore it on my father's memory, on my oath to Mstislav, on what remained of my soul.

Yet here I am again.

And I feel the beast stirring, eager for the dark water that first fed it.

Chapter II: Radalya's Scroll

The punt was a coffin of wood and pitch, built for black water, not honest sea. Flat-bottomed, narrow, tarred boards creaking at every shift. The cross-plank slick with moss, seams weeping oil that gleamed like old blood. Fragile as bone if caught broadside in a swell.

We slid between reeds tall as a man's reach, grey stalks rattling like bones in a charnel basket. Black water stretched mirror-still, broken only by our wake and the slow rings where fish rose to breathe. Bog-oak trunks jutted like stakes of some ancient fort, iron-hard from centuries of rot. Between them, moss spread red and yellow, disguising hollows deep enough to swallow a horse. Mist hung low, making the world seem half-born from water and shadow.

Three months since the Black Altar — since Illarion seized Saint Ilyin's burning arm. Three months of watching him stare into fire that should not burn.

Aboard *The Grey Hand* he kept the iron-bound chest close, ugly as sin, ash and bone smouldering inside. Saint Ilyin's arm — blackened yet unconsumed, the bones laid careful as relic or trap. Bogdan swore the saint's fire held power enough to heal kings and raise thrones. But I saw no cure in it, only judgment.

Illarion bent to the chest and whispered over it, as if to crown or bride. Bogdan circled him like an eel in deep water — hissing prayers, feeding him words, never letting him stand alone. Guarding, waiting, teaching, all at once.

I kept apart. The oath I had sworn — to kill Illarion if his sickness overtook him — no longer felt distant. Each time I saw him bent to that fire, I felt the noose draw tighter.

Better to chase relics than linger near that one.

So we hunted Rumours through reed-villages and tide-marked towns. Taverns thick with fish-smoke and wary eyes. Markov carried the talk, smirks and boasts spilling easy from him, hoping to draw loose tongues. I followed, each step pulled more by oath than hope.

A relic here. Saint's fire there. All lies.

Doors shut when we asked of old temples. No one wanted to remember.

Yet memory clung in the mire like moss to stone. Twenty years since Mstislav broke the Brackfolk, but not all had drowned. I'd seen it myself — Otets hanged with their knives still bloody, Volkhvy screaming on stakes while their reed-lamps guttered. Their Martial Houses pulled down, temples rebuilt as churches, iron crosses hammered where spirals once shone.

Christ proclaimed. But the mire bent Him to its own shape.

Ivan the Broad ruled now, or so it was said. A warrior once, broad-chested and salt-sworn, made Thane, now gone soft. He let Brack rites creep back so long as taxes came — peat, fish, hides. Priests fumed, governors quarreled, but the people endured. They twisted old ways into new. Crosses carved from driftwood, daubed with spirals of white clay. Hymns sung in the cadence of reed-chants. Prayers bent to silence, breath, and stillness.

In Driftlight we found it laid bare.

A church named for Saint Vira, but the Brackfolk whispered another name: the Temple of the Way. The altar stood over bowls of water filled with reeds. Children and men moved together—stances, steps, open hands. Half prayer, half strike. I saw the Otets in their drills, the Volkhvy in their stillness. Both outlawed, yet surviving beneath Christ's face.

The deacon led them—lean man in linen, voice clipped, hands precise. But beside him moved a woman with no title. Radalya Tide-Reader. All deferred to her though she claimed no office. Her eyes were old as peat-smoke. When she passed, it seemed even the reeds leaned in her direction. Then the cross.

Markov threw himself into the stances, fists snapping, feet stamping the rushes. He said it was for favour, for our quest. I knew better. The hermit monk at Dobroslav's cloister had told him he was too old for the Way of the Hand. Still he lingered, convinced patience could be outrun if he only moved faster.

Radalya saw him. She spoke in half-riddles, words like water slipping through fingers:

"A reed bends, yet its root holds. The hand forgets, but the body remembers. The water carries whom it chooses."

Markov lapped it up, eager as a boy. I stayed close—to guard him, and because I didn't trust her. Once she turned those eyes on me, and it was like she saw past scars and sinew to what lay beneath.

My soul is no thing to be examined.

So it went, dawn after dawn, until one evening she came with a scroll wrapped in oiled leather, sealed with dark wax.

"If your path is true," she said, "begin in Reedmarch. The great Mire has temples yet. Perhaps, if persuaded, they will guide you further."

Markov near snatched it from her hand, grinning like he'd won a prize. I saw something else. A gift, yes—but a gift that bound us deeper into the mire, and into her judgment.

Now Markov sat in the bow, one hand trailing in cold water.

"Think she was lying?" he asked.

"Radalya? No."

"Then why now, after months of shrugs?"

The scroll lay against his chest, bark-paper that smelled of fish and smoke. A pass to deeper waters—or a trap dressed as kindness. I couldn't shake the weight of her gaze when she'd spoken.

"Maybe she tired of your questions," I said.

"Hardly. I'm her chosen pupil."

Markov could charm, if you liked talk that ran like a brook—quick, restless, always noisy. But I doubted she heard him as he believed. There was design in her hand, only too subtle for me to read.

We rounded a bend. A town rose from the water, stilts and smoke lifting from mist like something half-born.

"This is the start, Yarik—I can feel it," Markov declared. "And you said my training was a waste of time!"

I hadn't. Though I'd thought it often enough.

Radalya had sent us true. But I knew enough of Brackfolk ways to expect little kindness.

It was a beginning, yes. Whether it led to fire's judgment or only death in the mire, I couldn't yet tell.

Chapter III: Reedmarch

Two dozen houses on stilts, built where the flood never withdrew. Reed walls patched with mud and bark, clay chimneys leaking smoke. Nets strung between posts, heavy with weed and small silver fish. Everything grey-brown, wet, patient—as if the land had grown these dwellings the way it grew reeds.

Reedmarch lay at the edge of law. Northmen called it a parish, bound to Crown and saints. But the Great Mire stretched east of Driftlight for leagues—a drowned heart no man wished to govern. On parchment it was quartered among four governors, but none would plant their hall within its flood. Beyond the reed line their writ ended.

Here, the only law was survival.

An old man sat on the floating dock, bone needle busy with a torn net. His hands moved from long memory, but his eyes followed our approach. Narrow dark eyes in a face carved by wind and water.

I nosed the punt against warped planking. "Peace on your waters."

He nodded once. "And depth beneath your keel."

The ritual words. But they felt wrong here, thin as mist.

"What brings strangers to Reedmarch?"

Markov stepped onto the dock with careful balance. "We seek direction. To those who teach the disciplines of the Hand."

The needle stopped. The old man studied us — first Markov, then me. His gaze lingered on the scars that marked my hands, the set of my shoulders, the way I held myself still. Reading us like tide-signs. Something flickered in his expression. Recognition? No — but maybe its cousin. The look a man gives when a story matches a face.

"Path leads inward," he said at last.

Nothing more. But his gesture toward the settlement carried weight — not welcome, but acknowledgment. We'd been measured and found... something. Not wanting, perhaps. Not yet.

The walkway creaked beneath our boots, lashed planks floating where earth failed. As we moved deeper, I noticed what Markov missed. Windows shuttering at our approach — not casually, but with the quick snap of people securing valuables. A woman gutting fish let her bone knife rest loose, edge turned outward. Children didn't just watch from doorways — they counted us, memorized our faces, then disappeared with purpose.

Runners, probably.

By the third house, men had emerged. Not obviously armed, but standing where they could see our path, working at tasks that kept their hands near tool handles. One man mending nets looked up as we passed, and I saw his eyes track the way I moved, the weight of my tread on the boards. His mouth formed a word — silent, but I could almost read it on his lips.

A name? A warning?

I'd seen this before in villages that expected raids. They weren't curious about strangers—they were cataloguing threats.

"Friendly place," Markov murmured, still wearing his trader's smile.

I didn't answer. The last settlement that watched us like this, we'd left at a dead run with arrows whistling past our ears. But there was something else here, something in the quality of their attention that made my skin prickle. Not just wariness of strangers. Something more specific. They had the look of folk with something to guard, who wondered why northerners would press this deep into the mire, and why now.

The headman's house stood at the settlement's heart, raised higher than the rest. A wooden cross was fastened above the door, the northern kind—but the plaster beneath was white clay, and faint spirals showed through where damp had eaten the paint thin. Inside, the air was close with smoke and lamplight, the smell of bodies that worked and sweated in reed and mud. Psalms had been carved into the beams, though I saw a sprig of dried reed tucked in the joinery, and a bowl of fish bones hidden beneath the benches.

Christ looked down from the walls. But the mire had not let go.

Men filled the walls. Not many—maybe a dozen—but they moved with the easy stillness I remembered from old battles, fighters who knew their ground. One whispered to another, eyes on me, and I caught only a fragment—too soft to make sense—before it died as they noticed me listening.

The headman sat cross-legged on reed mats. Lean, scarred, forty winters maybe. Ritual marks gleamed pale on his arms in the firelight. His eyes were dark water—no bottom, no light.

I knelt on the threshold. Markov followed, though his bow came too quick, showed too much eagerness.

"Strangers," the headman said.

The word fell into silence like a stone into deep water.

Markov tried his smile. "Honoured headman, I am Markov, this is Yaroslav. We come seeking wisdom. The Church teaches discipline, but we've heard the old forms endure here—the way of the Hand. We seek to learn, to grow in skill. To understand."

Something shifted in the headman's expression—not interest exactly, but calculation. His scarred fingers drummed once against his thigh. A signal? One of his men shifted position near the door.

"And who told you such things might be found here?" Each word careful, weighted.

"Travellers. Rumours in Driftlight." Markov's lie came too quick.

The headman's eyes flicked to me, reading something in my stillness. Did he see what his people whispered about? Did he know the name they almost spoke?

"Rumours, yes. Many of them. Of men gathering in the deep marshes. Of old banners being stitched in secret. Of disciplines the northerners swore they'd burned out." His smile held no warmth. "Dangerous things to repeat. The kind of rumours that end with a man's mouth full of bog water and his eyes left open to stare."

My chest tightened. A threat unspoken, yet sharp as any blade.

"Radalya Tide-Reader gave you passage, you say?"

Markov brightened, pulling out the scroll. "Yes. She said you might—"

The headman raised one hand. Palm out. Stop.

One of his men took the scroll, cracked the seal, spread the bark-paper in the firelight. The headman read without expression. When he finished, he looked up.

"She writes that you ask questions about the deep places. About things better left sleeping."

"We seek only to learn," Markov said. "The old ways. The forms of the Hand."

"Why?"

The question hung like a blade. Markov's smile faltered.

"To... to understand. To grow in skill. We've heard the masters—"

"There are no masters here."

Silence.

"Then perhaps you know where—"

"I know many things. The tides. The signs. Which men sink and which swim." The headman leaned forward slightly. "What I don't know is why two strangers paddle into my waters asking about sacred things. Speaking of temples and masters and binding forms. Unless..." His eyes lingered on me a moment too long. "Unless they come for reasons not spoken."

The weight of it pressed against my ribs. Not a name, not proof — just the quiet suggestion that northerners never drift this deep without purpose they keep hidden.

Markov tried again. "We mean no offence. We come with respect, with gifts —"

He pulled out his offerings. Silver coins. A knife with a bone handle. A flask of Driftlight whitefire.

The headman's mouth twitched. Not a smile.

"You think wisdom is bought like fish at market?"

"No, I —"

"You come to my hall. Speak of sacred things. Offer metal and drink." The headman's voice stayed flat, but something moved behind his eyes. "Tell me, stranger — what blood-price would you pay for your own mother's bones?"

Markov went white. "That's not... we wouldn't..."

"But you ask for ours."

The silence stretched. Water lapped at the stilts beneath us. The trap had been sprung from the moment we asked our first question. Maybe from the moment Radalya gave us the scroll.

"I think," the headman said, rising to his feet, "you misunderstand what you seek."

Markov tried once more. "If we've given offence —"

"Offence lives in the asking. Go back to your northern fantasy about mastering our people's discipline. You are not worthy of it. And no good can come from this path. One day you may thank me for saving your life."

We were clearly dismissed.

I spoke for the first time. "What about the blood price?"

In Mstislav's campaign I'd seen it paid. When words and gifts failed, the Brackfolk turned to ordeal. Success in single combat proved the worth of a request. Failure meant the bog. No parchment law carried more weight here.

The headman's flat eyes held mine. For a moment there was no warmth, only the weight of old custom pressed between us. Then — grudging, reluctant — he gave a slight nod, as one forced to admit the stranger knew the rule and had the right to name it.

"You may ask that way."

Markov's face went grey. "Yarik, what are you —"

I started to rise.

"Him," the headman said, pointing at Markov. "The one who asked. The one who offered coin for sacred things. He answers."

The headman stepped down from his platform. Lean muscle moved beneath scarred skin.

Markov shrank back. "I... that is... what exactly are we talking about?"

"We will fight. To the end."

I looked at the headman. "I called the blood price. I'll stand."

"No." The refusal cut flat across the room. "He gave insult, he pays the price. This is the only way."

Men moved to the walls, making space. Lamps were pulled back. Reed mats cleared away to show the wooden floor beneath, stained dark with old use.

Markov stood frozen at the edge of the circle. "I'm no fighter. Just looking for self-improvement. He's the warrior—"

"You asked. You pay." The headman's voice cut through Markov's protest. "Unless you withdraw your questions. Leave now. Never return."

Markov's jaw worked, but no words came. He looked every inch the merchant caught where he had no business being—afraid, helpless, already beaten. He flinched as the headman advanced, hands loose and ready.

"Please," Markov whimpered, stumbling back. "I'm just a trader—"

The headman moved like water over stone—fast, precise. His palm strike smashed into Markov's face before he'd even raised a guard. The wet crack of bone filled the hall. He reeled, blood pouring from his nose, arms flailing too late to protect.

The headman pressed in for the finishing hold. Markov collapsed to one knee, coughing, whimpering like a man already broken. He looked pitiful. Helpless.

Then his body jerked sideways, sudden as a hooked fish. A hand darted to his boot. Steel hissed, and the thin blade tore upward into the headman's thigh, deep and ugly. Panic had made him cunning.

The headman roared, staggering, clutching the wound. Blood welled fast—too fast. Markov didn't press the attack. He scrambled back on hands and heels, knife out, eyes wide, still half-blind with blood and fear. Every line of him screamed flight. Yet in that panic he was lethal. Perhaps that was why he'd lived so long—because cornered, Markov fought like a rat in a burning cage, teeth bared and mind stripped to survival.

Only once he had space—when no hand could reach him—did he begin to steady. The whimpers died. His blade leveled. Breath slowed. In place of fear, calculation returned. That was when he spoke, voice raw but words chosen, already turning from victim to negotiator.

"Herbs and pressure," Markov said through the blood running from his nose, the trader's mask slipping back into place. "You've got three minutes before you bleed out." He pulled a leather pouch from his belt. "I have bloodmoss. You have information. Shall we trade?"

The headman's men started forward, but he raised a bloody hand. His face had gone grey, but his eyes burned with something like respect. "You fight like a Driftlight whore. All softness until the knife comes out."

"I'll take that as a compliment." Markov kept the bloodmoss just out of reach. "The location."

The headman pressed powder into the wound, his breathing steadying. When he spoke, his voice carried odd formality—the tone of a man keeping the letter of a bargain while betraying its spirit.

"South channel. Past the Standing Stones. At the place of two drowned crosses, turn toward the morning sun." He met Markov's eyes. "Wait there. If you are worthy, the temple will take you."

Something in his phrasing made my neck prickle. Too precise. Too practiced. Like words he'd spoken before, to other seekers who'd never returned.

"And if we're not worthy?" I asked.

His smile was thin as winter ice. "Then the bog takes you instead. It's always hungry this time of year."

The other men laughed—short, ugly sounds. The headman's eyes flicked to Markov, then back to me. "The mire keeps what it claims."

We left Reedmarch as the sun touched the western reeds. The punt carried us into deeper channels, where the water ran black and still. Behind us, the settlement faded into mist.

Markov dabbed his split lip, cleaning the boot blade with careful precision. "Well," he said, "that went better than expected."

I looked at him. "How do you figure?"

"We're still alive. And we know where we're going." He grinned despite the pain.

I didn't answer. Behind us, I could still feel their eyes, heavy with suspicion, watching to make sure strangers left their waters. Ahead, the mist closed around us like a shroud.

Markov grinned through blood, easy in his rat's skin. Fear never shamed him—it only made him quicker, meaner, alive. I almost envied him for it. The rat survives by gnawing, but still remains a rat. The wolf inside me was never so merciful. It did not simply survive. It tore, it judged, and when it was done there was no laughter, no fear, no hunger left—only silence. The kind that hollows a man until even survival feels like death.

Chapter IV: The Standing Stones

We took the south channel toward the Standing Stones, as the headman commanded. His words clung like smoke from green wood, and his flat eyes followed me still. Wolf. The Brackfolk remember everything. A slight becomes a blood-debt. A name spoken wrong festers for generations. Here in the deep places, my past walks with me like a faithful hound.

The danger lies not just in the mire itself — though that's real enough. Midges that swarm thick as battle-smoke. Reeds sharp enough to flay skin from bone. Mud that takes men whole, swallowing them without ripple or cry. But it's the people who make this place truly treacherous. They watch from reed-beds and stilt-houses, marking every boat, remembering every face. Twenty years since the conquest, and still they wait. Patient as bog-water. Deep as old graves.

Perhaps that's the end I'm being drawn toward. Not glory. Not redemption. Just to sink into black water.

The punt slid south through channels that narrowed with each mile. Mist thickened around us until we could barely see the water ahead. Darkness came early, pressing down like a burial shroud.

Cold gnawed at us.

"We'll have to camp," I said.

"A fire will mark us," Markov muttered. The words came thick, blood still clotting in the back of his throat.

"Cold will kill us faster."

We found a knob of solid ground—willow roots and peat lifted just above the flood—and dragged the punt half onto the moss. I worked flint while Markov gathered what dry wood we could find. Not much. Everything here held water like a sponge.

The fire caught, grudging and mean. Orange light bled into the fog, making us visible from half a mile. But without it we'd freeze before dawn.

"Your nose is crooked," I told him.

He touched the bridge gingerly. "Feels straight enough."

"It isn't." I set down my flint and reached across the flames. "Hold still."

"Yarik, don't—"

I cupped the back of his head in one hand, grabbed the bridge of his nose with the other. Twisted sharp. The crack echoed across the water like breaking kindling. Markov yelped, half-curse and half-howl, blood pouring fresh down his chin.

"Saint's bones! You broke it again!"

"I fixed it. Another day and it would have healed wrong." I wiped my hands on my cloak. "Now you're only ugly, not misshapen."

He blinked tears from his eyes and began to laugh—wet, choking sounds mixed with blood. "Ugly? I'd still steal a woman's glance if you stood beside me."

"True enough."

I tossed him a rag. "Stuff that in before you drown yourself."

He pressed cloth to his nose, still shaking with laughter. "Always gentle, my friend."

The pain seemed to wake something in him. He rose and began moving slowly through the forms he'd learned at the Church of Saint Vira. His balance was better than before, his movements less rushed.

"Playing monk again?" I asked.

"Better than lying still, waiting for the bog to take us." He sank into a crouch, arms weaving like reeds in wind. "It helps me think."

"About what?"

"About why we're here. What we're truly seeking." His eyes caught the light, suddenly serious. "Three months, Yarik. Three months of questions that lead nowhere. Empty hands every time."

I fed the fire a twist of grass, keeping the flames low. "Better empty hands than a knife in the back."

"Is it? At least a knife would be honest."

He straightened, rolling his shoulders.

"The Brackfolk smile and nod and tell us nothing," I said. "Maybe there is no relic. Maybe we're chasing shadows."

"The relic is here," he said firmly. "I feel it."

"Feel it? Or want to feel it?"

"Think about what Radalya taught us. About the old saints, the way they transformed the ancient spirits." He moved through another sequence, more focused now. "Saint Ognevara wasn't just some northern invention. She was the fire-spirit of these marshes, dressed in church robes to make her palatable."

I thought about the witch—for that's what she was, whatever title the Church gave her. Radalya Tide-Reader, with her water-words and marsh wisdom, getting her hooks into Markov with cryptic teachings.

"You remember what she said about the Way of Purifying Fire," Markov continued, warming to his theme. "How the Church softened the saint's teachings because the true forms were too dangerous. Men died seeking purification. But in the deep places—"

"The spirits remember their first names," I finished. "Yes, I remember your lectures."

He ignored my tone. "If there's truly a temple in the deep marshes—a place where the old ways of judgment survive—it's not coincidence, Yarik. It's exactly what we've been seeking. Not just a relic, but the source itself."

"You're grasping at marsh gas."

"Then explain how Radalya knew." His eyes held that fever-brightness now, the look of a man convinced he'd found truth. "She knew about our quest, Yarik. About what we were really seeking. I never said a word about the relics, but she knew."

"You didn't tell her, did you?"

"Of course not!" He looked genuinely offended. "But she saw it somehow. Those strange eyes of hers, like she could read the desires written on a man's soul."

I remembered those eyes. Dark as bog-water, impossible to read. The way she'd looked at me that first day, as if she saw past scars and sinew to what lay beneath. I hadn't liked it then, didn't like thinking about it now.

"She gave us the scroll," Markov pressed. "Led us here. And now we're being pointed toward the deep places, where temples might still stand and spirits remember their names. Don't you see the pattern?"

The fire hissed against the damp, giving little warmth. I had to admit—grudgingly—that it was our best lead in three months of searching. Maybe our only lead.

"Even if you're right," I said, "walking in doesn't guarantee walking out again."

"No," Markov agreed. "But the bog will take us if we just keep wandering. At least this feels like... destiny."

I scowled at his optimism. "In my experience, destiny is rarely kind."

I let him settle back into his cloak while I took first watch, punt-rope wrapped twice around my wrist. His words followed me into the darkness like smoke. Despite my misgivings, I knew he was right about one thing—we'd run out of safer options.

Night fell like a held breath. Even the insects quieted. Mist beaded on my beard.

Near midnight, a light appeared on the water.

"Markov," I whispered.

His voice came soft from the darkness. "I see it."

A drift-lamp. Shell and oil and wick, floating without current or wind to guide it. It moved toward us steady as a walking man, then stopped ten paces from our island. The flame turned—no other word for it—until it faced east. Then guttered out, leaving us in darkness deeper than before.

"Omen?" Markov asked.

"Warning. We're being watched."

We spoke no more that night. When dawn came grey and thin, we ate cold bread and pushed off. The water ran black as old blood between banks of whispering reed.

The channel kinked around drowned stumps of bog-oak, their roots deep as centuries. White clay spirals marked some of the trunks—water-signs that made the eye want to slide away. I didn't look directly at them. In the old wars, men said such marks could lead you to drowning if you stared too long.

By what might have been noon, we reached the Standing Stones.

They rose from the water like broken teeth, black rock slick with moss and age. Some leaned toward each other until their tips nearly touched. Others stood solitary, marked with the same spirals we'd seen on the trees. The water around them had no current, no life—just stillness that felt heavy as prayer.

We drew the punt against the nearest hummock and stepped onto solid ground. Offerings lay scattered at the stones' feet: braided reeds, black feathers, a child's doll made from driftwood and grass. Everything smelled of clay and old smoke.

"Feels like a graveyard," Markov muttered.

"Is one," I said. "Sacred to them. Don't touch anything."

We stood without speaking. The stones seemed to listen. A wind moved somewhere high above, and the reeds answered in long, low breaths. When I looked again at the offerings, something new had appeared among them: a reed bracelet with a bone charm carved like a reaching hand. It hadn't been there moments before.

"Message?" Markov asked.

"Invitation. Or trap." I studied the bone charm. "With the Brackfolk, both is always possible."

A voice came from beyond the stones, soft as wind through marsh grass.

"Peace on your waters."

I turned, not too quick. "And depth beneath your keel."

She stepped from the reeds as if the green itself had shaped her. Brackfolk, narrow-built and pale, her dark hair bound with water-weeds. She wore the rough tunic and seal-hide boots of the marsh-dwellers, but moved with the fluid grace I remembered from the old campaigns. A hunter's walk. A killer's stillness.

At her throat hung a pendant of carved bone, worn smooth as river stone. Her eyes were darker than the water, impossible to read. A black crow perched on the stones behind her, preening its wings with careful attention before taking flight eastward.

"You were told to take the south channel," she said. Not a question.

"We took it," I said.

"These are the Standing Stones, are they not?" asked Markov. "Further south, the headman spoke of two drowned crosses, where we are to turn east and wait."

"That does not exist." Her mouth curved, though it wasn't a smile. "Unless one considers the drowning of two northern cross-bearers to be one. He sent you to die."

The words hung in the mist like a net. I felt the weight of them—no path, no landmark, only a death-sentence spoken as directions.

Her gaze lingered on Markov, on the way his hands dangled loose at his sides. She came close, closer than courtesy, and reached to him. Her fingers, wet and cold, closed around his jaw. He froze. She turned his face toward the light, studying the broken bridge of his nose, the dried blood along his lip. As her thumb traced across his mouth, she glanced briefly at the crow's retreating form. A small smile played at the corners of her mouth—satisfied, as if confirming something long planned. Then, slow as if feeding a flame, she dragged her thumb across his mouth, smearing the crusted red with a sheen of water from her palm. When she pulled away, a damp spiral remained on his cheek—a mark that would dry dark, like rot.

He blinked at her, startled, almost boyish. "What is it?"

"A sign," she said. "And a debt. This is the hand that drowns. All who see it will know."

Markov touched his cheek as if to wipe it off, but stopped halfway.

"You seek the temple," she said. Not a question.

"If it exists," I replied.

"It exists. Whether it will have you..." She shrugged. "That is another thing."

She stood a moment longer, the mist curling at her shoulders.

Markov spoke. "Do you know the way?"

"I know a path," she said, "but not whether it ends in knowledge or grave."

Markov stepped forward with his trader's smile. "We're grateful for any guidance. Perhaps we could arrange—"

She cut him off with a gesture. "No bargains. No coin. The temple chooses its own."

Her gaze found mine and held it. Recognition flickered there—not of my face, but of something deeper. The weight of old violence. The smell of blood that never fully washes clean.

"I know your work, Volkolak," she said quietly.

The name hit like a physical blow. I kept my voice level. "Do you?"

"My mother died in the reed-beds. Stabbed and drowned. You stood on her head as she went down in the mud."

The memory came sharp and sudden. I had seen her rise from the black water, mud streaked across her cheeks, steel flashing in her hand. She had been like a marsh-snake, quick and deadly, but her strike missed my neck by inches and then it was over. I cut her quick, cut her deep, felt the spray on my face, and drove her mouth into the mire. I stood on her with all my weight as she thrashed, then stilled. She was no different from the rest—just another death, another offering to the wolf that howled inside me.

But she would have had family. Sisters. Daughters. Faces I never saw. Names I never knew. And still the blood runs after me.

She stepped closer, near enough that I could smell the marsh-water on her skin.

"Her name was Vassa," the woman continued. "She had three children. Two sons who drowned trying to reach safety. One daughter who watched from the reeds."

My hand moved toward my sword hilt. Not threatening—just ready.

"And?" I said.

"And now fate brings you back here, to this place of remembrance." Her mouth curved in something that wasn't quite a smile. "To me for the way."

She paused, studying my face. Her eyes flickered with that strange inner light again, as if she saw more than what stood before her.

"I can lead into the deep, though whether and how you leave depends on how you answer for what you've done." The words came with certainty, as if she spoke prophecy rather than threat.

Markov glanced between us, tension singing in the air like a drawn bowstring. "What kind of temple are we walking into?"

"The kind that judges," she said. "The kind that drowns the unworthy in black water and feeds them to the deep things."

"Ah, the charms of the Mirefast," he muttered.

But his eyes had changed. I saw recognition dawning there—not fear, but something closer to wonder.

"The temple of judgment," he said slowly. "Where the spirits remember their first names. Where the old ways of purification survive." He looked at me. "Yarik, this is it. This is exactly what Radalya was preparing us for."

Markov's words rang with certainty, and I remembered the witch's knowing eyes, the way she'd sent us here with purpose I was only beginning to understand.

I looked at this woman—this daughter of a woman I'd butchered in the reed-beds—and felt the weight of all those accumulated deaths. They followed me everywhere, patient as shadows.

"What's your name?" I asked.

"Kharna," she said. "Though that name dies with me. I have no children to carry it forward."

The bitterness in her voice was sharp as winter wind.

"Will you come?" she asked. "Or will you add cowardice to your other sins?"

I met her eyes. In them I saw the marsh itself — dark, patient, remembering everything. But behind that darkness, something else flickered. The shadow of distant sight. The weight of words spoken by another voice, in another place.

Markov was right. Three months of chasing shadows had led us here, to this moment, to this choice. Perhaps it had always been leading here. Perhaps this was what Radalya had seen in those bog-dark eyes of hers when she gave us the scroll.

"We'll come."

She nodded once. "Then we leave now. The temple does not wait for comfortable timing."

She stepped into our punt without ceremony, taking the pole from my hands as if it had always been hers. The boat barely shifted under her weight. She knew these waters like blood knows its way through veins.

As we pushed off from the Standing Stones, leaving the bone charm among the other offerings, another crow landed where we had stood. It cocked its head, studying our departure with bright, intelligent eyes.

The reeds closed behind us without a sound, and we were swallowed by the mist-wrapped maze of the deep Mirefast.

Ahead lay judgment. Behind us, nothing but the long wake of our sins.

Chapter V: The Temple of the Drowned Waters

Mist pressed low over the channel, heavy as sodden wool, binding water and sky into one grey shroud. The reeds closed tight around us, each stalk beaded with cold water that dripped like tears onto black surface. The punt slid forward through a tunnel of green spears, air thick with the smell of peat and fish-rot. Every push of the pole came back slow, as if the mire itself leaned against us.

Kharna stood in the prow, narrow shoulders moving with the rhythm of deep water. She didn't ask which way to steer, never waited for my nod. At each branching of the channels she chose without hesitation, though the passages looked identical to me — reed, mud, and black stillness stretching in every direction.

"She walks these waters like a woman treading her own garden," Markov muttered, his voice still thick from the cloth stuffed in his nose. "Yet I see no markers, no signs. How does she tell one channel from another?"

"Brackfolk have eyes for these places," I said. "What's a maze to us is home to them."

But I watched her back, the set of her head, the way she sometimes paused to listen before choosing a direction. There was something more than familiarity in her movements. Authority, perhaps. The confidence of someone who knew not just the way, but what waited at its end.

Once she stopped at a heron's cry and held us motionless until silence returned. Another time she pulled a reed, tied it into a complex knot, and let it drift away behind us. Her knots were not markers for the eye, but messages for those who read the water.

When I asked why, she only said, "So they know we passed."

"They?" Markov asked.

She didn't answer.

The mist thickened until water and sky became the same grey shroud. Only the ripples from our wake proved we moved at all. Ahead, the reeds thinned into a narrow passage between two islands of peat and bone. Charms hung from willow branches—finger-bones and bird skulls, shells and twisted metal, all clicking together softly in the damp air.

Kharna rested her pole, studying the passage. "Here the temple takes its due."

Markov leaned forward, peering at the hanging charms. "Looks like a toll-gate. Shall I pass the lady a coin?" His grin was thin, more habit than mirth.

"No coin," Kharna said, turning those dark eyes on me. "Blood. Yours."

Cold walked up my spine. "Why mine?"

"Because you are the one the deep places remember. They know the weight of your hand. They wait for its measure." Her voice carried no emotion, as if she spoke of tides or weather. "The debt is written in water and bone. Only your blood can pay it."

I drew my knife. The steel looked too bright here, foreign in this world of reed and mud and patient darkness. The blade caught what little light filtered through the mist, throwing it back like a challenge.

"How much?" I asked.

"Enough to show the waters your worth." She watched my face, reading something there I couldn't name. "The temple judges by what is given freely."

I cut the ball of my thumb. Not deep, but the blood welled quick and red. I held my hand over the water and let the drops fall. They struck the surface without splash, spreading slow through the black water like ink through cloth. Each bead sank whole, carrying its red down into depths I couldn't see.

I watched the dark of the mire drink my blood and felt one darkness calling to another—the old dark of the marsh, patient and cruel, and the harsh violence of the animal that tears with its teeth. I thought of how man fights for supremacy even as the world presses forever to smother him. Men claim they are more than beasts, yet here at this threshold that demanded its toll I knew the cloak of skin we wear is paper-thin. Beneath it waits only ruin, howling, and fury at death.

The water stilled. The charms stopped their clicking. Even the reeds, which had whispered all morning, fell silent as though some vast hand had pressed upon the world.

Markov shifted on his bench. "Saints preserve us. I've heard quieter graveyards."

"Quiet keeps you breathing here," Kharna said. She lifted one finger to her lips, then traced a slow spiral in the damp air—a warding sign, or a binding. Her eyes never left my face as she made the gesture, as if marking me with something only she could see.

The silence pressed down like deep water. My own breath seemed loud. The punt's timbers creaked, and that small sound carried like a shout across the still channel.

The mist began to lift, revealing what lay beyond the bone-charms.

Something struck the punt's hull. Not hard—not enough to breach or break—but a deliberate nudge from beneath, as if the water itself had shouldered us aside. The boat rocked. Dark ripples spread from the point of contact.

Markov's hand went to his knife. "That wasn't wind or current."

"No," Kharna said. Her gaze stayed on the water, unreadable. "The Morskoi Zmey has risen. The water-lord takes note when blood is given."

The name coiled in the mist like a curse, old as the reeds themselves.

Markov paled, lips shaping it again as if afraid to speak aloud.

I stared at the black surface. No sign of what had touched us, yet I could feel it still—a presence sliding under the punt, long and heavy, testing our worth. My knuckles whitened on the pole.

"The mire knows you now," Kharna said, calm as naming the weather. "It tests who seeks the temple."

"Tests how?" I asked.

She smiled for the first time since we met. It was not a pleasant expression. "By seeing how you face what you have made."

The presence beneath us passed away into the dark, leaving only ripples and the memory of weight. But I understood then: this was no random creature of the deep places. This was judgment taking form, summoned by blood and ritual, called by a woman who knew more than she revealed.

The punt drifted forward. The mist lifted like a veil drawn back, and I saw what awaited us.

The temple rose from black water on stilts of bog-oak, ancient and twisted, their roots vanishing into depths that held no light. Reed walls hardened with clay bore white spirals that seemed to writhe when glimpsed from the corner of the eye. Bones crowned the roof-peak, drift-lamps hung green with slime. It wasn't built so much as grown — a thing raised from mud and memory, shaped by hands that knew the old ways.

"There," Kharna said, guiding us toward a landing made of lashed driftwood. "The Temple of the Drowned Waters. Where debts are measured and dues collected."

Markov stared up at the structure, his face grey as the mist. "Home sweet home," he muttered.

I said nothing. The temple pressed on me like the silence had — weight heavy as judgment, patient as the grave. Every bone that crowned its peak, every spiral that marked its walls, spoke of power older than kingdoms. Older than kings.

This was where the Brackfolk brought their deepest questions. Where they sought answers from gods that dwelt beneath the water, in the spaces between breath and drowning.

And Kharna had brought us here not as guests, but as offerings.

The punt bumped against the floating dock. Kharna stepped out first, her movements sure on the unstable platform. She turned and waited for us to follow, her dark eyes reflecting the temple's bone-crowned peak.

"Come," she said. "The deep places have been patient long enough."

I looked at the temple, at the woman who had led us here, at the black water that had tasted my blood. There was no going back now. The debt had been acknowledged, the contract signed in red.

Whatever judgment awaited in those reed-woven halls, I would face it standing.

But as I stepped onto the dock, I caught the edge of Kharna's smile—not a guide welcoming pilgrims, but a priestess content with the offering she had brought.

Chapter VI: The Children of the Hand

The dock creaked beneath our boots as we stepped onto the temple's platform. The structure rose above us like something half-remembered from fever dreams—reed walls darkened with age and weather, bog-oak pillars twisted by decades of flood and drought. This was no converted church wearing saintly icons over pagan bones. This was older. Deeper. A place formed in the old ways. One that had cast off Mstislav's conquest, or never been taken.

"Wait," Kharna said, her voice carrying the quiet authority of someone accustomed to being obeyed.

She moved to a shell-lamp hanging beside the entrance and cupped her hands around the cold wick. Words came from her throat—not the common tongue, not even the Brackfolk dialect I knew, but something older, liquid sounds that seemed to flow with the rhythm of water over stone. The lamp flared to life, casting dancing shadows across the bone-charms hanging from the eaves.

Footsteps echoed from within the temple. Heavy boots on wooden planks, moving with purpose. The entrance curtain—woven reeds bleached white as bone—swept aside.

The Otets who emerged wasn't what I expected.

He was young, perhaps thirty summers, with the lean build of a man who'd learned the martial disciplines early and never stopped practicing them. His hair was long and braided, in the manner of the old faith, and bound with carved bone. Seal-hide clung close on his shoulders, black with fish-oil sheen, and ritual scars crossed his forearms like shifting spirals in lamplight. Ritual scars crossed his forearms in patterns that seemed to shift in the lamplight. His eyes held the flat intensity I remembered from the best fighters—men who could kill without passion, without hate, with the same ease they drew breath.

Behind him came four others, not acolytes but fighters. Serpent-blades rode high across their backs, hilts jutting over the shoulder for a draw unhindered by reed or water. Either the law held no weight in these deep places, or they simply chose not to acknowledge it. Their movements carried the flowing grace of the Hand, each step eel-swift, each shift a form half hidden.

The Otets' gaze found Kharna first, and something passed between them—a conversation held in glances and the slight tilt of heads. His jaw tightened. Her chin lifted, stubborn.

"Otets Kazimir," she said. "We bring these men under the old laws. They seek the temple's judgment."

The manner of her speech was strange, but I didn't think that "we" was an error. Our guide spoke for more than just herself. Volkhva, then—one of the temple's sisters, not merely a guide.

"Do they?" His voice carried the same liquid cadence as the ancient words Kharna had spoken, but harder. Like water over sharp stones. "Or do you bring wolves to the fold, expecting us to feed them from our own flesh?"

The warriors spread out in the practiced way of men who'd done this before. Not threatening—not yet—but ready. I kept my hands visible and still. Beside me, Markov shifted his weight to the balls of his feet.

"The Awakened One teaches us to see clearly," Kharna said. "Without the veil of desire or fear. After winters of silence, two cross-worshippers come to us now, seeking understanding, and judgment. The wise trust the current, and do not seek to stop it."

Kazimir studied her face, reading something written in the lines around her eyes, the set of her shoulders. The argument they were having had nothing to do with us, I realized. We were just the stones they threw at each other in some deeper conflict.

"The current," he said, voice soft with something that might have been mockery. "Yes. Trust the water to carry us where we need to go. Even when the banks are crumbling."

"Especially then," she replied, meeting his gaze steadily. "The deep places know their own purpose."

Something passed between them—a conversation held in glances, in the tilt of heads, in words that meant more than they said. The tension stretched taut as a bowstring.

"Your timing," he said at last, "is unfortunate."

"Timing is rarely our choice to make."

"No." His smile was sharp as a blade's edge. "But it is always our burden to bear."

Kazimir stepped closer, his gaze moving between us with the calculating precision of a man sizing up opponents. The warriors behind him shifted subtly, hands never quite touching weapons but ready all the same.

"You move like a scout," he said to Markov, studying the way he held himself. "Light on your feet. Eyes that see the edges of things."

Markov nodded. "I was. Among other things."

"Other things." Kazimir's tone was flat. "Thief? Cutthroat? The usual trades of northern scum who prey on honest folk?"

"Yes." No shame in Markov's voice, just acknowledgment. "I guided travellers through places they shouldn't go. Took what I needed to survive. Served men I probably shouldn't have served."

Something flickered in Kharna's expression—approval, perhaps, of his honesty.

Kazimir circled him slowly, predator-like. "And now you come to us seeking what? Absolution? A new master to serve?"

"I met one of your people," Markov said quietly. "A brother from these marshes, living alone, in the west. He showed me movements—forms that were like nothing I'd ever seen. Physical, but more than physical." His voice grew stronger. "I asked to learn. He said I was too old."

"You are too old." Kazimir's lip curled. "The Way of the Hand begins in childhood, when the body can still be shaped, when the mind hasn't hardened into northern patterns of thought."

"Perhaps," Kharna said softly, "age brings different gifts."

The Otets' attention snapped to her. "Gifts. Yes. Always you speak of gifts and signs and the wisdom of teaching wolves to hunt with the pack." He turned back to Markov. "What makes you think we need another northern criminal stumbling through sacred forms? What gives you the right to claim what you spent your life ignoring?"

Markov was silent for a long moment. "Nothing," he said finally. "Nothing gives me the right. But I've lived as a petty thief, a hired blade, a man who never saw beyond the next meal or the next job." His hands moved unconsciously through a partial form—crude, imperfect, but showing genuine understanding. "If there's a way to be more than that—if there's truth you're willing to share—I'll earn whatever right I can."

"More than that." Kazimir watched the clumsy attempt at the form with obvious disdain. "You think enlightenment is something you can steal like a purse or learn like a trade route?"

"No," Markov said simply. "I think it's something you become. If you're worthy. If you work for it."

Then his gaze found me, and what little warmth had crept into his voice vanished entirely.

"And you." He moved closer, studying my face, my hands, the way I stood. "You have the look of iron about you. The smell of old blood." His eyes narrowed. "Not a teacher. Not a seeker. A killer."

I said nothing. There was no point in denying what any warrior would recognize.

"How many of my people died by your hand?" he asked, voice soft as silk over steel. "How many mothers weep because of your service to the northern crown?"

"I was a soldier," I said simply. "I did what soldiers do."

"What soldiers do." He tasted the words like poison. "The language of butchers. The excuse of men who close their eyes to the evil they do."

Kharna stepped forward, her movement subtle but deliberate. "The mire brought him to us wounded. Marked by more than mortal weapons."

"The mire brings many things," Kazimir replied without taking his eyes from mine. "Corpses. Plague. Poison that looks like clear water." He tilted his head. "What wounds could touch a creature like this that weren't earned honestly?"

"Perhaps," she said carefully, "wounds that teach rather than merely punish."

Something passed between them again—another layer of their ongoing argument. She was defending me, I realized, but not because of who I was. Because of who she thought I might become.

"The sisters have dreams," Kazimir said, his tone flat with disapproval. "Visions. Prophecies of transformation and redemption." His smile was blade-thin. "Pretty stories to tell when the real world demands harder choices."

"The sisters see what is," Kharna replied. "And what might be."

Movement caught my eye. Children emerged from the temple's shadows—boys ranging from perhaps four years old to their middle teens. They moved in formation, feet whispering across the wooden planks, arms tracing the slow patterns of the basic forms. Even the youngest mimed the draw from the back-scabbard, shoulders twisting, arms cutting down in the short vicious arcs the Otets favour in the mire.

They formed a loose circle, never stopping their practice, never looking at the confrontation between Kazimir and Kharna. But I felt their attention like physical weight. Here was the next generation of Brackfolk resistance, learning the old ways in defiance of conquest and conversion.

Kazimir followed my gaze and nodded grimly. "Yes, look at them. See what your king's peace has wrought. Boys who should be learning with steel in their hands must train in shadows, hiding their birthright like thieves. The youngest among them has brothers who lost their hands for carrying the serpent blade."

His hand lifted to the hilt jutting above his shoulder — not straight northern steel, but the old serpent-blade, oil-dark and curved like a marsh-serpent, edge gleaming with meticulous care.

"Tell me, butcher, how many of our fathers fell to your blade in the reed-wars? How many of our mothers died with your steel in their throats?"

I met his gaze without flinching. "I killed who needed killing."

The words were a shield, but thin as paper. Soldier was the cloak I had worn, the name that made slaughter sound like duty. Beneath it, I had wanted the fight — the tearing, the spray of blood, the hush that followed. The wolf had driven my hand as often as the Crown's command, and Kazimir saw it written plain. He knew the difference between a man who killed because he must, and one who killed because the beast inside him hungered and would not be denied.

"Needed killing." He tasted the words like poison. "The lies of the conqueror."

"The truth of soldiers," I replied. "Your people fought. We fought back. Neither side asked for quarter."

No quarter. Two words to cover all the blood, all the ruin. Yet I knew what lay beneath them. No quarter was not just necessity, not just law of war — it was the wolf in me, hungry and tireless, that drove me past mercy. It kept me alive where others fell, but at a cost carved deep. The scars I bore were not only on my flesh. They were the wolf's tally, proof that I lived by what devoured me.

One of the children — a boy perhaps ten years old — missed his footing and stumbled. Kazimir's attention snapped to him like a blade finding its target. The boy reddened but resumed the form, movements more careful now, more precise.

"This is what we have become," the Otets said, voice soft with something that might have been grief. "Children learning to fight in whispers. Warriors training with wooden swords while their enemies carry steel. A people who must hide their strength or watch it burned from their bodies."

He gestured toward me. "And you would have us welcome another northern butcher into our most sacred place?"

"I would have you remember," Kharna said, her voice carrying a new weight — not just authority, but power, "that the Volkhva speak with the voice of the deep places. That we see what the surface cannot reveal."

The air seemed to thicken around her words. Even the children's movements slowed, as if the very atmosphere had grown heavy with significance.

"The sisters dreamed of this one's coming," she continued, meeting Kazimir's gaze without wavering. "Radalya herself spoke of the wounded wolf who would seek healing in the sacred waters. You would deny what the Awakened One has shown us?"

Kazimir's jaw worked silently for a moment. Whatever authority he held here, whatever power his position granted him, it didn't extend to questioning the visions of the Volkhva directly.

"Dreams," he said finally, but his voice had lost its edge. "Riddles and prophecies while our children grow up in chains."

"The deep places work in their own time," Kharna replied. "Not ours."

He stared at her for a long moment, then nodded slowly. The fight had gone out of him, replaced by something harder and more dangerous.

"Very well," he said, turning to us. "If the sisters demand trials, then trials you shall have."

The silence stretched between them. Around us, the children continued their practice, but I saw how their movements had grown more intense, more focused. They were listening to every word, learning not just the forms but the shape of their people's anger.

Finally, Kazimir nodded. "The Volkhva speaks of judgment. Very well. Let the temple test what it has been given." His smile was thin as a knife-edge. "But understand this, northerner—the trials you face will not be gentle. The deep places remember every slight, every burning, every death. If you are found wanting..."

He shrugged, the gesture somehow more threatening than any spoken threat.

"Then the mire will have what the mire is owed."

Two of the warriors stepped forward. Not quite menacing, but their intent was clear. We were to be escorted, not guided.

"Your companion remains with you," Kazimir said, glancing at Markov. "The temple judges all who enter its halls. The debt you carry is not yours alone — it is the price of the north's peace. Whatever the temple demands, you will answer from the same ledger."

Markov straightened, jaw set despite the fear I could see behind his eyes. "Fair enough, Father. We accept your justice."

"Yes," the Otets said softly. "You will."

The warriors moved to flank us. Not rough, but firm. We were guided toward the temple's entrance, past the circle of practicing children, beneath the hanging charms that clicked like bone dice in the wind.

As we crossed the threshold, I heard Kharna and Kazimir begin to speak in the old tongue—words that flowed like water over stone, urgent and sharp. An argument, though about what I couldn't say. Whether to test us or kill us, perhaps. Whether mercy had any place in a world carved by conquest and resistance.

The temple's interior was larger than the outside suggested, stretching back into shadow and lamplight. Reed mats covered the floor in intricate patterns. Carved pillars rose to support a ceiling lost in darkness. And everywhere, the smell of incense mixed with something else — the deep, wet scent of things that grew in places the sun never touched.

"This way," one of the warriors said, his accent thick but his meaning clear.

We followed him deeper into the temple, leaving behind the argument at the door, the circle of children, the weight of twenty years' hatred made manifest in a young Otets' eyes. Ahead lay whatever judgment the deep places had prepared for us.

Behind us, Kharna's voice rose in the ancient tongue, sharp with authority, demanding something from Kazimir that he was loath to give. The sound followed us into the temple's depths like a current pulling us toward some dark convergence we couldn't see.

Radalya and Kharna dreamed of the wolf made whole in sacred waters. But Kazimir had the truth of it. Wolves do not heal. They bite, or they starve. The choice is never mercy — only death, or cruelty. The trials would not be kind.

Chapter VII: The Wolf and the Rat

They stripped us of our weapons in the antechamber—not roughly, but with the thoroughness of men who'd done this before. My sword went first, then the long knife, the boot blade, even the small skinning knife I kept for cutting rope. They worked in silence, efficient and thorough.

Markov's disarmament took longer. Layer by layer they peeled away his hidden arsenal—throwing knives from his sleeves, stilettos from his boots, the garrote wound around his left arm. He stood naked to the waist, pale skin goose-fleshed in the temple's damp air, while they searched every seam and fold of his clothing.

They left us with rough temple robes—undyed wool that scratched the skin—and led us deeper into the structure. The walls here were older, built from reed and clay that had hardened to something like stone. Bone-charms hung from the ceiling, clicking softly as we passed beneath them.

The chamber they brought us to was windowless, lit by a single oil lamp that threw dancing shadows across the walls. Reed mats covered the floor. A wooden bucket sat in one corner, empty.

"Sit," the guard commanded. We sat.

The door closed behind them with a wet wooden crack.

I should have known better than to follow Markov into this madness. Should have seen the trap closing around us from the moment Radalya offered her scroll. But I'd let his enthusiasm carry me forward, telling myself I was protecting him from his own foolishness. Now we sat in a

Brackfolk temple while men who remembered the old hatreds decided our fate.

Twenty years I'd served the crown, twenty years of campaigns and conquests, and it would end here—not on a battlefield with steel in my hand, but in a reed-woven cell, waiting for judgment from people whose gods I'd helped bury.

"Well," Markov said into the darkness, "this is cozy."

I didn't answer. The walls pressed close as a burial shroud, the weave gone unforgiving. Water dripped somewhere in the distance, patient as time itself.

"I'm thinking we may have misjudged our welcome," he continued, shifting on the thin reed mats. His voice carried that forced lightness he used when things turned bad—the trader's mask he wore to hide fear.

"Could be worse," Markov tried again. "At least the accommodations include a bucket. Shows they're civilized."

The silence stretched between us. Outside, night birds called from the reeds, their voices sharp in the still air.

Markov sighed and settled back against the wall. "You know what your problem is, Yarik? No appreciation for the finer things. Here we are, guests of a mysterious temple in the heart of the Great Mire, about to undergo sacred trials, and all you can do is brood."

"Sacred trials," I repeated. "That what you're calling it?"

"Better than 'waiting to die in a hole.'"

I almost smiled despite myself. Three months of travel, and he still believed things would work out. Still thought charm and luck would see him through.

"Get some sleep," I told him. "Tomorrow will be hard enough."

"Sleep. Right." But he closed his eyes anyway, or seemed to. His breathing didn't settle into the rhythm of true rest, though. Like me, he was listening to every sound beyond the walls, cataloguing threats, measuring chances.

I leaned back against the reed wall and let my eyes drift shut. But sleep wouldn't come. Instead, unbidden, sharp as winter wind, came the memory.

Mirameer, three years after the conquest. The last of the temple-schools, hidden in the deep marshes where we'd thought it destroyed. But children don't simply forget their lessons, and the Brackfolk had been teaching their young in secret—the old disciplines, the old prayers, the old hatreds.

We found them during the morning forms. Forty children, maybe fifty, moving through the ancient patterns in perfect silence. Boys as young as five, girls barely tall enough to hold the training spears. Their teacher was an old man with ritual scars covering his arms, speaking to them in the liquid tongue of the deep places.

Captain Rostislav gave the order. The children scattered like birds, but there was nowhere to run. The platforms were built over deep water, and we controlled the boats.

"Form them up," Rostislav commanded. "All of them. Every last whelp."

The children stood in a ragged line, youngest to oldest. Some wept. Others stared at us with eyes that held too much understanding. They knew what was coming.

But Rostislav didn't order executions. Not directly. He pointed to the pile of stones beside the platform—granite blocks quarried from the northern hills, each one heavy enough to anchor a boat.

"You will build," he told them in the common tongue, words carefully chosen so even the youngest could understand. "A guardhouse. Here, where you practiced your heathen rites. You will carry stone until it is done."

The old teacher tried to step forward. "They are children. Let me—"

Rostislav's sword opened his throat. The man fell forward, blood spreading across the reed mats like spilled wine. The children didn't scream. Didn't run. They stood and watched their teacher die, then picked up the stones.

It took them seven days to build the stone walls of the garrison that would house their oppressors. Another seven to build the walled courtyard where they'd be re-educated in the ways of the north. Fourteen days of watching children—some no older than those training here in this temple—carry blocks of stone heavier than they were, their small hands bleeding, their backs bent beneath the weight of their own subjugation.

We hanged their teacher's body from the rafters where he'd once led prayers. A reminder. A warning. A promise of what happened to those who taught the old ways.

I'd stood guard while it happened. Watched those children build the cage that would break them in spirit as well as in body. Told myself it was necessary. Told myself it was war.

Told myself a soldier's lies.

Now I sat in another temple, surrounded by more children learning the same forbidden disciplines, and felt the weight of every stone those young hands had carried settle on my chest like a burial shroud.

Eventually, the door opened. Kazimir entered, followed by two of his warriors. His eyes like dark pools of hate in the lamplight, ritual scars dark as old blood across his forearms.

"The trials begin," he said simply.

We were led to a courtyard open to the grey sky above. Wooden posts stood at regular intervals, scarred by old use. Iron rings had been driven into their tops, black with age and weather. The children I'd seen earlier formed a loose circle around the space, still moving through their practice forms but watching us from the corners of their eyes.

"Strip," Kazimir commanded.

We removed the rough robes. The morning air raised gooseflesh on my arms, made my breath visible in small puffs of vapor. Beside me, Markov shivered but said nothing.

They bound our wrists with hemp rope, then stretched our arms above our heads, securing us to the iron rings. The posts were set close enough that we could see each other clearly, far enough apart that we couldn't touch.

"The trial of endurance," Kazimir announced, his voice carrying across the courtyard. "Let us see how long northern strength lasts without northern steel."

He nodded to his warriors. They brought out long poles tipped with bronze—not spear-points, but blunt instruments designed to cause pain without killing. They took positions beside each post and waited.

"You may end this at any time," Kazimir said, looking directly at me. "Confess your crimes. Name the innocent blood on your hands. Beg forgiveness from those you have wronged."

I met his gaze without flinching. "And if I do?"

"Then you will die quickly instead of slowly."

The poles struck simultaneously. Blunt bronze against ribs, kidneys, the soft flesh of the belly. Pain flared bright and sharp, stealing breath, making vision blur. The children in the circle never stopped their forms, but I felt their attention like heat from a fire.

Again. The poles found nerves and soft places; pain bloomed like glass. Markov cried out—a short, sharp sound that cut off as he bit down on his tongue.

I didn't make a sound.

Time became meaningless. There was only the rhythm of bronze on flesh, the taste of blood in my mouth, the burn of rope against my wrists as my body tried to pull away from the pain. Sweat ran down my sides despite the cold. My vision darkened at the edges.

Markov broke first, as I'd known he would.

"Stop," Markov whispered. "I'll say anything. Anything you want. True or not. Just... please."

The rod clattered to the ground. Two guards hauled him upright, his legs buckling beneath him. Blood streaked his back in parallel lines. As they dragged him toward the temple entrance, his feet scraped uselessly across the wooden planks, toes catching splinters he was too broken to feel.

The courtyard fell silent except for the drip of his blood on the boards.

Kazimir turned to me, and I saw something terrible kindle in his eyes. Not the cold judgment of a warrior, but the hot fury of a man who'd been denied his revenge for twenty years.

"Now," he said, rolling up his sleeves and dismissing one of the guards with a gesture. He took the bronze rod in his own hands. "We discover what you truly are."

The first blow drove the air from my lungs. Kazimir's strikes were different—more precise, more personal. Each one carried twenty years of accumulated hatred.

"What say you, Volkolak? Will you beg as your friend has begged?"

The children had stopped their practice. They stood in their circle, watching with the patient attention of those learning an important lesson. This was their education—not just in the forms and disciplines, but in the price of resistance. The cost of defiance.

I thought of other children. Other lessons. Stones carried by hands too small to bear them.

"No," I said.

Time blurred. The courtyard faded to distant shapes. Kazimir's breathing grew laboured, sweat beading on his forehead as he worked. The bronze rod rose and fell with methodical precision. My ribs cracked. My vision greyed at the edges.

But I didn't beg.

When consciousness finally began to slip away entirely, I heard Kazimir's voice, breathless now: "Enough."

The beating stopped.

"Cut him down," he ordered, though whether to his warrior or to me I couldn't tell. "The northerner has spine, at least."

They lowered me to the reed mats, rope falling away from wrists rubbed raw and bleeding. I tried to stand and fell, legs too weak to hold my weight.

"Tend his wounds," Kazimir ordered. "Barely. I want him alive."

As the temple healers approached with their oils and bandages, I caught sight of Kharna watching from the shadows of the courtyard's edge. Her dark eyes reflected nothing—no satisfaction, no pity, no mercy. Just the patient observation of someone taking careful measure of what they'd been given.

The first trial was over. But in her expression, I saw the promise of trials yet to come—tests that would cut deeper than bronze, hurt worse than rope and iron.

Tests designed not just to break my body, but to strip away whatever remained of my soul.

Chapter VIII: Truth in the Deep Places

They came for us at dawn, separating us with the casual efficiency of men dividing livestock. Markov was led toward the temple's eastern wing, where I could see light streaming through reed-woven windows. I was pushed in the opposite direction, deeper into the structure's cold heart.

My cell was smaller than the first—barely room to lie down, with walls that wept condensation in the morning chill. A wooden bucket for waste. A clay bowl for water that came twice daily, never full. Food arrived once, if it could be called food: a handful of grain porridge thin as gruel, sometimes with scraps of fish so old they stank of rot.

The single window sat barely a hand's breadth above the waterline—too low for any mercy it might have offered. When the wind picked up or boats passed, black water would slosh through the opening, flooding the cell floor with brackish mire that never fully drained. The constant splash and gurgle meant no rest, day or night. What little light filtered through showed only the dark chop of water and the endless grey of reed and mist. I could watch my prison from the inside, but the window brought no relief— only the promise that the mire was always waiting, always ready to claim what the temple left behind.

The hunger came quick. Not the clean ache of a missed meal, but the gnawing weakness that steals strength from the limbs and clarity from the mind. By the third day, my hands shook when I tried to lift the water bowl. By the fifth, I spent most hours lying on the reed mat, conserving what little energy remained.

I felt my humanity peel away in that cell, thin layer by thin layer, until only the wolf remained. I was not a who bore oaths, but the brute hunger beneath. Each hour of weakness stripped another thread of conscience, until all that stirred in me was the beast that endures—half-breath, half-shadow, gnashing against the dark. And I hated it. Hated that what kept me alive was not faith, nor memory, nor duty, but the shameful strength that refused to die.

Markov survived too, but not as I did. He clung to shadows, to bargains, to the rat's cunning that scurried from trap to trap. I endured by the wolf's teeth; he endured by the rat's guile.

The walls here were old, built in the manner of the ancient temples where sound carried like water through hidden channels. I could hear fragments of what happened in the eastern wing—voices raised in instruction, the rhythmic whisper of feet moving through forms, occasionally Markov's laugh echoing across the courtyards.

They were teaching him. Using him for their purposes under the guise of instruction.

On the seventh day, I heard Kharna's voice through the walls, clearer than the rest.

"Your friend suffers because he will not speak truth," she was saying. "The deep places know what he has done. They wait for him to name it freely."

Markov's reply came muffled but distinct: "He's stubborn. Always has been. But not cruel. Not by choice."

"Come. See."

Footsteps moved away, but I could track their passage through the temple's bones. They paused at what must have been a crack in the wall—some gap in the ancient construction that offered view into my cell. I lay still, breathing shallow, letting them think me asleep.

"Look at him," Kharna whispered. "See how the north breeds its wolves."

Silence. Then Markov's voice, softer now: "He's wasting away."

"As did our children. As did our elders. As did all who stood in the path of his king's peace." Her words carried the weight of deep water, patient and inexorable. "Yet still he will not name what he has done. Still, he clings to the lie that his hands are clean."

"Maybe... maybe if I talked to him. Explained what you've shown me. About your people, your ways. He might listen."

"Truth is not taught, young shadow. It is discovered. When he grows weak enough, hungry enough, desperate enough—then perhaps he will find the courage to see himself clearly."

They moved away, leaving me alone with the knowledge that Markov had been watching me starve. That he'd stood there listening to Kharna explain why it was necessary, why it was just.

The doubt crept in like cold through stone. How long had he been observing? How many times had they brought him to peer through cracks and gaps while I lay senseless from hunger? The image of his face pressed to some hidden viewing slot, studying my degradation like a lesson in a book, settled in my gut like swallowed iron.

But worse than the watching was the tone in his voice when he spoke of me. Not the easy familiarity of our time on sea and land together, but something more distant. More careful. As if he were speaking of a stranger whose nature he was still determining.

Days blurred together. The hunger became a constant companion, gnawing at my ribs, making my vision dance with spots of light. Sometimes I heard them in the eastern wing—the soft percussion of training, voices raised in the liquid syllables of the old tongue, the scrape of wooden weapons against wooden floors.

Markov's laugh came less frequently. When it did, it sounded different. Subdued. More thoughtful.

Then at last they came for me.

Two warriors hauled me from the cell, my legs too weak to bear weight properly. They dragged me through corridors I hadn't seen before, past chambers where children moved through forms with silent concentration, past altars where drift-lamps burned with cold light.

The room they brought me to was circular, its walls marked with the spiral patterns that made the eyes water to look upon directly. Kharna waited in the centre, seated cross-legged on a reed mat. Beside her sat Markov.

He looked better than when I'd seen him last. His colour had returned, the gauntness filled out. Clean clothes replaced the rough temple robes. His hair had been washed and worked into the long braids of his captors. But it was his eyes that struck me most—the way they studied my face with a mixture of concern and something else. Something cooler.

"Sit," Kharna said.

The warriors lowered me to a mat across from them. The effort of staying upright made my vision blur.

"Your friend has been learning," she continued. "About our ways. Our history. The price your people extracted for their peace."

Markov nodded slowly. "They've shown me things, Yarik. Records. Testimonies. I never knew..." He paused, choosing words carefully. "I never knew how bad it was. What was done after the fighting ended."

I said nothing. Speech took energy I couldn't spare.

"He speaks of you often," Kharna said. "Your shadow-friend. He tells us you are not a monster by nature. That you followed orders, served your king, did what soldiers do in war. He believes your hands are stained by duty, not by choice."

Her dark eyes fixed on mine, reading what was written there.

"But I listen to the walls, Volkolak. I hear you in the dark hours when you think no one can see. And I wonder — what is it you dare not name, even to yourself?"

The hunger made thought difficult, but I forced words past my cracked lips: "You want confession? I killed your people. Men, women, some barely old enough to hold weapons. I burned your temples, scattered your worshippers, put down your resistance."

Markov shifted on his mat. Something flickered across his face — not surprise, but confirmation of things he'd begun to suspect.

"Yes," Kharna said softly. "That much we know. That much the mire remembers. But there is more, isn't there? Something that cuts deeper than duty. Something that stains blacker than orders."

I met her gaze and saw my own reflection in those dark depths—hollow-cheeked, fever-bright, worn thin by hunger and the weight of years. Behind my reflection, I saw something else. Patience. The infinite patience of deep water, waiting for stone to crack.

"The children building their own cages," I said finally. "The teacher we hanged from his own rafters. Boys who carried stones until their hands bled." Each word came like swallowing glass.

She listened, regarding me with her measuring stillness. "No. That is not it," she said at last, unsatisfied.

The silence stretched. Markov leaned forward slightly, and I caught the scent of good food on him, the smell of someone well-fed and clean. The contrast with my own stench—sweat and waste and the sour reek of starvation—was sharp as a blade.

"The woman with the curved blade," I continued, voice barely above a breath. "Vassa. Your blood. She came up from the water like something born from the deep places. Fast as a striking snake. I was faster."

"And?"

The words stuck in my throat like fishbones.

"And I killed her. Not because I was afraid. Not because she was my enemy." The admission tore from me like flesh from bone. "I killed her because I wanted to. Because in that moment, watching her die felt better than anything else in the world. The wolf in me sang—alive in a way nothing else ever had. She was woman and small; I was man and strong; I could make cruelty a choice. To dominate, to break—that power tasted like victory."

The words hung in the air like smoke. Markov recoiled as if I'd struck him, his face draining of colour. His mouth opened, closed, opened again without sound. The carefully braided hair, the clean clothes, the well-fed flesh—all of it seemed suddenly fragile against the horror in his eyes.

"You..." he whispered, then stopped. His hands trembled where they rested on his knees. "Sweet saints. You enjoyed it."

Not a question. Recognition.

"There," Kharna said, and for the first time since I'd known her, she sounded almost satisfied. "There is the truth the deep places have been waiting to hear."

She rose from her mat with fluid grace, looking down at me with those depthless eyes.

"Your shadow-friend believes you can be redeemed. That the darkness in you is accident, not nature." Her smile was sharp as winter. "We shall see. The trials are not finished, Volkolak. Before they end, we will know exactly what kind of beast wears your face."

She turned and left, robes whispering against the reed walls. The warriors moved to haul me back to my cell, but Markov raised a hand.

"Wait," he said, voice cracking slightly. "Let me have a moment."

They hesitated, then withdrew to the doorway. We were alone, but I could feel their eyes on us like physical weight.

Markov stared at me for a long time, his face cycling through emotions I couldn't name. Finally, he leaned forward, close enough that his words wouldn't carry to eager ears.

"They will kill you," he whispered urgently. "Kazimir wants you dead. Kharna... I don't know what she wants, but it's not mercy."

His fingers worked at his collar, and something small and cold pressed into my palm. A needle-blade. Thin enough to disappear into fabric. Sharp enough to part flesh or rope.

"Save yourself," he breathed.

Whether he meant escape or something darker, I couldn't tell.

His eyes searched mine. For a moment, I saw the old Markov there—quick, calculating, alive with the small cruelties of survival. Then something shuttered behind his gaze.

"I'm learning to see clearly," he said more loudly. His voice carried an echo of Kharna's liquid cadence. "The Awakened One teaches that truth is the first wisdom. Perhaps it's time you found yours."

He stood and walked away, leaving me with the guards and the echo of words that sounded like goodbye.

Chapter IX: The Wolfskin

The guards dragged me back to my cell, my legs too weak to carry me properly. I collapsed onto the reed mat, Markov's needle-blade a thin line of hope pressed against my palm, even if it were just to choose my end instead of having it forced on me.

The confession had carved something hollow in my chest — not relief, but a void left after twenty years of carrying rot. I was the Volkolak. Not just in name, but in nature. The beast that smiled while children built their own cages. The monster that killed for pleasure and called it duty.

Water dripped somewhere in the darkness. Each time I closed my eyes, I saw Markov's face in that moment of recognition — the horror, the understanding, the way his faith in me crumbled like wet clay.

Days bled into weeks, sleep coming only in fragments. Through the walls I sometimes caught his voice — at first clumsy, then steadier — answering chants, moving through forms. The sound grew more practiced as my own strength ebbed.

The needle-blade stayed warm against my palm through the long hours. A finger's length of sharp steel, thin enough to disappear into fabric. Sharp enough to part flesh or rope. I turned it over and over, feeling its edge, measuring its weight. Not much of a weapon. But enough. I might have chosen the coward's way then, despite the drive to live being strong, except that part of me thought such shameful release was more than I deserved.

When I woke, the taste of old blood filled my mouth.

The door to my cell opened. Not guards this time, but Kharna herself, carrying a clay bowl of what might have been soup. She set it beside me without ceremony and studied my face in the dim light.

"Eat," she said. "You will need strength for what comes."

After weeks of scraps and brackish water the real food shocked my gut, but steadied me enough to keep living. Real food, not the rotten scraps they'd been feeding me. Vegetables I could identify, meat that didn't stink of decay. My body accepted it gratefully. Whatever Kharna planned, she didn't want me dead yet.

"More trials?" I asked.

"Of a different sort." She looked out the window, peering through at something beyond. "The mire has been restless these past winters. Currents changing. Old paths opening that have been closed since the conquest."

"Meaning?"

She turned back to me, her dark eyes reflecting something I hadn't seen before. Not satisfaction at my confession, not the patient observation of a priestess weighing judgment. Something sharper. More immediate.

"Meaning your king's peace cannot last. The king fades, and his son is not even his shadow. Already the waters stir. There are those who would see blood spread across the reeds again."

I thought of the queen's warning before I set sail, Vezhena's low words in the Sea-Fort chapel: "Men are hungry, always hungry—for coin, for power, for safety. A pack of dogs.

Unless they feel the alpha's teeth, they will tear at each other until all lies in blood and ash. But the Grey Hand weakens."

Now I heard that hunger rising through Kharna's mouth.

"I am only a killer," I said at last. "The ways of politics and war are not mine to decide."

She studied me, head tilted as though weighing a relic. "That is where you are wrong. No man is only himself. The Mirefast fears the Volkolak, but it is not the Mirefast alone. Tell me, Yaroslav — do you fear him too?"

I felt the question crawl under my skin.

"Maybe there is nothing more to me now."

"And when did the wolf devour the man?"

I hesitated. The answer wasn't a date but a slow corrosion. A man sins once and tells himself it was a mistake, that it was not him. He blames fear, or rage, or drink. He repents and swears to do better. But true evil does not come in single strokes. It creeps in act by act, small choices that feel justified at the time. Good motives lead to bad deeds; bad motives sometimes to good. Loyalty, duty, anger, grief — each one leaves its mark, and you tell yourself you are still the man you were. As if a man was something other than the sum of his deeds.

It was in the Mirefast that Mstislav named me Volkolak, when he saw how good I was at being terrifying — at cruelty, at domination. He spoke it with pride, and I loved it. I embraced it. I acted on it. For sixteen years I wore the name like armour, patching the wolfskin deed by deed until there was no man left beneath. By the time they called me

Volkolak, it was no longer a name given. It was what I had become.

"Twenty years at least. Perhaps more."

I remembered the Straightsward campaign—the first time I killed not because I must, but because I wanted to see fear die in a man's eyes. Mstislav watching from horseback, his approval like strong wine. The man who had slaughtered my father became like a father himself, and I begged for his acknowledgment like a starving cur. He withheld, then granted it, once others began to whisper Volkolak and move aside when I passed.

"And what did such skill earn you?"

"More death."

"And what would you give to leave it?"

"It is my skin. Sewn onto me by my own hands."

She did not smile. "The wolfskin clings like rot. But rot can be burned away. If fire came for it, would you cling tighter—or let it burn, even if it took you too?"

I saw it then: the blood-stiff furs clinging to me in the mire, children's eyes wide as I passed. To burn the wolfskin would be to burn those faces also.

"There is no point asking."

"Yet you wish to be rid of it."

Silence stretched between us, sharp as a drawn blade. Was she testing me, or simply playing with me?

"Of course."

"That is the beginning," she said softly. "Perhaps there is no redemption. Perhaps there is only use. Even a blade that has cut the innocent may still cut the tyrant. Would you rather be thrown aside, or wielded once more?"

"I do not believe."

"Belief is not required. The tide turns, with or without faith. One life freely given can shift the waters. You were the wolf that hunted our children. Perhaps the deep places will make you the stone that breaks the wolf's teeth. Perhaps your death alone can teach such balance."

Before I could ask what she meant, footsteps echoed in the corridor outside. Heavy boots, moving fast. A warrior appeared in the doorway—not one of Kazimir's temple guards, but someone older, scarred by real battles rather than ritual cutting.

"Volkhva," he said, urgency tight in his voice. "They arrive."

Kharna nodded and rose. At the doorway she paused, looking back at me with something that might have been pity.

"The deep places remember everything," she said. "But they also know when to let the tide turn."

She left, taking the bowl with her. I was alone again with the needle-blade and the sound of my own breathing.

But not for long.

I pressed my face to the window, trying to see what was happening on the temple platforms. Glimpses of movement—warriors I hadn't seen before, bearing different house marks. Women in the flowing robes of Volkhvy, marked with symbols I didn't recognize. All arriving as the mist began to lift, summoned to council.

Voices carried across the marsh—not the liquid tones of the local dialect, but harder sounds, commands in the old tongue. Boats thudded against the docks, and soon the platforms rang with debate—not ritual cadence, but the clash of argument: supply lines, garrisons, whether Reedvault or Willowreach could stand if the northerners pressed south. Ships sighted in the southern channels. The words cut sharp, too familiar, and when I shut my eyes they became other voices—Mstislav's captains quarreling over the Mirefast, twenty years gone, as if war had never ended.

The noise swelled. Figures crossed the platforms beyond: volkhvy conferring in quick whispers, warriors testing weapons that should have been outlawed since the conquest. Women in robes inscribed with unfamiliar signs moved among them, and even scarred fighters shifted aside to make way, their authority unquestioned.

A council of war.

Hours passed. The debates grew louder, more heated. Through the window I caught fragments—urgent exchanges about readiness, about timing, about the cost of waiting versus the cost of striking first. Each word carved deeper into my understanding: this was not local politics, but the Mirefast deciding between endurance and revolt. And Kharna meant to lay my body on that scale.

The needle-blade grew warm in my palm. Weeks of turning it over had worn a groove in my fingers. One life freely given, she had said. Perhaps my death alone could teach such balance.

I waited in the dark, listening to the voices rise and fall like tide against stone, until the morning came for me.

Chapter X: The Council of the Deep Places

The door opened again at dawn — or what passed for dawn after weeks of stone and hunger. Two guards this time, moving carefully, almost respectfully. Whatever was happening beyond these walls had changed the way they looked at me.

"Come," one said. "The Volkhva calls."

They led me through corridors I had not seen in all the weeks of my confinement, past chambers where drift-lamps burned with cold light, past alcoves where children whispered prayers in the old tongue — a sound I had heard grow daily from beyond my cell, rising like tide. The temple breathed differently now—charged with purpose, alive with murmurs, footsteps, the creak of weapons being carried where none should exist.

The main hall stretched deeper than the building promised from outside, lost in lamplight and shadow. Reed mats patterned the floor in curling waves. Carved pillars rose to a ceiling swallowed by darkness. And everywhere, people.

Volkhvy in flowing robes marked with symbols from across the Mirefast. Otets with ritual scars dark against their skin, lean fighters' builds barely concealed beneath ceremonial dress. Delegates from distant settlements, tokens of bog-oak and bone tied at their belts. All gathered in a loose circle around the centre, where Kharna waited.

Markov stood beside her.

His hair had been worked into the long braids of the faithful, bound with carved bone. His posture was straighter, shoulders drawn back — but the stiffness of someone holding himself in shape. His movements echoed the Brack children's grace without their ease, each step a little too careful. Even his face tried at calm, but the set of his jaw betrayed strain. They had not remade him; they had pressed him into a form he was still learning to hold.

The guards placed me opposite, prisoner not participant. Every eye measured me. I knew immediately that the council had been told what I was. Not only a northern butcher, but the Volkolak. Some looked with hate, some with fear, some with the hunger men reserve for omens.

Kharna raised her hand. The hall hushed.

"Brothers and sisters of the deep places," she said, her voice clean and carrying. "You know why we have gathered. The northern king weakens. His son hungers for war. The governors speak of cleansing the southern waters once and for all."

Murmurs rippled, sharp with anger, hushed with fear.

"Some among us call for resistance," Kharna continued. "Steel against steel. Fire against fire. The old way, when strength was proven by blood spilled and enemies broken." Her gaze found Kazimir, standing among the Otets, his scarred hand already near his weapon hilt. "But I say there is another path. The way of the tide. Stone yields to it in time, not by force but by patience. As reeds outlast the flood, so we outlast conquest. What we preserve in silence endures when empires rot. That is our strength."

She gestured to Markov.

"Behold—a northern criminal, steeped in the worst of his people's ways. Thief, liar, servant of predators. Yet here he stands, learning our forms, speaking our prayers, finding peace in the discipline his kind mocked."

Markov stepped forward. He moved through a sequence of the basic forms — still clumsy, the rhythm uneven, but real enough to draw murmurs. The posture of a man trying to remember every lesson at once, or perhaps only the posture of a man desperate to remember his lines.

"I was lost," he said, voice steady and stronger than I expected. "I served coin instead of purpose. I hurt whoever stood in my way. But here, I have found something better. A way to be more than what I was."

Murmurs stirred through the crowd — some approving, some doubtful. More than one eye lingered on the tremor in his hands when he thought no one saw. Whether that tremor betrayed shame, effort, or fear of failing the part, I could not tell.

"And this one," Kharna said, turning to me. "The Volkolak himself. The wolf who earned his name in reed and blood, who broke our resistance and scattered our people. Behold him now—confessed, humbled, ready to face whatever judgment the deep places demand."

The silence stretched. I felt their eyes like weight on my skin, the hatred and fear of twenty years gathered in one place and poured over me. In that moment I knew my fate was sealed. They would kill me. The only question left was how.

Kharna had whispered that my death could serve a greater purpose, that peace might be bought with the blood of a monster. I did not believe her, not really. But I would die. Not with a sword in my hand, not on a battlefield, but as a sacrifice. I had never thought it would end this way. And yet I was ready. Beyond pride, beyond bargaining, I chose to be the hated beast brought low, as she required. Perhaps it would do some good.

"I have done great wrong," I said, and the words cut easy because they were true. "I have killed your people not only in war but for pleasure. I have broken your children, burned your sacred places. I have earned death a hundred times."

Faces shifted — some softening, some unmoved.

"But if there is a path to something better, if the deep places offer even a monster like me redemption, then I would walk it. At whatever cost."

Kharna's eyes lit, the barest smile touching her mouth. She had what she needed.

"You see?" she told them. "If even the Volkolak can be turned, then the north itself can be changed. Patience, not vengeance. Conversion, not fire. This is the way of endurance. This is how we preserve what matters."

The chamber stirred. Volkhvy nodded. Settlers whispered. Even some of the Otets shifted, uncertain. For a heartbeat I thought she might win.

Kazimir broke the silence.

"Pretty words," he said. His voice was harsh iron. "But reeds break in storm. Only steel keeps us from drowning again. Only blood for blood."

Anger stirred. The circle fractured — voices rising in old tongues, sharp arguments that clashed like blades. Kharna countered with measured calm, pointing to Markov's transformation, my submission, proof of endurance. Kazimir thundered back: the dead demanded vengeance, patience had bought only chains.

Then came the sound of boots outside. Not the careful tread of guards, nor the shuffling of more delegates. Heavy steps, each strike ringing with authority.

The hall froze. Even Kazimir fell silent.

The curtain swept aside.

She entered like judgment itself. Ancient—twice Kharna's age at least, her hair white as bone, her face seamed with scars from rituals I did not want to imagine. Her eyes burned like coals banked long but not extinguished. Heat rolled from her gaze, and when she looked at me I felt it as standing too close to a forge.

The assembled crowd drew back without conscious thought. Even the other Volkhvy lowered their eyes. I had seen that reaction before—when men recognized not just rank, but legend made flesh.

Her voice cracked like flame across dry wood. "I bring word from the hidden island, where the unquenchable fire still burns—the flame our ancestors carried from reed to reed, guarded through conquest and flood. The king dies. His son is weak, consumed by pride and rot. We have seen it in the flame."

A hush fell. Her presence was not argument, but judgment.

"The tide has turned," she said. "No reed outlasts the fire. No stone endures the storm forever. If we do not strike first, we will be drowned once more. And for that strike, we need blood. Blood to hallow the cause."

Her eyes took in Markov, then locked on me with terrible intensity.

"What foolishness is this?" She gestured at us with contempt.

Kharna stepped forward, but her usual composure wavered. Though her voice came smaller than before. "I do not question wisdom from the deep places. But surely if we can show that even the worst—"

"Still preaching patience, child?" the elder said, and something old and bitter passed between them. "Still believing wolves can be tamed rather than burned? These northerners must burn," she cut Kharna off, voice rising to fill every corner of the hall. "Not in secret, not in shame, but in fire that purifies. Fire that shows all the Mirefast what justice looks like when it finally comes."

The hall erupted—some voices rising in fierce approval, others crying protest. But the momentum had shifted like a tide turning. Kharna's voice rose urging patience, but she was speaking into a rising wind she could not stop.

The old Volkhva raised her scarred hand, and the arguments stilled as if cut by a blade.

"Prepare the stakes," she said.

The words struck me harder than chains. Around the circle, I saw faces transform—doubt hardening into certainty, mercy curdling into righteous hunger.

The guards closed in.

Beside me, Markov's careful composure finally shattered. His breathing quickened, the practiced calm of his new faith crumbling as the reality hit him. His hands shook as they bound them. The man who had stood so straight moments before now hunched with fear, all his transformation reduced to nothing. He shook like any man before the stake.

They dragged us both from the hall, past the watching eyes of those who had debated our fate. Some looked away. Others stared with the satisfaction of long-delayed justice finally served.

In the corridor, Markov stumbled, his words spilling in a thin whine. "No—no, she promised… Kharna said we'd be spared. She said…"

I said nothing. What was there to say? That mercy was a luxury the desperate could not afford? That conversion was a pretty dream when weighed against twenty years of slaughter?

They threw us back into the cell. Markov collapsed against the wall, shoulders shaking. The careful braids, the straight posture, the fluid movements—all of it meaningless now. He was just a frightened man again, facing a death he had not earned in the old way but could not escape in the new.

After all these weeks the needle-blade was still hidden in my robes, a splinter of choice no search had found. One life freely given, Kharna had said. Perhaps two.

But as I looked at Markov—this man who had tried to become something better only to be condemned for what he was—I knew the blade might serve mercy before it served escape.

Chapter XI: Ashes in the Dark

The cell stank of old rushes and damp stone. Markov crouched opposite, hands twisted in his braids, breath shallow as if the walls pressed on his chest. He looked at me once, then away.

"I should have helped you," he blurted. "Back there in the hall. I should have said something, stood with you. But I froze. Gods, Yarik, I only stood there, playing their puppet. Nodding like some disciple, mouthing prayers I barely understood."

His words spilled faster, thin and frantic.

"I wanted it to be true. Kharna's promise. That I could turn a page. Be more than Iron Bay scum. I thought if I spoke their words, bent my head, maybe I could be made clean." He let out a bitter laugh. "Clean. You know what I was at Iron Bay? Thirteen years old, catching rats with my bare hands to sell for meat. Once I tried to dress like a merchant's son, stole a coat, walked the docks like I belonged. They caught me before noon. Stripped me, beat me bloody, tossed me in the bilge-water. I remember crawling out, stinking like piss and tar, and thinking—this is me. A rat. Not a man."

He covered his face. "And now I tried to be a monk. A saint, maybe. But it was another lie. I believed my own lies, Yarik. That's the worst of it. I betrayed you, betrayed myself, chasing a dream I never had a right to. And now they'll burn us both."

He lowered his hands, and for the first time I saw it—fear not just of the fire, but of me. As if I might cut him down here in the dark for his weakness.

I let the silence stretch until he trembled.

"You did what you had to," I said at last. My voice scraped, flat as stone. "We're alive. That's what counts." He called himself rat, but I had seen worse—men fattened on lies who thought themselves good. There is no shame in a rat. No dishonour.

He flinched, as though waiting for more—curse, blow, judgment.

Instead, I pulled the sliver of iron from my robe. The needle-blade he had slipped me before, a thief's gift in the shadows. Small, but enough.

"There are two guards," I said. "They've weakened me, but not enough. I can still fight. You've got your tongue. Your fingers. Use them."

He stared at the blade, then at me. His lips worked, no words left.

"Think like the rat you were," I told him. "Rats live."

The lock scraped, iron on iron. Two guards came first, not ours but Kazimir's—scarred faces, eyes like stones, hands never far from their knives. Kharna followed with a reed-basket in her arms. I smelled it before I saw it—bread gone stale, dried fish, a skin of water.

"They will not last the day without food," she said. Calm, as if reason might still matter. "Let me give it to them."

One guard snorted. "They'll not last the day regardless."

But they let her through the outer gate. One stood in the passage, arms folded, weight thrown back. The other stepped near the bars, closer than caution allowed, his gaze on her instead of me.

She crouched, pushed the basket under. Her eyes met mine. She wanted me to see it — that she still believed her mercy could change something.

I moved as the guard bent low. No sound, only iron sliding between bars and into soft flesh. The needle-blade punched under his jaw, angled up. His breath caught in a wet gasp.

He jerked, struck the bars, tried to pull away, but I seized him by the throat and dragged him tight. His skin burned under my grip, hot blood pumping over my hand, spraying the rushes.

He tried to shout. Only a bubbling noise came. His free hand clawed at mine, nails raking. His legs kicked frantic against the stone. I pushed the blade deeper, twisting. His eyes bulged.

Kharna's cry split the air. "Stop — by the reeds, by the patient waters — stop!" She caught my wrist, tugging like she could break iron. "You don't have to —"

But I did. His strength was already ebbing, though his body thrashed. I crushed harder at his windpipe, the cartilage cracking. Blood gurgled in his throat, poured from his mouth. His boots slowed, twitching, then dragged limp.

The second guard swore and ran.

Markov staggered forward, hands clumsy but fast, brushing past the belt of the dying man. A moment later the keys flashed in his grip — iron familiar as old coins in his palm. He cursed as they clinked, fighting the lock with trembling fingers.

The guard in my arms convulsed one last time. I held him until he sagged, head lolling against the bars, blood pooling dark.

The lock gave. Markov swung the door wide, face pale and set.

Kharna had stepped back, shaking her head, eyes on the corpse. Her voice was broken glass. "It wasn't meant to be this way."

But it was. It always was.

We moved fast. No time for prayers, no time for Kharna's protests. I seized her wrist and hauled her close, blood still on my hand.

"You're coming with us," I said. Then, to Markov, "Grab the food."

She struggled, but I dragged her all the same. Markov snatched the basket, crammed fish and bread under his arm, water-skin hanging from his teeth as he fumbled the keys.

Shouts echoed through the passages. Feet hammering stone.

We ran. Reed mats ripped beneath our boots. Smoke from the lamps stung my throat as we burst through narrow corridors, Kharna stumbling against the pull of my grip.

"Which way?" I barked.

Markov's eyes flicked like a rat's, darting corners, remembering. "Left—then down the stair, past the carved door. Dock's that way."

He led, weaving through torchlight and shadows, the food clutched tight as any relic. Kharna clawed at my arm, begging me to stop, to listen, but I kept her close, iron grip at her elbow.

Voices rose behind us. Kazimir's men, the clang of weapons drawn.

We hit the stair spiraling down the cliff-face, torches guttering in the draught. Markov flew ahead, near falling, half-sobbing, half-laughing, his breath tearing ragged. I shoved Kharna after him, down into damp air thick with the stench of river-water. At the foot, a timber door groaned open, and beyond it the docks stretched out from stone foundations into the current — pilings slick with moss, boats chained close in the torchlight.

Markov leapt to the nearest, nearly spilling the basket in. He jammed it under the thwart and turned, hand outstretched. "Come on!"

I dragged Kharna to the edge. Her heels caught, fighting me even now. Behind us the passage roared with shouts, firelight flickering on steel.

There was no time left.

Kazimir's men filled the passage, torches spitting fire. Kazimir himself stepped to the front, scarred hand on his hilt, face set like carved stone.

"Let her go, Volkolak," he called. His voice carried over the water. "The tide will take you soon enough."

I hauled Kharna tighter against me, her back to my chest, my arm locked across her. She fought, weak against my grip, her nails biting my wrist.

"Get in," I told Markov.

He obeyed, scrambling to the oars, panic in every movement. The punt rocked, near tipping as he dragged himself aboard.

Kazimir's men spread along the dock. Bows lifted. Spears poised. The torchlight shook on their blades, on the black water.

"She comes with us," I said.

Kharna twisted in my grip, her voice raw. "Don't—don't do this. If you kill me, everything I stood for dies with me."

"It already died," I told her.

The first spear flew. I pulled her close, her body jerking as the point punched through her shoulder. She cried out, thin and breaking, blood soaking down her robe.

Another struck, lower. She stiffened in my arms, breath hissing out.

"Hold her, Yarik!" Markov screamed from the boat, his voice wild. He was already rowing, oars biting water in frantic strokes, pulling us from the dock.

Kazimir shouted, and the air filled with arrows. I kept her between us and the rain of iron. Shafts rattled off stone, skidded across her body. Each one drove her down heavier against me, her weight growing as life drained.

Her voice faded to a whisper. "You could have... been more."

I felt the breath leave her, light as smoke.

Still I held her, even as Markov dragged at me, shouting for me to get in. I clutched her like a shield, her body breaking each shaft, until we were far enough that their aim failed and the torches blurred small in the dark.

Only then did I lay her down across the thwart. Her blood mixed with the river-water at our feet, black in the torchglow.

Markov rowed with wild, jerking strokes, breath ragged, tears streaking his face. A strangled laugh tore from him, ugly as sobbing. 'We're… we're not dead,' he gasped, as if saying it might make it true.

I said nothing. My hands still carried her warmth.

She had spoken of patience, of reeds outlasting flood and fire. But in my arms she proved what I had always known: reeds burn like anything else. And I carried her ashes with me into the dark.

Chapter XII: The Beacons of War

We rowed until our arms burned and the torches were only faint sparks behind us. The oars dragged water heavy as lead, each stroke slower than the last. When the shouts faded into fog and no pursuit showed, we let the punt drift. We had nothing left.

Kharna still lay across the thwart where I had carried her, limp against the basket of bread and fish. Arrows jutted from her like stakes from a broken fence. I knelt and drew them one by one. Each pull was slow, wet, the shafts slick with her blood. Markov turned his face away.

We had no fire, no earth, no stone. Only black water and marsh grass. When the last arrow lay in the bilge, I lifted her by the shoulders. She was already cold, her robe stiff with blood and river-mist. I lowered her into the mire. The weeds caught at her sleeves, tugging her down.

Markov bent his head. His lips moved, but the words came broken—half-remembered scraps of psalm and blessing. The sounds sat rough in his mouth, like a thief trying on priest's robes. Still he forced them out, voice low and shaking.

I did not stop him. Prayer belongs to the dead, even if the tongue falters.

The marsh grass closed over her face. She was gone.

Peace may be worthy. But peace is never given.

For one heartbeat she had almost offered it — a kind of peace even in death, a sacrifice meant to cleanse rather than stain. But no peace is mine. My path has always been violent, as if some cruel demon held my leash and dragged me down the ugliest roads where other men fear to walk.

I had not loosed the arrows. Their archers had. And yet I had taken her and used her as our shield — pressed her living body between myself and death like a man who knows no other way. She had believed, even in me, right up to the end. Her eyes held something I could not name and did not deserve. And she was consumed by violence, pierced through because of what I am — because the truth of violence is easy and the truth of peace is hard, and I have never learned it. Perhaps I am not made to learn it.

If the saints look down, they will take her in hand and lead her to grace. She earned it with her blood. But for me there are only bad things waiting — I know this as a wolf knows winter is coming. I have always known it. And still I go on, dragging this weight, adding stone upon stone, for which I will one day answer.

The punt drifted in silence, weeds hissing at the hull. Then a glow flared through the fog, high above the waterline. Another answered it farther off, then another — red flames licking skyward until the horizon burned in broken lines.

Markov twisted to watch, face drawn tight. "They're hunting us. Lighting the way so we can't hide."

"No," I said. The firelight bled across the channels, jagged as wounds. "That's not for us alone. That's war. The rebels have shown their hand."

Markov swallowed hard, clutching the basket tight. The light painted his face raw and hollow. "Then they'll not let us reach Driftlight alive."

"They can't," I told him. "Two northerners loose with their secret? We're worth more dead than a dozen beacons."

The fires still burned behind us when sound drifted through the fog — faint, broken, yet real. The dip of poles, many at once. Shouts in the Brack tongue, stretched thin by the mist.

Markov stiffened, jerking his head from side to side. "They're close. They'll find us."

"Maybe," I said. The mire bends sound; what seems near may be a mile off. But every ripple told me the same truth: the enemy knew these waters. We did not.

I pulled at the oar. The current tugged westward, but west itself was only guesswork, hidden in fog. One channel looked like another, weeds shifting with the tide, each turn a trap. Even if we slipped Kazimir's men, the rebels would have eyes everywhere.

Markov hacked at the water with the oar, splashing more than pulling, his arms trembling. Each stroke looked less like rowing than a drowning man trying to claw forward.

My belly cramped tight. I had not eaten enough in days, yet I held myself from the basket at my feet. We might row for hours yet before finding shelter — better to keep our strength for the work than waste it feeding hunger that would only return.

Markov spat into the water — curse or prayer, I couldn't tell. His gaze darted at every sound, every swirl in the weeds.

The fog swallowed the echoes again, but it left the truth heavy in my gut: we were lost, hunted, half-dead already, and the mire had all the time in the world.

The current dragged us on through the grey hours, neither fast nor slow, just endless. My arms burned with every pull. The oar grew heavier until it felt carved of iron. Each stroke tore breath from my chest, left my head swimming.

Markov rowed wild, splashing more than pulling, but still he rowed. His mouth worked with curses, mutters, scraps of prayers. The water gleamed on his cheeks — sweat, river-mist, or tears, I could not tell.

I bent forward to pull again, and the world tilted. Black water surged up. My grip slipped. For a heartbeat I saw only weeds and fog rushing sideways.

Then hands clawed at my collar, dragging me back in a rush. Markov's face loomed, pale and frantic. "Don't—don't die, Yarik, not here, not in this stink—". His voice cracked, desperate, more fear of being left alone than of losing me.

I tried to curse him, but the words died in my throat. The oar thudded against the boards. My arms would not lift it again.

We could not stop. Stop meant cold. Stop meant the rebels or Kazimir's men finding us. So we took turns, one rowing while the other slumped against the boards, eyes closing in spite of themselves. The punt was coffin-small, tar seeping, water pooling at our knees. No place for sleep. Still, sleep came.

Sleep never lasted. A jolt would drag me back — Markov shifting, the oar striking the gunwale, water slapping hard against the hull.

Then worse. The punt lurched sideways, nearly throwing me into the black. I woke to Markov's cry, his hands clutching the thwart.

The water heaved, rising under us as if the mire itself had drawn breath. A pale back broke the surface, long and ridged, glistening like wet stone. It rolled past, longer than the boat, then slid under, leaving rings that spread wide into the mist.

Markov's voice cracked. "The Zmey. Gods, it followed us. We gave it blood already — why is it here?"

Her gift had been clean. What followed was not. The water could taste the difference.

I gripped the needle-blade, useless in my fist. For a moment I thought of pressing it to my thumb again, letting the water take its due as before. A drop, a cut, a contract signed in red. But that had been Kharna's bargain, not mine. I clenched my hand until the thought passed.

The arrows I'd pulled from Kharna's body lay at my feet, warped but sharp. I snatched one up. Markov lifted his oar like a spear, knuckles white around the shaft.

The water swelled again. For a heartbeat the broad head surfaced, jaw ridged, eyes black as peat-pools. It lingered, watching.

"It is never sated," I said. "Not while blood runs in men."

The punt rocked in its wake, boards groaning. We sat frozen, hearts hammering, every nerve waiting for the strike that never came. The creature slid under once more, and this time did not return. Only the circles on the water remained, closing slow around us.

Markov whispered, "It marked us."

I did not answer. The mire keeps its debts. Blood had been given, and more taken. Whether it was enough, only the water-lord could say.

Chapter XIII: Judgment in the Reeds

Hunger woke me the second day. My belly twisted on itself, but I forced my hands away from the basket. A strip of bread and fish would not bring me strength, only make the hollow deeper when it was gone. Better to row empty.

Markov was not so strong. He chewed at his crust with cracked lips, gnawing as though it might turn soft if he worked it long enough. Between bites he muttered, low but constant.

"My leathers. Gods, Yarik, I wore them near ten years. Thin as skin, supple enough to lie under a tunic. Took me half a lifetime to stitch in all the pockets, to balance the weight so no man could tell. You know how many times that armour saved me? I can't count. Steel glanced, knives stuck short, even arrows—"

"Quiet." My voice came harsher than I meant, cracked by thirst.

But he would not stop. "Every coin I ever stole, every trade I made—it went into those leathers. That was my life, hidden on my back. And now? Gone, gone with the rest. Like I was stripped bare. Might as well walk naked through this swamp for the crows to laugh at."

"Enough." I swung the oar, water shearing away with a heavy slap. The sound carried. I felt it ripple out into the reeds. "Noise draws ears. Do you want them on us already?"

He hunched but did not look at me. His hands clutched his sandals as if they too might slip away.

"I had nothing left, Yarik. Now even less."

I wanted to tell him we all had nothing—that I rowed barefoot with rags bleeding red, that hunger hollowed me too. But I swallowed it down. Words were wasted breath.

We rowed on in silence, arms shaking with each pull. The oars dragged heavy through water that felt more mud than current. Reeds pressed close on either side, whispering with every shift of the wind.

The silence did not last. A reed cracked to our left, sharp as a snapped bone. Both of us froze, oars lifted.

From the misted grass rose a shape — black, low, long. It moved with a ripple, not a step. Shoulders rolled under a sleek hide, tail twitching like a whip. The head lifted and I saw the eyes, pale in the fog, fixed on us.

"Saints," Markov whispered. His fingers tightened on the oar as though it were a spear. "A marsh-cat."

I had heard of them. Black as peat, large as wolves, living on fish, fowl, and men unwary enough to stumble from their punts. I had never seen one, and I prayed I never would again.

It padded closer, silent save for the hiss of grass against its flanks. Its body coiled low, ready to spring.

"Don't move," I said.

Markov did the opposite. He raised his oar high, lips peeling back from his teeth. His voice shook. "Back off, beast! Back into your mire!"

The cat froze, ears twitching. The sound carried, thin and sharp across the water. For a heartbeat I thought it would leap, claws first, straight into the boat. My hand closed on the needle-blade, though I knew it would do little more than open my own veins with it.

Then the cat hissed, a sound like steam from a crack in the earth. It turned, slow, and melted back into the grass. The reeds closed behind it, as if nothing had passed that way at all.

I let out a breath I had not meant to hold. My hands shook on the oar.

Markov laughed, thin and nervous. "Saw the devil in its eyes, Yarik. It would have taken us both, I swear it."

"You nearly gave it cause." My voice came flat and raw. "Next time you open your mouth, think which ears are listening."

We rowed on, but the cat did not leave my mind. More than once I thought I saw it pacing in the reeds, black and low, keeping stride with us.

Markov's strokes faltered. His voice came ragged. "We can't last like this, Yarik. Not on scraps and swamp water. There's a garrison at Saint Cuthbert's Hollow to the south. Food. Men who guard their own. Better to risk them than starve."

I kept pulling, jaw tight. "The Hollow has soldiers, yes—and priests. They'll see gore on us, robes torn, no flocks, no reason to be there. You think they'll call us pilgrims? They'll call us murderers. And word will reach Driftlight faster than we can."

He shook his head, near pleading. "And north? Past Reedmarch, Blackfen, Drownbank? Rebels choking every channel? That's worse. Driftlight's south too, if we can cross open ground."

His hands trembled on the oar. For once, his fear made sense. The thought of food, of dry ground, bit into me sharper than hunger itself. I nodded once. "South, then."

We turned the punt, bent our backs to it. For a time the channel seemed to yield. The water pulled steady, reeds parting. But then it closed. A dead wall of grass. We forced another way, and it bent us back in a circle. Again, and the bank shifted as if the mire itself had moved while we rowed.

No matter how we pressed south, the current turned us. The channels narrowed, split, rejoined in ways I could not map. Fog thickened, veiling distance. It was like rowing inside a maze that breathed, each passage closing even as we entered.

And always, when the reeds thinned and the water caught us again, we were facing north.

Markov cursed, voice cracking. "It doesn't matter what we choose. The mire's chosen already."

We had barely yielded to the northward pull when a figure slid into view through the fog — a low punt nosing along the channel edge. A man stood in it, reed cloak over his shoulders, short reed-bow slung across his back. He had not seen us yet; his eyes searched the banks, not the water.

Markov's breath caught sharp. He set his oar flat, hands shaking. "A scout."

I nodded once. If he raised his head and spotted us, a single shout would bring a dozen more.

We pushed the punt silent into the reeds, breath held. The man drew closer, dragging his pole. His face turned, narrow and pale in the mist. For a heartbeat I thought he might pass.

Then his gaze snapped to us. His mouth opened.

We struck first. Markov surged up, oar swinging. I leapt with the needle-blade. His cry rang out, high and ragged, before the water took him.

I held him under, blade working, the iron taste thick in the air. His body convulsed, then sagged. We dragged him across the thwart, stripped him in silence — cloak, tunic, reed-bow and its quiver of bone-tipped arrows. I passed the bow to Markov; he tested the string with a thief's quick fingers, nodding once. Street rats learned to use whatever came to hand. Boots too small for me, but Markov jammed them on with a shiver of relief. I wrapped my feet in torn cloth, tighter, thicker, until they bled less.

The man's eyes still stared, wide and empty. Markov would not meet them. We weighted him with the pole, let the reeds close over him. But I knew sound carried farther than bodies sank.

Markov's whisper trembled. "They'll have heard."

I kept rowing. "Then row faster."

For a while the fog stayed close, muffling all. Then the sound came — faint but certain. Another pole striking water. Then another, farther off, answering.

Markov's face drained white. "Patrol."

The reeds bent with a shifting wind. Through the mist, firelight flickered, small and moving — torches on the water.

"They heard him," I said. "And they're hunting."

The torches grew into three, then four, bobbing through the fog. Men's voices carried, Brack tongue sharp and fast, calling back and forth across the water.

We bent to the oars, though every stroke tore muscle and opened sores. The punt slid fast as we could drive it, but the patrol spread wide. They knew the mire, every turn and cut. They were not chasing; they were herding.

Twice we veered into reeds, hoping to lose them. Twice we struck dead ends, channels that closed like jaws. Each time we backed out, slower, weaker. The torches came on, steady, patient.

Markov muttered prayers between curses. His head snapped at every sound, and once he hissed, "There!" A black shape slid the reed-line — the marsh cat, still following. Pacing us like a shadow, eyes pale in the dark.

"Let it stalk," I said. "Better one beast than six."

We pushed north, where the water widened, driven by currents we could not fight. And there Drownbank waited. Houses on stilts, driftwood lashed into rafts, torches burning at the piers. Figures moved along the bank, voices rising. The cry of the dead scout had reached them before us.

A longboat pushed out, broad and low, six men aboard. Spears and bows glinted in torchlight. They came fast, cutting across the channel to block our way.

We could not outrun them.

"Reeds," I hissed. We shoved the punt into a thicket. Water climbed to my knees, mud sucking greedy at my boots. Markov floundered beside me, bow clutched, the little needle-blade I'd pressed into his hand glinting faint.

"Close range," I told him. "Point-blank, then drop the bow. Eyes, throat, groin. And don't stop."

He swallowed, nodding too fast.

The longboat slid past, oars hissing, then a shout. They had seen.

Six men came splashing, torches behind them painting fog into fire. Not soldiers — reed-folk. Shorter than us, narrow-shouldered, their weapons little more than fish-spears, rusted knives, a wood-hafted axe. Faces tight with fear as much as fury.

The first lunged, spear thrusting. I met him with the oar, wood jarred near in half. The point scraped my sleeve, tearing cloth, but I rammed forward with all my weight. The shaft drove into his chest and he folded back, wind gone, water up to his chin. I swung again, cracked the oar across his skull, felt the wood split as he sank.

Another waded close, chest bare, knife held high. Markov's bowstring snapped sharp, the arrow burying in his throat at arm's length. The man toppled gurgling, clutching at the shaft as the mire dragged him under.

A third came howling, knife flashing. Markov loosed wild — the arrow skidded off ribs. The man slammed into him, blade raised. Markov shrieked, dropped the bow, and drove the needle-blade into his gut. Once, twice, again, until they both went down thrashing, water clouded red.

Three still pressed me. My oar was splintered, arms heavy as stone, breath scalding my chest. One jabbed high with his spear. I knocked it down, but the iron head punched my thigh, fire ripping me open. Pain near dropped me. I twisted, dragged him off balance, then clubbed his face until bone gave way.

Something in me tore loose. Not strength — hunger. The wolf-skin on my back, claws in my chest. My snarl filled the reeds.

The fifth rushed in. I wrenched the spear from my thigh — the iron head still slick with my blood — and drove the butt into his chest, hard enough to knock the wind from him. He staggered back, off balance. I spun the shaft in my hands, point forward now, and rammed it through. The iron burst from his spine. He twitched once, sagged against me. I shoved him off with a snarl, water and mud leaping high.

The last saw Markov atop his victim, stabbing frantic, and raised his axe for the kill. I hurled myself at him. We went under together, reeds and mud filling our mouths. His hands clawed my face. I caught the axe-shaft, wrenched it free, smashed his jaw with the butt. Again at his throat. He flailed, choking, but I pressed his head down into the mire and held. Held until the bubbles stopped.

Then silence. Only our gasps, the lap of water, the groan of the empty longboat drifting against the reeds. Markov crouched low, the needle-blade trembling in his fist, his breath ragged sobs. His eyes were wide with horror, as if he couldn't quite believe his own hand had done it.

The mire around us was thick with floating bodies.

"We're not done," I said. My voice was flat, raw. "Not until the current takes us."

We hauled into the punt, bodies slick, clothes torn, weapons clutched like relics. My leg gave out, spilling me across the thwart. Markov shoved us off, hands shaking on the oar.

The current caught, dragging us into the main channel. Behind us Drownbank burned brighter, voices rising in anger. Ahead the water ran swift and black, carrying us south.

Something moved at the edge of the reeds. The marsh cat slid out, black hide slick with water. It padded silent through the shallows to where a corpse floated, seized it by the neck, and dragged it toward the grass. The body vanished as if it weighed nothing at all.

For a heartbeat the cat's head lifted. Its eyes found mine. Pale, unblinking. Then the beast blinked, and only hunger remained. It vanished into the grass, its prize dragging behind.

The silence stretched, broken only by the weight of the dead around us. Then pain hit like a second spear thrust. My leg buckled, dumping me against the thwart. Hot blood poured between my fingers, more than cloth could catch.

Markov's eyes went wide. "Saint Danilo, Yarik—how deep?"

I looked down. The wound gaped like a mouth, edges ragged where the spear had torn through. Dark blood welled steady, not spurting but constant. Too much, too fast. Mud still clung inside it, grinding with every breath.

"Deep enough." My voice came thin. Already the edges of sight wavered grey.

"We have to go. Now." Markov seized the oars, hands shaking. "They'll send more boats. The whole settlement will come."

I tried to help, but my arms had no strength. The world tilted with each stroke. Behind us, Drownbank's torches multiplied—angry lights spreading along the waterfront like fire through dry grass.

"Which way?" Markov's voice cracked. "Yarik, which channel?"

I forced my eyes open. The current pulled strong here, southward toward the sea. Toward Driftlight and Imperial waters.

"Let it take us," I managed. "Current runs fast... south to the bay."

The punt caught the flow, suddenly swift beneath us. Markov shipped his oars, letting the water do the work. Smart—rowing would only tire him, and we needed speed more than steering.

We swept through channels that opened wide, the mire releasing us at last. My head rolled against the gunwale, the cold mist a mercy against my burning skin. Time became liquid—minutes or hours, I couldn't tell.

The world swayed. Black water, lantern lights drifting. My thigh burned hot, then cold. Mud still clung inside the wound, grinding with every shiver of the boat. I could feel the blood seeping, feel the mire inside me.

"Stay with me, Yarik. You bastard, don't you fade." Markov's voice rasped, too loud for the fog. "Look at me. You've stared down worse."

I tried to answer. What came out was a groan. My head sank against the gunwale, mist cold on my cheek.

"Not yet. Not now." I felt him slapping my face, but it was far away. "I row, you breathe. That's the bargain."

I tried. But the darkness kept pulling, soft as warm water. Each time I surfaced, we were somewhere else — different banks, wider channels. The blood made a pool at my feet, black in the starlight.

"How far?" I managed.

"I don't know. But the water's getting broader. Saltier." His voice carried hope now. "We're heading for the bay."

Lights appeared ahead — not the angry red of torches, but the steady yellow of harbour lanterns. The current swept us toward them like a tide.

Lantern Quay loomed, pilings and ropes black against the torchlight. Faces turned as he rammed us in, wild, half-mad. Dockmen shouted, the air thick with fish oil and lantern smoke, but he staggered through them wild-eyed, half stumbling, half dragging me. His eyes flicked to the blood pooling at my feet and panic hollowed his face. With a grunt more desperation than strength, he heaved me awkwardly over his shoulder.

"Help! Clear a way!" His voice cracked like a whip. "Wounded here! Make room!"

I half knew the quay beneath us — nets strung high, peat carts creaking. They blurred, spun. People pressed in, but he shoved through, cursing, bellowing, spitting like a mad dog. The hill rose above, Ostrov stone dark in the mist, Ivan's hall and the bell-tower shadowing it.

Each step jarred me deeper into the dark. I remember the tide-bell tolling once, far and hollow, though maybe it was only the blood roaring in my skull.

Then doors. Broad, iron-bound. His fists slammed them like hammers.

"Open! By Christ and the saints — open in Ivan's name! He's dying!"

A bolt scraped. Light split the dark. Men's voices, rough, wary. Then another, deeper, carrying through the smoke-hall — Ivan's voice, broad as his chest: *"Who pounds at my hall in the dead of night?"*

The door swung wide. Heat and smoke wrapped us, close as a cloak.

I saw the marsh cat's eyes again — pale, unblinking — and felt the wolf-skin drag tight across my shoulders. Hunger, waiting. Judgment.

Then the dark took me.

Chapter XIV: Driftlight

I dreamed of Anya.

Not in shrouds, nor as bones in the earth, but as she was in Skeld when the first ice glazed the harbour stones. She sat by the hearth in her grey wool dress, sleeves pushed back to show her strong forearms. Her hair fell loose over one shoulder, catching the firelight like spun copper, and it smelled of smoke and fennel from the fish she had cleaned that morning.

She was mending a net whose knots had come loose — one of mine, no doubt, torn on the rocks near Seal Point. The hemp lay spread across her lap like a wounded thing, and her fingers moved quick and sure, coaxing order from the tangle. She clicked her tongue when a strand refused, the same sound she once made when I tracked mud across her floor.

The firelight bent across her face, catching the lines at her eyes. It caught the lines at her eyes — laugh lines, worry lines, the map of years beside the sea. Her mouth was set in a small frown of concentration, the whole world narrowed to her work.

"Hold this," she said, not looking up, passing me a length of cord as if I had never left, as if I had never traded her warmth for oaths and blood. Her voice was as I remembered — low, steady, touched with the north. "Keep it taut, but don't pull. The knot needs room to settle."

I took the cord, clumsy as a boy. The hemp was rough in my palms, familiar in a way that made my chest ache. I tried to hold it as she wanted, but my hands shook and the tension sagged.

She shook her head — not unkind, only certain I would never master a fisherman's patience. "Too tight or not tight enough," she said. There was warmth in it, the warmth of old complaints worn smooth by use. "No feel for the give and take."

Salt thickened the air, mixed with peat smoke and the green tang of seaweed on the racks outside. The tide crept in through the stones underfoot, leaving patches that never dried. Gulls cried sharp beyond the window, and waves hushed against shingle.

She looked up at me then and smiled. Not the smile of saints in painted glass, but the quiet one that said I was still here, still whole, and that was enough.

"I miss you," I told her. The words felt thick.

"I know," she said. "I've been waiting."

I reached to touch her hand, to feel the callus on her palm, the band worn thin by years of work. I needed to know she was real.

The cord slipped. The fire guttered. The light fled. The smell of fennel and peat gave way to rot and blood. Gulls' cries twisted into men's voices, harsh and urgent.

My fingers closed on nothing.

I woke aching in every bone. The wound in my thigh burned as if it had waited for her to leave before striking. The dream clung like mist, already fading, yet I swore I could still smell the smoke in her hair.

A shape sat in the half-dark, boots hooked under the stool to keep it from rocking.

"About time," Markov said. "Three days I've been watching you fight fever and blood loss. I was running out of heroic last words to whisper over your corpse."

His voice was low, careful. He watched my face the way a river man watches eddies—reading for pull.

"You've looked better," he added. "Also worse. Mostly worse." A beat. "Hungry?"

"Thirst," I managed.

He had the cup ready. Tilted it so I wouldn't strain. Didn't fuss. Didn't look at the wound.

"I swore you'd wake," Markov said. "Even Krull wagered against you—said the wound would fester before dawn. Still, I bet against him. Never trust a medic who drinks more wine than his patients."

"You won?"

"Not yet. You've got to live the week for me to collect. But when you do, I'll be the richest pauper in Driftlight." He leaned back, smug as a cat. "Already ordered new leathers. And knives — a matched pair, balance like a gambler's thumb."

"With what money?"

"Persuasion," he said, tapping his temple. "Merchants here will trade half a hide just to hear themselves believe a good story. I promised fifty sols on delivery — imperial sols, mind you, not the reed-scrip they print in Driftlight. The kind with the crown's seal, hard and heavy. Worth twice their weight down here."

"And you have none."

"Not yet. But you keep breathing, and I'll have more than enough."

"Who lost most?"

Markov's grin spread. "Illarion. Couldn't resist. I told him you'd outlast the lot of us. He called it blasphemy and bet I'd be digging your grave by morning. I goaded him — small wagers, then larger. He doubled and doubled again. In the end, he swore my service for life against a chest of sols that would buy me a house on High Mound."

I looked at him. "A lifetime of service."

"Ahh… you're too stubborn to die," he said, leaning close. "So drink up, heal up. I'll fetch your broth, change your bandages, sing you lullabies if I must. Then you'll be back to killing everyone except me, and I'll be rich. We both profit."

I drank. The water tasted of iron and old wood. He let the silence sit, then set the cup down where I could reach it again.

"All right," I said at last. My voice rasped, but it held. "I won't die. Not yet."

I shifted against the boards, the wound hot in my thigh, but I forced my eyes steady on him.

"Now tell me. What did I miss?"

Before Markov could answer, the door scraped open.

Bogdan stood framed in the lamplight, cloak damp from the night. His eyes had that distant gleam again, as if he had come straight from prayer, or dream, or both. He looked from me to Markov, then back again, and made the sign of the cross in the air — slow, deliberate.

"You are needed," he said.

"For what?" I asked.

"The council gathers." His voice carried no inflection, as though he were naming the weather.

Markov snorted. "And what business has a half-dead soldier at Ivan's council?"

Bogdan ignored him. His gaze lingered on me, heavy as a hand on the shoulder. "They wait."

He left the door open. The hall beyond was lit by rushes, their smoke bitter in the draft.

Markov muttered under his breath. "Mystic bastard could just say please."

Before I could rise, another shadow filled the doorway — one of Illarion's drilled boys, no more than sixteen, eyes hollow from nights without sleep. He carried a bundle in his arms: rough-spun tunic, wool leggings, a cloak too short in the hem. Guard's garb, scrounged from Ivan's store.

Bogdan nodded as if this too were ordained. "You cannot stand before princes and thanes in rags."

The boy set the clothes down without a word, gaze sliding from my face to the floorboards. I took them piece by piece, slow with the pain. Markov steadied me when I swayed.

The tunic clung damp to my back, smelling of tallow and another man's sweat. The leggings were patched at the knees, the cloak moth-eaten, but together they made me pass for more than a beggar. No boots — raw soles on cold stone— but at least I would not stumble into council half-naked in a monk's ruin.

I tied the rope-belt hard across my waist and stood. The floor lurched, but I set my jaw and bore it. They would not see me crawl.

Bogdan was still waiting when I limped to the door. He inclined his head once, nothing more, then turned and moved ahead of us, silent as smoke.

Why he wanted me at Ivan's council I could not guess. Perhaps to bear witness. Perhaps to keep me in his orbit, as he always did when omens weighed heavy.

I followed anyway.

We followed Bogdan down a passage lined with stone from upriver, dry-laid but proud against Driftlight's sagging wood. The air shifted as we walked — less fish oil and reed-smoke, more beeswax, wine, fat, and the peat-reek bite of whitefire stored somewhere below. Ivan liked his comforts.

Rugs from the North lay across the floor, thick enough to swallow the sound of bare feet. Antlers were nailed high along the beams, tusks from southern boars set in iron brackets. Between them hung shields, their paint bright still — red crosses, crowned lions, a stag on green.

A harp leaned unused in the corner, strings slack with damp. On a side table stood silver cups chased with the King's seal, though the rims were tarnished where Driftlight's salt had bitten them. A man could tell himself he still lived in Velgrad here, if he did not breathe too deep.

We passed servants bowing low, Brackfolk girls in patched wool carrying trays of fruit and wine. Ivan liked them thin, silent, and frightened. They glanced once at me — a barefoot soldier in borrowed guard's cloth — then looked away quick.

The voices of men carried down the hall before we reached the chamber. Loud, hot, clashing.

"…if Drownbank rises, we must cut it at the root—"

"…saints witness, Greenfen burns—"

"…Reedmarch! Always Reedmarch!"

Bogdan did not pause. He moved straight to the great door, carved with knotwork of vines and beasts. The wood was oak, iron-banded, thick enough to bar a siege. He set his hand to it, but turned first, looking back at me as though to weigh whether I would stand or collapse.

I stood. My leg burned, the bandages tight beneath the leggings, but I would not falter here.

The voices on the far side rose sharper, then stilled all at once as the hinges groaned.

We stepped into Ivan's council.

The chamber stank of smoke, sweat, and spilled wine.

A long table stretched from the hearth to the high seat, oak planks wide as a coffin-lid, scarred by years of knives and cups. On it lay the wreckage of hours: trenchers slick with grease, bones gnawed to gristle, bread ground to crumbs beneath elbows. Papers had curled in the damp; maps were blotched with ale. Candles had burned to stubs, wax pooling across the margins where governors had jabbed with their fingers.

Ivan sat at the head, not as I remembered him.

Once he had been Ivan the Broad: chest like a barrel, laughter that could shake a camp, a spear that never missed. He used to carry a pouch of salt for luck, swore by Saint Stepan, and said a man should fight like a butcher and pray like a widow. I had liked him. Most of us did. He made fear feel smaller.

But the man before me was Ivan the Fat. His belly spilled across his belt, sweat shining on the rolls of his neck. He wore fur heavier than the season, a show of wealth rather than need, and a torque of silver that cut deep into his flesh. His face sagged; his eyes did not. Quick, restless, knife-bright. A man could still be dangerous long after his edge had gone blunt.

Driftwood and bone hung from his chair in place of banners. The title of Thane of Mirefast lay on him like a cloak he had never earned, and the Brackfolk still bent their ear more to the bog than to him. His wife was gone, his hall filled with visions and bluster, but his grip on the table was thick and red as ever.

The council around him was a rabble. A priest in black wool with ink-stained fingers. A scarred woman in half-unbuckled armour. Two wine-flushed governors. A captain in driftwood mail. Six voices, none in tune.

They had been at this for hours — I could smell the sour of their sweat, the exhaustion beneath their anger. They spoke of upriver towns and borderholds, of levies and levies not yet called, but it was not policy I heard, only men and women fraying, each more afraid of losing face than losing ground.

And among them, standing tall, was Illarion.

He had dressed to impress. His doublet was velvet dyed storm-blue, cut tight across the shoulders, the seams stitched with silver thread. Jewelled clasps caught the firelight, and at each hip hung a sword — twin blades, as was his way, hilts chased in brass, polished bright enough to blind. Few men could wield two at once, but Illarion wore them as though they were birthright, proof of his difference.

He held himself rigid, jaw set, eyes alive with fire. His words came quick and sharp, too sharp for courtesy, yet they drew the room like iron to a lodestone. He carried the bearing of a man certain he had been born to command.

And yet — there was something wrong. A tremor in the hand that smoothed his cuff. A flicker in the muscles of his jaw when he clenched too long. Sweat at his hairline where the hall was cool. Small betrayals the others missed, or ignored, but I had seen them before. His strength was real, but it carried a flaw, and the flaw was widening.

The governors shifted uneasily, caught between awe and doubt. To them he was the King's son, a man of blades and ambition they might harness. To me he was more dangerous than any of them knew — a flame that burned hot, but never steady.

Ivan raised his hand, fat fingers glistening with grease, and the noise fell ragged to silence. His eyes, sharp beneath the folds, turned on me.

"Yaroslav Krovin," he said, and his mouth split in a grin. "Saints save us, you live yet. I told them the wolf never dies."

I inclined my head. My leg burned where the cloth rubbed the wound, but I kept my weight steady.

He leaned forward, jowls quivering, and his voice turned hard. "Tell them what the mire does to armies. Tell them what we saw with Mstislav. They prattle about marches and victories. They forget the ground eats men quicker than any sword."

His gaze was not plea but command. He needed me to carry his point, to win this quarrel. What he had not counted on was how my presence would feed Illarion's fire instead of dampening it.

I cleared my throat. "The Great Mire kills slow. Not in battle, but in silence. Men sink in peat. Sickness eats them. Blades come from fog, then vanish. You can march a thousand in, and count a hundred back."

I saw some blanch. Others scowled as if I had robbed them of courage.

"They are not rabble anymore," I added. "I saw training schools. Boys drilled with spear and bow. Serpent-blades worn openly, not hidden as once. And at their hidden temple in the mire, a war council — dozens of Brackfolk bands, not scattered, but gathered. They are organized. Mobilized. Significant."

One of the priests leaned forward, ink still black on his fingers. "You speak of their hidden temple. Then tell us where it lies, so we may put torch to it."

The hall hushed, every eye weighing me. Markov would have spun a lie if he could, but he had no lie to give. He had never known the way — only that we were led blind through reed and mist.

"The way is not mine to give," I said. "We came to the Standing Stones, two days south of Reedmarch. From there a guide took us—" I stopped. I would not speak her name. "—through channels that bent like a maze. No chart marks them, and even if it did, the mire itself twists. Islands shift, currents change, banks close where they were open. The fog clung in the throat, the oars pulled sideways as if by unseen hands. There was more than mud and water at work. The place is guarded by something older, something that does not let strangers walk free."

Murmurs stirred — some derision, some fear.

"When we fled," I went on, "half-starved and beaten, ribs raw, the wound in my thigh tearing at every stroke, we tried for Saint Cuthbert's Hollow. The channels moved beneath our oars. Every southward way closed. The current turned us north. The mire itself is alive with dark magic. If you march an army in, you will not find a temple. You will find hunger, and the mire will take you whole."

"Convenient," the priest spat. "To speak of their heresies but not of their halls."

"Not convenient," I answered. "True. Their temples are not guarded by walls but by water, by mist and memory. Even if I gave you a name or a channel, it would not be the same when you sought it."

Silence pressed close. To some it sounded like evasion. To others, like warning. In truth it was both.

A clerk, ink still wet on his fingers, spoke from the door. "My lords — Saint Cuthbert's Hollow is fallen."

The room stilled. He swallowed. "The monks are dead. The reliquary is gone."

The table stirred like a hive kicked open.

A priest with ink-stained fingers struck the wood with his fist. "And why? Because we let their heresies rot within the Church! Driftlight crawls with false deacons and women preaching. They twist the holy forms into mire-chants. The first blow must fall here — in this city — cleanse the altar, then the marsh."

"Madness. The crown bleeds timber and whitefire through Ironholt. If the rebels seize it, Velgrad will freeze in its own hearths. The forges will go cold, the ships lie unfinished. Trade first. Guard Ironholt, and the rest can rot."

A scarred woman slammed her tankard down. "Rot? Drownbank rises already. If we do not cut them, they'll be at these gates before your ships reach Ironholt."

Ivan's lips curled back. He had heard all this before. "Enough. You waste air. We hold Driftlight. We entrench. Ships already sail for Velgrad. Reinforcements will come." He thumped the board. "The King will send ships. Armies. Then we grind them flat."

Murmurs of dissent broke, but before any man could rally them, Illarion's voice cut through.

"And until then?"

He stood, storm-blue velvet flashing at the seams, twin swords gleaming at his hips. His jaw was rigid, his eyes lit with something that burned too bright.

"They struck at me. Tried to storm the Grey Hand and take me in the night." He let the words hang. "An heir of the Crown, hunted in Driftlight's bay. That is no small insult. That is war on the bloodline itself."

The table stilled. Even Ivan's fat fingers twitched on the wood.

Illarion went on, voice edged like steel. "Now is no time for patience. Drownbank must burn. From there we march through the mire — Reedmarch first, then deeper if need be. Root and branch. Burn them. Salt the ground. Let them learn what fire means."

The hall broke.

"Madness—"

"Sense at last—"

"You'll drown them all—"

"Let him try, he'll hang us with him—"

The shouting rose until it was only noise — priests clamouring for purity, governors for trade, captains for strikes upriver. Ivan slammed his fist on the board, the blow rattling cups and maps alike.

"Enough!" His voice rolled through the hall, louder than all of them. "This council is adjourned. We meet again tomorrow, with heads cooler and bellies filled. Then we decide."

Some sagged in relief, others nodded, already thinking of wine and rest. Ivan leaned back heavy in his chair, wiping grease across his furs as if the matter were settled.

But Illarion did not sit.

"No."

His voice cut clean, and every eye turned. He stood rigid in his storm-blue doublet, both hilts flashing, his face set with fire that was almost a sneer.

"No more food. No more wine. No more waiting while the mire laughs at us. They struck at me — me, the Queen's son — and you would sleep on it? Pray for ships? You think Velgrad will save you?" He spat the word, heavy with scorn. "Velgrad sends nothing swift. Its throne wavers, its court whispers and stalls. Do not put your faith in Velgrad. I stand before you. I am the Crown."

The uproar swelled again, but this time some voices turned Illarion's way.

"A strike upriver—sense at last," barked the scarred woman, slamming her cup.

"Burn Drownbank before it festers," another agreed.

Ivan thumped the board, fat hand sending a platter rattling. "Enough! You think to march half-fed men into the mire at night? You'll drown them before dawn. We wait. We hold Driftlight. Reinforcements will come."

Illarion's jaw set, eyes flashing. He leaned forward, voice like steel on stone. "I've the Grey Hand — the King's own warship. The greatest hull afloat, and near enough to truth for any boast. Give me every ship, every man. We march tonight. Not tomorrow, not when Velgrad bestirs itself, not when the mire has grown bold. Tonight."

The hall faltered. Those who had cheered his fire glanced away. One muttered, "Supplies must be readied…" Another, "A strike, yes, but with caution…" A third raised his cup and murmured, "Your courage is beyond question, Highness." Placation, not pledge. Demurs where he had sought assent.

Illarion's face hardened. The silence stung him more than shouts. His gaze fixed on Ivan, sunk in furs, sweat beading on his neck.

"Cowards," Illarion hissed. "All of you. And you—" He pointed at Ivan, the gesture sharp as a thrust. "You were once Ivan the Broad. Now you hide behind your meat and your grease. The mire broke you, and you call it wisdom."

Ivan surged half to his feet, face purple, but Illarion's cloak had already snapped as he turned. The twin swords at his hips clattered as the doors slammed in his wake.

Silence held. No voice rose. No hand steadied.

Chapter XV: Ivan's Plea, Illarion's Claim

I woke to the smell of peat-smoke and herbs. My thigh throbbed but the fire had ebbed; the fever was broken. A Brack woman sat by me with a bowl of broth cooling in her lap. She had the hands of a fishwife, scarred and red at the knuckles, but she worked as nurse. She pressed me to drink, and I did, though every swallow felt like pulling reeds through my throat.

Markov ducked in behind her, eyes already roving for food. "Up, wolf," he said. "You've slept through supper and half a day besides. Let's find the kitchen before Ivan's hounds lick the pots clean."

I let him help me rise. My body felt hollow, ribs like planks, the wound pulling each time I breathed. Still, it was good to walk. Gratitude stirred in me for Ivan—he had housed us, tended me. I thought of thanking him.

We followed the smell of bread and fish down a narrow stair. The kitchen door stood open, voices within, raised and raw. We meant only to steal a crust, but we stepped into a quarrel.

Ivan was there, red-faced, huge shoulders stooped over his son.

The boy was no child—fifteen, with arms already corded from oars and drill, but his face still carried the soft edges of youth. Sandy hair hung lank with sweat. He stood defiant, chin thrust forward, yet his hands shook with more than anger.

"You'll not go back to him!" Ivan bellowed, voice cracking like timber. "I've lost enough to that mad princeling—I'll not lose you too!"

He cuffed the lad hard across the ear, but the boy wrenched free, teeth bared like a cornered animal.

"I will! I'm no coward!" The word spat from his lips like poison. *Coward.* Illarion's word, not his own, yet it fit his mouth as though bred there.

Ivan's face darkened. "Coward? Boy, I've bled for this realm before you could lift a knife. I've stood in shield-walls while you were still at the breast—"

"Then why cower now?" Borislav's voice cracked, high and fierce. "Why let the mire-rats burn our holdings while you feast and grow fat? Prince Illarion has fire—he'll drive them back to their holes!"

"Prince Illarion has madness!" Ivan roared. "He'll march you into the bog and leave your bones for the crabs! Is that what you want? To die for his glory while he watches from dry ground?"

The boy flinched but held his ground. "Better to die fighting than live hiding. You taught me that once. Or have you forgotten what honour means?"

Ivan surged forward, hand raised, but Borislav shoved him back. The boy had grown strong—stronger than his father had reckoned. Ivan stumbled, caught himself against the table, and for a moment looked older than his years.

"You know nothing of honour," Ivan said, voice gone low and dangerous. "Honour is keeping what is yours alive. Not throwing your son's life away for a madman's dream."

"And what of our people?" Borislav's fists clenched at his sides. "The fishermen burned out of Greenfen? The families butchered at Thornwick? Do we abandon them too for the sake of safety?"

"We wait for reinforcements. We hold what we can —"

"We wait while they die!" The boy's voice broke, tears bright in his eyes though his jaw stayed set. "You taught me the sword, Father. Taught me to lead. But when it matters, you tell me to crouch behind walls like a merchant's son!"

Ivan's shoulders sagged. For a heartbeat he looked not like the Thane of Blackreef but like any father watching his child walk toward fire.

"Boy," he said, and his voice carried all the weight of years. "You think I fear their blades? I fear their purpose. You see Prince Illarion's fire and think it strength. I see a boy drunk on his own legend, leading good men to death. That is not courage — it is waste."

Borislav shook his head, sandy hair catching lamplight. "He's the King's son. He carries mandate —"

"He carries nothing but pride and madness!" Ivan slammed his fist on the table, making bowls jump. "The King is days away by ship, if he comes at all. Here, now, we are all that stands between Driftlight and the flame. I'll not see it fall for a prince's dream of glory."

The boy turned then, and his eyes found mine across the kitchen. Appeal, perhaps, or challenge. He saw in me what his father had once been: a man who rode toward danger rather than away.

"Tell him," Borislav said, voice thick with unshed tears. "You've served the King. You know what duty means. Tell him we can't sit idle while the realm burns."

I felt Ivan's eyes on me too, heavy with expectation and fear. The boy stood straight despite his trembling, waiting for my words to tip his fate.

"I've served the King," I said. "I've seen men rush to their deaths calling it duty. When the fire cooled, all they left behind was ash and widows."

Borislav's face hardened. He had hoped for support and found only cold truth. "Then you're both cowards," he said, but the fire had gone from it. He sounded suddenly young again, a boy trying on a man's convictions and finding them ill-fitted. He pushed past us, head high but shoulders tight with hurt. The door slammed behind him, leaving silence heavy as fog.

Ivan stood breathing hard, one hand pressed to the table as if it were the only thing keeping him upright. Servants busied themselves with pots, but their glances betrayed pity.

He caught sight of me then, really saw me. Tried for a smile, failed. "Parenting," he said, voice rough as sailcloth. "Harder than any war. The boy will get himself killed chasing that prince's shadow."

He stopped, as though he might speak treason, then only shook his head.

At last he said, "Save him, Yaroslav. Talk to him. He won't hear me—sees only a fat old man where his hero used to stand. But you… you still carry the wolf-skin in his eyes. He might listen."

"I can take a look," I said. "No more than that. I can't promise him safe from his own path."

"That's enough." Ivan set a hand to my shoulder, weight of years in his grip. "You've saved me more than once."

"I don't remember it."

He grinned a little then, weary but real. "That's because you were busy bleeding. But I remember. Thornwick Bridge. The Greenway crossing. Always in the worst of it, drawing fire where weaker men fled. You think that's forgotten?"

I thought it flattery, a ploy to bind me closer. Yet his eyes were too tired for cunning, too full of honest fear for his son.

By next dawn I kept my word and went down to the yard. Rain had rinsed the stone clean, leaving every joint dark, reeds already pushing up where Driftlight's wall gave way to mire. No chapel, no hall — only mud, rope circles, barrels split for shields, a rack of blunted spears. Yet it felt claimed, reshaped, as surely as any chapel by its saints.

The veterans stood easy in the press, druzhinniki of Velgrad, hard men in well-kept mail and plate, shields slung, swords sharp, bows strung. They had held lines under fire, and it showed in their calm. A thin edge of discipline among the noise. The sotniki worked among them without fuss: Mikhail the Butcher tested shield grips, running his ruined hand along the rims and swapping out a cracked board before it could fail; Sava One-Eye checked the bowstrings, leaning close to hear the twang, nodding when the note rang true; Petyr with the bent spear walked his men through thrust and brace, haft angled just so against a charging foe; Radovan barked over the axe-men, reminding them when to hack and when to hew; and Krill, lean as rope, crouched by the packs, weighing rations and water, marking what would last a week and what would rot by dusk. Their presence kept the press from boiling over, order stitched into the crush of bodies by habit older than these boys had years.

Once, in the old wars, a sotnik commanded a full hundred. Illarion had five, and not a hundred men between them, yet the name mattered. He dressed scraps in the shape of an army, and by naming them so, he made them believe it.

Before them stood twenty-five Velgrad men in five even ranks—not boys, not conscripts, but druzhinniki who had held lines under fire. Their silence was heavier than any shout.

Beyond them came the youths gathered by Illarion in Stormhold City, ten in all, paired and set at the head of five groups of Driftlight boys. Illarion called them desyatniki — leaders of ten. In truth they were little more than drill-sergeants, but titles lent weight, and weight bent raw ore into shape. Their task was plain: to test, to drive, to raise their allotment or break it.

The Driftlight lads, near fifty of them, stood in rough squares, ten to a group. Barefoot, patched, knuckles raw from training. Yet even in their hunger they no longer shifted or muttered as rabble do. They waited. They watched their desyatniki. They held their stance until told.

Borislav was among them, hair plastered by mist, shoulders squared in clumsy mimicry of the older youths. He strained to belong, and in the shape of the warband there was room even for him. I had known that joy once, when the mire first tasted my blood.

What had been scraps and strays three months ago now stood as a company. A blade hammered from raw ore, not yet sharp, but no longer formless.

Illarion paced the front, his voice ringing hard as steel on stone.

"Three months past, no one knew your names. Now you stand as my blade. And a blade is only worth what it cuts."

At his word Desyatnik Kendric, scarred jaw, stepped into the Driftlight ranks. He pointed at a boy barely fourteen. "Hit me."

The boy hesitated. Kendric's hand closed on his wrist, turned him, pressed him into the mud until the mire swallowed his cry. He rose smeared, chest heaving. Illarion's voice cut across the yard.

"Pain does not flatter. It shows what you are — and what you must become."

So it went down the line. Youths set upon each other, some dropped in moments, others lasting longer. The Stormhold lads struck hard, drove Driftlight's to their knees, then dragged them up again to face the next. Weakness was not spared, only used.

I watched them rise to it. However brutal, they found their place in it. Illarion taught the first rule: the world is cruel, but a man may climb through it if he learns when to bow and when to bare his teeth, whose boot to kiss and whose throat to cut. In that order he can find belonging. And I felt the old hunger in me as I watched those who rose to the challenge. It feeds something in us — this hierarchy of wolves — gives shape to the howling emptiness. There are other lessons, gentler and harder, but I have never learned them.

The sotniki and druzhinniki stood silent at the edge, watching, but never stepping in; it was the desyatniki alone who broke the boys, while the veterans' presence hung like iron behind them.

A tall boy named Tomek was called out. Illarion asked his name, then stripped it away. "Your name is what I choose. Your worth is what I decide. Your life is mine to spend. Do you accept this?"

"Yes, my liege."

"Then strike the one beside you. Drop him — or Desyatnik Veynar drops you both."

The choice was plain. Tomek struck. Not hard enough. Illarion's face stayed still. "Again."

The second blow sent the boy to the ground, blood on his lip. Veynar pressed a boot to his back and kept him there. The rest learned by watching.

The yard became a contest measured in bruises. The strong lifted higher, given place, given food. The weak were pushed down, made to crawl, but even crawling had its place. Borislav flung himself into it, taking blows, giving them back, eyes alight with the strange joy of finding a rank in the order.

Through it all Illarion moved like a conductor, shaping cries and strikes into a rhythm. Not rabble, not brawl — ranks formed under his hand, each boy tested, each place set.

When they sagged breathless, Bogdan stepped forward, cloak heavy with rain, bone charms knocking like teeth. His voice was smooth, carrying.

"Brothers, do you know whose steps you follow? Saint Danilo, who stood with a dented helm and gave his life so others might retreat. He was no king. Only a boy. As you are boys. He died young, and he died worthy."

He pressed thumb to brow. Some did the same, whispering Danilo's name once, as custom holds.

"Your bruises are your helm, dented but unbroken. Let pain temper you. Let hunger sanctify you. Those who endure will die as he did — with no shame, no surrender."

Captain Soroka stood apart by the wall, rain streaming from her hood and soaking the tar-bound braid that hung heavy against her shoulder. Broad in the frame, pale-eyed, she said little, as ever. Her cloak dripped steadily onto the rushes, but she made no move to shake it off. Still as a moored ship, waiting her turn.

Her vessel waited below as well—the Grey Hand, broad-keeled and stubborn as her captain. Ninety men weighed her deep for the upriver run, too many for channels that shifted like lies, but if any sailor could force her through mud and shallows it was Soroka. She had the sea in her bones and patience like ballast.

Princes and priests fill halls with words; the captain needed none. I had seen her ignore his orders once, in the waters of the Kladovek, and walk away rather than risk wreck on hidden stone. She would carry us now—not for him, not for me, but because the river and the keel demanded it.

Among the druzhinniki I counted bows strung and ready, a dozen at least. Enough to blacken the air over Drownbank's palisades. Bogdan would see to fire; the oil-jars stacked near the yard's edge were proof of that. And the desyatniki — Kendric, Veynar, and the rest — were killers already, eager to drive their allotments into the breach.

Illarion had gathered all he needed: ship, captain, fire, arrows, blades. Nothing lacked but the will to strike, and that he carried in excess.

The rain fell hard, and Illarion let it beat against his face. "Enough. Go rest. At first light we sail."

He lifted his swords. Steel flashed under the torches.

"Look at you. Driftlight gave you nothing. No armour. No name. You were rabble. Hungry. Waiting. I gave you steel. I gave you purpose. I gave you fire. Now you are mine. My fire-blades. Each of you, all of you. Ivan waits for ships. Ivan waits for death. I do not wait. Fire does not wait. It burns. It takes. At dawn we go to Drownbank. At dawn its walls burn. At dawn the mire learns who leads its sons."

Their cry came hard and joined. Not boys' voices now, but a war-shout that struck the yard like surf against stone. For the first time I heard not hunger, but belief. Belief is sharper than hunger. Hunger weakens. Belief drives men into the fire smiling.

Chapter XVI: Toward Fire at Dawn

The yard emptied slow. The sotniki gathered their druzhinniki and marched down the quay, the hardened core of Illarion's warband. The Stormhold youths—the new desyatniki—fell in beside them, striding proud to the Grey Hand as if they had worn rank all their lives. Soroka's sailors followed with Bogdan's oil, two jars to a pole under her pale watch. Bogdan came last, bone-charms whispering as he shepherded the fire aboard like a priest with flock.

The Driftlight recruits slouched off into alleys and stilt-houses, back to reed-mats and smoke-huts, their bruises proof enough of service. A few lingered in the torchlight, trading jests or nursing split lips before drifting into the dark.

Illarion's gaze cut across what remained and fixed on one boy.

"Borislav."

The name came sharp as steel. The lad froze, then stepped forward, shoulders squared though his lip still bled from the drills. Illarion's mouth curved, not in warmth but in recognition.

"I know you," he said. "Ivan's cub. Broad in the shoulders, quick to strike. You stood your ground."

Pride lit the boy's face, but Illarion let the silence stretch, praise measured out like a miser counting coins.

"A fine name. Borislav. Worthy, though untested."

The boy flushed. "I will prove myself, my prince. I will fight for you, lord —"

Illarion's voice cut like a whip. "Not lord. I am your liege. Say it."

Borislav stammered, blood on his teeth. "My liege."

"Again."

"My liege!"

Illarion's smile was quick and sharp. "Better. Remember it. I am no man's master for coin or bread. I am the King's son. I am your liege, and you are mine to spend."

The boy dropped to one knee in the mud, bowing his head. "Then I am yours, liege. By steel and by fire."

Illarion struck him across the face. Not blessing but brand. The slap cracked loud enough to echo off Driftlight's wall, a cruel seal of service. Borislav staggered but did not rise until ordered.

"Up," Illarion said. "Marked. Not as child, but as man."

Borislav rose trembling.

"You will come to the Grey Hand before first light. You will help me into my armour. You will walk at my side — into fire, into ruin, into the very gates of hell."

The boy's face was bright with blood and triumph both, shoulders squared as if the blow had made him taller. He fairly glowed, smiling so wide it seemed his face might split.

I watched, silent. Illarion's choice was no accident. He had plucked Ivan's son from the rabble and set him apart, binding him with praise and pain both. The boy thought it honour. He did not see how sharp a snare it was.

If Ivan feared losing him before, now he had true cause. A squire beside the prince was no safer than a torch in a powder-store. Illarion would burn through men and boys alike to prove his fire.

I had given Ivan no promise to guard his son, and even if I had, I was in no state to keep it. My wound still pulled with every breath. I could scarcely protect myself, much less a boy racing headlong into a prince's ruin.

Illarion's eyes slid from the boy to me.

"Krovin," he said, voice flat as iron. Then, after a pause that stretched too long: "You're still breathing."

Not quite surprise. Not quite disappointment. Something caught between the two.

"Hard to kill," I said.

His mouth twitched — not quite a smile, but close. "So I've heard. Drownbank. Six men in the reeds." He stepped closer, low enough that his words wouldn't carry to the boys still lingering nearby. "With a spear through your leg."

There was something in his tone I couldn't place. Respect, maybe. Or hunger. The way a man might look at a sword he couldn't afford but couldn't stop wanting.

"Lucky," I said.

"Luck." He repeated the word like it tasted bitter. "Is that what you call it when you kill six rebels with a broken spear and crawl out of the mire half-dead?" His eyes were bright with something that might have been fever, might have been need. "I have seventy boys who think they're warriors. You know what they are? Farmers' sons playing with steel. Pretty to watch, but they'll break the moment they taste real war."

I said nothing. Let him talk.

"Tomorrow we burn Drownbank. I need those boys to stand when the killing starts. To hold when men scream and bleed and beg." His voice dropped lower, urgent. "You know what that looks like. You've stood in it and not broken."

He wanted something from me. Needed it. But beneath the need, I caught something else—a flicker of resentment, quickly hidden. The look of a man asking for help from someone he'd rather strangle.

"I can barely stand," I said. The wound pulled even as I shifted weight. "My leg's not healed. I'd be more hindrance than help."

"Then be a hindrance that knows which end of a sword kills," he said at last, restless hand falling back to his side. "I don't need you whole, Krovin. I need you there. When the pretty boys see you standing, bleeding, still swinging your blade—they'll think they can do the same."

Borislav was watching us from across the yard, trying to look like he wasn't listening. Other boys clustered near, heads turned our way.

"You want me as warden," I said.

"I want you as proof." His voice carried an edge now, sharp enough to cut. "Proof that men can stand when everything falls apart. That weakness doesn't have to mean death." He leaned closer, and I smelled the sour sweat of fever on him. "These boys worship pretty victories. Clean kills. They need to see what real war looks like — ugly, bloody, desperate. They need to see you."

"I've no armour. No weapon," I said. "Mine were stripped by the rebels."

For a heartbeat his eyes narrowed, measuring the truth of it. He wore twin swords, bright at the hilts, polish enough to blind. My hands were empty. Greyfang — the northern sword the Queen once pressed into my hands — lay lost beneath a sunken causeway, price paid for the burning relic now locked in Illarion's aftcastle on the Grey Hand.

Illarion's fingers brushed the hilt at his hip. Not threat — consideration. As though he weighed the cost of putting his steel in my hands.

And in that gesture lay the knot of it. I had never been asked to guard him; my place at his side was only cover for the Queen's command. Yet by chance, and by my own folly, I had sworn him an oath that bound us tighter than kin. Not to save him. Not to crown him. To kill him, clean, before he was broken and useless. That oath sat between us, heavier than steel. He had wrung it from me drunk and desperate, and yet he trusted it more than he trusted blood. He knew I would kill him if the rot took him. He hated me for it, and leaned on me for it, both in the same breath.

I saw the hunger in his eyes, and the hate, and the twisted reliance that lay between them. He wanted me armed. He wanted me broken. He wanted me ready to strike at his enemies — and ready to strike at him, if the time came.

And I agreed, because where he walked, my oath walked with him. If I stayed behind, I could not keep it. Only by standing at his side could I judge when the rot had taken hold, and only by standing close could I end him when the moment came.

"I'll come," I said.

Relief flickered across his features, quickly masked. "Good." He straightened, voice rising enough for the boys to hear. "Dawn. Don't keep me waiting."

He turned away, then stopped. When he looked back, his smile was sharp as winter wind.

"And bring Markov. He'll fight and die with the rest. I need every blade. Even lying thieves."

Borislav left the yard with his head high, the welt on his cheek red as a brand. A few Driftlight lads clapped him rough on the shoulders before peeling into alleys and stilt-houses. He strode past them, not homeward to reed-mats, but up toward the stone rise where Ivan's hall shadowed the quay.

I followed.

He noticed me quick enough, but he did not slow. "Come to tell me I'm a fool?" His voice cracked between defiance and hope.

"No. I swore no oath to change your mind. Only to see you live long enough to make it your own."

That earned me a glance, quick and uncertain.

"You've got wealth," I said. "Use it. Armour, real armour—not just boiled leather. Boots that won't rot in the mire. A spear is fine, but that blade you took from your father's wall is too long for marsh-fighting. Better a short sword. Or an axe you can swing in close quarters."

He bristled at the correction, but listened all the same.

"Thieves will be worse than rebels," I went on. "Even among your brothers. Watch your back. Guard your kit. And honour your oaths. Men forgive theft easier than treachery."

His smile flickered. "You sound like my father. Always warning, always weighing. Never seeing the fire in it." He kicked at the mud, scattering torchlight in the puddles. "He was a hero once. Now he hides behind meat and walls. He doesn't understand me."

That struck familiar.

Ivan had never spoken of his father with anything but scorn. Murderer, coward, braggart—he cursed him as easy as breathing, wove the words into every story until the men laughed and made wagers on what sin he would name next. A fool, a bully, a drunk—on and on, never an ounce of mercy. Yet I remembered the day word came his father was dead.

I remembered the night word reached camp that Ivan's father was dead. No curses then, no boasts. I had gone to his tent by chance, meaning only to ask for orders. The flap was half-closed, lamplight leaking thin across the mud. Inside, he sat hunched over his cot, shoulders broad as an ox yet caved in, hands locked white on his knees. His breath came ragged, as if the news had driven a spear into his chest. The air smelled of tallow smoke and damp canvas; I could hear the cords creak as his weight bowed the frame.

He looked up when he noticed me. For a heartbeat I saw it plain — eyes red, face slack, the grief of a son who had hated too long and found himself emptied when the hatred was taken. Then the mask snapped back. He forced a grin, even a bark of laughter, and waved me in like nothing was wrong.

"Disappointed, that's all," he said, voice too loud in the close tent. "Wanted to be the one to kill the old son of a bitch myself."

It fooled no one. Not me, not the lamp smoke that curled like a funeral pyre above us. But he held to the jest, and by next day the tale had grown teeth again — coward, braggart, drunkard. The men laughed, and he laughed with them. Only I carried the memory of that first look, raw as any wound.

Now I saw the same wound festering in his son — the need to prove himself against the very man whose praise he craved. Borislav's scowl was near the same: boy's anger, but rooted in something older, sharper. He wanted his father's blessing, and hated him for withholding it. Pride and hurt together, red as any gash.

"You think me old," I said. "Maybe I am. But I've buried more young men than you've named. Take my counsel, or don't. Remember it when the mire closes in."

He gave no reply. Yet I saw him weighing the words, even as he turned his face away to hide it. His stride did not falter.

The hall loomed above, windows glowing faint with hearth-smoke, bell-tower lost in fog. Borislav squared his shoulders as though the sight alone proved him grown.

I thought only of Ivan—my old comrade, fearing the son who would not hear him. If the boy had seemed lost before, he was further gone now. And I had promised nothing.

Still, I walked beside him until the doors took him in.

Later that night, when the hall's noise had ebbed to silence and only the tide-bell tolled faint through the fog, I sat wakeful by the shutter. The room looked east across Driftlight's quay. Mist drowned the city, lamps swaying dim in the murk, their glow paling against the bulk of the Grey Hand. Even at anchor she loomed broad and heavy, a beast waiting to swallow men whole. At dawn she would carry us upriver. Into Drownbank. Into fire.

I leaned on the sill, thigh aching, the stink of peat-smoke thick in the rafters. The yard lay empty, but I still heard the echoes—boys' voices cracking in shouts, Illarion's hand branding them his.

For a moment I thought of rousing Ivan, telling him plain that his son had taken the oath regardless of him. But I let the thought pass. The man had burdens enough, and the truth would find him soon enough in the fire.

The door creaked. Markov slid in, a bottle clutched like contraband. "You brood too loud," he said. "It rattles the beams."

He sat beside me, pulled the stopper with his teeth, and winced as the fumes rose. "Driftlight's finest. Peat and rot in equal measure. Saints preserve us." He handed it over.

I took a swallow. The whitefire clawed down, smoky as a burned bog, nothing like the clean spirit of Velgrad. My eyes watered.

"You've learned not to choke," he said. "Practice makes perfect." He drank deep himself, coughed once, then grinned thinly.

I set the bottle between us. "The Grey Hand sails at first light. Illarion wants us aboard."

Markov laughed sharp. "Of course he does. March the wolf and the rat into the bog to prove his fire. Why not? Saints know the ship's heavy enough without our carcasses weighing her deeper."

He shook his head. "Channel's deep enough, current runs fast from Drownbank to here. But the Hand's no river boat. Soroka will have to thread her through shoals with ninety men and oil stacked to the gunwales. One slip and we're aground with rebels swarming the banks."

I said nothing.

Markov glanced at me sidelong. "You'll go anyway."

I met his gaze.

He swallowed, then tried for levity. "Just don't expect me to stand tall when the prince charges. You remember Stormhold. I found the deepest hole in the rubble and stayed there till the screaming stopped. Best decision I ever made."

His grin faltered, shame creeping in around the edges. He had confessed it before, and still the truth bit him raw.

"You're still here," I said.

"Aye," he muttered. "Cowardice has its merits." He took another swig, wiped his mouth with the back of his hand. "But this? Drownbank? Even a coward can tell when the dice are loaded against him."

The whitefire burned in my gut. Outside, the tide lapped slow against the quay, steady as a death-drum. The Grey Hand loomed, waiting.

Markov pushed the bottle back into my hand. "Drink, wolf. If we're fools enough to see dawn, might as well meet it warm."

I drank. The fire clawed deeper. Neither of us spoke again.

The ship swayed in the dark, waiting to drag us all into the mire's teeth.

Chapter XVII: Proof of Oath, Proof of Fire

First light came thin, washed grey through the river mist.

The Grey Hand loomed at the quay's end, black hull tarred and ribbed with iron. Driftlight's stilt-piles strained beneath her weight, timbers creaking as though the town itself feared her mooring. The smaller craft alongshore seemed like minnows beside a pike — traders and fishing punts pressed back into the reeds, their owners staring wide at the warship they had no right to share water with.

Ninety feet stem to stern, beam near twenty-two, her waist full as a whale's, her keel biting deeper than the Driftwater liked. Two decks rose in her aftcastle, a tower of oak and tar that shadowed the quay like a watch-post. Her single square sail — black wool patched white where the king's sigil stood — hung furled, thick as curtain-cloth. Pennant frayed but still snapping, shark-tooth fringes biting the wind.

Below, twenty benches ran each side, oar-ports tarred and ready. In her hold lay pitch casks, salted fish, and cordage enough for a season. She had been built for sixty souls and war besides — bows strung across her rails, oil-pots slung by the mast, shields stacked like a wall along her gunwales. More than that was folly. With ninety aboard she would ride heavy, her belly grinding the shoals, but men crammed anyway, shoulder to shoulder. Sardines in oak.

I remembered her when she was sharper — lanterns gleaming, brass bright, crew quick in the rigging, sails clean as judgment. She had sailed with the king then, and I had walked her deck with my oath like a chain about my throat.

Now she waited in silence, scarred, tar-streaked, her breath held like a beast led inland to slaughter. Built for the open sea, she was bound upriver, into channels too narrow for her shoulders, into waters that would never forget.

The veterans stood easy in the press, druzhinniki of Velgrad, hard men in well-kept mail and plate, shields slung, swords sharp, bows strung. They had held lines under fire, and it showed in their calm. A thin edge of discipline among the noise.

The desyatniki were a different sight— Stormhold youths in mixed leathers, a patchwork of boiled hide and scavenged studs. Each carried a spear or dagger, a few short bows slung over shoulders, the kind stolen from kin or pressed into hand by Illarion's command. They strutted among their tens, voices too sharp, eager to show authority they barely owned.

The Driftlight recruits hunched in rough squares, barely armed—staves cut from reed or ash, fish-knives polished bloody, whatever Illarion had scrounged from storehouses. Some had short bows of Brackfolk make, bone-tipped, seal-gut strings. Enough to shoot, not enough to win. Bare feet stamped the planks, raw with cold, but they held their ranks.

Borislav stood apart even here. Studded armour cinched proud across his shoulders, sword at his hip, dagger sheathed bright. He looked like he belonged among the veterans, though his cheeks were still soft with youth. His eyes never left Illarion, hungry as a hound for command.

Illarion had dressed in plate—one of several he kept, iron chased with storm-blue trim, pauldrons rising sharp, breastplate polished enough to blind. He moved heavy in it, but the weight only lent him presence. Borislav had buckled the straps before dawn, and now he trailed in his prince's shadow, close as a squire to his knight.

Markov kept to the gunwale, half in shadow. He looked unarmoured, a thin cloak and smirk for disguise. But I knew better. He liked his leathers thin and hidden, knives stitched where eyes wouldn't catch them, garrotes coiled under sleeves, blades pressed into boots. An arsenal carried light, as if survival could be sewn into seams. He didn't want to be there, and his eyes measured the riverbanks more than the men.

The Captain had the tiller, muttering sharp to her sailors, barking when hands slipped knots. She did not like it—sailing upriver into the Mirefast's dark heart, through channels that shifted like lies. "The Driftwater swallows ships whole," she growled. "This hull was built for sea, not for reeds and mud." But still she steered, because the Grey Hand obeyed her hand more than any prince's dream.

On the quay a small crowd pressed close. Mothers and fathers had come to see off their sons, faces raw with fear. Some prayed aloud, clutching icons or reed-knots. Others waved, voices breaking. The boys answered with eager shouts, proud to be seen as warriors. The older men kept their silence, knowing what lay upriver. The dock bell tolled once, deep and hollow—the tide-bell that had marked Driftlight's hours long before there was a northern ship in her harbour. Its voice rolled across water and fog alike, farewell and warning in one.

"Anchor up! Cast off!" Captain Soroka's voice cracked sharp across the deck. Ropes slapped the water, oars bit, the Grey Hand began to pull free. The quay slid past slow, the crowd walking with her until the pilings ended.

Then Ivan came. He stood at the end of the dock, broad as ever, furs thrown over bare shoulders, no guards to flank him. His eyes found his son on the deck — Borislav standing proud in his studded armour, cheeks flushed with youth and fear. For a heartbeat father and son faced each other across the widening water. No words passed. No blessing. Only a silence heavy as stone.

Illarion stood beside the boy, plate bright in the dawn, gaze locked on Ivan as well. The silence widened — Thane, son, and prince bound in a knot the tide would soon pull tight.

The Grey Hand pushed upriver slow, her keel too broad for the Driftwater's tricks. The channel shifted under her like a living thing — sandbanks here today, gone tomorrow, shoals that moved with every tide. Captain Soroka barked sharp, sailors straining on poles and sweeps to keep her from grounding. Every time the hull jarred shallow, the men flinched as one. Too many aboard, too heavy, and the river wanted to swallow us whole.

The deck stank of bodies. Ninety men crammed shoulder to shoulder, no space to lie down, no food ladled, no piss-pot. Those with courage leaned over the rail; those without fouled their boots, and the reek grew. Sweat and breath steamed in the morning chill, ropes creaked, oars groaned. The river mist never lifted, pressing low, thick as wool.

Tempers frayed quick. The desyatniki barked at their tens, eager to prove themselves hard. Boys shoved for elbow-room, cursed each other, squared their shoulders like they were already veterans. A fistfight broke before noon, two Driftlight lads grappling until one bled. The Stormhold youths dragged them apart, but their grins told the lesson plain: bruise quick or be made to.

Markov crouched near the stern, chewing nothing, eyes restless on the banks. "We're being watched," he muttered. "I can feel it."

I didn't deny it. The reeds hid more eyes than we'd ever count. But a ship like the Grey Hand—broad-hulled, bristling with bows and oil—made ambush folly. No Brack raiders would waste men striking her in open water. That was the comfort. The trap would be farther on.

"Empty town or death pit," Markov whispered, "no other choice."

He was right. Drownbank would not be half-manned. Either abandoned, lures left to draw us deeper, or packed with knives and fire. Either way, the march into the mire was folly. A prince's pride, not strategy.

After the flare came the slump. Hours dragged. Oars dipped slow, the river steady, the banks sliding past reed by reed. Men muttered, spat, shifted weight until the deck rocked with the motion. Some sang half-remembered marches, voices cracking. Others dozed standing, heads bumping shoulders. The Driftlight boys pissed over the side, jeering when the current sprayed back.

The veterans kept still, conserving strength. They had seen marches like this before—twelve hours with nothing but their own stink and the river's pull.

The Captain never left the tiller. Her voice cracked constant, cursing the current, snapping at the oarsmen. The Grey Hand heaved with every shift of the channel. The deck pitched once, hard, when her belly scraped mud. Men yelped like startled hens. She steadied under Soroka's hand, but her jaw was set white. "River's rising against us," she growled. "She'll take the unwary."

By dusk the bravado had burned off. The boys slumped in knots, too hungry to chatter, too weary to fight. The deck was slick with piss and sweat, and the stench clung in every breath. Illarion had not shown himself since dawn. His absence pressed heavier than his presence—men waiting for a word, a shout, anything to turn this day from slow rot into meaning.

Twelve hours the river carried us, and by nightfall we were only deeper in its teeth

Borislav came for us as the Grey Hand neared the last bend, where the Driftwater curled west three miles short of Drownbank. Mist clung low, the reeds close, the smell of smoke where there should have been none. The boy was flushed from running, studded armour bright in the dim, his eyes lit with pride borrowed from his prince.

"My liege calls," he said.

So we went aft, Markov and I, limping through the press to the stern-castle. The Prince's chamber was narrow and close, tarred planks sweating river damp, the lamps smoking thick. Iron polish and wet wool soured the air.

Illarion waited in plate—storm-blue edged, pauldrons like knives, the breastplate polished until it spit back lamplight. Bogdan stood close, bone charms whispering against his chest with each breath; his smile was the kind that absolves and condemns at once. Two guards leaned along the wall, iron faces, fingers loose at hilts. Borislav lingered by the table, a folded cloth held like a sacrament.

I came with my old shield only, scarred and warped from Stormgrave Isle. No sword. No armour. A limp that still marked every step.

Illarion's eyes found me and did not let go. He lifted a chestplate from the table — plain iron, straps waiting as if for living shoulders. Beside it lay a sword in its black scabbard, the mouth gaped an inch: dark as oil, its edge catching the light like a fin of water. He set them forward with the smooth courtesy of a man making an offer into a demand.

"Yaroslav Krovin," he said, low and sure, his voice filling the room. "You bled for my father. You stood in fire and did not break. Stand with me now. Take these. Be armed again."

His hand rested on the scabbard. "Pryaz," he said, almost tender — speaking the name as if it were both benediction and brand.

The word landed like a cold thing. Pryaz — the Binding. Not only a name but a sentence. To take it would be to let iron weave itself through oath and flesh. He had named the snare before I had stepped into it.

He did not let his grip go. "But not for nothing," he added. "I want your oath. Not only to fight. To guard what matters most."

He nodded. Borislav moved as if on a rope and unfolded the cloth on the table.

It was not the black field I had known — no Crown's grey hand. The white gleamed under lamplight, painted with a crown in red, its points singed and black at the edges where the dye had bled. A new banner. Illarion's banner.

Silence closed like a lid. The boy's head stayed bowed; he made no sound.

"Swear it. To this banner. To me. Before witness." Illarion's voice sharpened, a blade thrown. Bogdan's eyes flashed —

hungry and pleased. The guards watched the way iron watches for cracks. Markov said nothing; I felt his gaze like a thin blade at my ribs.

The weight settled on me. To guard a banner was to guard the man beneath it. To swear to defend it was to bind myself to him. This was no loyalty to the King's black field — this was fire and crown, the prince remade.

And Pryaz lay there, its scabbard swallowing lamp-smoke, the steel promising an oath I refused to speak. I had sworn one vow — to kill him if the rot took him. To lift that blade would be to take another oath, a different noose.

There were eyes on me. Witnesses. No silence possible. No way out.

Smoke curled slow in the close air. Illarion's hand still rested on the chestplate, patient as a thing that had waited long for claim. Borislav's head did not rise. Bogdan's smile showed teeth like judgment. Markov's mouth was a thin knife-slit.

I stood with only my old shield. No sword, no helm, a limp that slowed me. Death in the press was certain. Yet breaking an oath was worse than death. Worse than chains, worse than the stake. Oath-breakers were remembered only in shame.

But to swear to him — to this burning crown — was no better. It was a pledge not to the King, but to his son. Fire instead of iron. Ambition instead of rule. If I swore, I would be his, body and blade.

If I refused, the Prince might cut me down then and there. He needed loyalty shown, not withheld, and his guards were close.

The weight of it pressed hard as the deck itself. I thought of what oath I carried already: to kill him clean if the rot consumed him. That was enough.

At last I drew breath. "I will guard you in the melee," I said. My voice came flat, iron on stone. "I will stand with your banner. I will fight as I always have. But…."

Then the floor shuddered. A long groan ran through the timbers, followed by a thunderous crack. We staggered as the Grey Hand lurched sideways, her belly grinding hard. Men shouted outside, the sound of oars clattering, rigging snapping. The lamp swung wild, smoke spilling thick.

"Saints!" Borislav gasped, catching the table as it slid.

Illarion's sword rang as he half-drew it, not at me but at the unseen. "What—?"

Shouts rose from the deck. "Aground! We're aground!"

We rushed to the door, stumbling into the pale mist. The river had narrowed, no more than fifty feet of true depth, the current pressed tight between reed-banks. The Grey Hand listed hard to port, her keel caught but her deck still above water, trapped like a beast in a snare. Water churned black against her flanks.

And under that water, faint in the shifting current, I saw the shape: cut trees, chained together in a lattice, laid crosswise to bar the channel. A trap built for us.

The first arrow hissed from the reeds and thudded into a ratnik's mail. Then another, and another. A rain of shafts clattered across the deck. Men cried out. The Driftlight boys cowered.

The trap had sprung.

Chapter XVIII: The Black Blade Taken

Arrows sang. Iron rang. The Grey Hand shuddered with every impact as though the whole ship groaned at once. Boys screamed, pressed flat to the deck, their hands clamped to heads as if that would stop a shaft. Veterans shouted them to rise, to string bows, but their voices were lost in the storm.

Illarion did not flinch. He planted himself midships, plate bright as a beacon, and bellowed orders above the din. "Shields to the rails! Archers forward! Hold fast, you sons of Velgrad!"

His voice cut through the panic, but no voice could conjure discipline where none had been forged. Driftlight lads scrambled, grabbing for bows, loosing wild into the mist. Most arrows struck water, some even our own planks. Only the veterans' shafts found flesh; I heard rebel cries from the reed-line, thin but real.

At the stern Borislav fought with a length of cord, lashing the prince's new banner to a pike-pole. He raised it high, the white field stark against the smoke and fog, crown-and-fire painted crude but proud, the strokes raw, unfinished. "For my liege!" he shouted, voice breaking, but it carried.

Illarion's mouth curved in fierce pride. "Hold it high, boy! Let them see!"

The boy did, though the pole shook in his hands, his knuckles bone-white around it. Arrows hissed close; one split the wood near his grip. He staggered but held on, face set, as if the banner itself were armour.

I had nothing. No sword, no shield. Only my limp, my empty hands. I shoved boys back from the rails, barked at them to stand straight, but it was nothing. A hollow show. Already rebels were loosing steady from bank and reed-line, twenty bowstrings singing. Our lads dropped shrieking, or fled to the mast-foot for cover.

Illarion's gaze caught mine, fierce above the rim of his plate. The breastplate he had offered me still lay in the aftercastle. The sword too. I had refused once. But to stand unarmed now was worse than cowardice. It was uselessness.

"Saints damn me," I muttered, and turned.

Markov slipped after me as I forced through the press and into the aftercastle. The door thudded shut behind us, muffling the storm of arrows. The room smelled of tar and damp wool. On the table lay iron and steel: the chestplate plain but well-forged, the sword oiled and sharp, waiting.

Markov's grin was thin, feral. "Better to be a target in iron than meat in rags."

He seized the straps, wrestling with buckles meant for other hands. The plate sat wrong on my shoulders, heavier than I was used to, the balance foreign. His mutter never ceased — half curses, half jests. "Lift — hold still — saints, this plate's a coffin if you fall, but it keeps the blood in, eh?"

The weight dragged at my shoulders, heavy as oath and grave both.

I strapped on the scabbard and drew the blade. *Pryaz.* The Binding. Black steel, northern-forged, polished to a dark mirror, its edge gleaming thin as frost. Illarion's steel — his pride, his vanity, his claim. It felt colder than iron had any right to, the grip tight in my palm as though it knew me.

Cruel steel, too fine for my hand, a prince's weapon dressed in shadow.

Not Greyfang. That had been a gift, a debt of duty from the King himself, a sword that bound me to a man I loved like a father. This was different. This was Illarion's darkness made bright at the edge, his fire caught in black iron. I had not sworn the oath he demanded, yet by taking up Pryaz I felt the weight settle on me all the same. The blade was sharp, but the binding sharper.

Outside, the din shifted. Ropes creaked, men shouted, oars splashed. A deeper crash followed, and screams cut short.

Markov's eyes flicked to the beams. "Hear that? One of the boats gone under."

Another roar: Soroka cursing, her sailors shouting to balance, the slap of poles against water. More cries, wild with panic, then drowned.

Markov muttered, "Gods help the bastards in mail."

I pushed through the door, iron dragging at my shoulders, Markov at my back. The mist hit like a wall, wet and sour with blood.

The deck was changed. One landing craft was already overturned, men thrashing in the current while the weight of armour pulled them under. Hands clawed at the hull, then slipped away; the river swallowed them, shield and steel alike. Soroka's sailors leaned over with poles, hooking a few, but most vanished beneath.

The second boat still fought toward the shallows, packed to breaking with boys and veterans both. Shields bristled at its prow, arrows hammering them flat. Some shafts punched through anyway, men toppling overboard, swept off by the black current.

On deck the shield-bearers held the rails, covering high, archers shooting cover fire into the reeds. One Driftlight lad stumbled out of cover screaming, an arrow through his thigh, until another cut him down to silence.

Bogdan crouched at the waist of the ship with a knot of men, bone-charms rattling, oil jars hefted in their arms. He muttered prayer or curse — I could not tell — and pointed toward the reeds as though willing them to ignite by word alone. Soroka stormed down from the tiller, soaked cloak snapping, her hand seizing the nearest jar.

"Not on my ship," she snarled, voice sharp as any blade. "You'll burn us with them."

Bogdan's smile was terrible—kind and merciless both. "Better ash than rot."

Her voice was low, steady as the tide: "Better breath than ash."

The men wavered. Illarion, roaring in the centre deck, did not turn—he was too drunk on the fire of his own shouts, his plate clanging as he swung like a man anointed. The jars remained sealed.

In the reeds the second boat struck home. Veterans splashed into waist-deep water, shields locked, spears thrusting. Points clattered against iron as they pressed for the bank. Rebels met them there, short spears stabbing, knives flashing. Boys shrieked, hacking at grass more than men. The fight churned red in the shallows.

Archers loosed in cadence from the deck. The veterans shot steady, their shafts finding throat and eye among the swimmers still in the water. The Driftlight boys followed clumsy but numerous, their wild volleys harrying any rebel bold enough to linger.

While the main assault raged in the shallows, a handful of rebels tried a different approach. They came from downstream, swimming hard against the current — half a dozen men with nothing but knives between their teeth and desperation in their hearts. No mail, no shields, just muscle and courage enough to try the Grey Hand's stern where the hull rode lowest.

The first man's fingers found the rudder chains. Then another, clawing up the ship's transom while our attention was fixed forward. By the time the watch spotted them, three were already over the taffrail, water streaming from their bare skin, blades bright in their fists.

"Boarders aft!" The cry split the air.

I limped to the rail. Every motion tore my thigh, every breath caught in my chest, but I raised the shield all the same. The first rebel shaft smacked the iron rim, numbing my arm to the shoulder. I shoved it down, bared teeth, and loosed a roar that carried as much pain as rage.

Markov stayed tight to me, knife flashing when a rope snaked over the rail, cutting it free, grinning like a rat in a slaughterhouse.

Around us, the veterans formed a line, shields locked, jabbing down at fingers and faces as they appeared. One crushed a dripping rebel's skull with his spear-butt before the man could find his footing. Another drove his spear-point through a swimmer's throat; a third wrenched a man back over the side, stamping on his fingers until he dropped into the black current with a splash that turned red.

The last swimmer fell back into the current, throat opened by a veteran's blade.

In the shallows, our shieldmen shoved forward, boots sinking, shoulders braced, until the rebels wavered. Two of their leaders went down, one skewered through the belly, another felled by a shaft from the Hand. Their line bent, then broke. Survivors dragged their dead, stumbling back into reeds.

The return fire thinned. Shouts of retreat carried thin on the mist.

Grey Hand held. Blood slicked her planks, bodies littered her rails, but she had not burned, had not broken.

Illarion raised both blades in triumph, voice ringing like a king's proclamation. "You see? Fire does not falter. Fire burns all!"

The veterans said nothing. The Driftlight boys wept or retched against the gunwales. The banner lay trampled underfoot, its white cloth blackened with mud and blood.

My chest heaved as though I had run a league. The weight of the prince's breastplate dragged me down, my thigh burned with every breath, and the sword near slipped from my grip. The world tilted, and I sagged against the mast, wood hard and slick with spray.

Markov was there at once, his hand braced under my arm. He pressed close, voice pitched low so only I could hear.

"Still upright," he said. His grin was too wide, sharp as a cut. "I'll tell the lads you slew a hundred, and you can call me liar when they bring the ale."

I let the sword clatter to the deck. My breath came ragged, my leg near gone under me.

"Easy," he muttered, shouldering me heavier. "Don't rob me of my winnings now. You collapse proper later, when I've got coin in hand."

I tried to answer but only a rasp came, and he shook his head, forcing a laugh that sounded too thin. "I'll take that as a yes."

Borislav bent to gather the banner. The pole was split, the cloth fouled with mud and blood, bootprints ground into the painted crown. He clutched it to his chest like a wounded thing, his face raw with shame.

Soroka came forward, cloak dripping, her face pale with salt and smoke. She looked not at Illarion but at the water sliding black past the hull. "We're still grounded," she said. Her voice carried low but hard enough that all near heard. "The channel's closed behind us, the current rising against. If the mire wants us, she has us."

Illarion raised his swords higher, as though to drown her words in steel. The Driftlight boys tried a cheer, thin and ragged. The veterans only stood silent, their shields split, their blades red.

Victory, he called it. I saw only a ship caught fast, bleeding from her scuppers, and a river that had not yet taken its due.

Chapter XIX: Anointed in Blood

We pulled the dead in as best we could. Some we fished from the reeds with spear-shafts, others we dragged up the bank by belts still slick with blood. Forty-five lived. That was the count when the noise stilled, when no more cries answered, no more hands clawed at the hull.

The Driftlight boys were the worst of it. Thin limbs tangled in oar-ropes, faces blank with mud, eyes wide though no breath came. The Stormhold lads fared little better — leather patchwork cut through by arrow or knife.

Among the veterans the tally was smaller but heavier. Three druzhinniki down, men who had held true lines in fire before ever setting foot in this mire. One sotnik gone too — Krill, lean as a drawn blade, the man who had lived through a dozen sieges. Drowned here like a common recruit, dragged under by iron that had carried him through wars enough for any man. His helm washed ashore, dented, empty, staring back at us from the mud.

We laid them side by side on the bank. Some still twitched when we touched them, but not for long. Those too far gone were given steel quick, before they could beg. The rest lay still, open-mouthed, as if the sky above had stolen their last word.

No priests sang them down. No bells marked the passing. Only the reeds hissing in the wind, and the stink of blood soaking earth already sour.

Illarion stood among the wreckage, helm off, hair plastered to his brow with sweat and spray. His plate was streaked dark where blood had run, not his own. He gave no sign of the weight on him. His voice came harsh but steady.

"Soroka—take what crew you need. Fetch the capsized boat downstream. Cut the *Grey Hand* free and meet us at Drownbank."

She gave a single nod, pale-eyed, and was gone with her sailors.

Illarion's gaze fell next on the banner. The pole lay snapped across the deck, white cloth fouled in mud and boot-marks, the painted crown smeared black. Borislav knelt over it, clutching the torn length to his chest as if it were a wounded thing.

The prince strode to him. His gauntlet cracked across the boy's face once, twice, until blood welled at his lip. Borislav staggered but did not loose his grip.

Illarion wrenched a fallen spear from the deck, hefted it, and for a heartbeat I thought he would drive it through the boy where he stood. His knuckles whitened on the shaft, his eyes bright with that fever that never left him.

Borislav froze, breath sharp in his throat, waiting on the blow.

It never came. Illarion lowered the spear, hard, into the boy's hands. "Tie it on," he said, voice flat as judgment. "Hold it high. And if it falls again, so do you."

Borislav clutched the banner-pole as though it burned him, his face raw with shame and terror. His lip bled where he bit down, holding back words that would not save him.

Illarion turned, voice rising to the survivors. "All warriors ashore. We march. Drownbank is a mile upriver. It burns tonight."

His eyes fixed on me. "Every blade. Every back. Even you, Krovin."

I tried to rise. The deck was slick, red underfoot. My boot slid, and I went down hard, hand skidding through blood gone tacky in the sun. The plate dragged me further, weight pressing until I could scarcely breathe.

Markov caught my arm, cursing under his breath. "He can't walk in this coffin."

Illarion did not so much as turn. "Then he'll crawl."

The blood stank of iron and river-mud. My thigh screamed with every shift. I braced on one knee, teeth set, but the armour pinned me as surely as chains.

"Take it off," I rasped.

Markov stared at me, wide-eyed. "What?"

"Take it off. Now."

He hesitated, jaw tight, then dropped to his knees. Fingers fumbled at buckles slick with gore, curses spilling as straps tore free. One by one the plates slid off, clanging on the boards, heavy as coffins falling shut.

The air came easier without it, but lighter did not mean stronger. I felt only the weakness beneath, ribs hollow, leg raw, breath shallow as a child's.

Markov shoved the last strap clear, eyes darting toward Illarion. "Better to die naked than drown in steel," he muttered.

I said nothing. The humiliation was mine to carry.

The ferries ground in shallows, spilling men into mud. Some hauled survivors up the bank, laying them in rows. Others bent low with knives to be sure the fallen stayed fallen. Groans ended quick. Steel is the only mercy the mire understands.

Weapons were stripped, purses torn, boots stolen off stiffening feet. The Driftlight lads clutched at what they found—knives still wet, bows strung with gut, spears nicked from reeds. Their hands shook but they held fast, as if steel alone could prove them men.

Illarion stood watching, plate bright with gore, face unreadable. Then he said only one word:

"Bogdan."

The priest came forward without question, bone charms rattling at his throat. He seemed almost to have been waiting. He stooped beside a corpse—a rebel youth no older than our own—and dipped his hand in the blood pooling beneath the ribs. When he rose, his palm was crimson, fingers dripping.

"Brothers," he said, voice low but carrying. "You ask for strength. Here it is."

He walked the line of men, scattering blood with his fingers. Drops spattered cheeks, helms, bared throats. "This is your blessing. Not oil, not water—blood. God's gift."

Some flinched when it struck their eyes, some bowed their heads. None dared wipe it away.

"You think pain is curse? It is blessing. You think wounds mark weakness? They mark you chosen. Pain is holy water, scalding you clean, making you sharp."

He turned back to the corpse, pressed both hands deep, and flung the wet across us. It fell like rain, red and stinking. "Take it! Let it sanctify you. You are not rabble. You are fire's altar. And fire does not falter."

Illarion watched, silent, eyes bright.

But I knew what the prophet made of them. Every palm he marked took on a debt that could only be paid in more blood or in long, hollow silence. I saw the power in it. Trembling recruits stiffened, ready to stand again, to follow though death might come — not by justice, but by stronger hands or by cruel chance. He hardened them, yes, gave them courage by making them cruel. And we needed them hardened more than we needed them good. That is the soldier's bargain. I know it well. Made in blood it will serve, but it is still a devil's bargain.

Bogdan raised both arms, voice swelling. "Tonight, the mire learns God's fire. Tonight, your blood and theirs join as one. Not in shame — never shame — but in triumph. Burn. Kill. Rise."

The men gave no cheer. But when he stepped back, faces were smeared red, eyes hard, jaws set. They had been anointed, whether they believed or not.

Illarion gave a sharp nod. That was all. The march began.

We left the *Grey Hand* moored in silence, her timbers scarred, her scuppers still running red. Soroka and her sailors stayed with her, bent to the work of freeing keel and salvaging the capsized boat. The rest of us went upriver.

The bank was firmer than the true mire, but no easy ground. Roots clawed from the soil, earth rose and fell sharp as waves, and trees pressed close, dripping river-mist onto helms already heavy. Each step jarred my thigh raw, every rise took the breath from me.

Illarion strode at the head, plate bright, pace brutal. Borislav stumbled after him, banner clutched like a crutch, face still swollen from the blows. Behind came the sotniki and druzhinniki, silent, eyes forward, blood drying on their mail. The Driftlight lads dragged their new-won blades like prizes, eager for another clash.

Bogdan walked among them, voice low, steady, repeating fragments of his sermon. "Pain is gift. Blood is holy. Fire does not falter." The boys mouthed the words without knowing it, lips moving as if in prayer.

Markov kept beside me, shoulder near mine, curses spilling with every step.

"Madman prince," he hissed, tripping on a root. "Drives us into another slaughter before we've licked the blood from our boots."

He spat, dragged a sleeve across his mouth.

"Stubborn wolf, dragging that leg as if you were twenty again, when any sane man would lie down and let the mire take him."

His breath came hard, but his tongue didn't slow.

"And me — me the greatest fool — following you both, when I could be drunk on reed-ale and cheating fat merchants."

I did not disagree. But held my tongue. I had no breath to waste on words.

I limped in his shadow, half-blind with sweat. My ribs felt scraped hollow, my breath ragged, but still I walked. To stop was worse.

A mile upriver feels longer when each step is bought with pain. The trees thickened, the path rose and fell, the river flashing dull through breaks in the green. Men stumbled, swore, rose again. None dared slacken. Illarion never looked back.

We did not know what waited at Drownbank — another ambush, another wall of reeds bristling with arrows. Only that we would meet it on foot, bloodied already, driven forward by a prince who refused to yield.

The mile dragged us hollow. By the time the river bent and the huts of Drownbank came into sight, we were forty-five shadows with blood still crusted on our mail, half our strength gone, the rest staggering under the jars of oil and the weight of scavenged steel. Some limped barefoot, boots lost in the current. Others clutched weapons too heavy for them, dragging spearpoints in the dirt.

Illarion drove us to the last rise and stood there, helm under his arm, breath harsh in his throat. We lifted shields, braced spears, waiting for arrows to find us. None came.

Drownbank sprawled below the slope, stilts rising from the shallows, rafts chained together, smoke thin from cold hearths. No shield-wall. No spears in the lanes. Only women, children, and the frail stood watching. An old man with a stick. A mother with an infant tight to her chest. A girl no older than Borislav clutching a reed basket.

Illarion's jaw clenched. His eyes swept the empty lanes, the sagging nets, the figures too weak to flee. Fury took him — the fury of a man robbed of his enemy. He had driven us through blood and mire for this. No warriors. No ranks to break. Nothing to crown his fire but silence.

He raised his sword high, and for a heartbeat he said nothing. His breath rasped, the blade bright in the grey light. Every man waited.

Then his voice broke the stillness, flat as a hammer striking.

"Burn it. Any who raise a hand — cut them down."

The words hung. For a heartbeat no one moved. Even the Driftlight lads froze, blades trembling in their hands, eyes darting from him to the people below.

Illarion's gaze swept them, sharp enough to draw blood without steel. His teeth bared. "Do it."

The pause shattered. The veterans moved first, their faces hard, their swords certain. Men who tried to bar doors or lift poles were struck where they stood. Others dropped tools, dropped to their knees, and were shoved aside as the fire spread.

Cries rose from the lanes. Women begged, clutching children close. Elders shouted oaths, warnings, prayers. Dogs yelped and scattered into reeds. The huts rattled with shrieks as men poured down the slope with torches and blades.

Borislav stood above it all, banner pole clutched in both hands. His face was white, lips bitten bloody. The cloth shook in his grip, but he did not cry out. He only held it high, stiff as wood, horror plain on him as the burning began below.

I dragged myself up the slope, each step tearing at my thigh. By the time I crested the rise, my leg gave out entirely. I fell to my knees in the mud, breath gone, helpless as a man shackled.

Below, fire ran wild. Steel flashed in narrow lanes as resisters were cut down. A woman screamed inside one hut, then flames took her voice. Children wailed as rafts were shoved off, the river their only refuge. Oil burst from jars, reeds popping, thatch collapsing in sheets. Smoke climbed black into a sky too grey to care.

I had seen this before. In the mire under Mstislav. At Stormhold's gates. In nameless villages that never found their way to a map. It is always the same. The strong spend their fury on the weak. Blades meant for warriors bite softer flesh. Fire meant for armies eats roofs and cradles instead.

Men call it victory. They drink, boast, sing of it. But there is no glory in a burning town, no honour in the cries of children. Only the old truth: war is not fought on fields, clean and bright. War is fought in mud, in alleys, in kitchens. War eats what cannot fight back—because when the spears are broken, they are all that's left.

I knelt there through it all, unable to rise, watching smoke climb thick into the sky, the heat of burning thatch pressing against my face, the screams threading through my ribs like knives. I could not stop them. I could only watch, and remember.

And in that remembering, I knew: this was not the mire's cruelty. It was ours.

Chapter XX: The Cost of Fire

By the time we limped back to Driftlight it had been a day, no more, but in my bones it felt a week. The cries still clung in my ears — thin screams cut short by steel, the wet crack of timbers splitting, the hiss of flames eating thatch. The mud pulled at my boots with every step through the quay, black and stinking, thick with ash the river had not yet carried off.

The Grey Hand rode heavy at her moorings, scuppers still weeping red into the current. Men carried the dead off the ship and laid them in rows on the wet planks of the quay — some from Drownbank, some our own. Bodies bore wounds clean enough — arrow-holes, spear-thrusts — but others were charred beyond naming, their mail fused to blackened bone. Families pressed close along the dock's edge, moving between the rows with careful steps, searching faces that would never answer their calls. A woman with grey braids fell to her knees beside a boy whose features were mud and ruin, her wails cutting through the evening air. Others stood silent, hands pressed to their mouths, already knowing what they had come to find. The smell hung over everything: burnt flesh, river-rot, the sweet stench of blood gone thick in the sun.

Markov walked close beside me, sharp-eyed, his tongue working constantly though no words came. He had the look of a man hunting whitefire — needing the burn in his throat to scour out what he had seen. His hands shook when he thought no one was watching, fingers opening and closing as if they still gripped a blade slick with someone else's blood.

Ivan's hall stood above the stilt-streets, its stone lifted proud against the sagging timber around it. He had not come to the quay. Not to greet his son, nor to see which sons had failed to return. Pride, or shame, or fear—I could not tell. But when we climbed the narrow steps to his door, the boards groaned under his pacing. Back and forth, back and forth, like a caged bear waiting for news of his cub.

He stopped at the sight of us, his face caught between scorn and desperate need. His eyes swept over me—the mud caked to my leggings, the blood under my nails, the way I favoured my wounded leg—then fixed on the space behind me, searching.

"Well?" The word cracked out of him.

I gave him only two words. "He lives."

Relief broke across his broad face like surf on stone, washing away the careful mask he had worn. His shoulders sagged, and for a heartbeat he looked older than his years. Then pride rushed back, or the pretence of it. He barked for food, for ale, for servants to bring meat enough for a feast though none of us could stomach the thought of eating.

"Sit," he ordered, trying to cloak his fear in command. His eyes fixed on me, taking in the grey pallor of my skin, the way my hands trembled against the table's edge. "You don't look well. Healer!"

I dropped onto the bench, my leg screaming as it bent, chest hollow as a drummed-out cask. The hall spun for a moment, torchlight blurring into streaks of gold. I said nothing. Only set steel on the wooden table—Illarion's sword, still streaked where blood had dried in the fuller like rust in a groove.

The blade lay between us, catching firelight along its edge. Ivan's gaze lingered on it, on the nicks and stains that told their own story, but he did not reach to touch it.

He wanted more. Proof of his son's courage, a tale to match his own memories of battle. The truth sat heavy on my tongue: Borislav white-faced and shaking, clutching a banner like a talisman while men died around him. The prince's hand across his cheek, the crack of palm on bone that left him reeling. The way he had stood frozen on the hill above Drownbank, watching the slaughter spread below like spilled wine.

I said nothing. My silence weighed heavier than any answer.

Markov leaned forward before the pause could grow too wide, tongue quick and silver.

"He stood like a mast in a storm," he said. "Arrows hissing close, men dropping on either side, and still the boy never flinched, not once. His voice carried above the din — stronger than the clash of steel. Drew their fire like iron draws a lodestone, and never bent. I saw veterans take heart from it. Your son, Lord Ivan — he gave them spine when their own failed."

All true in fragments, polished smooth with lies that gleamed like gold in firelight. Ivan's shoulders eased as the words washed over him. Pride touched his weathered face, thin and fleeting but real as rain. He straightened in his chair, the years falling away, seeing his son as he wanted him to be — as perhaps, in some small way, he had been.

I let him keep it. Some truths are too sharp for a father's heart to bear.

The servants brought bread and meat, ale that foamed white in wooden cups. Ivan raised his drink high, proposing toasts to victory, to courage, to sons who carried their fathers' honour into fire. I drank as custom demanded, but the ale tasted like ash in my mouth.

The next morning Illarion held a funeral.

The corpses we had hauled home lay covered, sailcloth cut white and draped as if linen had been theirs in life. Hands folded, torchlight catching cloth as though it were silk. Men who had died choking on river-mud were made martyrs with a brushstroke.

Illarion stood at their head, plate scoured bright though it still stank of smoke. His voice carried over Driftlight's quay, smooth and sonorous, the sort of words you might think a priest had written for him.

"They did not fall in beds, nor of plague, nor of cowardice. They died as warriors. They spent their blood for fire, for crown, for God's will. Let them be remembered as they stood — steel in hand, flame in heart. Let no man say their names are forgotten."

One by one he called them, dragging names out like coins from a purse: druzhinniki from Velgrad, Driftlight lads whose mothers sobbed in the crowd, Stormhold youths still soft with down on their cheeks. Each name was dressed in honour, each death made holy in the prince's telling.

He named twenty-seven in all. That was the number we had brought home under sailcloth. The rest were still out there — dragged under by current, tangled in reeds, or gone down in armour too heavy to rise. Forty-five dead, but only twenty-seven lay on the quay for mothers to touch and name.

Bogdan moved between the rows, his bone charms rattling, but he carried no basin of oil. He dipped his fingers in the blood clotted on armour and touched it to the foreheads of the dead. "Pain is gift," he murmured, voice rising with each anointing. "Blood is holy. Fire does not falter." The crowd shivered, not knowing if he blessed or damned them.

I remembered the riverbank: boys tangled in oar-ropes, faces blank with mud, Krill dragged down in iron like any raw recruit. No priest then, no names carved in stone, no linen. Only reeds whispering as the wind took them.

And yet—on the quay that morning, it was hard to deny the grace of it. Mothers clutched their sons' names as if they were relics. One woman, bent and worn, caught Illarion's gauntlet and kissed it, whispering thanks through her tears. Thanks—for giving a shroud where there had been none, for making her boy matter in a world that had no room for him.

I could not fault that. Even if it was theatre, even if it was half-lie, it gave them something the mire had stolen: meaning.

But as the pyres were lit and smoke climbed straight into the sky, I thought of the other dead—Brack children with skulls caved in, women cut down clutching infants, old men with nothing but sticks in their hands. They had no sails for shrouds, no names spoken, no pyres. Only shallow graves upriver, and the silence of mud.

Chapter XXI: The Squire's Rise

They drilled again the next day, because that was what the living could do. Forty-five in the yard above the quay, though it looked fewer with the gaps. A handful of Driftlight boys had slipped home to reed-mats in the night, their courage drowned with their friends. A couple of new ones crept in—cousins, brothers of the dead—hungry to claim a place. The number hardly changed. We were stronger for the loss of the weakest, but the cost was ruinous. Forty boys wasted at Drownbank, fed to fire before they had even learned to stand.

The veterans carried the line now: twenty-two druzhinniki in scarred mail, four sotniki walking the yard with old patience. Only three Stormhold youths remained to bark the tens, their pride thinner with so few to echo it. Sixteen Driftlight boys shuffled between them, trying on their fathers' shadows and finding them too large.

Illarion watched from the steps, helm under his arm. His sickness had flared again: the left eye swollen, weeping pus, his hands shaking so badly that every gesture seemed like fury. Yet his voice came softer than before, almost gentle. He corrected grips himself, showed stances, sent the weakest to fetch water rather than let them faint. Between drills he spoke of fire: fire as judgment, fire as crown, fire as gift.

Bogdan moved among them with his bone-charms whispering, daubing rebel blood across foreheads until the stench of it turned my stomach. Illarion gave the stances; Bogdan gave the sacrament. One raised their bodies, the other raised their fear. Together they taught the men what to believe.

It became routine — sword, shield, and blood.

The training shifted. No longer only bruises and punishment, but weapons in hand. Illarion set each sotnik to their craft: Radovan with the axe, Sava teaching the bow, Petyr the spear, Mikhail's ruined hand still showing boys how to make a shield bite like steel. Then he turned to me.

The prince's own sword was already mine — a gift bound with an oath I had not wanted, yet could not shed. He pressed me to use it now, to show the boys how to stand, how to strike, how not to falter when the weight jarred their arms. I limped through the drills, thigh stiff but closing at last, each cut dragging less pain than the day before. They saw me sway, and they saw me steady again.

It felt wrong to teach. I had never been patient, never good with words. A sword I could swing, but shaping others to hold one seemed beyond me. Yet I found the boys watching close, copying even the hitch in my stride. Markov smirked at the edge of the yard. "Look at them aping your gait. Wolf pups learning to hobble."

He met with merchants, bartered coin and promises, and boys who stood their ground left the yard with boiled leather or a helm that fit closer than rags. The crowd noticed. Mothers came to watch, not just weep. Men muttered approval. The warband looked less like rabble each day.

One morning Borislav stepped forward unbidden. His lip was still split, the welt on his cheek not faded, but he called the boys into order and led them through the holy forms — kneel, rise, bow, strike, hold. His voice cracked, but the sixteen Driftlight lads moved with him. Not well, not yet, but in rhythm. His split lip bled when he shouted, yet he stood proud in the pain, as if to bleed was proof of worth.

I saw his father in him—easy strength, the kind that draws men forward. Not cruel, but fierce and eager, needing only a cause. Even men twice his age watched and smiled. And I, too, felt the pull of it.

But I knew what I was watching. Here was good clay, still soft. We could shape him into something fine—or fire him hard and sharp and use him until he broke. The world has need of sharp things. Gentle things do not win battles. I hoped then he might one day stand where I stood, watching younger men bleed and learn the hard path of war.

Illarion stood watching, his trembling hand tight on the helm's rim. I saw the thought take root in him even before he spoke it: boys who bent so easy might be bent into more.

The next morning brought Illarion to Ivan's hall, bright in fresh plate, with Borislav walking at his side like a favoured hound. The boy wore his bruises like honours—the split lip, the scrapes from arrows, the welt where the prince's hand had marked him. His spine was straight despite the weight of what he carried.

Ivan received them in his great chamber, the one with carpets from Velgrad and shields that gleamed with disuse. He sat heavy in his chair, eyes moving between his son and the prince who had claimed him.

"Lord Ivan," Illarion began, voice smooth as oil on water. "Your son proved himself in the fire. When arrows fell like rain, when lesser men broke, Borislav held my banner high. He stood when others cowered. He answered when I called."

Each word was honey over steel, calculated to bind father and son deeper into his design. Borislav straightened, eyes bright. Ivan's chest swelled despite himself — here was proof his boy had found courage, had proven worthy of his blood.

"I have elevated him," Illarion continued, hand settling on Borislav's shoulder with paternal weight. "He is my squire now, marked by battle, tested in blood. In my service, a young man of courage might rise without limit."

The praise carried its own threat, subtle as poison: *Your son belongs to me now. His future rests in my hands. Oppose me, and watch it crumble.*

Ivan shifted, reading the currents well enough. "You honour our house."

"I honour merit," Illarion replied, then let his gaze drift to the weapons adorning the walls — swords that had never drawn blood, mail that protected only memories. "But merit alone cannot win wars. It requires arms. Support from those who see clearly."

The dance began in earnest. Illarion spoke of duty to the Crown, of rebellion spreading like plague through the mire. He painted Driftlight burning, Ivan's hall reduced to ash, Borislav's bright future snuffed by rebel steel. Each image was a weight pressed onto the scales.

"My forces grow stronger," the prince said, pacing now. "But strength requires arms. Your storehouses could serve the realm's need."

Ivan's weapons, locked in vaults against emergencies Illarion claimed had already come.

Then Illarion's tone shifted, became intimate, conspiratorial. "There is another matter. A delicate one." He paused, letting the weight settle. "Your churches harbour a problem, Lord Ivan. One that threatens us all."

Ivan's brow creased. "What problem?"

"The discipline practiced there—you know of what I speak. Young men drilled in their temples, bodies hardened through holy forms, old rites dressed as prayer. Ancient Brack traditions, training warriors beneath the cross."

The accusation was delicate but clear. Ivan's jaw tightened. He knew the practices Illarion meant—the conditioning, the group exercises, the way boys emerged from church discipline harder, more cohesive than when they entered.

"Are you suggesting—"

"I suggest nothing," Illarion said smoothly. "I observe. Young men, trained together, bound by shared ritual, led by priests who may not share your loyalty to the Crown."

The threat was implicit but unmistakable: these church groups could become breeding grounds for rebellion, cells of resistance within Driftlight's own walls.

"Better to channel such energy toward proper service," Illarion continued. "Give these young men true purpose— service to their prince, their realm. Transform potential danger into proven strength."

Ivan's silence stretched. Illarion pressed forward.

"All I require is escort—your guards to accompany mine as we recruit these volunteers. A show of local authority to legitimize the process." His smile was sharp. "Better they serve willingly under your blessing than be forced to serve after they've turned rebel, no?"

The calculation was brutal in its simplicity: conscript them now while calling it service, or fight them later when they'd joined the enemy.

"Some priests have expressed... concerns about these practices," Illarion added, playing another angle. "Father Anatol mentioned them to me just yesterday. Called them 'troubling deviations from proper worship.' Perhaps removing the temptation would serve the faith as well as the Crown."

Ivan's face had gone still as stone. His eyes flicked to Borislav, who stood silent, bruises dark against pale skin. The boy was proof of what Illarion offered—purpose, advancement, belonging. But also of what he demanded in return.

"You make compelling arguments," Ivan said at last, voice carefully neutral.

Illarion's smile widened. "I make honest ones. The mire breeds danger, Lord Ivan. Better to face it with every blade we can muster than to leave potential allies idle—or worse, let them turn against us."

He gestured toward the dusty weapons on the walls. "Your arms could equip loyal men. Your authority could smooth their recruitment. And your son..." His hand pressed briefly on Borislav's shoulder. "Your son could rise high in the service of a grateful prince."

The web was complete. Military necessity, security concerns, religious propriety, paternal ambition—all woven together into a trap that felt like opportunity.

Ivan looked at his son one last time—the boy who had found purpose in another man's service, whose future now hung on decisions made in rooms like this.

"Very well," he said. "You shall have what you need."

Illarion's smile was triumphant, but he kept his voice humble. "The Crown will remember your loyalty, Lord Ivan. As will I."

As they left, Borislav walking proud beside his prince, Ivan remained in his chair, staring at walls lined with weapons that would soon arm other men's sons. The game was played, the pieces moved.

He had thought to protect his boy by keeping him close. Now the boy walked at another man's side, and Ivan sat staring at walls that would soon arm other sons. I could not say if it was wisdom or surrender.

Chapter XXII: Whispers of the Fire-Coven

The Church of Saint Dobry stood damp in the river-mist, its stones black with soot, reed-smoke clinging to the rafters. At dawn the parishioners gathered, Brackfolk mostly, moving through their forms in silence: kneeling, rising, hands pressed palm to palm, heads bent low. No priest to lead them now—the deacon gone north with silver—but still they prayed. The old rites lived in the bones.

Illarion broke them. He came with Ivan's guards at his back, mail clinking, boots loud on the worn flags. His plate caught the lantern-light, gaudy as a saint's icon, and the sound of it turned all heads.

Borislav trailed close, stiff in studded leather, a folded parchment shaking in his hands. His lip was still split from the prince's blows, but his eyes clung to Illarion as though the man were father and god both.

"Read," Illarion commanded. His voice rang harsh against the quiet.

The boy unrolled the parchment. His tongue caught on the first line, letters scratched careful by Bogdan's hand. He stumbled over each word, halting, lips fumbling syllables, but he forced them out.

"Let it be known," Borislav read, "that Prince Illarion, rightful heir to the Crown, led his faithful warriors against the rebel stronghold of Drownbank. Vastly outnumbered, our men charged through fire to seize victory. The rebels, cowards all, hid behind women and children, using innocents as shields. Yet our Prince's righteousness did not falter. With sword and flame he cleansed the mire of their poison. Twenty-seven heroes gave their lives, their blood sanctifying the ground. Victory was total. God's will was done."

He stumbled on "sanctifying," lips fumbling the syllables, a boy tripping over letters he scarcely knew, forced to mouth victory like prayer. Still he pressed on. His young voice echoed in the nave, fragile and certain both.

Ivan's guards moved among the parishioners, not striking, only looming. Men were told their names would be taken, their loyalty recorded. Boys were nudged forward, reminded what the Crown expected of its sons. Some stepped out willing, proud to be marked. Others hesitated, but the weight of steel at their backs bent them faster than any prayer.

When Borislav finished, Illarion took the parchment from him and nailed it to the church wall with the point of his dagger. The words hung there like scripture, black ink wet as blood, nailed to stone.

I watched the Brackfolk eyes — dark, resentful, silent. They bowed through their forms again once the prince had gone, but the rhythm was broken, the silence soured. The boy's words lingered in the air, a false gospel binding them tighter than chains.

Outside, Illarion's tally grew. By dusk he would claim near two hundred in his ranks. Boys pressed into tens under desyatniki, fathers promised spears and service. The training yard filled with voices again, the crack of whips, the stamp of boots.

But the yard did not ring only with northern drill. Illarion had seen more. At Saint Dobry's dawn rite he had watched boys bow and rise in silence, hands pressed, movements slow as tide. Prayer, they named it. To him it was stance. Guard. Strike.

So he took their silence and clothed it in steel. Each morning he set the boys through those same motions, but with spear-shafts gripped in their hands, shields on their arms. Kneel, rise, step, thrust — no longer only mercy, but form turned weapon.

The Brack called it discipline, holy endurance. Illarion called it fire. "These are echoes," he told them, "of what God once burned into your fathers' bones. You prayed with your bodies; now you will fight with them. Each dawn you will bow, and each dawn you will strike."

They obeyed. Not only boys — fathers too, pressed from pew to yard, their breath hissing through teeth as old movements woke muscle memory long buried. The silence of the church spilled into the yard, but no longer patient. It struck in rhythm with the crack of whips, the clash of shields.

What Mstislav had drowned, his son raised again — not Brack blades, not outlawed serpents, but spears and northern steel. Prayer warped into drill, endurance bent into fire.

While Illarion reforged his army, Markov and I made an overdue visit to the Church of Saint Vira.

It crouched at Driftlight's edge, stone pressed against reed, its walls black with centuries of smoke.

Inside, the altar stood bare. No cross, no silver icons, no painted saints gazing down. Only pale outlines on the walls where frames had hung, edges darkened by lamp-smoke. The nave felt hollow for it—stripped of weight, of splendour. And yet the air did not feel empty. Faith clung to the stones, not to silver or paint. It was no longer ancient temple, nor wholly Christian sanctuary, but something in between, the shape of belief bent but not broken.

She was there—Radalya Tide-Reader. No robe, no office. Only the same reed-grey cloak I remembered from the short weeks before, when she bent a hall without raising her voice. She bent this nave now by kneeling alone, hands folded, eyes shut. Prayer, though to the saints or to the Awakened One I could not tell.

When she looked up, it was without surprise. Her eyes were peat-dark, old as smoke.

"Yaroslav Krovin. Markov Zaytsev." Not accusation, not welcome. Only the naming.

Markov stepped forward, jaw tight, voice edged with heat. "You bent me with your forms. Gave me words, a taste of silence, made me believe I was more than I am. Tell me plain—was I only your pawn? Or your fool?"

Her gaze lingered, not cold but steady. "You were never pawn, Markov. Nor fool. I showed you water. You chose to drink. The water shows what a man carries; it does not change his skin. The path you walked was your own, though it carried you where the current wished."

Markov's smirk faltered. Hurt sat raw on him, thinly masked. "Current or no, it near killed me."

She turned her eyes on me. "And you, Yaroslav Krovin. You wonder if I am rebel, thief, traitor. You weigh me as you would a shield wall, searching for the crack where a blade might fit."

Her words struck true enough that I said nothing.

She had sent us toward the drowned gods' temple. That thread was enough to knot suspicion. And the missing silver—was it theft, or had she let it go? A woman who could bend men might also choose what to lose. My thoughts knotted and unknotted, never clean.

"You've chosen to stay," I said, at last.

"The deacon fled," she said. "North with the church silver. That is the way of frightened men." Her mouth curved without warmth. "But Driftlight is not mine to leave. It listens still."

"You worked with Kharna," I said.

The name was a blade. She did not flinch.

"Not worked with her, but I knew her," she said. "She walked among us once."

Markov's jaw worked before the words came. "She's dead. I thought she could bend the mire itself, make men follow. But in the end she went down like any other—arrows in her chest, weeds in her hair."

Radalya's eyes did not waver. "She died protecting you."

"She died for nothing," I said. "And afraid."

Radalya's gaze held mine, peat-dark and steady. "All fear death when it comes. But fear does not stain the current. She died as vessel, not as nothing."

I thought of the spear that struck her shoulder, of the arrows that thudded into her one after another as I held her close, of lowering her into the mire, weeds catching at her sleeves as the water pulled her down. Not the death of saints. A shield of flesh.

Radalya saw our doubt and shook her head. "The water holds more truth than men's eyes. Do not think you see it all."

Always, she spoke in riddles. I could not know the truth of her. My hand ached for the knife at my side, and the simple answer of steel. She saw that too.

"You wonder if I am a revolutionary," she said. "I am not. The Awakened One teaches patience, Christ the Sufferer teaches mercy. In dark waters it is hard to see where one ends and the other begins—but both preach peace. I do not believe in knives hidden under prayer. I will guide my people to endure, not to strike."

Her voice was calm, but not weak. Yet beneath it I caught a flicker—weariness, perhaps, or the strain of holding silence in a city that howled for knives. A stone can stand against the tide, but even stone feels the pull.

Markov's voice cut in, hard. "Then tell me of fire. You spoke of it once—flame that does not die. I heard her, the elder at the council, speaking of an unquenchable fire still burns. She turned mercy into war. Don't give me riddles, Tide-Reader. Where does that fire burn?"

For the first time, Radalya's eyes flickered. "There are whispers," she said at last. "Of women who keep flame older than our prayers. Not temple, not church, but a circle apart. They say the fire unmasks: it strips lies, bares oaths, shows truth in its blaze. Their leader is Vrasida—ancient, scarred, eyes like coals banked long but not quenched. Even Volkhvy bow their heads when she speaks."

Markov's breath caught. "A fire-coven."

She inclined her head. "So men name them. But their path is peril. The ways of fire were cast aside for good reason. In the old days they anointed men in oil and sent them blazing into their enemies—martyrs who left only ash. Too many burned their own kin with them. So the rites were broken, outlawed, left to rot. Or so we thought. Now they stir again. Whether truth or blasphemy, their blaze spreads."

"Where?" Markov pressed.

Her voice stayed calm, certain. "I do not know where their fire burns, only that its heat is felt even here. To seek it is peril, yet perhaps it lies in your path. Water bends. Fire consumes. Choose which you would follow."

The nave held silence, thick as peat-fog. I had meant to measure her danger. Instead, she measured us.

Dangerous, yes—but not in a way a knife could solve.

Chapter XXIII: The Prince's Fleet

The council met in Ivan's hall, long tables dragged close to the hearth, torches smoking down the walls. I had stood in rooms like this before—armies stripped to coin and ships, each man clawing for his portion. It always smelled the same: wax, wet wool, sweat under perfume.

The Bishop spoke first, soft hands weighted with gold rings that had never gripped a sword. But his voice carried the iron his fingers lacked—sharp with grievance and sure of its righteousness.

"Desecration," he spat. "At Saint Cuthbert's Hollow. Blood spilled where relics lay, rites profaned under the Prince's sanction. If the Thane tolerates such blasphemy, do not ask why heaven sends us fire in return." His eyes flicked to Illarion's empty chair, the words bait and prayer both.

The captain of the watch answered him, armour creaking as he shifted his weight—mail new, belly old. "Blasphemy I leave to priests. My men are fewer every week. The Prince takes them young, the rebels take them dead. If Driftlight is to stand, I need steel. Open the gaols, scrape the dregs— better thieves with knives than no knives at all."

The merchants muttered next, broad sleeves heavy with embroidery, fingers on their fat purses.

"Ironholt is silent. Our cargoes rot in warehouses. Rebel tolls choke the channels. Every day our ships sit idle, coin bleeds away. If Ironholt falls, Driftlight's trade dies with it. The fleet must sail." Their words smelled more of silver than blood, but silver feeds mouths as surely as bread.

Then the master of coin rose, pale as a fish pulled from the deep. His ledger lay open before him, thumb stained with ink. "The treasury is hollow. Pay is owed to men and fleet alike. Grain rises dearer with every barrel lost upriver. Without levy, without tax, we cannot fund war. The choice is simple: sols, or surrender."

At last the river-reeve shouldered through with a warped marsh chart. He rolled it flat with his palms, weights set at the corners—stone on driftwood. Ash stained whole reaches red where wax had been rubbed hard into the vellum and bled.

"As near as we can tell," he said, but his eyes did not lift from the map. "Scouts go out and do not return. Two hands sent east this fortnight; three came back. The rest are reeds and guesses."

He laid a nail to the marks. "Reedmarch's channels are gone to us. Their poles cut our knots and send them back in baskets. Willowreach bows to the reed-flag. Blackfen burns slow—Reedhaven, Crownmarsh both pressed."

His finger drifted upriver. "Here—east Mirefast. Redharbour's backwaters, the Standing Stones line—rebels breed like frogs after rain. South is not clean either: Stonefield and Ashern flare and go dark, then flare again."

He tapped the top of the isle. "North—Watcher posts blink out. Upland crossings held at dusk, lost by dawn."

He dragged a knuckle through the centre. "What we hold is this spine of water from Driftlight down to Ivan's Keep, and a few stone ostrovs that still take a supply barge if the wind is kind."

It was not a map so much as a wound. The red made a crescent about Driftlight, thin at first, thickening, the ends drawing in. The mire was not merely lost; it was closing.

The red crescent on the map spoke louder than any councillor's voice. Yet still they argued, as if words could hold back the tide.

The hall seethed, each tongue sharpening against the other. Ivan sat broad in his chair, sweat gleaming down his neck. His hand twitched for the salt-pouch he once carried, but it was not there. He muttered oaths that convinced no one.

Then the doors burst wide. A man staggered in, mud to his knees, one arm bound with bloody cloth. His cloak hung in rags, his boots cut through. He fell hard on the rushes, clutching them as if the mire still pulled him under. We gave him a cup. He drank deep, wine spilling down his chin, then choked out the words.

"Ironholt's harbour burns."

The hall stilled.

"The rebels struck by night," he gasped. "Shipyards first. Hulls on the stocks, every vessel at anchor. What ships did not sink were scuttled or dragged aground. On land, a hundred at least, digging earthworks, ladders, rams against the northern gate. Lord Kozlov holds the keep, but our men are cut near half, and food shorter still. A week, my lords. A week and the Crown loses the city."

The Bishop clutched his cross, claiming judgment had come. The merchants cried for the fleet. The watch-captain demanded men. The master of coin whispered of doubled levies. The noise swelled until no word held meaning.

That was when Illarion entered. He had not been called. He strode in polished bright, though fever burned behind his eyes. Borislav walked at his side, and the guards parted as if they had known he would come. His eyes swept the chamber — not to the map, but to the faces around it. He read their fears like a hunter reads tracks, knowing which lever would move each man. Then he bent over the table, gauntlet tracing the coast.

"Two hundred and fifty stand in my ranks. The Grey Hand carries a hundred. Ivan holds six warships. Thirty men each, fifty if you pack them like grain." His voice cut the chamber clean.

Ivan's jaw worked. "Four," he said at last. "Four only. Driftlight keeps two — without them, the town is naked to the reeds."

"Four stuffed to the gunnels," Illarion said softly. "Boys stacked like cordwood. And you call that safety." His gaze slid to the merchants. "Trade lies strangled, does it not? What profit in ships left idle while Ironholt burns?"

The merchants seized his words, pressed them into Ivan's ears. "All six, Lord Thane. Let him save the port. Let the fleet earn its keep."

Ivan's lips thinned. "Four," he repeated, though the sweat on his brow told the rest.

"Then another ship," Illarion said. "A craft swift and shallow, to cut the blockade."

Silence. Then one trader shifted uneasily. "Vedek's zubatka," he admitted. "Forty men, built for trade."

Ivan's face darkened, but Illarion's smile curved like steel. "Done. Four warships. The Grey Hand. And the Zubatka. Enough to break their hold."

Ivan sagged, the decision stolen from his mouth before he spoke it. Borislav stood proud at his prince's side, the bruise on his cheek fading to yellow, the banner tight in his grip.

I could have spoken. Could have warned Ivan what it meant to yield his fleet into Illarion's hands. But I kept my silence. Ironholt needed saving, that much was true. Yet Driftlight was being lost in the same breath, its hall bent to a boy's fire.

I had seen cities fall to siege, to hunger, to betrayal. Driftlight was falling to something slower and more dangerous: a crown men placed on Illarion themselves. Men follow conviction more than banners. When every road leads to ruin, they cling to the one who strides forward as if he knows the way. In such certainty lies both valour and cruelty, born of the same flame. Illarion embraced that flame with zeal. He made the beast his gospel, and men knelt gladly to it.

But fire spends itself in one coin alone. It burns until blood quenches it—and then demands more. That price was coming. I saw it already, yet held my tongue, and by that silence set the circlet firmer on his brow.

Chapter XXIV: The Burning Crown

She had been the King's ship. The Grey Hand. Born in Hookmarch when Mstislav's coffers were full and his crown secure — after the northern coasts were broken, before the mire had yet risen against him. The shipwrights cut her ribs from the oldest oaks, hammered her nails with bronze, tarred her seams black as judgment. She was the greatest vessel ever launched from Hookmarch's slipways, meant not only to carry men but to bear the weight of a kingdom's pride.

Her black wool sail bore the white hand of Mstislav, stark on night-cloth, a mark that made men kneel at the sight. I had marched her decks then, when her timbers still smelled of Velgrad oak and the blood-oath spiral carved into her prow gleamed fresh with pitch. Broad-shouldered, tar-black, she had been built for judgment, never bending to storm or siege, carrying sixty men like a blade carried its edge.

Now Illarion had renamed her. Called her *The Burning Crown*.

He made a ceremony of it. Driftlight filled the quay — mothers and fathers pressed shoulder to shoulder, merchants hanging from balconies, children lifted high to see. The men of the warband lined the rails, helmets gleaming, mail polished, each one standing straighter as if summoned to account. Borislav held the new banner tight to his chest. Bogdan stood near, bone charms rattling, ash smudged on his brow, silent but watchful.

Illarion stepped up to the stern-rail in full plate, cloak thrown wide. In his fist he held a scrap of black wool torn from the old sail, soaked in oil until it dripped. He raised it high, voice carrying clear across the water.

"The Mirefast does not wait," he called. "The rebels do not wait. The fire in their reeds will not wait. If the King himself were here, he would not wait. And so I do not wait. The Crown is here, and it burns in our hands. Driftlight—your sons stand ready. Mirefast—your strength will not be lost."

He struck flint, set the black wool alight. Flames licked, curled, devoured, until smoke trailed upward and ash dropped from his fingers into the tide. A cheer rose — not forced, but raw, eager, carried from quay to deck to shoreline.

Borislav unfurled the new cloth, crown painted bright and wreathed in flame, and raised it above his head. The boys roared, the veterans clashed shields against rails, Driftlight's townsfolk shouted until the quay itself seemed to shake. Mothers wept but raised their voices too, pride breaking through fear.

Then the sail was hauled aloft. The great square no longer bore the hand. A slab of white canvas had been stitched across the black wool, seams crude but bold. On it Illarion's sigil blazed—crown aflame, points blackened at the tips as if already ash. From a distance it looked like glory. Up close the patch sagged, stitches strained, paint bled—but no one cared. To them it was no scar but a promise. The greatest ship Hookmarch ever built, scarred and tarred by war, now bore fire where once it bore judgment.

Borislav stood at the prow beneath a matching banner, proud as if he carried more than cloth. Driftlight's boys shouted until their throats broke. On the quay their mothers clutched each other in silence. The mire had already taken their sons. Now fire would take more.

I kept to the quarterdeck rail near Soroka. She had sailed the Grey Hand for years, through sleet and storm, though only since Stormgrave had she worn the captain's coat—when her master lay gutted on his own deck and she stepped into command before the blood dried. Now she stood watching while Illarion scrubbed the King's mark from her mast.

Markov leaned close, voice pitched low enough the prince could not hear. "How many years did she sail with the Hand on her sail? Ten?"

Soroka's jaw tightened. "Grey years. Hard years. She held."

He tipped his head toward the patch. "And now the Hand's buried under rags, fire daubed bold as if men forgot what fire does to wood."

Her mouth thinned, eyes fixed ahead. "Ships live by keel and mast. Paint's only skin."

He smiled, sly. "Still—first royal mark you ever sailed under, patched over like a trader's botched crest. Must sting."

Her eyes snapped to him, cold as frost-sky. "You don't know the first thing about ships. Or about me."

Markov raised his palms in mock surrender and slunk aft.

Soroka kept her gaze on the sail. She didn't speak again, and I didn't press her. The crowd's roar still echoed off the water, but she stood unmoved. She had commanded this deck only months, yet I had seen her steady through storm and slaughter. She didn't need to say what was already plain: names could change, colours could cover, but a ship remembered.

The oars took us out past the piers, Driftlight's harbour falling behind, the water turning darker, salt-sharp on my lips. Ahead lay Ashenbay, broad and grey, the tide drawing us south.

We rowed south, and by dusk the isle showed itself — black stone rising from grey water, walls square and close-fitted, as if hammered by the sea itself. Ivan's Keep.

It crouched low against the tide, no spires, no banners. Only thick walls, a squat hall, and towers built for signal-fire. A cistern lay inside, and vaults deep enough to feed a garrison through a year's siege. No storm had ever broken it. No army had ever tried. Mstislav had raised it during the Mirefast War — stone by stone, season by season, until it stood like a fist thrust into the sea. Built to guard what he had won, to hold what he meant to keep. But Ivan preferred the comforts of Driftlight to the cold halls of his fortress. So its shutters were closed, its quays empty. A fortress built to last, left hollow.

Illarion spat over the rail. "Stone without fire is rot. That's what Ivan leaves for crown and kingdom — a husk."

Borislav shifted at the prow, hands white on the banner-staff. "It could still hold. If the city fell, the keep would stand."

Illarion laughed once, sharp. "Stand for what? Silence? Dust?" He turned away, cloak snapping.

I watched the dark bulk slip past, the gulls circling it as if it were a carcass. The keep had been raised to guard the southern reaches, to be hammer and shield if war came by sea. It still could. But a keep without a lord is only stone. And stone remembers nothing.

By the next dawn the decks rang not only with oars and orders but with prayer turned drill. Illarion had commanded it — *discipline of holy fire,* he named it. At first light every boy was driven from his bench, made to kneel, rise, bow, strike. Not empty-handed as in Saint Dobry's nave, but with spear or sword gripped stiff in their fists.

Bogdan bristled, bone charms clattering. "These are heathen forms," he spat. "Reed-prayers, drowned rites. They profane fire with water's silence."

Illarion hesitated, not wanting to cross him, but he was too committed already. To withdraw now would be weakness. "Then find a way to sanctify them, prophet. Scatter your ash, whisper the saints' names, burn the sin from them. I need soldiers. They need faith. I want discipline every dawn, every deck. Make them my fire."

So Bogdan scowled but muttered blessings all the same, smearing soot across brows, turning silence into sermon.

Markov stood apart, arms folded, gaze caught half in longing. I knew why. The Temple of the Drowned Waters had near broken him, promises of discipline turned to chains, silence turned to shame. Yet when I pressed him low — *Better to bow than to break* — he gave a crooked smile, spat once, and joined the line.

The boys shifted to make space. He moved with them, awkward at first, then smoother, his body remembering what his mind denied. Sweat caught in his hair, his breath came steady, and for a moment he looked not thief nor coward, but something else.

The veterans watched from the rail, laughter rough. "Play-fighting," one called. "Dance-steps." Another hawked and spat. To them only blood proved steel.

But the Brack youths bent serious, their stances sure, their silence deep. What had been prayer in reed-temples now sharpened into drill on warships. I watched and felt unease knot tighter.

The prince had bound silence to fire, discipline to steel. Could he truly turn the Mirefast to his will — or had he only lit the fuse of what his father drowned?

The aftcastle chamber stank of pitch and wet wool, timbers creaking with every roll of the sea. Illarion sat by the stern window, storm-blue plate dulled to grey in the weak light. Bogdan crouched near the brazier, bone charms rattling as the ship pitched, lips moving in silent prayer or curse. Outside I could hear the guards' mail clinking as they shifted — two Stormgrave veterans who followed the prince like hounds.

Markov had asked for private words. Now he stood before Illarion, throat working as if the sentences stuck there like fish bones.

"My prince," he began, voice thin. "Yaroslav and I have been thinking —" His eyes flicked to mine, seeking support he wouldn't find. "Ironholt is a siege. Men die at sieges. Good men, useful men. Men who might serve you better elsewhere."

Illarion's gaze never shifted. "Speak plain. You've never cared for other men's deaths before."

Markov's grin was sharp as broken glass. "We'd be better used finding what we came for. What really matters."

"The relics." The words fell flat from Illarion's lips.

"When we were at the temple, there was a war council. The Brackfolk were divided—some wanted peace, others rebellion. The cautious voices were winning." Markov leaned forward, words quickening. "Then she appeared. Vrasida. Swept in like wildfire, and they bent to her—Otets, Volkhvy, every voice. One word, and the hall turned to war."

Bogdan's head lifted from the coals, eyes bright in the firelight.

"Two things she said that matter," Markov pressed on. "First, that her visions came in *unquenchable fire*."

Silence stretched. Only the creak of timber, the hiss of water against the hull.

"What do we chase but fire that doesn't die?" Markov's voice rose, daring. "What's in your strongbox but that same flame? Find her, find the coven, and maybe we find the next relic. That's why you need us—following my nose, hunting the source. So we can all get out of this bog of knives."

Illarion didn't move. Only turned, slow as a drawn blade, toward Bogdan.

"Well, priest?" His voice was low, dangerous. "Is this another of his lies?"

Bogdan's smile showed teeth in the brazier's glow. His eyes fixed on Markov, unblinking, as if seeing him for the first time.

"The fire shows me... yes. His tongue will lead us to what we seek. The flames speak through him, though he knows it not."

The words struck like cold iron. Markov's grin faltered, eyes cutting to mine as if asking whether I believed it.

Illarion rose, cloak brushing the planks. His hands trembled—fever or fervour, I couldn't tell. "Even a thief's tongue can carry flame, it seems." His gaze sharpened. "But relics can wait. Ironholt comes first. When we take their priests and elders, they will tell us where this coven hides. Then we burn it from them and take what fire they keep."

"And the second thing," Illarion said, voice silk over steel. "What else did this Vrasida say?"

Markov swallowed. "She said the King is dying."

The chamber went still. Even the ship seemed to pause in her rolling.

Illarion's smile was thin as a knife's edge. "Did she now." He stepped closer, close enough that I could smell the fever-sweat on him. "Hear me, thief. If you ever speak those words again—to anyone, anywhere—I will cut out your tongue and feed it to the gulls. Do you understand me?"

Markov nodded, all his cleverness fled.

"Good." Illarion settled back into his chair. "We sail to Ironholt. We break their siege. We take their leaders and wring from them what they know. Then—and only then—do we hunt your prophet and her fire."

Bogdan's eyes lingered on the brazier, flame reflected bright in the dark. His smile never wavered.

I stayed silent, deck groaning beneath us. Prophecy or madness — in the end, fire burned the same. And we sailed straight toward it, willing or not.

By morning the coast drew close again. The sea widened south of Driftlight, the water darker, sharper on the tongue, as if the salt itself carried knives. Even in summer the Southern Sea bit with winter's teeth. The boys pulled cloaks tight and muttered of home; the veterans only rowed on, their faces hollow.

Yet before oars bit water, the prince called the boys to the deck again. Dawn meant drill now as surely as bread. Borislav took the lead, voice cracking as he barked the forms. Kneel, rise, thrust. Their breath steamed, their feet thudded the planks, rhythm like a heart the ship itself had grown.

Illarion's voice cut across the deck. "Boris. Five names. Now."

The boy spoke them quick — two Driftlight lads, a Stormhold youth, a veteran's son, and a reed-born boy with peat-dark eyes.

The drills recommenced.

Illarion snapped the correction again when Borislav faltered: "Not wave — strike! Fire, not water!" Weapons thrust forward and bodies stomped with a violence that shook the deck.

Soroka leaned close to me at the rail, voice dry. "He means to bind the fleet tighter than rope."

When done, Illarion descended and spoke to the new leaders. "You five will lead. You go to every ship. At dawn and at dusk the forms are drilled—no exception. When we reach Ironholt, I will board each deck myself. If I see slackness, if I see no improvement, I will bleed the fault from your hides. Do you understand?"

The words struck harder than any whip. Even the veterans glanced aside, grim. To them it was still pageantry, but they heard the steel beneath it. The Brack youths bent to him, their silence louder than words.

"Up. Go. Burn the fire into your charges — and know this: I will come. If you fail, you will teach the deck how to bleed."

I had seen armies kneel before banners, kings, saints. But never had I seen prayer itself forged into weapon. The Queen had once named Mstislav God's own hand, and the King did not deny it—but Mstislav's wars were marches, sieges, tactics. We prayed before battle and cursed the saints after, yet the fight itself was steel and hunger and mud.

Illarion's fire was different. He did not pray for strength; he made strength of the prayer itself, as if God were oil to be poured on the blade. Zeal married to drill, conviction hammered into steel. Such fire could harden boys into warriors faster than any wound—but it would burn them hollow just as fast. I knew this. I watched it happen. And I did nothing, because wars are always fed with boys, and I had long since ceased to believe I could change the feast.

We passed the fishing stilt-villages first. Ashern, its piers strung with nets that snapped in the wind, smoke thin above the reeds. Men stood watching from the platforms, women pulling children back from the rails. Not a cheer, not a curse. Only silence.

Further down the peat cliffs rose sheer, black and root-hung, the land crumbling into the water. At Stonefield we saw huts clinging to shale, smoke rising from sod chimneys, faces gathered on the slope. They did not wave. One old woman spat into the surf, as if to ward us off.

Last came Rosnolt, where a ruined tower leaned half-buried in reeds. Children stood on the quay throwing stones at our hulls until their fathers cuffed them hard. The stones clattered off harmless, but the sound carried further than any welcome.

Illarion called them cowards, his voice carrying across the deck. Borislav barked agreement, raising the banner higher. But I watched the shore and thought otherwise. These folk had seen too many sails already — grey, black, red. All of them brought fire. And fire never stayed long.

The sea stretched ahead, iron-grey and empty.

Dawn broke low and colourless. Mist dragged across the sea like torn cloth, the sun a pale coin behind it. The boys rowed stiff-armed, teeth chattering, breath white in the air. Even the gulls had gone silent.

Then the cry came from the prow. "Sails!"

Men surged to the rails. Illarion stepped from the stern, cloak snapping, face hollow in the damp light. He needed no spyglass; the word alone set his smile. Fire lit in his eyes, fever or fervour, I could not tell.

Chapter XXV: What the Sea Remembers

The mist peeled back in torn veils, and sails showed ghost-grey on the horizon. Not warships, not built for iron and storm, but hulls enough — twelve at least, decks crowded full as anthills. Could have been five hundred men, could have been less. From a distance they all looked the same: patched sails, oars churning, too many bodies for too little wood.

Soroka leaned to the rail, squinting through the haze. "Converted traders. Barges. One Zubatka, stolen or bartered. They'll try to run for the river-mouth."

She meant west — back to the reed-water they had come from. There the shallows would take us, deep keels driven aground, and their light hulls would vanish into channels no map marked. Already their oars thrashed white, bows swinging, straining for home.

But they were too far out, sea-wind hard against them. They had risked open water to cross Ashenbay, and now the trap was shut. The bay spread wide, no cover but mist.

Illarion only smiled. He stood tall by the prow, helm off so the boys could see his face, bright as if he had already claimed victory. "They sail without colours. That is no fleet. That is kindling."

Bogdan knelt by the stern brazier — a squat iron pan chained to the deck, meant for cooking or charms. He fed it strips of pitch-soaked rag. His bone charms rattled with the ship's roll, clinking like teeth. Beside him, deckhands hauled buckets of clay jars up from the hold, sealed with waxed cloth and heavy with tar. They were buried in sand to keep them from breaking. One slip, one spark, and we would burn before ever casting them.

"Light them," Bogdan whispered, eyes bright as the coals. "God judges by flame. Fire makes truth of rebels and kings alike."

Soroka's voice cracked like rope under strain. "Keep your torches down. At sea, fire kills us as quick as them. Steel and oars win ships, not pitch."

Illarion's smile never bent. "No. Fire crowns. Fire devours. Light them."

The veterans muttered, but the boys cheered, thin voices snatched by wind. I watched Soroka's jaw knot. She spat into the sea and gave the order anyway. Only then were torches struck from the brazier, their flames licking against the morning mist, and pitch-pots passed hand to hand, stinking of tar and oil.

Then the drum began, slow and heavy. Not for hearts, but for order. Each beat carried across the waves, answered by the other ships. Strokes for speed, rolls for turn, silence for hold. Our line bent south, sails fat with wind, each hull matching the flagship's cadence.

The rebels bent west, straining to reach the river-mouth. But the bay was wide, the current against them, and our oars pulled harder. Their crescent began to wheel back toward us, forced to fight where they had no refuge.

The drums quickened. Our oars bit deep, throwing spray white against the black water. The rebels wheeled clumsily, half their hulls still straining for the river, the others swinging bows to meet us. I could see their decks now: men packed shoulder to shoulder, some with reed-helms lacquered in pitch, others bareheaded, clutching reed-bows or water-spears. Too many to count clean, only the press of bodies like a threshing floor.

Arrows came first. Thin whines, a scatter into the waves. One thudded into our sail and stuck quivering, another skittered across the planks near my feet. A Driftlight boy screamed when a shaft split his arm, high and sharp as a gull's cry. Veterans dragged him down, stuffed cloth in the wound, shoved another boy forward to take his place at the rail.

"Hold until they close!" Soroka's voice cut sharp, but her command was already drowned.

Bogdan raised a torch high, its flame guttering in the wind. "Cast for judgment!"

The first pitch-pot arced out, clay shattering on a rebel deck. Tar splashed and caught, a hungry flower of flame climbing fast across planks and men. Screams carried thin over the water. The boys on our deck cheered, shrill and breaking, as if their voices alone might keep the fire fed.

Another pot flew, then another. One missed and burst against the waves, black slick writhing on the surface until it caught and burned in a trail across the water. A barge lit, sails sagging in fire, men shrieking as they flung themselves overboard. Some sank fast in seal-hide coats heavy with tar, some clawed uselessly at the water but all chose the black current over the fire. For a heartbeat it looked as if Illarion's madness was right — that fire had crowned us victors before steel ever touched.

Then a pot slipped. A Driftlight boy, hand slick with tar, fumbled his throw. The jar burst against our fore-rail. Tar climbed fast into the rigging, rope flaring, mast-edge alight. For a heartbeat the mast looked lost, sail curling black in the heat. Men shouted, clawing for buckets. Soroka's voice ripped the deck raw—"Chain, water, drown it or she's gone!" Her fury cracked louder than steel, but Bogdan only howled louder, as if the flames themselves were his psalm.

Smoke rolled, bitter and black. Ahead, the rebel crescent tightened, their oars biting in rhythm now, bows bearing down. The fire had opened the battle, but it had not ended it.

The gap closed fast. Rebel oars churned foam, bows cutting low, hulls turning inward like a crescent net. Ours drove steady on the drum-beat, spray sheeting the rails. The first crash came sudden as thunder.

Vedek's zubatka struck a fishing craft head-on. Her sharp prow punched through rotten planks, splinters flying. For a heartbeat the rebel hull clung like a split log, then broke, water flooding. Men poured over Vedek's rail instead of drowning, knives flashing, teeth bared. I saw him grinning back, short axe in one hand, burying it in a man's skull.

To starboard, one Driftlight warship caught two barges at once. Hooks flew, bit deep, ropes tautened, and the hulls ground together. The veterans braced shields at the rail. Boys behind them jabbed with spears too long for the deck, thrusts wild and clumsy. A rebel's axe smashed a boy's face in, teeth scattering across the planks. Another went down kicking, throat torn. The veterans closed ranks, shields locked, their blades working short and sure. They gave no roar, no flourish—only the grim rhythm of men who had done this before, hacking until nothing moved.

The deck listed underfoot, water pouring over planks. Smoke from the mast-fire curled low, stinging eyes, blackening breath. I glimpsed Soroka on the quarterdeck, mouth open in fury, arms cutting the air — no sound reached through the din.

A pot burst against our second warship's side, tar blazing up the hull. Men stamped and splashed, beating the fire down with soaked cloaks. Soroka bellowed for distance, but her voice vanished under screams and steel.

Our own deck shuddered as arrows bit, shafts hissing into sailcloth, planks, men. One caught in the meat of my shoulder, half-spent — a sting, not a kill. I tore it free, tossed it over. The air stank of pitch and brine, of wet wood ground against wet wood.

The rebels had not broken under fire. They had closed. And now it was knife-work — wood to wood, breath to breath.

The rebel zubatka came hard, prow sharp as a spear. Their oars bit deep, spray shearing white. Soroka's voice tore from the quarterdeck: "Starboard or we'll ground her!" No one heeded. The rebels struck, hull to hull, hooks biting wood, ropes taut as bowstrings. Our timbers screamed.

They came over the rail like wolves, lean men with hair bound, arms tattooed, serpent-blades curving in their hands. Not rabble — Brack fighters born for these waters.

Illarion was already at the prow. He had drawn both swords. In his right, a narrow blade long as his arm, its edge so fine it hissed through air. In his left, northern steel, lean and bright as frost. Together they flashed like twin razors, cruel and eager for blood. He screamed as he fought, but no one could hear. Not command, not order. Only rage, loosed like a furnace. Twice a rebel's stroke near took him, once low at the knee, once high at the throat, and each time his guards crashed in, shields and steel saving him. He gave no guard, no shield, only strike upon strike, every blow to kill, his fury carried on the backs of other men.

Borislav clung behind him, banner raised. Crown-and-fire crude on white, a target brighter than steel. Rebels surged for him, serpent-blades flashing to cut the cloth, the boy. I limped through the press, every step fire in my thigh. A rebel swung for the boy's head. I caught the haft, turned it, drove my blade up through his jaw. He spasmed, piss flooding his breeches as he went down. Borislav sobbed but did not let go. His hands were flayed raw, locked to the pole as if terror itself clenched them.

Bogdan staggered back as steel rang, his chants breaking off. He could howl fire from the stern, but here where blood slicked the deck, he fled below like any man who had never carried more than bone and prayer.

No sign of Markov.

Then one found me — a Brack warrior, hair braided with shell, serpent-blade in his grip. His stance was the Hand: coiled, patient, the curve of steel promising a single cut, a single end.

I raised *Pryaz*, its edge bright as water, its weight heavier than oath or chain.

My limp betrayed me, stumble in every step, and once it near cost me. His blade hissed past my thigh, so close I felt skin split, blood running hot. Only the black blade's cruelty kept me upright, biting deeper than my stance deserved.

He pressed, fast. His steel slid past guard, nicking my side. It burned cold, sharper than any northern edge. He grinned, teeth black with rot, and I knew he wanted me bled slow.

I feinted high, let him take the bait. When he struck for my leg, I pivoted on the good one and rammed Pryaz down. It cracked bone at his collar, spray hot on my lips. He sagged like a fish hauled from a net, breath rattling until it stopped. I nearly went with him, knee giving, pain tearing through me.

Across the deck Borislav staggered, banner whipping. Rebels dragged him down, hacking at the pole. I lurched in, shield high, bashing one back. The black blade punched low under his guard, ribs cracking wet around the edge. He coughed blood in my face before I shoved him off. Borislav gasped, eyes wide, but still his fingers would not open.

At the prow, Illarion screamed still, both swords whirling, no guard, no thought. His guards ringed him, shields braced, but a Brack slipped through — tattoos black across his chest, serpent-blade high, mouth wide with an oath I half-remembered from the war. He struck sideways, perfect and clean.

The steel kissed Illarion's face from brow to jaw, carving it open. He reeled, blood fountaining, breath bubbling. His legs buckled, swords sagged. For a heartbeat he looked broken, crown and fire slipping from him.

His guards closed, shields battering, hacking the Brack down in a storm of steel. They dragged Illarion upright, face torn, left eye drowned in blood. He sagged between them, still clutching his swords, trying to scream, but what came was only a wet gurgle.

The mast still burned, rope spitting sparks. Soroka's roar cut through it, harsher than Illarion's: "Buckets! Chain! Douse or we're ash!" Veterans heaved water up from the sea, boys beat at flame with cloaks, sparks stung bare flesh. For a moment the ship was a funeral pyre. Then the sail sagged wet, mast scorched but standing.

I turned to check on Borislav, only a heartbeat — a fool's heartbeat. Too late I felt the air change behind me. A rebel was there, serpent-blade already raised, arc perfect for my neck. I threw my shield up, too slow. The steel split my shoulder open, leather parting, flesh tearing, and spun me hard into the rail. Fire lanced down my arm as I rolled, choking on blood in my teeth.

He came again, grinning through blackened teeth, pressing like he already owned me. I fumbled my shield half-raised, sword clumsy in my hand. His stroke should have finished me, but he stumbled on the slick deck. That slip saved me. I rammed Pryaz under his ribs, felt bone grind, breath bubbling wet against my face. We went down together in a tangle of limbs and blood.

The press thinned. Rebels faltered, oarsmen breaking rhythm, some casting off ropes to pull back. Their Zubatka still clung, but her oars were sheared and her stern split wide. Men fought on her deck like trapped beasts, every step closer to drowning.

Vedek's prow punched another barge broadside, splintering her open. The hull rolled, men screaming as water poured in. Firepots still arced, but fewer now, hands too slick with tar and blood. One barge sagged low, sails ablaze, another drifted blind with oars cut.

Soroka drove our drum faster, voices hoarse from shouting commands I could not hear. Her hands carved shapes in smoke and spray, the fleet answering. Our three warships closed their line, pressing the rebels east, away from the river-mouth, away from escape.

For a heartbeat it seemed the Brack would rally. A knot of them leapt our rail together, serpent-blades flashing, teeth bared. One carved down a boy, another drove a veteran to his knees. Borislav staggered, banner dipping low. The guards struck back, shields hammering, blades short and brutal. The rebels tumbled into the sea. Their line broke with them.

Oars scattered, hulls pulling away, men diving from decks to swim for smoke. Some tried to vanish into the mist, but the bay was too wide, too bare. Their cries carried long, thin as gulls, until the sea closed them.

Illarion still stood at the prow, blood thick on his face, left side torn open from brow to jaw. His guards held him upright, but his mouth only spilled a bubbling croak. The boys cheered anyway, shrill and broken, because silence would have been worse.

The fight guttered out. Two barges burned to the waterline, another sank stern-first, oars sticking up like broken ribs. A handful of hulls had already slipped back into the haze, too far gone to chase; they would carry word upriver, a wound that would fester later. The rest lay finished—some smouldering, some wallowing half-sunk, crews throwing down blades or gone quiet beneath the water. Vedek's zubatka limped, prow split from the ramming, but still afloat. Of our own, one warship lay scorched, another listing with wounded. The Burning Crown herself was blackened at mast and rail, ropes still smoking.

Our dead lay thick. Boys sprawled where they fell, some curled like children, some torn open so their insides steamed in the cold. A veteran sat against the mast, throat gaping, staring like he could not believe it. The scuppers ran red, chunks of meat and clots swirling with the wash. Vomit streaked the planks where boys had retched until nothing was left, their sobs breaking into silence. Smoke hung heavy with the stink of blood and burnt hair. Between it all rose the sounds that linger longest — the thin cries of the wounded, and the rattling breaths of those dying slow, each one scraping out into the dark.

Krull moved among the sprawled bodies with a butcher's speed, thumb to neck, eye to wound. Some he bound, some he left. "Rot'll have him by night," he muttered of one, rolling the boy's head aside and moving on. His curses were the only last rites most would get.

Illarion dropped to one knee at the prow. He jammed both swords into the deck to keep from falling, gauntlets locked white on their hilts. Blood streamed down his face, his chest heaved, and still he forced the word out — half gasp, half snarl, spitting red with every breath. "Victory."

The boys answered anyway, their cheers thin as reeds, mouths moving more from fear than faith.

Borislav knelt beside him, the banner still clutched though the cloth was hacked to ribbons, its crown-and-fire smeared black with blood. His face was streaked the same — some his own, most not — and he gagged until he vomited across the planks, retching in time with the ship's roll. Still he would not let go of the pole. Tears cut clean lines down his cheeks, and yet his hands stayed locked white around the shaft as if it alone kept him upright.

Markov slunk up from below, clothes clean of blood, grin pasted brittle on his face. "Still breathing," he muttered, as if that alone were triumph. None answered him. Even the boys looked away.

Soroka only spat, hands black with soot. "Victory," she said low. "We lost men. They lost wood. Tell me which the sea will remember."

I had no answer. Only smoke in my throat, blood on my hands, and the sight of Illarion half-blind, his face torn open from brow to jaw.

Chapter XXVI: The Scar Made Crown

Smoke still clung to the bay when the last rebel craft faltered. Their oars dragged water without rhythm, men slumped over benches, the mast a blackened stump. At last a spear went clattering to the deck, then another. One voice cried out for parley, cracked and hoarse. Soon others followed, hands raised, blades flung down like scraps to dogs.

They came close under our hull, heads bent, arms lifted. Some shouted of quarter, of ransom, of names they claimed would buy them safe passage. One swore his father was reeve of Reedvault and would pay gold enough to fill a hold. Another spat promises of maps—hidden channels through the Standing Stones, secret paths north to Blackfen. Their words tumbled like coins on a table, desperate, glinting, none worth the weight of the dead already floating.

Vedek's men leaned over the rail, jeering back. Some of our boys whispered that prisoners meant ransom, meant food and coin if nothing else. A veteran muttered it was better to chain them to oars than sink whole hulls. For a breath the crew believed it—believed the fight had ended in surrender, that survivors meant spoils.

Nets were cast. Dozens were hauled up like fish, some bloodied, some barely standing. They were bound fast, wrists lashed with oar-rope, forced to their knees along the deck.

Not all met their fate the same. A few begged still, voices cracking, eyes wide as boys. Others cursed us in their Brack tongue, lips split, teeth red. One knelt silent, chin high, the line of his throat bare as if daring the knife to find it.

Another prayed, words half-Christian, half to the drowned gods of the mire.

To the crew it seemed finished. Captives meant ransom, or labour, or at least the show of a victory claimed. Some of the boys even smiled, boasting they would drink on rebel coin when next we made port. They thought mercy a prize already won.

They had not yet reckoned with Illarion.

They brought him to the mast, where light struck cleanest through the morning haze. Tomas Krull demanded it — the ship's medicus, a thin man with hands that stank of old wine and camphor. I had seen him work before. He had pulled arrows from dying men, sewn bellies back together after sword thrusts, burned infected flesh with hot iron when nothing else would serve. His satchel held bone needles, scavenged silk, a curved hook for digging metal from flesh.

"Not below deck," he said, voice flat as hammered tin. "Air moves wrong down there. Humours turn foul. Do this in shadow and the wound will rot, no matter how clean I stitch it."

Illarion's jaw clenched. For a breath I thought he would order it done in his quarters anyway, away from the stare of boys and veterans alike. His eyes cut to the faces watching — some hungry for spectacle, others grey with their own pain. The hesitation showed like a crack in stone.

Then his spine straightened. "Here, then. Let them witness."

But I saw what he hid. Fear lived in the way his fingers knotted, the way his breath came too quick. Not fear of death—he had stood in sword-reach without flinching. Fear of the knife. Fear of crying out like a child. Fear of letting them see him break.

Borislav stepped forward, clumsy in borrowed gauntlets, and began unlacing the prince's plate. Each piece came away heavy with sweat and blood—cuirass lifted with a grunt, pauldrons dragged off like millstones, gauntlets peeled from hands gone white. By the time the last strap fell, Illarion sat smaller, mortal in damp linen that clung to his ribs.

The cut gaped from left brow to jaw, edges black with clotted blood. His eye floated in red.

Tomas set his tools on a cloth, each one clean-wiped with wine. Needle, thread, hook, small pot of honey for the wound's edge. "This will hurt. No wine for the pain—wine thins blood, makes healing slow."

Illarion gripped the stool's arms until his knuckles went bone-white. He did not look at Tomas or the needle. He looked at Bogdan.

The prophet moved close, bone charms clicking soft as rain. His voice wound out low, speaking of fire that sealed instead of destroying, of pain as God's chisel carving kings from common flesh. Each word wrapped around Illarion's shaking breath, steadying it.

The first stitch went in. Silk thread pulled through torn skin with a wet whisper. Illarion's face twisted, a hiss escaped him before he could bite it back. Shame flashed across his features—that he had made sound, that they had heard.

Two boys in the watching crowd exchanged glances. I saw doubt flicker between them like a flame guttering in wind.

Illarion saw it too. His jaw locked down, teeth grinding until I heard the sound. When Tomas made the second stitch, Illarion forced his eyes open, forced them to meet the watching faces. "It does not master me," he rasped through clenched teeth. But I thought it as much for himself as for the watching men.

Tomas worked steady, each pull of thread drawing flesh together. No mercy in it, only craft. Between stitches he dabbed honey at the wound's edges—old knowledge, learned from campaign surgeons who knew honey fought the rot better than prayer.

Bogdan pressed a bone charm to Illarion's temple, whispering of crowns earned in fire. The prince shuddered but kept his gaze steady on his men, daring them to see weakness where he showed only will.

By the last knot, sweat had soaked through his shirt, jaw muscles corded from the strain of silence. Tomas tied off the thread, wiped blood from his fingers with wine-soaked cloth. "Deep as a ploughshare's cut. If the rot takes hold, you'll lose the eye."

Illarion rose on legs that shook despite his will, Borislav steadying his arm. He turned slow, deliberate, so every man could see—the black stitches stark against pale skin, the ruin that would mark him forever. Blood still wept at the edges, but he held himself straight as a banner in wind.

The veterans watched with something like recognition. They had seen him opened and bleeding, seen him refuse to break under the knife as other men break under the sword. The scar would mark him as one who had paid in flesh. The boys stared, eyes wide, memorizing what they saw — not just pain endured, but pain transformed into something harder than steel. One Driftlight lad pressed fingers to his own cheek, tracing where the prince's wound lay, as if to mark himself with the same fire.

I understood then what made Illarion more than ambitious. He demanded of himself what he demanded of others — to be greater than what birth had given him. Not through blood or title, but through will made visible. He needed witnesses not for vanity, but for proof. That a man could choose what he became, stitch by bloody stitch.

For a long breath the deck held its noise. The only sounds were small — winecloth dragged, a gull somewhere off the shivered horizon, the faint rasp of a boy's breath held too long. A lad near the rail touched his lip and tasted the salt and the iron and swallowed. Another clutched his oar as if it were a rosary. The crowd did not scatter; it waited as if some ordinance had been struck and all were bound by it. In that hollow, Illarion's wound ceased being a wound and became a mark placed upon the world.

Scarred and standing, Illarion turned at once to judgment. The captives knelt in rows, wrists raw where rope had burned flesh. Sixty men in all — Brackfolk by their flat brows and coppered skin, hair braided with reed-thread, hands folded in gestures our boys didn't know. Even kneeling, they looked other beside our pale plates and northern wool.

He questioned them there before all. Some spoke quick, eager — Ironholt under siege, ships burning in the harbour, ladders set against the northern wall. Others lied smooth as merchants, spinning covens and fire-holders to please his ear. A few held silence until the rope and the lash loosened their tongues, then spat curses in their own speech.

Bogdan rose, bone charms clattering. "These are rebels against Crown and God. Their tongues speak serpent-lies. Fire is mercy for them."

Soroka answered without heat, only ship's sense. "Our losses are significant. Here are sixty hands to replace what we've lost. If the wind dies, we're dead in the water. Drown them and we are lighter — for a season. Keep them and we move. That's the law of the sea."

A veteran captain spat agreement. "Collar the able ones. Two watchmen per bench. Whip the slack backs. Those that break, cut loose and feed the fish."

Illarion let their words fall like rain on deck. Then he turned to me with that slow smile that held no warmth. "And you, Krovin? Judging silent as always?" He gestured toward the bound prisoners. "Tell me — what should a king do with rebels?"

The question landed like a blow. Memory rose: my father and uncle on High Mound, standing proud until Mstislav's blades cut them down. I had bent. I had given my blade and my name, and learned what it meant to live by another man's word — you turned his choice into your work and wore its stain.

I spoke not as a captain but as a man with an oath in his mouth. "Let those who swear to serve live."

Illarion's ruined face brightened. He stepped closer; pain and smoke clung to his breath. "Bound by oath? What... worth has a muck-worshipper's word? I should show mercy —" he attempted to sneer and then grimaced at the pain, "to cross-defilers?"

He paced—whether to consider or to draw out the theatre, I could not tell. Finally he stopped, looking at the prisoners as if they were crops to burn or harvest.

"You... will renounce your drowned saints," Illarion rasped, the stitches pulling as he forced the words. Blood thickened his mouth, broke his voice raw. "Swear... to Christ— to me—" he coughed red onto the planks, then swallowed it down, dragging the words out ragged. "Take His name and mine, and you live. Pull oars. Eat bread. Refuse—" his jaw clenched against the pain, "—the sea takes you."

Then he fixed me with that thin, sharp smile. "As you wish, Krovin. The able-bodied go to the benches. You will witness their oaths. And if any break faith—or try to slip their bonds—you see them killed."

The deck held its breath. Soroka's jaw worked. Bogdan's eyes flared like banked coals.

Forty-five of the captured swore the words. Fifteen refused and were shoved over the rail with weights tied to their ankles. They sank quick, water closing over them with barely a splash.

Forty-five of the captured swore the words. Fifteen refused and were shoved over the rail with weights tied to their ankles. They sank quick, water closing over them with barely a splash.

I watched their heads vanish. Fifteen men who would not break—who chose cold water and choking over a lie spoken aloud. There is a word for such men: faithful, or foolish, or both. I did not know which. I knew only this: God was not an oath that bound me as it bound them. Other oaths I would die for, but not the name on my lips in prayer. Perhaps that is why there is nothing left in me to save.

The survivors were driven to the oars and collared — iron rings hammered shut around necks, chains linking them to benches. The metal bit deep, already drawing blood where it rubbed bone. Two guards took position behind each pair, knives loose in their belts. The youngest prisoner — a boy no older than Borislav — sobbed as the collar closed, but his hands found the oar and began to pull.

I watched it all and tasted bile. Illarion had not asked because he needed guidance; he had asked to make me complicit. He had bound my voice to his will so that when the blade fell — and it would fall — my word would guide it.

Forty-five men lived who might have drowned. But what lived was not what they had been. They pulled our oars with Christ's name fresh on their tongues and iron fresh on their necks, and I could not tell which death would have been kinder.

I did not yet hate Illarion for the question. I hated myself for answering.

Chapter XXVII: Silence and Fire

The prince's door stayed shut. For three days Illarion had not shown himself, not even to the boys who waited for his blessing or the veterans who brought reports of wind and weather. Only Tomas Krull passed in and out, carrying wine and clean linen, his face grey as old parchment. Sometimes Bogdan emerged, bone charms rattling, ash still clinging to his fingers.

The whispers spread like rot through wet timber. *He's dying. The wound's gone poison. The priest keeps him breathing with charms and prayer.*

I had seen this before. Absence breeds more fear than presence ever could. A commander who vanishes becomes either dead or divine in his men's minds. No middle ground remains. Bogdan knew it as well as I did. He did not fight the silence—he shaped it, letting each closed door and whispered prayer build Illarion higher.

Borislav stood guard at the aftcastle door with Illarion's two veterans flanking him, men who had bled through a dozen campaigns. He gripped his spear as if the haft alone could keep death at bay. The older guards watched in silence, but the deckhands whispered—"Playing watchdog for a corpse." The jibe struck, yet he never moved. His whole purpose hung on the door behind him. If Illarion lived, he was squire and chosen. If Illarion died, he was nothing. So he stood, hollow-eyed, sleepless, holding his post like a drowning boy clinging to driftwood.

Illarion's silence loosed what he once held tight. At dawn Bogdan strode from the prince's quarters, palms black with ash. Soroka was waiting at the rail.

"I will tend the dead," he declared, voice ringing across all six ships. "Each vessel will receive the proper rites. God's judgment must be spoken over every soul."

Soroka's jaw hardened. Hands steady on the wheel, cloak dripping salt spray, she gave him no deference. "My ships. My dead. My duty."

Bogdan's smile showed teeth. "Your sailors are yours, Captain. But warriors are not claimed by wood or sail. Their blood is God's, and I only speak what He commands." He touched the bone charms at his throat, their clicking sharp as breaking twigs.

"No fire on my ships," Soroka said, voice flat as beaten iron. "I'll not have you burn my men to ash for your theatre."

"Fire lives in words as well as flame." Bogdan's eyes caught the morning light, bright and certain. "I need no torch to speak God's will."

They faced each other across twenty feet of deck, rain beginning to spatter the planks between them. Neither yielded. Neither looked away.

"As you will," Soroka said at last. "But you touch nothing aboard without my word."

Bogdan bowed to her, though I thought I saw a hint of mockery in it. "Of course, Captain. I seek only to serve."

That night, when the deck had emptied and only the watch remained, I found Soroka kneeling by a sailcloth bundle. The dead sailor inside had been young—seventeen, maybe eighteen—with hair still soft as wheat stubble. She murmured his name, quiet prayers I could barely catch over the sound of water against the hull. No fire. No theatre. Only grief, honest and plain.

She noticed me but did not rise, only acknowledged my presence with a glance. Small, but grateful. In that moment something settled between us—an understanding that needed no words. For her, this was what mattered. Not the spectacle of death, but the weight of it. The knowledge that each name had carried hopes and fears and the particular way a man held his head when he laughed.

I stood beside her in the darkness, listening to rain drum against the canvas above.

Morning brought the storm of Bogdan's ceremony. Rain lashed the deck, turning everything slick and treacherous. The dead lay in rows, wrapped in sailcloth, faces hidden but still somehow accusing.

Bogdan stripped to the waist, bone charms clattering against his ribs. Ash darkened his palms—where he had gotten it without fire, I could not guess. His skin showed pale as fish-belly, marked with old scars that seemed to writhe in the uncertain light.

He moved among the bundles, voice breaking between rasp and roar. Each name he spoke like a nail driven into wood. Each touch of ash against sailcloth marked another soul claimed for God's vision.

"Pain is the crown!" he cried, rain streaming down his face. "Wounds are the altar! These men died not as beasts die, but as warriors chosen for God's table!"

He spoke of fire that needed no fuel, of deaths that purchased grace, of blood that sanctified the very planks it stained. His words sounded like gospel, but none I'd ever heard. The language twisting beautiful and terrible together. The men watched in dread and awe. Some crossed themselves. Others only stared, feeling power beyond their understanding.

When he finished with our ship, Bogdan moved to the next vessel, then the next. His authority swelled with each deck he commanded. Bare, soaked, compelling, he strode from ship to ship like some elemental force made flesh. By the time he returned, the men looked at him differently. Not just as priest, but as something more—a man who could speak with the dead and make the living see beyond death.

Funerals matter—not just to shepherd souls home, but to honour sacrifice, to wrest meaning from deaths that might otherwise mean nothing. A boy who sees his friend dropped overboard like carrion fights worse the next day. A boy who hears his name called in fire or prayer will bleed knowing it matters.

Whether God's hand moves in all things, I cannot say. What I know is that the dead are beyond pain. That is mercy enough. And no matter the power Bogdan wielded, I preferred Soroka's quiet prayers to his sound and fury. I wished then that on my death I might have only a quiet word to ease my passing.

Chapter XXVIII: Smoke on the Horizon

A quarrel broke before noon — two Driftlight boys needling a collared Brack with jeers sharp as hooks. When he spat back, they pounced, fists and boots landing harder than their courage ever had in battle. Soroka stormed down from the quarterdeck, her voice sharper than steel. She tore them apart with a curse and a cuff to the nearest ear.

"No idle hands on my deck. If they cannot pull rope, they'll sweat under shields." She jabbed a finger toward Mikhail. "Keep them busy, Butcher. Drill them till they drop. No man rests while I command."

Mikhail had them form shield-walls, break them, advance in step and wheel by companies. His ruined hand made him inventive: he showed them how to hook a rim with his elbow, how to use weight when grip failed. All the while he muttered recipes under his breath, as if battle were butchery and he still worked his father's trade. "Salt the edge. Cut clean. Bleed it dry." The boys whispered he could taste death on the wind like a cook tasting soup.

When he was done with them, he handed off the drill to Petyr. Lean and scarred, Petyr drilled them with spears — how to brace against a charge, thrust low into gut, wrench free before the next stroke. He taught them to keep rhythm by heel and breath, not by fear.

Then Sava laid the bow in their hands. His voice was quiet, but his eye missed nothing. He taught how to string fast, loose smooth, count arrows as if each were coin from a dying purse. "Don't waste a shot. Every shaft you throw into the sea robs your brother's life."

Then Radovan took his turn. Heavy-shouldered, axe in hand, he showed the boys how to strike from overhead, how to block with haft, how to drive a man back by weight alone. He barked fewer words than the others, but every swing landed like a hammer, and the boys flinched even at the air he split. One lad dropped his axe outright, and Radovan only snorted. "Then you're meat, not man."

I took the sword and shield, showing stance and timing, how to cut where armour weakens, how to guard when the man beside you falls. "Too high," I told one lad whose sword wavered like a reed in wind. "A man's guts sit lower than his heart. Aim for the belt, not the throat."

Markov had been pressed into teaching knife-work, much to his disgust. "They'll stab themselves before they stab rebels," he complained, watching a boy fumble his grip for the third time. "It's like teaching sheep to bite wolves."

But he showed them anyway—how to hold the blade, where to cut for quick death, how to strike from surprise. The boys hung on every word, hungry for any edge that might keep them breathing.

"Remember," Markov said, demonstrating a throat-cut on empty air, "in close quarters, the man who hesitates feeds the fish. Think too long and you're dead too quick."

One boy raised his hand. "What if they surrender?"

Markov's grin was sharp as his blade. "Then you pray Krovin is the one watching. He knows mercy. I don't."

The boys stared at him like he was some blood-slick hero. I knew better. Markov could talk a good game, and he had hands quick enough to cut a throat when cornered. But he was no killer at heart, and never had been. What kept him alive was not the knife, but the wit to know when not to draw it. But that lesson he did not teach.

That night the rain came — not hard, but cold and endless, the kind that soaked through cloak and bone until a man shivered even with fire in his belly. The deck stank of wet wool and pitch. The collared Brackfolk hunched under the benches, shackled together, scraps of crust between them, huddled like half-men. Our crew fared better — hot broth ladled from the pot, dried meat, coarse bread. No feast, but enough to remind us which side of the chain we were on.

We sat close around the pot: Mikhail with his ruined hand, Petyr thin as a pike, Sava quiet and watchful, Radovan heavy-shouldered with axe across his knees, gnawing his crust down to splinters. Markov leaned back against the rail, grinning as if the cold rain were nothing but another jest.

On the deck before us, the boys moved through the forms by rote — step, cross, back, forward, kneel — while Borislav barked rhythm. Their bodies obeyed, but their eyes were dead with fatigue.

Markov snorted. "Look at them. Empty shells. That's not training — that's penance."

He stood, took Radovan's axe without asking. "Step, cross, back, forward, kneel — bah. Even when they stomp, it's prayer, not war. But watch." Hefting the axe, he moved through the forms: step jab, cross strike, back guard, forward cut. The rhythm turned dangerous in his hands.

He handed the axe back and turned to us. "What did we do all day? Drill them, then hand them to Bogdan. Two halves that never meet. The forms are patterns. So are our drills. We just need to take them back to what matters. They were killing forms once, before the serpent-blade was banned. Let's make them ours."

Radovan grunted. "Patterns are useless once the fight thickens."

"Maybe," Markov said. "But most fights end in the first few cuts. If we give them even two good strikes, it might save their necks. And ours."

Sava spoke up, flat as ever. "Most of these recruits aren't worth training. A handful have good eyes and hands. The rest are ballast."

Markov smirked. "True enough. I thought the same trying to teach fat Mikhailov how to walk soft. The boy stomps like a mule with rocks in its guts."

That earned a laugh, even from Radovan.

Markov pressed the point. "So we don't waste time. We split them. Mikhail takes shield-hearts. Radovan the axe-men. Petyr the spears. Sava the bows. Krovin the sword and board. Me the knives. Each boy drilled where he's sharpest, all day, every day—no wasted motions, no dull pattern. Honed until the rhythm itself kills."

No one argued. Even Radovan only gnawed his crust and kept silent.

I watched Markov—the self-proclaimed coward, the rat who always found a crack to slip through—and I marveled. He had no hunger for killing, not truly, but his wit turned even prayer into war. Illarion's command, Bogdan's zeal,

Markov's craft—the forms were already becoming something none of them had intended.

The days bent into rhythm—northern drills and holy fire woven like warp and weft, sweat and smoke binding the crew tighter than rope.

Between drills, Bogdan seized his turn. Only days before he had spat that Illarion's discipline was heresy—drowned rites profaning fire. But something shifted in him. Perhaps cunning—seeing a chance to make the boys his. Perhaps pragmatism—with the drills now ordered and praised, he could not afford to be left aside. Whatever the reason, he bent them to his will. He smeared soot across brows, drove knees to the planks slick with rain, and lashed chants of fire and oath to Borislav's movements. What had begun as reed-prayer he recast as gospel, each bow and strike hammered into sermon.

But between drills, the whispers never stopped. The prince was dying. The prince was healing. The prince was being reborn in fire. Only Bogdan and Tomas Krull knew truth from Rumour, and neither spoke. Once I saw Krull toss a bundle of bloody bandage over the rail. The gulls fought over it like entrails.

Still, dread spread faster than rain, seeping into every corner of the ship. When men did not know if their commander lived or died, they began to doubt everything else—their orders, their purpose, their chances of seeing home again.

The voyage crawled on under inconsistent wind. The oars groaned constantly now, pulled by boys whose backs ached and collared Brackfolk whose eyes held nothing but endurance. The former rebels had learned their rhythm, pulling in time with the drum, but no warmth passed between them and their guards.

By the fourth day, even I began to wonder if Illarion would emerge at all.

Then the rain thinned. The mist pulled apart like torn cloth. On the horizon, a smudge of smoke rose dark against the grey sky.

Ironholt burned, and we sailed toward it like moths drawn to flame.

Chapter XXIX: The Crowfen Gate

We rounded the Horn of Rosnolt, a black spit of rock that hooked into the sea like a broken claw. The southern coast of Mirefast sprawled ahead—reed-beds giving way to peat cliffs and low ridges where spruce and alder clung like teeth in a rotten jaw. The wind carried their resin, sharp enough to taste, mingled with the sour reek of kelp drying on the rocks.

The waters here never warmed. Even in summer they bit like steel. Spray froze to salt crust on the rails; the oarsmen blew on their hands when the gusts turned. Gulls wheeled, black-backed and lean, their cries harsh as hinges. The boys said they sounded like souls not yet drowned.

Eastward the coast narrowed, and we bent into the Crowfen Channel, where reed-beds crowded close and the tide snarled through stone jaws. The sound of it was like a beast growling in its sleep. Crows wheeled above the fen, ragged flocks breaking and reforming, their wings a scatter of black against grey sky. Markov muttered that they had come to measure how many of us would be theirs. Veterans said nothing; they had seen enough drowned men to know the count was never wrong.

Beyond the channel the bay opened, wide as a gate, and Ironholt stood there on her rise.

The bay bent like a crooked arm around Ironholt, shallow at the mouth and deep where the town clung to its stone rise. She had begun as a garrison, a squat keep and barracks hammered down to hold the southern shore. But war and drink are kin, and here the Mirefast peat gave both. From the stillhouses came whitefire—clear and sharp, reeking of smoke, burning down the throat like swallowed flame.

Markov swore it could strip paint from a hull; I said it was better suited to cleaning wounds than drinking. Yet beyond the mire it was a delicacy, casks fetching fortunes from Ashenbay to Velgrad, praised by men who thought peat a flavour rather than rot.

That was Ironholt's wealth. Timber floated down from inland forests to feed her wharves, but it was whitefire that swelled her coffers. The quay was lined with warehouses, taverns fattened on soldiers' pay, and merchant houses whose sons counted coin by the barrel. They said the Crown's fleets would not march a week without her drink.

Now that wealth had made her a prize. The rebels ringed her fields with trenches and palisades. Smoke already rose from the outer wards, and from further off the dust of wagons bringing stone for engines. Timber once cut for planks now braced their ladders and towers. Whitefire once rolled onto ships now soaked rags for firepots hurled against her gates.

From our decks we saw it plain: a town fattened by its own fire, bleeding it out drop by drop.

The bay kept its breath as if it, too, were waiting for a sickness to pass. Smoke curled from Ironholt like a hand trying to hide something it could not hold. From the quarterdeck we watched it thicken, a slow, patient black that climbed over roofs and turned the sun to a coin dulled by ash. Men pointed. A boy spat. The mast creaked and the oars that had rowed us this far sat like useless ribs along the benches.

The aftcastle door did not open.

Four days. That was the measure men had begun to use when the night stretched and no order came: four days, four meals, four watches. Desyatniki and Driftlight lads muttered prayers. Soroka walked the deck with the gait of someone counting losses she had no name for yet. She barked at the boys to keep the ropes clear, to keep the hull tidy, as if neatness could steady a thing gone loose.

The fleet pulled closer, oars biting until we were within reach of Ironholt's piers. The town lay right there — smoke curling behind her walls, the cries of gulls drowned beneath the heavier rhythm of our own drums. Each warship struck the beat in turn, steady as heart and bone. On deck the men made ready: buckles tightened, blades whetted on stone, bowstrings plucked and tested. Quivers were upended and arrows counted, each shaft tapped against the rail as if that could make it truer. Stormhold lads checked their helms three times over, while Driftlight boys muttered that their hands had gone slick with sweat. Even the veterans grew quiet, feeling the weight that comes when the sea itself seems to lean toward the shore.

They braced themselves against the benches, waiting for the call to board, for the surge that would throw us into rescue or ruin.

Then the drums fell silent. One by one they guttered out, until only the slap of water on hull remained. The ships held in line, black prows facing the harbour mouth. From the walls of Ironholt I thought I saw movement — shapes gathering, a banner lifted, hands raised to point. They had seen us. They must have thought the hour of relief had come, that the fire on their roofs would be quenched by fire from the sea.

But no order came. Our fleet sat in the bay like teeth clenched against speech. Each captain held his deck and waited for a command that never left the aftcastle. On our rails, the boys still clutched at their buckles, their blades, their bows, all dressed for a charge that never came. Veterans stared flat-eyed, already knowing what it meant. And the city — our city — went on burning while we watched.

Evening fell, and still the line of ships held the bay. The sun went down behind the peat-cliffs and turned the smoke above Ironholt the colour of dried blood. Men kept their gear close as if orders might come with the dusk, but none did. Soroka walked the deck twice, then three times, her shadow long against the planks. At last the boys slumped where they sat, armour rattling as they nodded into uneasy sleep.

Night came, black and raw, the water cold as iron. Watchfires flickered along the rebel lines, specks of orange against the dark. From the town came shouts and the distant crack of timbers, each one carried clear over the still water. We lay awake, counting them, until we stopped counting because we could not bear the numbers. Once, the aftcastle door opened. Bogdan came out, his hands still black with ash, eyes bright with fever-light. He walked the deck slow, bone charms rattling at his belt. The men watched him like he might give word, but he only turned back through the door and shut it behind him. No explanation, no command. Just silence.

At dawn the gulls screamed again. A skiff tried the bay-mouth, a handful of rebels testing, and Vedek's men volleyed until the craft went crawling back, boards splintered and oars shattered. The boys cheered thinly, but no order followed. By full light the fleet still sat, sails furled, anchors biting. Men oiled blades that would not be drawn, checked arrows that would never fly. The town burned, and we kept watch like mourners at a bier.

By the second evening the engines fell silent. All day they had thrown stone into the wards, thudding like the heartbeat of some great beast. Now the hill above the town lay still, the two catapults hunched against the sky like broken cranes. Men still moved about them—shadows hefting buckets, stacking stones—but no shots came.

Smoke clung to the walls below. Sections were broken jagged, gaps where you could see the dark teeth of houses inside. Part of the town was already fire-eaten. Once or twice we saw figures running along the breaches, defenders or rebels we could not tell. It seemed the enemy had pressed into the outer streets, for fire ran not only along the walls but behind them. The keep still held—its banners stiff in the wind, a knot of defiance at the town's heart—but how long can a knot hold when the rope is burning through?

The rebels sat their hill, banners limp, waiting. A handful of skiffs prowled the channel mouth, daring the reef, but none came close after Vedek's volley. For a moment it felt like stasis again, three sides staring at one another—the rebels on their hill, the garrison in its keep, and us, sitting in the bay with our sails furled.

The confusion bled everywhere. From the town, no sally came. From the rebels, no charge. From us, no rescue. Only smoke rising, the gulls crying, and men staring across the water wondering which silence would break first.

On our decks the murmurs thickened like the smoke. The veterans spoke first, low and bitter. "Better to let the rats starve," one said, spitting into the scuppers. "Storming a town half-lost is nothing but a meat-grinder." Another counted on his fingers, the way soldiers do when they measure distance and death. "Three walls broken. Engines still whole. We'd lose half the fleet in an hour." Their voices carried the tone of men who had seen it before, who feared waste more than shame.

The boys did not carry it so well. Driftlight lads who had sworn for glory kept their bows tight across their knees, arrows already fletched between their fingers. They whispered of charges through fire, of storming ladders, of lifting the siege in a blaze that would make them men. Waiting was worse than dying for them — it made them feel like cowards before a fight they had not even been given.

The arguments fed one another. Old soldiers against young, profit against pride. The rope of our company frayed in the silence, every strand tugging a different way, yet none daring to move without the hand that should have pulled them tight.

Then a veteran beside me spat and muttered, "They're turning them."

I followed his gaze. The crews on the hill had dragged the frames half-about, ropes creaking, straining as the great arms were reset. No longer aimed at the walls, the engines now faced the harbour. Their shadows crouched like beasts ready to spring.

"Docks," I said, my throat tight. "They mean to smash the docks."

The knowledge spread along the rails. Men shifted, muttered curses. Soroka swore under her breath. We all knew what it meant: if the piers went, we would land under fire, or not land at all.

The first stone came down hard on the quay, shattering timbers into spray. The sound cracked across the bay like thunder. A second followed, splinters whistling, men ducking on instinct though the shot fell short. They were finding their range, and soon enough the firepots would follow.

The waiting stretched until even the gulls fell silent. Then at last the aftcastle door creaked. Tomas Krull stepped out, his surgeon's smock stained with vinegar and blood. He pulled the air in like a man drowning and let it out with a curse. His face was drawn, lips tight, as if every question hurled at him were a weight he refused to carry. He gave no word, only stalked across the deck and spat into the sea.

Not long after, Borislav was called in. The boy's armour hung loose on his frame, and his jaw worked like he was chewing stones. He crossed the threshold with the look of a man who had been summoned to judgment, and the door shut behind him.

We waited again. Men shifted, muttered, touched their blades as if the metal might steady them.

Then Illarion came.

He emerged in full plate, burnished bright, helm closed. The sickness that had held him vanished beneath steel. Not a stumble nor tremor showed in his step. He climbed to the command gallery above the stern, slow and deliberate, until he stood where every ship in the line could see him. The light struck his armour and it answered, fire chasing across the plates like a living thing.

Borislav followed close, pale as wax, eyes wide, as if the helm beside him had hidden not a prince but a revenant. When they reached the gallery, the boy unfurled a scroll with trembling hands. His voice cracked at first, then grew steadier as he read—while another stone screamed over the bay and smashed into the quay, timbers shrieking as they splintered. Men flinched at the crack, but Borislav pressed on.

"Men of Driftlight, Stormhold, Velgrad – sons of the Crown, hear these words.

Before us stands Ironholt, jewel of the southern coast, a fortress raised by our fathers, a harbour whose strength has built ships for king and kingdom. Her wealth is timber and whitefire, but greater still are her people – children of the King, kin to us all.

Now traitors have risen against that bond. They have broken oaths sworn before God and saint, set fire to their own hearths, and dared to raise hand against their lord. They crouch upon the hills like jackals, casting stones upon their betters. Such men are not rebels but apostates, enemies of Crown and Christ, serpents gnawing at the roots of the realm."

Another stone arced, fell short, and burst the tide into spray. Borislav's voice wavered, then stiffened again, as if he had not heard.

"But look you now! The Crown has not forgotten its children. The King's hand is not withered. The fire of judgment has not gone out. I, Illarion son of Mstislav, stand clothed in steel, bound by oath, chosen by flame. By the saints and by the fire that does not lie, I proclaim: Ironholt shall not fall.

Lift your eyes to her walls – not broken stone, but ramparts of our cause. Hear her cries as your own mother's voice, calling sons to shield her from the knife.

This day we strike. Not for gold or plunder, but for the sanctity of the realm, for the oath of every man sworn to the Crown, for the children of Ironholt who wait to be delivered. We are their shield. We are their fire."

The next stone struck close enough to send shards of dock flying, the crack echoing through the bay like a tree splitting in storm. Still the boy finished, voice hoarse:

"Therefore carry my word to every ship, every bench, every blade: in the name of the King, the saints, and the fire that judges, I command the assault. Let treachery be ash, and loyalty endure forever."

The scroll at last went still in Borislav's hands. His voice cracked on the final words, and he lowered it with a tremor, but Illarion gave no sign. He did not speak. He only stood, helm lifted, armour blazing in the new sun. He was faceless, voiceless, an idol hammered from steel, fire chasing across him in every gleam. The boys cheered raggedly, beating weapons against shields, trying to drown their fear in sound. The veterans held their tongues. Their silence was the harder truth.

Then Soroka's voice cut the air.

"Beat to oars!"

The order struck like a blade. Drummers lifted mallets, and the first heavy strokes rolled across the decks. Oars slid into water, the fleet pulling as one. The line of ships surged forward, hulls shuddering, spray bursting white against their prows.

Rebel skiffs scattered, their oarsmen darting for reeds rather than face a charge. Arrows hissed after them, shafts hurling men into the tide. The warships pressed on, driving straight for Ironholt's quays.

From the walls we could see smoke thick as a pall. From the harbour, nothing but silence — the docks bare, no enemy to contest them. That silence was its own omen.

Still the drums thundered, faster, louder, until timbers shook and men shouted with every stroke. The fleet bore down on the city, and Ironholt's burning roofs loomed closer with every pull.

Chapter XXX: The Quiet Had Teeth

The oars bit harder, and the fleet surged as one. Spray fanned white from the prows, the drumbeat rolling in our ribs. Rebel skiffs skulked at the harbour mouth, thin as reeds against hulls built for war. When our bows rose out of the mist they broke like minnows, oars flashing for the shallows. A few hurled javelins back over their shoulders; arrows answered, cutting men into the tide. The rest vanished quick as they had come.

We drove on. The bay-mouth narrowed, piers jutting like broken teeth. Quays shuddered under our keels grinding stone, timbers shrieking like bones under a lash. Gangways slammed down, iron-bound and heavy, and men poured ashore—Velgrad veterans first, shields locked, then Stormhold lads, then Driftlight boys tumbling after, armour clattering like pots down a stair.

The rebels did not contest the landing. That silence froze the breath in every man. No charge, no arrows, only the thunder of stone falling from the heights. A boulder struck the next pier and split it like kindling, the shock running up through the planks into my bones. Men screamed as they pitched into the water; others crouched low, clutching shields against a sky that might spit death at any heartbeat. To stand there was to feel the whole weight of the hill above you, unseen hands winding back the sling.

A second stone smashed down on one of our ships, timbers cracking, mast twisting like a broken limb. The hull lurched, water rushing through the split. Men leapt for the pier, some too slow—crushed flat where they stood. The chained oarslaves had no chance. Still fixed to their benches, iron dragged them into black water. Their voices cut short. The tide swallowed them whole.

Soroka's curse cut the din, sharp as steel.

"Too slow! Move, you bastards, move!"

Her voice lashed veterans and boys alike, driving them off the gangways and into the streets before the next shot could find them. She spat toward the aftcastle, fury plain. "Waited 'til the bastards turned the engines. Botched from the start. Ships win harbours," she spat, "but men lose them."

The stones kept coming while we crowded the quays, each one a thunderclap that made the timbers shiver beneath our boots. Splinters flew like knives, and every man's eyes flicked skyward, waiting for the weight that might choose him next. To stand there was to feel your own grave swinging through the air, hidden until it fell.

The column formed slow, too slow. Boys jostled in the front ranks, shields clutched tight, armour clattering as if they shook inside it. Veterans cursed and shoved them forward, keeping lines from tangling. Officers barked names, voices lost in the roar. A stone burst against the pier, throwing men sideways, collapsing one rank into another. It was order only in name, fear hammered into shape by discipline.

I saw old soldiers set their jaws, spit black with ash, eyes never leaving the sky. One muttered to another, not caring who heard:

"No man should linger on a dock in range. They're bleeding us before the fight."

Then Soroka's whistles split the din. I turned in time to see the warships pulling back, hulls scraping free, oars biting hard. The gangways had been hauled aboard. The ships were gone, dragging smoke and splinters with them, slaves bending low over their benches to save themselves. Whatever waited ahead, there would be no retreat to water.

Illarion came ashore last, as if the tide itself bore him. From a distance he looked the prince he named himself. Close by, the armour seemed to bear him more than he bore it.

His stride was slow, deliberate, measured so no stumble could be seen. I saw his gauntlets tighten and release, like a man bracing against something inside his skull. When he spoke, the sound came low and muffled through the helm — short words, torn by breath, as if the steel itself had swallowed half of them.

"Up… the hill."

The words barely reached me. Borislav leaned close, head bent like a servant, then lifted his face and cried them loud enough for all:

"The prince says the hill is the goal! The traitors wait there — jackals on the heights!"

The Driftlight boys roared, beating their shields, spears thrust skyward, as if the streets ahead were open fields and the sun itself would bear them uphill.

Illarion forced another phrase, thick and broken.

Borislav's voice cracked but carried it high:

"The prince commands we break them! We strike as one, the Crown's glory made fire!"

The boys howled louder, as if sound alone might make them strong.

The drum began, slow and steady, each beat rolling through smoke and fear.

Recruits in front, veterans behind, archers strung and watching the roofs. The column marched off the docks and into the town.

We stepped into the wards. The stones stopped. The silence was worse.

The wards lay bare. Boys ran ahead, kicking barrels aside, dragging beams into gutters. Their voices were too thin, too sharp, trying to sound bold and sounding only afraid.

No rebels. Only dogs barking in alleys, a child crying once then cut off, the crack of fire chewing through timber. A few townsfolk slipped past us, clutching bundles, faces hollow as ghosts, vanishing into the smoke without a word.

The drum kept its beat. Step by step we made for the hill, and still the silence pressed close, heavy as chains. The harbour had been a graveyard. The town promised something worse.

The veterans kept their mouths shut until we'd pressed deeper into the wards. Then one spat into the ash at his feet.

"No man gives up a harbour unless he's dug in deeper."

Another grunted, checking the edge of his axe.

"They'll bleed us in the alleys. He dreams of banners. We'll find smoke and knives."

I heard truth in it, heavy as stone. The prince dreamt of fire on the hill, but I smelled only smoke.

Illarion gave no sign. He walked forward, slow as shadow, helm sealed tight, faceless as an idol hammered from steel. The boy carried his voice, the armour carried his frame, and still the men followed, driven not by sense, but by the promise of fire on the hill — into streets already half a grave.

They had made it barely two streets in when the town closed its teeth.

A thousand small sounds: a plank kicked, a wheel overturned, the quick slap of something running along a roof — and then the world changed. Men at the front felt it before they saw it: the alley narrowed, timbers slammed together, a barricade born from kitchens and carts rising like a wall. The boys at the head ran straight into it, shields meeting wood with a sound like flesh. Behind the barricade hands shoved poles through cracks; something hissed and glass broke.

Reed-bows whispered from the roofs — short arcs, sudden, a scatter of bone-tipped shafts that found faces and shoulders. The first who went were the eager ones: Driftlight lads who had run too fast, laughing at their own courage. One of them looked at his hand as an arrow drove through the palm and his laugh broke into a gurgle. Another had his throat split open; his head lolled and he died still trying to shout.

A firepot hit the barricade like a thrown heart. Oil hissed, black and hot, and the scent of burning hair rose. Men slammed shields to slow the flames, but it ran down cloaks, pooled at boots. Someone screamed that a roof had gone; the sound of falling tiles came like rain. The alley became a corridor of smoke and cursing.

Petyr planted his spear at the barricade like a stake. He did not charge; he braced and shoved. Where spears could find purchase he forced gaps, levering rotten axle and plank with veteran strength. Boys poured past him in that small opening—eager, blind with wanting—into knives and hands that were already waiting. Petyr's face stayed a mask of effort. Bodies smashed against his flanks and slid away. He stood while the young died before him, and for each one his jaw tightened like a vise.

Radovan was where timber split and metal met wood; his axe rang with every swing, sending splinters into the smoke. He fought like a man who believed brute force could defeat cunning—big blows, furious, a roar in his throat that steadied the lads behind him. He tore a gap through a cart, ripped a shutter free, and in that bright labour his eyes shone. He cleaved a man trying to leap the barricade and his axe came back wet and black. Radovan moved like a hammer until something small and slick—oil, a thrown brand—caught his sleeve. He spat flame from his mouth and kept chopping. He kept on until the smoke hid him, until I could not see whether he still stood.

From the roofs Sava's voice barked orders and the rhythm changed. He had taken his archers through a side-street and up into the houses; now he ran the rooftops, stringing shafts in fast, precise volleys that drove some of the rebel archers back. His shafts found heads above the barricades, and where men on the ground would have been butchered blind, Sava's men bought us moments—vital moments—by cutting off the worst of the angles. He cursed like a captain and his voice threaded over the din. He lived and he shot, and in those few minutes his fire kept whole ranks from folding.

Mikhail moved among the boys like a butcher among calves—cruel in speech, relentless in order. Where panic flared he slammed a shield into a shoulder and drove the lad on. "Plant! Plant! Watch your left!" he barked, and the command had the hard edge of practice. The discipline he'd beaten into those boys saved more than it had ever cost. One of them, a thin thing with a new scar, followed a shield-wall and lived because Mikhail shoved him into place when the barricade gave.

A cry rose near the breach—ragged, not the sound of a fighter. I saw Tomas Krull there, no scalpel in his hands now but a short blade wrested from a corpse. He had been pressed into the line, a healer dragged into butcher's work. His smock was black with other men's blood, not his own. He tried to stand behind Mikhail's shield-wall, jabbing where gaps opened, but his grip was poor, his stance a half-step slow. A spear drove through the smoke and took him under the ribs. He folded without a word, eyes wide as if still trying to reckon whether the wound belonged to him or another.

The boys who saw it faltered; the man who had bound their cuts the night before lay choking in the muck. Mikhail cursed and shoved them forward anyway. We had no space for mourning.

The street became a press. Smoke spooled up between houses and the sunlight turned red through it. Knives slid between ribs. Arrows thudded into timber and man and the cries of the dying were close enough to taste. I drove Pryaz in and out, the blade heavy, taking men where I could find a seam—an armpit, the web of an elbow. Each cut was an answer and a question. I killed to stay alive; I killed and felt no honour in it. The weight of the breastplate made each movement clumsy and slow; I felt every life I took as if it were a chain put onto my neck.

Borislav stood not two strides from me, the banner over his shoulder bright against the smoke. Veterans circled him like a small shield-wall around a child. He did not falter. He did not drop the cloth even when a shard of tile grazed his cheek and sent red running down his lip. The men made space so the banner might fly; the men died to keep that space.

The killing widened. Where the barricade had been forced open, the rebels pressed into the lanes like water finding a breach. They came with crookfang knives — short recurved blades meant to catch and tear — and with broken eel-forks, twin-pronged spears hacked down to staves. Rage gave edge to reed and bone. They did not fight like men who wanted honour but like people who would rather burn a town than hand it over. Civilians were trampled or cut down trying to crawl from doors; a woman with a child on her hip screamed until a veteran smothered her cry with a sword hilt to the jaw, and then there was only the low sound of her dying.

We answered. We butchered through rooms and courtyards, stabbed through shutters, hauled men out by their hair and finished them where they crouched. Some veterans moved like ghosts — efficient, terrible. Mercy went out with the smoke. The street filled with the kind of red that stains memory.

By the time the first clearer of the barricade was done, the alley behind us was a smear of bodies and the air tasted of iron and burning. We had won a narrow inch of ground by killing for it, and the victory felt filthy and small. The drum counted the dead and called for more.

That was when I saw it plain: no single charge, no field to win — just a hundred small deaths ground out in alleys and rooms. It felt less like a fight than a machine built to chew men into bone. The town did not give a field to be taken; it turned itself into a machine to eat men.

They came down from the hill at last, the roar of them louder than fire. A flood of bodies poured through the breaches and lanes, not a charge in order but a breaking wave of rage. We shrank at once. Streets that felt wide as a square became tunnels; doors turned to knives. The town swallowed us room by room.

The first man before me swung a tethered hook, a claw of iron on a cord meant to catch and drag. The breastplate turned it, screech of metal on metal, and I drove Pryaz into the gap at his ribs until he folded. Another came with a cleaver black from butchering pigs, hacking wild. He caught my shoulder once, and I felt the weight of the plate take it, the edge biting only leather. I cut him under the chin and the blood came in sheets. My wounded leg gave no protest now; I had forgotten it in the crush. My breath rasped raw.

They kept coming — faces ash-smeared, eyes wide with hate. A boy no older than fifteen thrust a spear at my chest. The point slid off the plate, but it left me open. Another man rushed in with a mallet and cracked my helm so hard sparks swam in my sight. I killed them both, quick, dirty, the blade dragging heavy in my hand. Every cut was work. Every cut was survival.

The street stank of blood and smoke. Roof-tiles rained down. Screams from houses rose and cut short in the same breath. I saw Radovan through it all, huge in the haze, still swinging his axe though his cloak and hair had caught fire. He burned like a torch and kept chopping, bellowing until the sound turned to a roar of flame in his throat. When he fell it was not to any blade, but because the fire took him whole.

Petyr lasted longer. He stood braced with his spear, prying at another barricade, holding space so others could pass. A rebel knife caught him low, another from behind. He sank to one knee still thrusting. By the time I reached him he was gone, staring glassy-eyed past me as if the fight had marched on without him.

Borislav clung to the banner as if it were breath itself. The veterans kept a ring about him, but a pot of stone and pitch fell from a roof and burst among them. I saw men reel, one with his face gone, another staggering blind. Borislav tried to lift the pole again, lips red with his own blood. He crumpled, banner slipping from his hand into muck.

Before I could move, a Stormhold youth—pale, sweating, a face I half-knew but could not name—snatched it up and raised it high. He howled as he did, as if shouting could keep him alive. The cloth flared in the smoke again, bright against the ruin.

Trumpets cut through the din, sudden and sharp. From the keep gates the garrison burst out at last, horsemen leading, hooves striking sparks on stone. At their head rode a captain with a red sash, Ironholt's badge stitched rough into it—a white flame on black cloth. They burst from the keep's broad gate into the open of the market square, lances striking true, rebels scattering before hooves and iron. But the square funneled quick into lanes too narrow for charge. The mounts skidded on ash and blood, riders wheeling, hacking with blades too long for walls so tight. They had broken the first press, but the town's teeth closed again, swallowing horse and man alike. They broke the first press, but the mire of streets swallowed them quick, mounts wheeling, riders hacking with swords too long for such close walls. Still, their charge gave us breath.

My breath came ragged. The breastplate dragged me down, heavy as chains. Still I killed and killed again, every swing of Pryaz a sentence, every face that fell another memory etched in black.

Illarion came late into the press. Once he would have been at the fore; now his steps dragged, the weight of plate pulling at shoulders already bowed. For a breath I thought he might fall, then he steadied, and the fire on his armour turned doubt into splendour. He moved slow but shone all the same, a walking idol among men. The boys cheered at the sight of him, even as arrows hissed and firepots shattered at their feet. To them he was the promise made flesh. To me, the promise already cracked.

He waded forward, sword in each hand, shields clanging from his breastplate as if nothing could break him. I saw men strike at him—spears thrust, knives raked, clubs swung—and each blow rang from his steel or slid harmless down the plates. He stood in it all, faceless, wordless, his armour answering in place of any cry. For a heartbeat it seemed he might be what he claimed: fire clothed in iron, unbroken.

Then the hammer came. Heavy as a smith's, it dropped out of the smoke and struck the side of his helm with a crack that split the din, a sound I felt in my teeth. His whole frame lurched, arms splayed wide. For an instant he was no prince, not even a man—only a tower folding in storm.

He went down. Steel to stone, slow and terrible.

The press swallowed him. Rebels surged to strike, clubs and blades hacking down, sparks flying where steel met steel. His guards flung themselves over him, shouting, their bodies taking the blows that should have ended him. It was chaos—men heaving, hacking, dragging. His body moved only by their will, armour scraping against cobble, inch by inch pulled back toward the keep. They strained with it, bent double, blood streaming as they forced him out of the kill-pit. He looked lifeless, heavy as iron without a soul inside. I could not see his face. I could not hear his breath. Only the weight of him, dragged away like a corpse, helm dark, limbs slack.

They dragged Illarion into the garrison at last. I saw his shape borne past a doorway on a ragged litter, men bent under the weight of his steel, helmets glancing against beams. They dragged him with difficulty; his arms and legs flopped like a thing emptied of heat. The drag of cuirass on stone made an ugly sound. The garrison closed behind them, a door slammed like a verdict.

For a breath the street lay full of bodies and the sound of panting men. Then faces hardened, eyes cleared as if by a cut. The fall of the prince had become a blade sharpened into the men. They rallied as if sewn together by that very loss—shouting, pushing, binding wounds and seizing standards. Where confusion had been, purpose snapped like a line. Illarion's absence—his dragged-though-not-dead body tucked behind garrison doors—became a reason to kill harder, to make the loss not vain.

The line did not break. It surged.

We fought on with his body gone from sight, smoke and screams closing in, and still the thought beat in me with every step: if he lived, he lived only by miracle.

They tore the town apart until it had nothing left to give.

What had been cramped slaughter became an ugly, systematic killing: veterans moving with the cold economy of men who had died and learned the price; boys running with a terrible new steadiness, raised by the need to not be next. The trumpets from the keep had cut through the smoke—and the horsemen pushed down lanes with lance and mailed fist, forcing the rebels back from pockets they had hoped to hold. Horses slipped on blood and ash; riders swung blades that did not fit between shutters and eaves, but even so, the charge scattered the first press and gave us breath.

We hunted them house to house. Doorways were broken, rooms cleared with spear and axe, crouched men dragged into the street and finished where they knelt. Where the rebels tried to stand in narrow rooms we burned them out or hauled them into light and cut them down. The smell was hot iron and smoked hair; it soaked into wood and the soles of boots and stayed when the men stopped shouting. I moved like a machine—Pryaz a dull, relentless work, the breastplate taking blows I no longer felt. My leg ached but it was a far thing now, buried under other hurts.

A handful of rebels fought with the kind of madness you get from defending a home and a life. One old man I caught with a water spear had hands that trembled from cold or fear and eyes ridiculous with stubbornness; he thrust and I shoved him back, and when he fell his face did not look like an enemy's so much as the town's own. A girl—no more than a girl—tried to fling a pot of oil and missed, and the thing shattered between us. A veteran shoved her aside; she tumbled, and I felt the shock like a stone in my gut. There was no music to this. Only work, and the moments between which men took breath so they could kill again.

Then the surrender began to clatter out of the alleys, small and shameful. First single hands behind a shutter; then whole knots of men shook white cloth. The cries for mercy were drowned in smoke and steel, but one by one the hands lifted, and the killing slowed.

We set the town to the sword until it sighed and could not sigh any more.

I walked among the dead and could not tell which pain was mine and which belonged to the place. The boy with the banner stood, chest heaving, hands black with blood and smoke. The streets were a map of worked ruin: bodies stacked, smoke curling, dogs nosing at gore. Ironholt stank of us. The quiet had teeth.

Chapter XXXI: Between the Dead

Radovan lay black as pitch, shoulders hunched like he still braced for the next swing. The fire had eaten his face, left only a mask of char and a mouth curled open. His axe lay beside him, haft burned through, head sunk half into the timber of the street.

Petyr was not far — flat on his back, eyes glazed, mouth slack like he'd meant to spit and hadn't finished. His spear was planted still, point skewed sideways as though he'd been trying to keep it upright when the end came.

I sat between them. My armour creaked once and then stilled. The street around me was movement — Sava shouting men toward the hill, boys pulling at beams to make pyres of the rebel engines, Mikhail corralling captives into knots. All of it came through like echoes from another room. Here it was only the two of them, and me, and the smoke hanging low.

They had not been good men. Radovan was quick with his fists, mean with his tongue. A bully, cruel in small ways that left marks even when he laughed after. Petyr cheated at dice, lied when it cost him nothing, liked to watch men squirm. I had cursed both of them more times than I could count.

But I remembered them. That was the curse of it. You remember the bastards as much as the saints.

I remembered Radovan not for his temper, but for a day on Strayhorn Isle, the first campaign. We'd broken a village, smoke still in the thatch, and for once the drums were quiet. He'd been boasting over stew that he could fish better than any man alive. I told him he was full of it. So did half the company. He swore he'd prove it. Next morning he went out, and for some reason I went with him.

The sun had come up red over the water, flat and bright. He hardly spoke all day. Neither did I. We just sat with lines in the tide, waiting. The gulls wheeled, the sea stank, and the fish bit slow. Still, he caught enough for us to eat. And for that day he was not a bully, not a fist, not a flame in a man's skull. He was just a boy from nowhere with a line in his hand and the smell of salt on him. I have carried that day longer than all his cruelties.

Petyr I did not meet until Steelwatch Isle. He had that grin then — the one that meant trouble, always on his way to it or back from it. I hated that grin. But I remember a night different from the rest. We'd just taken a town, half the roofs still smoking, and the boys were restless. Petyr had gone quiet. Then I saw him watching a girl. One of the locals, dark-haired, slim as a reed. She looked back.

He fell for her, or thought he did. Maybe it was only lust, but it softened him. He carried a lock of her hair after, tied in cloth. Told me once he'd go back for her when the wars were done. We both knew he never would. He couldn't even keep a promise at dice. But he kept that lock, and he looked at it sometimes when he thought no one saw. That, I remember.

Now he lay with his eyes blank to the sky, and Radovan blackened to ash beside him. And I sat there, caught in the weight of years, the bonds made in mud and smoke. Not good men. Not saints. But my comrades.

A horn sounded, thin in the smoke, and from the quay came the creak of timbers as Soroka's ships edged into the harbour at last. The fleet was back under oar, black sails looming through haze, prow cutting through wreckage. I heard her voice over the water, harsh and flat:

"This is no harbour. It's a grave."

I stayed where I was, between Radovan and Petyr, the din passing around me like a river around stone. My hands stank of ash and iron. I let them rest on my knees.

Then the voice came.

"Where is the Prince of Fire?"

Bogdan. His ash-dark hands were raised, bone charms rattling as he strode into the square. His eyes cut through the men as if the answer should leap from their mouths.

No one spoke.

He asked again, louder, the words carrying like a curse. "Where is the Prince of Fire?"

I thought of answering, but the weight in me was too heavy for speech. My mouth opened and closed again.

Still silence.

At last a veteran leaned close to him, whispering low. I saw Bogdan's shoulders stiffen. His cloak snapped in the breeze as he turned, charms clattering with every step. He swept off toward the keep, not walking but near to running, like a mourner turned fanatic, desperate to reach his altar.

The noise of men filled back in where he had passed—chains clinking, boots dragging, Soroka's curses rolling down from the quay.

And then another set of boots came light near me. Markov crouched at my side, grin pale, knife still sheathed. He looked down at Radovan's charred husk, at Petyr's blank stare, then at me. His grin slipped a little.

"You look like hell," he said. A pause, almost gentle, then the edge slid back in. "Which is to say, you look the same."

Chapter XXXII: The Sealed Hall

The keep's hall was not built for this many bodies. Its roof beams sagged low, blackened by years of smoke; the air hung thick with it now, torches clawing more soot into the haze. The stone floor was slick in places, worn by boots and stained by blood dragged in from the yard. The smell was layered—iron and sweat, wet wool steaming, the sour bite of sickness already seeping from the table in the centre.

The crowd pressed close. Soldiers stood in knots, armour buckled but helms in hand, eyes fixed forward. Civilians lingered at the edges, wives and traders with lips pressed thin, drawn by the rumour of a dying prince. The local priest clutched his wooden cross like a weapon, lips moving in silent measure, as if louder prayer might drown the whispers. The captain of the garrison—cloak of colour still torn from the charge at the gate—kept his hand on his sword, scowling at every shuffle. Near him stood the governor of the province, Lord Kozlov, lean in velvet worn thin at the cuffs, his face pale with sweat; his eyes darted, not to Illarion, but to the men watching him.

I pushed into the press. Shoulders, curses, sweat against my cheek. Markov slid in behind me, light as a knife through cloth, letting my weight clear the path. Elbows yielded, grudging, until at last we broke through to the centre.

Bogdan was already there. He stood bent low over the table, palms streaked black with ash, charms clicking as he muttered. His voice carried just enough to be heard over the hush, words pitched like a prayer or a claim.

Illarion's armour had been stripped and stacked nearby like the shed skin of an iron serpent; only his helm remained, set on a stool close by. The dent was a crater in the steel—where a war-hammer had met helm and head and buckled everything inward.

Then I saw him.

They had laid him on a captain's table dragged before the fire, oak scarred by blade and time. A cloak was folded under his head to soften the boards. His body looked smaller without the plate, swallowed in sweat-stained linen. The cut across the left side of his face, done five days ago, had been stitched with vinegar, silk, and prayer, but the flesh had turned against itself. The line from brow to jaw was swollen, the stitches pulled loose, yellow pus crusting the gaps. The skin around it ballooned, one eye sealed shut, the other buried in swelling until it showed only a slit. The whole right side of his face bulged dark and angry, purple-black under the skin where the bone had cracked.

His lips were split and caked. Blood streaked his teeth. A sour stench rose from him—rot mixed with vinegar, sweat, and the faint copper of blood. It clung to the back of the throat.

For a moment I thought him dead. Then a rasp came, shallow and animal—wind dragging through reeds.

Someone near me muttered, "That's no prince, that's a corpse." Angry voices rose at once—curses, shushes, the hiss of boots scuffing the floor.

Another said low, "Fire burns quick. Look what's left."

Kozlov's, face white as wax, whispered sharp to no one in particular: "If he dies here, ruin will come to us all."

Markov leaned closer, his eyes narrowing, not with pity but with measure. "How did he fight? Even move? He must have gone in blind, half-dead already."

I looked at the ruin on the table and knew he was right. The wound had festered from the first stitch. He had likely lain beside death for days, and still he dragged himself into steel, hid his ruin in a helm, and stood in the line. Whether it was shame that drove him or pride, it made no difference. Grit carried him there. And grit has weight. His presence in the ranks mattered. When he fell, the men raged as if fire itself had been struck down, and that fury bore us through.

That was when Bogdan looked up from his muttering, his red-rimmed eyes sweeping the crowd. The whispers died as his gaze found them, one by one.

"You see death creeping close," he said, voice carrying to every corner. "You smell its breath on him. But death is not master here. There is power greater than rot, greater than fever, greater than the hammer that struck him down."

The doors scraped shut, the garrison hall sealed against the night. The hearth blazed high, fire clawing at the beams until smoke pooled thick as burial shrouds. Candles stood in ranks along the walls, flames twisting in the heat, wax hissing as it spilled onto stone. The air hung heavy with incense and sweat, with the smell of men pressed close in wool and mail.

None dared speak above the prophet's voice.

Bogdan stood over the makeshift altar. His palms were ash-black, his eyes red as coals, beard wild with sweat and fervor. Bone charms at his throat clicked with each breath, dice cast by death itself.

His words began as whispers, muttered prayers that seemed to rise from the stones themselves:

"Hear, O Lord, the cry of the faithful. Behold Your anointed, struck down in Your service, marked by fire for Your glory."

The whispers grew, became chant, rhythmic as a heartbeat. *"As David was chosen from the sheepfold, as Moses was called from the burning bush, so too is this prince sealed in flame, crowned in pain, made holy through suffering."*

The garrison captain dropped first, mail clanking against stone. His head bowed low. One by one the others followed—soldiers with scarred hands, merchants clutching their purses, Lord Kozlov pale and trembling. Even the wives pressed against the rail went down, skirts pooling round them.

Markov bent beside me, lips tight, and I bent too. Only the local priest remained standing, cross clutched in white-knuckled hands, lips moving in desperate Latin. *Pater noster qui es in caelis...*

Bogdan's burning gaze fixed on him. In three strides he crossed the space between them, seized the priest's collar, and dragged him down beside the rest. The cross clattered to stone, forgotten.

"There is but one voice in this holy place!" Bogdan thundered. His words echoed off the rafters, seemed to shake the very foundations. "One blood, one fire, one God who judges by flame!"

The chanting resumed, deeper now, more urgent:

"Blessed is he who sheds blood in righteousness. Blessed is he who offers flesh for the salvation of the faithful. By blood we are cleansed, by blood we are sealed, by blood we are made whole."

The door to the hall creaked open and men arrived with items he had demanded: one with a bronze bowl green with age, another with a knife, edge flashing sharp in the gloom, a third with a white cock held fast, wings bound. The bird thrashed once, weak and useless against the grip. They laid the bowl where he instructed, the knife in his hand.

"Blood speaks louder than words," Bogdan intoned. *"Blood seals what prayers cannot. Blood calls to the throne of the Almighty and demands His answer."*

Bogdan's eyes flashed, and the soldier held forth the cock over the bowl. The blade flashed. The bird shrieked once, then sagged. Hot blood spilled into bronze, steam curling red in the fire's glow.

Bogdan plunged his arms deep, crimson to the elbows. Blood dripped from his palms like sacramental wine. He raised them high and every candle seemed to lean his way.

"By this blood I mark Your chosen! By this blood I claim Your mercy! By this blood I seal his wounds and call Your fire!"

He touched brow, then breast, the sign in blood across his heart. Then he turned to Illarion.

The prince lay still as death upon the table, breath thin, face a ruin of swelling and pus. Bogdan's bloody hands hovered, trembling not with fear but with power passing through him. He pressed his palms to Illarion's ruined face. Blood mingled with the weeping wounds. The prince's skin burned fever-hot beneath. Bogdan's body shook, his voice rising until it filled the hall, terrible and whole:

"Out of the depths I cry to You, O Lord! Let Your ears be attentive to my supplication! If You should mark iniquities, who could stand? But with You is forgiveness, that You may be feared. By

fire and blood, by ash and bone, by the agony of the faithful and the prayers of the penitent, I beseech You — let this cup pass, and let Your will be done on earth, with Your chosen one!"

The blood on Illarion's face glistened in firelight, pulsing with each shallow breath.

Every soul in that hall held its breath. Hope flared, fragile as flame. And in that silence, with smoke thick as shrouds and blood steaming on the altar, it felt as though God Himself leaned close to listen.

Chapter XXXIII: Names in the Wind

We moved the worst of the wounded to the governor's hall where the floors could be scrubbed, others to the long warehouses by the quay where men could lie flat and the doors be propped open for air. The rest we laid where we could—on trestles, on benches, on shields stripped from dead men.

We counted the dead because the living needed a number to lean on. Rough tallies only; no clerk stood ready with a pen. A hundred rebels, give or take. Seventy-five of ours. The boys kept miscounting by tens, wanting it lower. I didn't correct them. Numbers do not comfort; they only make the ground real under your feet.

Soroka set her crew to fixing the quays—ropes, spars, patching seams, water-casks filled. She heard my report without change in her face, then jerked her chin to Vedek. "One hull upriver. Driftlight must hear from us, not from carrion." Vedek spat in his palms, grinning like battle had reset his bones, and made for the boats with that rolling stride sailors keep—half swagger, half balance against a wave no one else felt. Men rowed with bandaged hands. The oars knocked against the tholes with the dull sound of teeth in a drunk mouth. The zubatka slid free into the swell and vanished beyond the smoke-line, a dark insect on iron water.

We laid our dead in two places. Ours—Velgrad, Stormhold, Driftlight—under the broken bell-frame, wrapped in sailcloth where we had it, in cloaks where we didn't. Bogdan led the rites there, voice strong, palms ash-dark, boys trying to stand like men, veterans staring at the cobbles. The names went out one by one, thin in the wind.

For the rebels there were no names and no bell, just a trench beyond the east wall where the ground dipped and the smoke would blow away from the houses. Pitch went in after the first row, then brush, then another row. I won't pretend I minded the division. Mercy isn't blindness.

Borislav woke long enough to ask for his father. The words came slurred through split lips, but the meaning was clear. He looked at me like I could haul Ivan from the sea by his beard, as if command meant I could summon what was missing.

"Where is he?" His voice cracked. For a breath I caught Ivan's shadow in him—the same stubborn jaw, the same hunger for proof that the world would bend to his will.

"In Driftlight," I told him. "Word was sent."

I did not tell him what word had gone: that Borislav had fallen in battle but had not yet joined the dead. That his father would spend the journey not knowing if he came for a son or a corpse.

Borislav nodded once, careful, like his skull might crack if he moved too quick. Then he tried to rise—elbows braced, jaw set with Ivan's will. The effort lasted three heartbeats before he sagged in my arms, strength gone like water through a broken cup.

I eased him back onto the pallet, his head heavy against my arm. The boy who had stood beneath Illarion's banner, who had read proclamations to the fleet, was gone. What remained was a child's face, soft with fever, asking for his father with the trust that fathers could fix what had been broken.

"Tell him I held the banner," he whispered. His eyes fluttered shut before I could answer.

He slept, shallow but steady. I sat beside him longer than I should have. Command could wait. The boy had earned that much.

Illarion lingered—half-shadow wrapped in mail, his plate loosed at the straps, breath coming in ratcheted pulls as if the skin of the room might tear with each sigh. No surgeon could be found who would promise more than a prayer and a poultice; medicine here was thin as bread. It was in that hollow between one strained breath and the next—where hope and fear met—that Bogdan settled himself to the work, certain in the sort of faith that moves a man to lay his hands where flesh has been rent.

The prophet had turned the hall into a shrine. He came with palms blackened by ash and a cock cradled under one arm. Before the prince's cot he cut its throat, caught the blood in a bowl, and pressed it to Illarion's lips and brow, murmuring words that were half-prayer, half-command. He swore the prince still breathed because God willed it through him.

People gathered to see. At first only servants and a few boys, then more — guards, townsfolk, even Lord Kozlov at the door. Some came curious, some already believing. Bogdan's voice carried smooth as poured tar: the wound was judgment, the pain a gift, the fire God's test upon His chosen.

The rafters thickened with iron-sweet reek. Mothers clutched children close; veterans folded their arms, listening despite themselves. Whispers spread before the rite was

done: that each drop shed lengthened the prince's days. I did not doubt Bogdan's strength, only its end. We live and die at God's will, and no man decides the measure. I had seen too many prayers left unanswered to mistake blood for promise.

As I left the rite, I overheard the argument on the stair—Markov's voice sharp with impatience, the captain grinding like iron on stone, Kozlov thin with fear. They stood near the keep's outer door, and their words carried up on the draft.

"He needs a healer, not another sermon," Markov was saying. "The man's skull is cracked and his flesh is rotting. Prayer won't close wounds or cool fever."

The captain spat into the rushes. "There is no healer. The rebels killed old Marcus when he wouldn't tend their wounded. Slit his throat and left him for the crows."

"There's a country healer," the priest said, voice quick and nervous. "A Brack woman. Half-day's ride north toward Ravenholt. She tends fevers and sets bones," he added, as if that would make the suggestion safe.

The captain's face darkened. "A Brack? You'd trust one of them near the prince?"

"She's a healer first," the priest insisted. "Not a rebel. She'd tend anyone who came bleeding to her door."

The governor wrung his hands, sweat beading his forehead. "If the prince dies here, the King's wrath falls on us all. My head will roll first."

Markov laughed—sharp, hollow. "Then fetch her."

The captain shook his head. "My men won't be used to fetch some witch from rebel country."

"Her soul may be astray," the priest muttered, "but her hands are sure. She is the only healer near enough to matter."

Fear won out where courage might have held. "We have no choice," Kozlov said at last. "Fetch her. Gold for her services, whatever she requires." He turned to Markov. "You go."

Markov blinked, surprised. "Me? I don't even know where—"

"Half-day north on the Crowfen," the priest supplied. "Near the old mill."

Markov shrugged that careless shoulder that fools quiet men into trusting him. "Fine. Yaroslav comes with me."

"I didn't volunteer," I answered.

His grin sharpened. "Maybe not. But if there are rebels, someone needs to be able to kill them."

The captain threw up his hands. "Travel by day. Trust no one. Don't linger."

Markov nodded as if this had been his plan all along. I wondered, as I always did when the Brackfolk's names turned up on a map, how simple any of this would be. Nothing involving them ever was.

We burned our dead after sunset. Not all at once; Ironholt has little wood that isn't a wall or a door. Sailcloth burns fast. Pitch burns fast and ugly. Bogdan read the names over each pile. Some names were wrong. He read them wrong anyway. The boys took turns with the bell-rope until the bell rope broke.

The rebels' trench went up with a cough of flame, pitch catching quick, then sagged into a long red bed like a smith's fire left to burn itself out. The smell came first—sweet and foul, the same every time, meat turned against itself. I knew it before the heat reached me. I knew it from other heaps, other pits, other nights when we shoveled bodies like cordwood and set them alight. Soldiers learn the work by rote: drag, stack, pour, burn. Nothing holy in it. Only keeping the ground clear.

I stood close enough for the heat to sting, but it stirred nothing in me. Not hate for the rebels, not pity either. Only the memory of a hundred other pyres—Stormhold, Drownbank, nameless heaps in nameless fields—each one leaving the same emptiness after, like a tooth pulled from the jaw.

A lie is easier to die for than the truth, and the truth is that most men die badly, for nothing, and are burned in trenches when it's done. But they died believing in something—glory, God, their brothers beside them—and that was something. Perhaps all a man can have.

I would have prayed for them, once. When I was young I had words for the dead. Now prayer comes hard, and when I try, I do not know if I am asking for their souls or my own.

Chapter XXXIV: The Tale Grew Wings

The quay still stank of blood and char when dawn found us. Ironholt's walls smoked where the stones had cracked; gulls wheeled low, tearing at what the river had carried back. The town breathed like a man after a beating — still alive, but every breath hurt.

Soroka waited by the galley. Sixteen oars, shallow-drafted, low to the water. Built for rivers, not for seas. She had command of it herself, and would not hear of taking the Hand upriver. *The Hand,* she called it still, when Illarion would not hear. The great ship would stay moored with the other two, a steward set over them until she returned.

The galley's crew was simple: sixteen fighting men to row and guard, two sailors to trim, Soroka at the tiller, Markov and me at her side. No Brack oarsmen this time.

I had not yet stepped aboard when Mikhail and Sava came. They stood as if they'd rehearsed it — Mikhail with his ledger under one arm, Sava with his jaw set like stone.

"Three mornings since the prince fell," Mikhail said. "The men need command."

"Not mine," I answered.

"His door is shut," Sava said. "Yours is not."

I told them command would ruin me. They told me command had already chosen me.

So they pressed me with the first matter: the prisoners. Seventy-five in all. Sava wanted some cut down — better to thin the herd than risk an uprising. Mikhail said the town needed hands more than it needed graves.

I turned to Soroka. "Do you have chains for seventy-five?"

She did.

So I gave the order: work them. Guard them. One boy and two townsmen for every five. No more than that. Sava spat, but he did not argue.

Markov drew me aside. His grin was too thin for comfort. "Seventy-five captives you've chained. But seventy-five idle soldiers are near as dangerous. Put them to work, or they'll find their own mischief."

He had the right of it. I told Mikhail and Sava to see the garrison captain. Soldiers and townsmen both would labour: rubble cleared, walls patched, fields turned. Hands busy, mouths shut.

And the Discipline would continue. Morning and night, all of them drilled—boys and veterans both. Since Markov was coming upriver, I ordered Borislav to lead if he had the strength. If not, then one of the seconds he had chosen on the ship. The forms would hold them straighter than fear ever could.

With that, Soroka called the men aboard. The galley pushed off slow, oars biting into black water. Sixteen strokes carried us past the burned quay, past the stench, into the reeds. The Hand and the other ships dwindled behind us, their masts stark as gallows against the sky.

I had not wanted command, but command had found me. And every order, once given, weighs heavier than steel.

The river here was clean and broad, the banks rolling with fields and forested ridges to the north. No swamp-rot, no reed-choke. Only the pull of sixteen oars, steady as a heartbeat.

Soroka held the tiller, broad shoulders square against the current, rope-scarred hands sure on the steering oar. Not pretty, not soft, but solid as ballast stone. I caught myself watching. She caught me back.

"You think too loud," she said.

"Better than not thinking at all."

"Is it? A man can think himself into deeper water than he needs."

She turned back to the current, but her eyes had already read me.

Markov prowled between the benches, goading the oarsmen. "Stroke, stroke—you call this rowing? I've seen fish flop straighter."

The boys grinned, trading jibes, laughter rolling easier than it had in weeks. They'd left Driftlight as farm sons and fisher's brats. Now their hands were raw with callus, their jokes edged with the knowledge of death.

Markov winked at me. "Don't look so serious, Yarik. Sun on the water, no one screaming—paradise."

"Give it time," I said.

"How far to Ravenholt?" a rower called.

"Oh, not far," Markov said cheerfully. "Just through rebel-held waters to convince a Brack witch to come tend our half-dead prince. Simple as breathing."

The stroke faltered. "You said she wasn't a witch."

"Did I? Well, probably not. Probably just a perfectly ordinary healer. Nothing to worry about at all."

I gave him a look.

"Don't mind me, lads. I'm just naturally cautious. It comes from spending so much time around Yaroslav here. His pessimism is catching."

"My pessimism keeps us alive."

"And my optimism keeps us sane. We make a fine pair." He stretched like a cat in the sun.

For a little while the river carried us, and despite Markov's best efforts to the contrary, something like peace carried me. The sun was warm, the water clear, and for once no one needed me to decide who lived and who died. It wouldn't last—nothing good ever did—but for now, it was enough.

By midday Ravenholt came into sight. The river widened, shallows bristling with stilt-houses where nets hung grey in the sun. Most of the town stood inland on firmer ground, log walls dark with sap from fresh-cut pine. Behind it the forest pressed close, straight trunks waiting to be felled and floated down to Ironholt.

It should have been safe. The rebel host was broken, their fire spent. But word travels faster than boats, and the townsfolk on the quay did not smile. Men leaned on axes, women pulled children close. They had the look of people who had learned that any company of armed men might be their ruin.

Markov stepped off first, hands spread wide. His smile was easy, the kind that made men forget he carried knives.

"Good day, friends! Fine weather for honest work, isn't it?"

An old woodcutter eased forward, axe loose in his grip. "We've heard news from downriver. Battles and burning. Which side are you?"

"The Crown's," Markov said, his cheer softening to respect. "We stood at Ironholt. What remains of us."

The man's gaze swept over us. "You fought the rebels there?"

"Aye. Broke their siege. Scattered their host. Cost us dear."

A woman's voice rose: "Is it true? About the prince?"

I saw Markov's confusion flicker for just a moment before he smoothed it over. "What do they say?"

"That he fought like the heroes of old," she said, eyes bright. "Cut down a dozen men, blood streaming like tears of fire."

The boy beside her blurted, "Saint Mikhail come to earth!"

I kept my face still, though I felt Markov glance my way.

"The prince is… valiant," he said carefully.

Murmurs spread through the crowd — "ten men, fifteen — alone he charged —" — until the woodcutter's hand brought

silence again. His weathered face softened. "If you served with honour, you're welcome here."

Markov bowed his head. "We need a healer. A woman skilled with herbs."

The first woman nodded. "Yelka. Lives up Owl Creek, west through the trees. You've wounded?"

Markov let the moment stretch, then gave a solemn nod. "Aye. The prince himself."

That set them alight. Voices clamored — *the prince is here, the prince is dying, someone must help him.*

The woodcutter raised his hand again. "Follow Owl Creek to the cottage with blue stones. But mind — she chooses who she helps. Crown or rebel makes no matter to her."

"Then we'll trust she sees the justice in our cause," Markov said.

We turned back toward the galley to choose our party. I shook my head. "A dozen men? An avenging angel?"

He grinned. "You heard them. I didn't say a word."

"Saint Mikhail come to earth," I muttered.

Markov shrugged. "Well, he did take a hammer to the skull. That part's true. Curious, though, how the tale grew wings so fast."

"Stories travel quicker than truth," I said. "And they pick up ornaments along the way."

I thought of Illarion as I'd last seen him—broken, fevered, barely breathing. Then of the crowd's shining faces, already speaking of miracles.

"Let's hope he lives long enough to disappoint them."

Chapter XXXV: Yelka

We climbed the pine path six in all—four soldiers with spear and shield, Markov with his sly tongue, and me limping at their head. The forest swallowed sound. Trunks rose black and straight, bark flaking like old scabs, the air sharp with resin. Needles softened our tread, so that breath and creak of leather seemed loud as drums. Sunlight fell in bars across the slope, gold on one side, shadow on the other.

"*We* broke their siege?" I asked.

Markov arched a brow, walking loose at my shoulder. "Guarding the ship, keeping prisoners from cutting our throats—I did my part. Without me you'd have come back to an empty deck."

"You make cowardice sound like a duty."

"Not cowardice," he said smoothly. "Strategy. Somebody had to mind the boat."

Behind us the town had already vanished, smoke and stone swallowed by distance. Here the world narrowed to pine and silence. Even birds kept still. We went quiet, each man scanning shadows between the trunks, hands close to hilts.

The track bent and began to fall. Water showed through the trees—swift, black, foaming white where stones broke its flow. Owl Creek, though no bird called from its banks.

A house stood just beyond the bend, raised on a knoll above the water. Its logs were fitted clean, roof freshly thatched, fence mended. Yet something in the shape of it unsettled—windows narrow as slits, shutters painted dark, bunches of dried herbs hanging from the eaves. Smoke curled pale from the chimney, thin as a ghost's breath. A garden sprawled behind it, neat rows of plants I didn't recognize, some with leaves that seemed to shimmer in the filtered light.

We spread wide across the yard, six men circling careful — soldiers with spears low, Markov strolling as if it were a tavern door, me feeling the creek's murmur like a warning.

The house stayed still. Only the water muttered, and the pines leaned close above.

Then a shadow slid over us. On a bare branch above perched a raven — broad-shouldered, sharp-beaked, blacker than pitch. Larger than any I'd seen, its eyes caught the light like hammered glass. It tilted its head, slow, deliberate, and the weight of its gaze set my skin crawling. One of the soldiers muttered a prayer, as if the bird had marked more than flesh.

The latch shifted without sound, wood moving as if the wind had touched it.

What stepped out was no bent crone spinning at her wheel. She was young — perhaps twenty-five winters — straight-backed, her face striking as blade-cut stone. Black hair fell in a single braid thick as rope down her back, woven through with small bones and bits of silver that caught the light. Her skin was pale copper, marked with faint scars along her hands and forearms — the kind healers earn from sharp tools and impatient patients. But it was her eyes that held you: not the dark brown of black folk, but pale green as winter ice, steady as deep water — and wrong. Too old for her face, too sharp for mercy, as if some ancient thing peered out through borrowed flesh.

She wore Brack garb cut close to her frame — wool dyed deep brown, embroidered at collar and cuffs with patterns that seemed to shift when you weren't looking directly at them. A leather belt hung with pouches and small tools, and around her throat, a necklace of polished stones that seemed to drink in the light.

Beside her padded a beast that was no dog. Wolf blood ran in its veins — coat black as night, shoulders high as her waist, yellow eyes that never blinked. It moved like liquid shadow, muscles flowing under fur, head low and ready. When it breathed, I could see teeth long enough to shear a man's throat.

"Sit, Grendel," she said, voice carrying the authority of someone used to being obeyed by dangerous things.

The beast settled on its haunches but kept those predator's eyes fixed on us, ears pricked forward. Even at rest, it looked more coiled than still, as if in an instant it might leap upon us.

None of us moved. The soldiers shifted uneasily in their harness, suddenly aware how far they were from help. Markov, for once, seemed at a loss for words — his usual grin frozen, eyes caught like a boy seeing his first naked woman. The young men stared as if lightning had taken human form.

She let the silence stretch, studying each of us in turn. When her gaze reached me, it lingered, and I felt the weight of evaluation. Not the way a woman might size up a man, but the way a hunter measures prey.

"You're Yelka," I said, making it a statement rather than a question.

Her mouth curved, not quite a smile. "I am."

Markov recovered first, though his voice came out rougher than usual. "We're honoured to meet you, lady. Your reputation—"

"Travels faster than you do," she cut him off. "I know why you're here. The prince lies dying, and you need someone foolish enough to risk her life for northern coin."

One of the soldiers stepped forward, bristling. "Show respect. You speak of—"

She looked at him, just looked, and he stumbled backward as if struck. The wolf-thing's ears twitched forward, and a low rumble came from its throat.

"I speak of a man whose skull is cracked like an egg, whose blood runs with poison, whose breathing grows weaker with each sunset." Her voice was matter-of-fact, clinical. "A man who should have died three days ago. If he clings still, it is not pride alone. Something waits for him. Whether it is gift or curse, I cannot yet tell."

Markov found his footing again. "If you know so much, then you know we need your help."

"Need." She tasted the word. "An interesting choice. Not 'want' or 'request' or 'humbly beseech.' Need."

"He's dying," I said simply.

"Men die. It's what they do best." She stepped down from her threshold, moving with a predator's grace. The wolf kept pace at her side. "The question is why I should care about this particular death."

"Because you took an oath," one of the soldiers said. "Healers swear to aid any who—"

Her laugh was sharp as breaking glass. "I swore, but not to your priests. Not to your lords." Her eyes flicked over us, unreadable. "My laws are older. Older, and less forgiving. I mend, yes—but not all wounds are meant to close. Sometimes healing means finishing what lingers."

The raven above us cawed once, harsh in the silence. She glanced up at it, and for a moment her face hardened—as if she weighed our fates against the raven's croak and waited for its judgment to fall.

"Besides," she continued, attention returning to us, "what makes you think your prince wants to live? Perhaps he's ready for the long sleep. Perhaps this fever is mercy, not curse."

"He wants to live," Markov said. "He has... unfinished business."

"Ah." Her eyes lit, though the light seemed older than wonder. She stepped forward, the wolf pacing in perfect measure at her side. "Yes. Flame has taken him. But fire is never faithful. Sometimes it crowns, sometimes it devours. What waits to be made whole may raise him—or burn through him into all who follow."

She stopped in front of us, close enough that I could smell the herbs on her clothes, see the flecks of gold in her pale eyes.

Turning to Markov, she said, "Tell me, courier of need, what is it that *you* believe?"

Markov swallowed, the grin slipping from his face. For once he didn't reach for wit. "If we don't save him, not only the Mire burns. The Broken Isles will come apart in blood."

Her eyes narrowed, studying him as if weighing a coin. The wolf's growl faded; even the raven tilted its head, listening.

"Honest," she said at last. "Surprising."

The tension broke like ice cracking. She stepped back toward the door, braid swaying against her spine. "I'll come. But not for coin. Not for oaths. Not even for your prince. I'll come, because fire like that never rests. It finds a hand to shape it, or it burns the world to ash."

The soldiers shifted uneasily; no one cheered.

"There are conditions," she went on. "No priests at my shoulder. No questions when I work. And when this is done — whether your prince wakes or goes to the pyre — you will owe me. Not coin, not land. A debt of fate. I will call it, and you will answer, or all this suffering will have been for nothing."

Markov found his tongue. "What kind of debt?"

Her smile was thin as frost. "The kind I'll name when I choose." Markov tried for a grin, but it slipped, leaving something closer to unease.

I thought of Illarion gasping on the captain's table while Bogdan smeared him with blood. Of boys drilling with hollow eyes, waiting for commands that would never come. And then this woman before me — small, slight, without banners or command or throne.

Yet even the hardened men shifted their stance when she passed, wary without knowing why. It was not the power of steel, nor of oaths. Something quieter, more unsettling. The kind that slips past armour and finds you where you sleep.

I distrusted it. Perhaps I even feared it. I have spent my life among men's violences—knowing how to use it, when to unleash it, what it cost. This was something else. Yelka's power I could not name, could not measure, could not master. And that made it dangerous.

But the prince was dying. If there was anything left to save, it would not be saved by steel, or prayer, or the spilling of more blood. Perhaps it would take this—the thing I could neither understand nor trust.

"We accept."

She nodded once. A whistle left her lips, sharp and low. The wolf rose, silent, still watching us as if we were meat. The raven launched from its branch, wings black as sails, and settled on her shoulder. It croaked once—flat, harsh—like judgment in a tongue none of us knew. Yelka tilted her head, listening. Her mouth curved, not quite a smile. "Perhaps you're worthy. Perhaps you're not. The raven will know before I do."

"Give me an hour," she said. "Then we'll walk together and find out if the world's path leads to ruin or glory."

With that, she vanished into the house.

Markov let out a long breath when the door closed. He leaned toward me, voice low. "Think we can trust her?"

I kept my eyes on the wolf, which hadn't blinked once.

"Doesn't matter. We already have."

Chapter XXXVI: Ash and Consequence

Ravenholt met us with fish-smoke and sap. Nets hung grey from the stilt-rows in the shallows; farther in, the log walls shone where fresh timbers bled resin. Word had run ahead of us. By the time we reached the market stairs the crowd had already opened a lane without anyone saying a thing.

Yelka moved the lane open as if the town itself was a reed she parted by will—staff like a spear in her right hand, pack drawn tight, the wolf close enough that its shadow touched her boot, the raven tracing slow, patient circles like a measuring eye. Men lowered axes. Women touched brow and breast and did not look away. Not fear. Reverence, the old kind that keeps its voice down.

Her staff rang the steps—wood on stone, wood on plank— as we dropped to the quay. She stopped at the waterline and waited, wolf sitting in one smooth fold of muscle, the raven stooping to her arm with a croak that made the dock-ropes twitch. She didn't call for a boat. She didn't need to. The town knew what was required.

Soroka came down the gangway with rain in her braid, eyes narrowed against the salt and the stare of the crowd. She looked Yelka over—the lean of her, the pack, the beasts— and Yelka met it, staff grounded, not a finger of her shifting.

A glance passed between them, cold and precise as a coin. Soroka's chin dipped not in greeting but in calculation—this woman was a hazard measured and found noteworthy.

"Captain," Yelka said.

"Healer," Soroka answered, and stood aside.

The oars dipped soft, steady. No one spoke. The men kept stealing looks—at the wolf curled tight at Yelka's boots, at the raven circling where the river widened. Even veterans shifted on the benches. Nobody liked the wolf. Every blink of its yellow eyes made their shoulders stiffen.

Yelka kept to herself, staff across her knees, gaze on the current. She hadn't said a word since we left the quay.

Markov leaned close. "I was joking, you know. About fetching a Volkhva. This won't work. Even if the men don't gut her, Bogdan will never let a heretic near the prince."

Soroka's voice came flat from the stern. "Not a Volkhva."

Markov turned, startled. "Then what?"

Her eyes stayed on the river, jaw set. "My grandmother called them znakharki. Not priest, not witch—something older and slipperier. They bargain with what the priests name sin and keep the breathing from leaving you."

The men muttered uneasily, not grasping. Soroka kept on, as if the words had waited years to be spoken.

"I grew up on Sealwatch Isle. Nothing there but cliffs, storms, and seals fat as men. The sea took what it wanted. My father drowned before I knew his voice. My brother too, when the surf broke the boat under him. Only my mother and me left, and she sick with lung-rot. The priests prayed. She still choked. Then the znakharka came. Bent old woman, hands like knots of rope. She boiled peat and salt, held a coal beneath a bowl and set her palm on my mother's breast; the coughing slackened as if some rope inside the chest had been loosened. Not healed—only leased back a few months of breath. Without her, I'd have been orphan before I was twelve."

Her hand tightened on the tiller until the wood creaked. "The priests called her danger and named it theft: that she took God's due. On Sealwatch, we measured differently — ask only whether a hand will keep the lungs from folding. If it does, we pay its price."

She looked at Yelka then, not kindly, but not with scorn either. "That's what she is. Not temple, not witch. Necessary."

For a moment, no one answered. The oars kept pulling, the raven croaked once overhead, and the wolf blinked slow, untroubled by their fear.

Then Markov, recovering, flashed his old grin and whispered to me, "And definitely not a bent old woman."

We brought her from the quay. Men parted like reeds for the wolf at her heel; the raven circled, black against the smoke. The wolf heeled like a blade to her heel at the twitch of a finger; the raven obeyed no hand, circling on its own measure and croaking once, a verdict delivered from some other court — as if one beast answered her, the other answered only the dark.

Ash clung to Ironholt's streets; people muttered of Brack rites and kept their distance.

When we reached the keep she halted. The raven stooped to her arm with a croak sharp as iron, not obedience but acknowledgment, as if it chose to share her burden for a time. I shoved the hall doors wide. The reek hit — ash, blood, unwashed bodies. Men knelt in the murk; Bogdan's voice rose thin and bright through coughs. On the captain's table Illarion lay like a failed statue: the grey of old wax, lips split with fever, ribs barely stirring.

Yelka's breath caught. Then she strode forward, shoving past soldiers. She pressed two fingers to his ribs, waiting for the shallow lift. Nothing in her face showed mercy. "This is no place to bargain for breath. Leave him in this haze one hour more and the smoke will claim him whole."

Bogdan spun, bone charms clinking, palms black to the wrist. "How dare you? That man is the prince—the anointed." His eyes searched the hall. "Who is this woman?"

Markov leaned in, grin sharp as a knife. "Prophet, meet Healer. I'm sure you'll get on splendidly."

Bogdan snapped, "I don't need your mockery, thief." To the captain: "Take her from our altar. She defiles it."

She met him square, the wolf bristling at her heel. "This is no altar. It's a shroud. Smoke preserves flesh, not breath. If he stays here, he will not wake."

"Heresy!" Bogdan's fury broke ragged. "Smoke drives out rot. Blood binds him to the Lord's hand. We give him to the flame—"

Morwen croaked overhead, harsh enough to make men flinch. Yelka did not look up.

"If your flame chokes him," she said, "what mercy is that?"

A murmur stirred the hall. Kozlov dabbed at streaming eyes, the captain cursed under his breath.

Bogdan stepped close, fury trembling in his chest. "Who summoned this Brack? Would you trust weeds and waters, not the Lord? You would lay hands where only fire should touch." His voice demanded assent—and found none. Faces turned away.

Yelka laughed, brittle as broken glass. "Weeds grow where fire fails. You choose one gift and call it God. I take what keeps breath moving. If your faith were enough, why was I called? You've stood over him for days, and still he fades. Tell me, prophet—stronger under your smoke, or nearer to death?"

Bogdan's voice dropped, fervent, almost pleading. "If we cease, he dies. By God's mercy he lives." Then, sharp: "Infidel! You would strip him from the Lord."

"And I say if he stays here, he dies choking." Yelka's voice was flat as iron. "Better he live to be judged in God's time than smothered in yours."

"Better the body fall than the soul be lost!" Bogdan spat.

The governor hacked into his handkerchief, voice raw. "Enough. We see no healing—only stench. Captain, carry him to the church. Let her try. At least let us breathe."

Bogdan flinched as if struck. He threw himself over the prince, clutching his wrist like a father torn from his child. When the men lifted Illarion, the priest's face broke—anger, terror, grief mingled. Dragged back, he strained forward, teeth bared but striking no blow for fear of the prince. His cry cracked: "If he dies, it is on your heads. I gave him to the flame. God will judge!"

Yelka did not answer. She was already giving orders: cloth, boiling water, steady hearth. Men moved fast, grateful for command, grateful to escape the haze. The wolf padded at her heel; the raven wheeled into the grey sky.

But Bogdan's words lingered as they carried the prince out. The hall smelled suddenly less of smoke, and more of consequence.

Chapter XXXVII: Rain on Saint Radegund's

The light was falling as we carried him to Saint Radegund's.

Through Ironholt's streets the day went with us—long shadows drawn out on wet stone, the last smoke of the fires drifting low between the houses. Rain slicked the cobbles, turning every step into a slip, the weight of the prince heavy on our shoulders. Lanterns guttered to life in doorways, oil-flame trembling as if the town itself feared to breathe. Faces watched from windows and alleys, pale in the half-dark, but none came near. Only the rasp of boots and the groan of stretcher poles marked our passage.

The church stood just beyond the garrison walls, half-ruined from the rebels' sack. Its doors hung crooked, one split clean through; the rafters above the nave were open in places where the dusk came seeping down with the rain. The walls still held, and the vault would keep out the worst of the weather. The flagstones were bare, washed by storm instead of blood. It was more than we'd had in the keep's hall.

She measured the nave with a single glance. "He needs wide air and cold stone under him—rooms that do not steam," she said. "This will do. It will not lie to me."

Her voice had the snap of command folded over something quieter—an insistence that would take things without asking. She set men to work: sweep, clear smoke, drag new timber, lay hearth. Each motion she named as if striking a tally against the debt she carried. She demanded a frame, a cot for herself, a broad table, a basin for a single coal, and well-water brought without priest's blessing. No one argued; the men liked orders that turned the air from smoke to breath. Illarion's personal guards were glad enough to trade the reek of the keep for this ruined nave, even if saints and rebels both had abandoned it.

Then she turned to Markov. "You stay," she said.

He blinked, mouth half-ready with a jest. "Me?"

"Your hands are steadier than your mouth," she said, unrolling bandages. "Hold him true. Don't let him roll. Do not flinch."

Why she chose him, none could say. He was no surgeon, no orderly, only a thief who lived by knives. Perhaps she saw something in his grip, or perhaps she wanted him bound close where she could watch. He started to protest, but her gaze cut him short.

So it was settled: the prince on his bed, fire kindled at the basin, the nave turned infirmary, and Markov drafted into service he had not asked for. Her wolf lay at the threshold like a second hearth, head heavy on its paws, pupils fixed and slow as a tide. It did not sleep; it kept measure of her — more guard than companion. High in the rafters Morwen perched and shifted — one quick scrap of sound — then became still and watchful, a black coin turned on its edge. The beasts defined her field: Grendel to hold her back; Morwen to judge what she offered.

I left the healer to her work and went to see to the men.

In the yard outside the garrison Mikhail leaned on his shield, Sava stringing a bow beside him. Their talk stopped when I came near, but I caught enough to know the healer was on their tongues like everyone else's. A Brack girl with beasts at her heels, now tending the prince — half called her witch, half saint.

Mikhail only spat. "Whatever she is, she knows her craft. The prince still breathes."

Sava nodded, eyes dark. "That's more than Bogdan ever gave him."

I left it at that. Words about healers did no good.

The slaves were locked apart, collars chained to the wall under guard. Two of the Driftlight boys had tested the lock with stones and got cuffed bloody for it. Elsewhere, discipline held. The town had been stripped of corpses, wells cleared, bread and fish gathered for the men. A day's labour, enough to quiet nerves, though the smoke still hung heavy.

By torchlight the company gathered for Discipline. The yard was close with sweat and damp wool, steel ringing as men fell into their places. Borislav came to me then. His colour was better, the fever gone, only the bruise under his eye left him boyish.

He nodded toward the church. "You trust her?"

"She's a healer," I told him. "She's a healer enough. Whether that makes her safe for your prince — I couldn't say. Bogdan has the Lord's ear. Let her ply her craft. If the two of them cannot save him, nothing will."

He lowered his head at that, then looked back to the men. "Shall I lead them?"

"You can."

The words struck him deep. He straightened, lips pressed tight, as if I'd handed him a crown. When he took his place at the front the men cheered, not forced, but glad. He led the forms with voice clear, steps sharp, and they answered him with rhythm.

I stood aside, my leg aching like an old unwanted companion, and watched.

It was late when Markov came to me.

He dropped beside the fire, shoulders sagging, eyes ringed black. "The prince lives," he rasped. "Which makes me, by all rights, a surgeon now."

I gave him a look. "You smell more like boiled linen than a surgeon."

He snorted. "That's the glamour of it, Yarik. Boil water till your arms ache, fetch knives, hold him down while she cuts." Suddenly he laughed. "Oh, you missed some excitement. The prince's guards nearly gutted her when she pressed the blade to his cheek. Thought she meant murder. Then she looked at them—calm, knife glowing red—and they froze like hares. I swear I've never seen anything like it."

He rubbed his wrist as if it were a treasure. "She struck me. Flat of her hand. Said I was holding wrong. Her hands are small, but sharp. Like claws dressed as fingers."

He rubbed his cheek as if remembering the sting. For a moment the grin faltered, and something like caution passed across his face — then it was gone, drowned in the daze she left him in.

I just stared, dumbfounded. "You're going to fall for a witch."

"She's not a witch. Soroka said so. She's a… znakharka."

"She's here to do a job. Not to bed you."

"You don't see it. She's beautiful, Yarik. Not the soft kind—sharp beautiful, like glass. And dangerous—saints, when she held that knife, every man in the room knew she could have cut any throat she pleased. And there's something else. Like she breathed smoke into me. I kept thinking if she touched me again I'd—"

"She'd eat you alive."

He only grinned, dazed. "Maybe. Maybe that is the way," Markov said, dreaming. "Imagine small hands trained to pick pockets and pull throats—her little wolves."

"Enough."

But he only leaned back, staring into the beams with that foolish smile, lost.

A znakharka, he called her. Soroka's word did not make it truth. When I thought of her hands, I remembered the way her fingers curved as she worked—shapes that looked nearer to command of death than any midwife's kindness.

Chapter XXXVIII: The Rope's Lesson

The prince lived through the night. And the next.

For Yelka it was pure labour — heat and knife and stitch. Her hands never stopped: setting a blade to the coals, rinsing cloth in steaming water, pressing a finger to his ribs to count the shallow lifts. For Markov it was worship, though he called it help. He fetched water, steadied limbs, carried cloth—always returning to the sight of her hands. She cuffed him more than once, and he wore the blows like favours. Though once I caught him watching her too long, his smile thin. "She doesn't look at him as a man," he muttered, not knowing I heard. "More like…" But he did not finish.

Bogdan would not stay away. He planted himself outside Saint Radegund's with his bronze bowl, feeding it with blood each morning and night. His prayers rose sharp over the square—half psalm, half curse—calling fire against heathens, railing at heresy, demanding that God's gift burn and heal as it pleased Him.

The rest of us bent to rhythm. Morning discipline until the boys sagged: shield-wall under Mikhail, spear-forms drilled by a veteran in Petyr's stead, bows under Sava, knives under Markov, sword and board at my hand. Borislav took Radovan's place with the axe, and swung until his palms split, jaw set though each blow near unbalanced him. They drilled until their arms hung limp, then went to labour — hauling stone, patching roofs, dragging corpses from the alleys. Work until the light went.

Then the discipline again, torches burning low in the square, bodies stumbling through the forms until they dropped to their knees. Only then were they released to eat. Then to sleep.

That was war. Not charge and clash, but waiting. Men tell it as fire and fury; in truth it is rations, watches, latrines. Again.

Bogdan squatted at the church steps, bronze bowl at his knees, stones blackened with old blood. His arms were raw, his lips split from chanting. A few folk lingered nearby — women with baskets, a crippled veteran, one of our own boys off watch. They listened, or stared, or crossed themselves before hurrying on. Some stayed. That was enough.

"They've taken him from me," Bogdan said as I came near. "The Brack witch, the captain, even his own guard. They shut the doors while his soul hangs by a thread. It should be my hands at his side."

Above him, atop the church, Yelka's raven sat like a black question, head tilted, watching the prayered hands below; once it croaked, flat and low, as if to puncture the air.

"You've blood enough here," I told him.

He shook the bowl, thick clots shifting. "I keep vigil, then. I call fire where they cannot shut me out. Better the street hear truth than silence. These folk—" he gestured to the onlookers—"they know who still speaks for God."

I looked at them. Some curious, some frightened, some already drawn in. Bogdan's words had weight, and he knew it. He spoke for devotion, yes. For care of the prince, perhaps. But more for himself, and the place he would not lose.

"You want him back in your hands," I said.

"I want him raised. If he dies, his blood is on them. If he lives, it is fire that carried him through, not herbs and stitches."

"Then burn your fires," I told him. "God does not need you at his bedside. He will listen in the street."

He searched my face, anger and hunger both burning there. For a moment I thought he might spit at me. Instead, he lowered his eyes to the bowl, muttered something I could not catch, and raised his voice louder for those still listening.

I left him there, with his prayers and his blood and pressed inside St. Radegund's.

Inside the church the air was clearer than I expected. A fire burned bright on the hearth, yet no smoke clung to the rafters. The air hung sharp, almost cold. In the corner lay the wolf, head on its paws. It watched me with eyes that did not blink, as if measuring my weight. The raven was nowhere to be seen—likely out among Ironholt's carrion, feasting where the dead still drew scavengers. Only the wolf watched, ears flicking.

Viktor and Andrei stood inside the doors. Illarion's personal guard. They had served him well and faithfully, putting their lives on the line time and again. I respected the service they gave him. They would not be shifted easily.

"He needs quiet," Viktor said. His voice was gravel, his nose long since broken and left crooked.

"I've no wish to disturb," I told them. "Only to see."

Andrei's eyes fixed hard on me. "You refused him."

They may not speak often, but they hear everything. Their loyalty is iron, and they had not forgiven me for refusing to swear.

For a breath we stood silent, the firelight catching on their helms.

"You're right," I said. "My oath is to the Crown and the realm. I've carried enough words already. But I took up his plate and sword. I tried to give them back; he would not take them. I never swore, yet the weight clings. It's an oath unspoken, and only he can cut it free. Until he rises, the men need a hand to hold them steady. That's mine."

That eased them. Viktor's mouth tightened, almost a smile. "Young men think they choose. Old men know better."

Andrei glanced at me, then back at his comrade. "Mikhail and Sava look to you, so the rest follow. That's plain enough. But we are sworn to him. You understand."

"I do."

They exchanged a look, silence longer this time. Then Andrei said, lower, "He's not himself. Breath rattles. Eyes open, but no thought there. She" —his lip curled—"works her craft. Threads, herbs, muttering I can't name. Still… he breathes."

"Better than the priest," Viktor muttered. "Bogdan would've burned him where he lay."

That won a thin smile out of me. "Then you're glad to be quit of him?"

They didn't answer, but the look they shared was enough.

I gave a single nod. "Keep your post. He's your prince. My duty is to keep the men from tearing each other apart until he rises."

That sat well with them. They stepped aside. Not invitation, but not denial either. Soldier to soldier, we understood each other.

Markov looked up at me as I approached, smiling through his weariness. "He opened his eyes," he said, grinning as if the words themselves were a cure. His hands were raw from steam, his tunic stiff with linen-rot, but his eyes were bright.

Yelka worked by the hearth, sleeves rolled, knives and cloth laid out with a soldier's neatness beside bowls of herbs and powders. The fire burned too clean, too bright—its light sharp and steady like a held blade. Markov hovered near her shoulder as if the glow itself kept him bound.

The prince lay stretched on the boards, armour and filth stripped away. His body was thinner, wasted by fever, but his skin was cool, his sweat gone. His lips were cracked, his eyes open but glassed, fixed on nothing. His chest rose and fell in shallow rhythm, each breath uncertain whether it belonged to life or to death.

I had seen that look before. Not here, but in the wars when Mstislav broke the marsh-holds. We fought men who should have stayed buried. *Strigoi*, the Brack called them—

bodies that rose in silence, eyes open, mouths slack. We said it was sickness, fever that left the body walking after the mind had gone. But I remember Sealwatch ditch, when they swarmed us gnawing their own kin. That was no fever I knew.

I watched Yelka's hands as she worked. Sharp hands, sure hands. She stitched with bone needle, wiped blood with reed-cloth, pressed her palm to feel each breath.

"You've kept him from death," I said. "But is he alive?"

Her eyes flicked up, calm and sharp. "He breathes. That is enough—for now."

"Maybe," I responded. "Though I've seen eyes open with only darkness within."

She did not flinch. "If darkness takes him, it will be his own. My hands only lend him back his breath. Whether it serves mercy or ruin—that choice is not mine."

I thought of Ravenholt, how the folk made way for her—heads bowed, women crossing themselves. In Mirefast there are death-houses where Volkhvy keep the last rites: washing, silence, the prayer that closes a life. But I had heard of darker rooms too—where black-book readers devote themselves to the craft of death, and from that darkness draw power enough to raise the unquiet. I did not know her craft. I only knew the prince's hollow gaze, and the raven that watched as if it understood. We had sought her as healer. But her hands moved like a woman too practiced in stitching the flesh of the dead. I did not know if we had set his soul in mercy's hand—or something darker.

"We need the man, and the soul," I said at last. "Not a dead-walker."

"I would not do such a thing," she answered, plain as if naming a tool in her pack. "What lies here is only the prince, wounded and mending. Nothing more."

I noted she had not said *could not*. Only *would not*.

The fire burned too clean. The wolf lifted its head, eyes never leaving mine.

I said nothing more.

Order fell to me, though I never sought it.

Men cannot hold peace in their hands and be content. Give them bread, they quarrel over the crust. Give them silence, they fill it with strife. Stillness presses on them like earth, and they mistake it for the grave, so they struggle against it. Beasts, once fed and sheltered, will lie quiet. Men invent grievance. Perhaps it is pride; perhaps only fear of rest. Whatever the cause, peace never lasts.

So when a collared rebel cut a guard's throat and ran, it was no surprise. Sava's arrow struck him through the back before he cleared the gate. Mikhail dragged him to the square, and the men gathered. They looked to me.

There was no law here but the law I spoke. So I made it plain.

I stood before them and gave judgment: "He has spilled blood under guard. There is one punishment. He will hang, and all will see it. Let every man know — betrayal brings only this."

I bound the rope myself and fixed it to the gallows-beam. Then I pulled until his feet left the stones.

He fought long. His throat worked against the cord, each breath a wet gasp. His face darkened, eyes filling until blood ran red from the lids. His tongue swelled, his body shuddered like a fish on the bank. There was no scream, only that rattling choke that told us he still felt it. I knew the life had left him when his bowels gave way, spilling down his legs. After that the twitch in him was only the body's memory.

It was long, and it was ugly. Not the quick snap of a soldier's mercy but a lesson carved into the belly of the men who watched. When the last shiver passed, Sava cut him down and slung the corpse high on the wall for the crows.

That was justice, and I owned it. I hoped it would not be asked of me again.

Dusk.

The men gathered for evening discipline. The collared sat apart, resting before they were locked up for the night. One of them called out.

"Otets."

I did not know who he meant until Mikhail said, low, "He means you, Volkolak."

I went to where he knelt.

"I am no Otets," I told him. "Say your peace."

He bowed his head. "I swore to Christ. I swore to the prince. Let me serve. Not just live — serve. I fought with sword and shield. I would move within your Way."

My Way. He meant the Discipline, or my part in it. As if I were an Otets of old, leading a temple of followers in forms of martial spirituality. But the Discipline was not mine. It was Illarion's, Markov's, Borislav's. Theirs, drawn from the old Way of the Hand, and before that the serpent-blade. Never mine.

"No," I said. "An oath to live is not an oath to serve."

He lifted his chin. "I saw you today. I saw what law means in your hand. Better to serve that than rot on a chain."

"You rebelled."

"I have a family," he said. "A wife, two boys. They live still because I joined. I must feed them."

I said nothing. Men are pressed into service. I have pressed them myself.

"Let me prove it," he pressed. "Give me shield and form. Give me place."

I turned away. "Back to your line."

They led him off. But his words stayed with me long into the night.

Chapter XXXIX: The Prophet's Bargain

I do not sleep well. Often sleep will not come at all; when it does, it brings the dead with it. Drink mutes them for a night, never forever. The captive's long death sat under my lids like a stone. His eyes — the way they bled and would not close — kept me walking the streets until the light smelled of paint and wet rope.

It was before dawn. Men were already at the broken parapet, hauling planks and mud, muttering that walls are always more faith than craft. They build worse than they destroy, and yet the idea of a wall holds a town more than the wall itself.

Voices cut across the yard: sharp, rising, edged with prayer and steel. Saint Radegund's door stood half-open; the square smelled of boiled wax and something raw. Bogdan and Yelka were there — the prophet and the healer.

Bogdan's voice shook, yet his words rang like scripture. "He came to me in the night. The prince hangs by a thread of breath. If we wait, the flame will gutter. Let me pray, let me bleed if God demands it — but let me act, now."

Yelka stood like a reed that would not bend. Her braid hung loose, eyes shadowed as if pulled from sleep. The wolf at her heel snarled, teeth white in the gloom; above, the raven crouched black against the paling sky, croaking once as if weighing the quarrel.

"He needs breath and clean air — not your sacrifice," she said, her voice flat, law not plea.

Illarion's guards hovered: Viktor grinding his jaw, Andrei caught between prophet and healer like men who had heard truth in both.

Bogdan turned to me, eyes bright, unblinking. "Yaroslav. God has shown me. The prince is dying. You must help — this is not a choice."

Markov slid from shadow like a rat that refuses drowning. "Nightmares aside," he said, trying to make prophecy small, "the prince's fever broke. The rasp's gone. He'll sleep if we let him."

Bogdan's eyes cut through him like smoke. "You speak of fevers and breath, but I speak of what God showed me. I saw him laid out. To his left a serpent, long as a river. To his right a crown. The serpent rose and its back bore the heads of men, their mouths torn wide with wailing. And the prince turned to me, pleading, begging I come. This is no dream. This is truth."

The raven croaked again, harsh and flat, and the men shifted uneasily.

I weighed the prophet's words. Bogdan was many things, but not a liar. If his vision was true, we stood at a crossroads. Yelka's craft could stitch and steady flesh, but beyond that, life or death turned on will — and perhaps on God.

"What will you do?" I asked.

"Only take his hand," Bogdan said. "Lead him back to safety. Offer him God's fire as shield."

I turned to Yelka. "There is no harm in prayer."

She bit her cheek. For a long breath she stared at the door, at the saint carved smooth by years of hands. Then she stepped aside, not surrender but calculation, yielding only enough to see what the fire might show her.

Bogdan's relief flared quick and greedy, like straw catching flame.

We went in together. The church swallowed us: candles guttered, cold smoke clung to the rafters, the carved mouths of saints stared like judges.

Illarion lay still, more corpse than man. Bone and sinew, lips split, one eye sealed, the other dull as river-stone. Breath shallow, no surer than the gutter of candles. When his eyes opened, they fixed on nothing—the stare of one half gone already.

Bogdan moved as if the place were already his. He climbed to the head of the table, brushing Illarion's hair back almost tenderly. His eyes burned.

"Here," he said. He pointed at me. "The right hand." To Markov: "The left."

Markov twitched, but obeyed. We took our places, anchors at the corpse's sides. Bogdan raised one hand, the other hovering near Illarion's temple.

Then he began.

Not shouting—low, heavy, torn from marrow. Scripture twisted into plea, curse braided with vow.

"Saint Ilyin, Burned One — your bones still shine in ash. As flame clung to you, let it cling to him. Do not loose him to the pit. Bind

him back. We walk the valley of death but fear no shadow. It is your fire that keeps him. Keep him still."

He shuddered once, but drove the words on.

"Lord of flame, hear me. I will pour blood till my veins are dry, I will give tongue, hand, breath, whatever you ask. Only give him back. Let him wake, and I will call no other name. Let him breathe, and I will serve no other master. Take me, but spare him."

The air thickened: smoke, sweat, candle-grease—but more than that, weight. My palm on Illarion's arm prickled, as if something stirred beneath ruined skin.

Viktor fell to his knees before the words were done. Andrei only stared, lips moving soundless. Yelka's eyes stayed open, green and steady, refusing to kneel, yet listening—whether in fear or calculation, I could not tell. Markov's grin stretched thin, faltering.

Bogdan's voice sank deeper, quickening into command. Prayer became chain, chain became summons. He was not asking—he was ordering, as a general orders men to their deaths. A fierce power pressed from him into the wasted body. I knew that power. I have carried it all my days: the spirit that drives men to rise when they would rather fall.

And I believed he could do it. Drag a soul back from the dark by sheer will, lash it to flesh the way I've lashed men to battle when they begged to break.

"Rise, Illarion. Rise though the pit holds you. Rise though the worm waits, though the dark calls your name. Rise, prince of fire. Not yet. Not now. Your oath is unspent, your crown unburned. By the saints who suffered, by the flame that judges—I bind you to this flesh. I chain you to this breath.

Live!"

Illarion's chest heaved. Lips cracked. A rasp broke from his throat, then words:

"Black." Hardly more than breath. He swallowed, eyes rolling, then fixed beyond us. "Land… no. A tooth. A fang."

His fingers scraped the blanket. "Cold," he muttered. "Ice…"

A tremor seized him. His eyes flared wide. "Fire," he croaked. "Bones… in a brazier." The last word slurred, breath broken into cough.

His head sagged back. His chest rose shallowly, then again. His eyes stayed open, glassy, caught by visions none of us saw.

Bogdan bowed his head, whispering thanks as if God Himself had answered.

Markov swallowed hard, jest gone from him. His glance slid to Yelka, frowning as if he'd glimpsed something nameless.

Yelka's eyes shut tight, her shoulders taut as if bracing against herself. The wolf pressed close at her leg, snarling low. The raven croaked harsh above, mocking every vow. She would not kneel—but she did not look free either.

I did not move. My hand stayed on Illarion's arm, hot beneath the skin. Fever's ramble, perhaps, nothing more. Yet Bogdan's dream had brought us here: serpent and crown, a prince begging for rescue. Illarion's words were stranger—no plea for aid but a riddle of tooth and fire. One vision chained him here, the other pointed past.

Fever or fate—I could not tell, nor which was worse.

And Yelka—when she opened her eyes again, something fixed hard inside them. She had seen more than fever. Whether it steadied her or frightened her, I could not say.

Chapter XL: The Prince Reborn

Illarion slept most days and nights, but no longer like the dead. He drank broth, swallowed water, even chewed a strip of boiled fish. His colour had not returned—still wax-grey, lips split, face swollen where the bone had cracked—but the fever had broken, and breath came strong enough that we no longer leaned in to count the lift of his ribs. When he stirred, his eye opened clearer, not glassed and vacant. On the third day he tried to rise and near toppled, yet the strength was there. Not enough for war, but enough for life.

Yelka ruled the church as hers. Not healer only—priestess, judge, keeper of a law none of us could name. Her temple of healing, she called it. She barred Bogdan's bowl, his blood, his ash. No smoke, no sacrifice, no incense to sting the air—only the fire she tended in the hearth, knives boiled till they glowed red, herbs steeped till their bitter steam filled the rafters. She said her arts had saved him, not prayer.

Bogdan spat at that. Said the church was God's, not hers, and that it was God's hand that had raised the prince. They near came to blows. I ended it: Yelka would keep it clean—no blood, no smoke—but Bogdan would have his services, three a day, psalms and sermons echoing against the stone. Neither thanked me.

Her beasts made the place stranger still. The wolf lay close by the hearth, yellow eyes catching every flame. The raven kept to the roof-beams outside, black against the sky when it wheeled, or hunched on the cross when it stilled. Life and death, flesh and omen. Some days the wolf pressed its muzzle to the prince's hand as if to tether him to breath. Other days the raven stared through the open door, eyes fixed as if weighing the hour of death. Yelka never spoke of it, but I saw where her hand fell—always to the wolf. Yet her eyes… they lingered longer on the bird.

The people swelled around us. At first it was only our own men, whispering resurrection. Then townsfolk. Then Brack from the reed-villages. They came with reeds and fish, with woven charms, with hands cracked from peat and salt. Some crossed themselves, some bowed as if before the Awakened. They pressed to the door, eager to glimpse him, or even touch the wall where he slept.

By the week's end they came from the countryside— farmers, wives, boatmen. Ironholt's church turned pilgrim hall. And Yelka walked among them with the calm of one who had always expected such a crowd. She did not welcome them, nor turn them away. She only let them come, as though their gathering confirmed some measure she already carried. Candles burned in every niche, offerings crowded the steps, smoke of cookfires curled in the square. And above it all, Yelka's raven perched on the cross, black against the sky. Some called it the Awakened's eye, some Saint Petron's messenger. Each day more came, as if the bird itself had summoned them.

Bogdan's voice fed them. He stood at the steps with his bowl, proclaiming flame and oath, naming Illarion not healed but raised, not spared but chosen. His words spread like tinder. The crowd swayed at his psalms, even when they spat at his curses. I heard men mutter: saint, prophet, prince reborn.

Markov muttered too—but only when Yelka passed. He lingered near her hands, fetched water, watched the wolf as though it might tell him secrets. I knew that look—he wanted what steadied her, though he called it help.

And with the pilgrim form the countryside and beyond came word and rumour. The king had come with a fleet. Ivan's host marched from Driftlight. The north was aflame. Families fled south, and Ironholt filled with the tide. The church groaned under bodies and candles, prayers and smoke.

I watched it all, bone-tired. I will not say it was no miracle. The prince was near death, and lived. Yelka's craft, Bogdan's prayers—both cut deeper than I can name. To a soldier, such power is only terror. What I know is this: belief is as strong as blood. And men will make of it what they will.

Ironholt's walls stood patched with fresh-cut timber, the palisade mended where Mstislav's fire had gutted it three moons past. Smoke still lingered in the gaps between the boards like trapped ghosts, and the ground beneath reeked of pitch and the salt-sweet of old blood. The scent clung to everything—clothes, hair, even the water we drank tasted of ash.

I stood on the rampart looking south, where the sea spread dark beneath the dying light. Always the sea drew me with invisible chains. Its black water was hunger made manifest, but also promise—the only promise that had never broken faith with me. I had given it blood enough to paint a ship's hull red, years that should have been spent in safer beds, brothers whose names I still whispered to the waves. Yet I yearned for it still, as a man yearns for his first love even after she has cut his heart from his chest. The sea was not mercy, but it was truth. And truth, I had learned, was rarer than mercy.

A harsh croak shattered my brooding. Morwen dropped from the air like a black omen, talons scraping against stone worn smooth by a thousand storms. Her feathers ruffled with a sound like dry laughter, and she fixed me with eyes that held the cold intelligence of winter nights. Then she turned her head with deliberate disdain, as if to make clear that I was beneath the notice of one who had seen the world's bones.

"Leave him," came a voice behind me, carrying the weight of old forests.

Yelka climbed the steps with the measured pace of one who had walked darker paths than these wooden stairs. Her staff clicked against stone with each step — ironwood bound with silver wire, carved with symbols that seemed to shift in the corner of my vision. At her side, Grendel paced with the fluid menace of his kind, yellow eyes never leaving me as they came to stand close enough that I could smell the wild on them both. She laid a weathered hand to the wolf's neck, steadying him, though I could not tell which of them drew comfort from the touch.

"You watch the sea," she said.

"I've lived half my life on it." The words came out rougher than I intended. "The other half preparing to return to it."

"It is alive," she answered, following my gaze to where the water met the darkening sky. "As the forest is. It breathes with the tide, hungers with the storm, speaks in the language of salt and foam. You know its voice."

"And you know the forest's." I studied her profile — sharp as cut glass, Brack-blood plain in every line. Scars marked her, but they did not mar; they only deepened the strangeness of her beauty, as if she had been shaped by harsher hands than nature alone.

Her mouth curved, not quite a smile, more like the expression of someone tasting a bitter memory. "Then we are kin, of a kind. Both servants to powers that care nothing for the small wants of men."

For a moment there was silence between us, filled only by the eternal conversation of wind and water. The salt breeze came sharp and clean, tangling her black hair and carrying with it the promise of storms building beyond the horizon. The raven shifted its weight and croaked again, as if to remind us that it was listening, that it remembered every word spoken in its presence.

She was the one to break the quiet. "Do you know the tale of when fire fell into the marshes?"

I glanced at her sidelong, noting how her grip tightened on her staff. "A Brack story?"

"My mother's story," she said, voice lower than I had ever heard it, like wind over reeds at night. Her eyes stayed on the horizon, unreadable as storm-water.

"She said fire once fell into the marsh. Some called it gift, some judgment. It burned clean at first—healed wounds, lit the dark. But hunger has no end. Men bled for it, women starved for it, children were given to it before they could speak. The fire made them strong, yes—but cruel, as winter is cruel. So the elders bound it. Urn, earth, tears—cast into water black enough to hide even fire. Swore it must never rule the reeds again."

Her mouth tightened, and for a breath she faltered. "But chains break. Mstislav came. He burned, he drowned, he shattered. And in that breaking the fire slipped its leash. Rebels clutched it to their breasts, called it strength, called it justice. They built shrines in peat and smoke. The fire fed on all blood — tyrant's, rebel's — it cared for neither cause. Only hunger."

Morwen croaked, harsh and sudden, and the sound seemed to please her.

"And now," she said, softer, "they whisper it returns when kin rise against kin. Not as saviour. As reckoner. Not to heal — but to settle debts."

Her voice went flat. The wolf pressed against her leg, steadying her; the raven's wings beat once, black against the dusk, and it rose into the air, disappearing into the gathering dusk.

I felt a chill that had nothing to do with the evening wind. "You know of our quest."

Her eyes glinted with something that might have been amusement, if amusement could cut. "Markov has a mouth that runs like a river in spring flood. Even when he thinks it is whispering sweet words to win a woman's heart."

"Damn him," I muttered, though without real heat. The fool's loose tongue might be our undoing yet.

She tilted her head, mocking but not entirely unkind, like a peddler humouring a buyer who cannot tell brass from gold. "Do not damn him so quickly. He speaks truth sometimes, though it comes by accident more often than design."

"Can you help us?" I asked, knowing the answer would cost me, knowing I would pay it anyway.

"Remember when I said there was a price for my aid?"

"I remember." How could I forget? Nothing came free in this world, least of all from those who walked the spaces where ordinary folk feared to tread.

"You will take me with you on this fool's voyage."

"We don't even know where we're going," I said, turning back to the sea.

"To the Black Fang, of course," she answered, as if naming sunrise. "Where else would you go, when every path bends there?"

I stilled, the weight of prophecy settling on my shoulders like a burial shroud. I turned to measure her. "Can you help us find it?"

"I might. But not yet. First sails come from the north — can you not smell them on the wind? Salt, tar, the sweat of desperate men. A choice must be made before any voyage. Then we will see what the currents reveal."

"Markov," I growled, thinking of his loose tongue and looser promises. "He'll be the death of me."

She shook her head slowly, eyes holding depths I could not sound. "Listen to him. Even when he babbles like a brook, listen. He is more important to what comes than he knows — more important perhaps than any of us."

"He's a fool," I said, though the words tasted less certain.

"A fool," she said softly, voice shading toward tenderness, "lets the king see himself. Without the fool's mirror, a king is blind to his own face, deaf to his own voice. And blind kings doom kingdoms."

"King Mstislav is not here," I said.

Her gaze moved slowly over the broken town, over smoke drifting from the rebuilt walls like ghosts of burned dreams, over the folk moving with the careful steps of those who know the ground beneath them is not solid.

"No," she said at last, her voice like a grave closing. "But there is a king here already. Made of smoke and ash, and the weight of choices not yet made. Not yet crowned—but crowned he will be. Whether he rules the living, or a kingdom of ash, that is the only question."

And in her eyes I saw fear again—not of the crown itself, but of what it would demand of her when it came.

Chapter XLI: The Hand Extended

Ironholt swelled.

Word of safety spread faster than fire. The walls still stood, the garrison bent but not broken, and within the palisade there was room enough for all who fled the mire. They came with sacks of grain, bundles of reeds, children on their hips. Townsfolk with nothing left but their hands. The king's banners moved flew in Crowholt, Greenfen, and Driftwatch provinces. Ivan's levy had broken from Driftlight and marched south. The marsh was at war. South was the only road left.

They came also for the prince. Illarion's name carried farther than our sail ever had, and with it came whispers: the fire-touched, the Awakened, the Anointed, the one who would judge. They pressed into Ironholt not just for safety but to see him, or the shadow of him, or the flame they thought clung to his breath.

Bogdan fed that hunger. He made the nave his pulpit, the altar his stage. Three times each day he called mass, and men filled the aisles until there was no space left to kneel. Voices rose with him, ragged at first, then swelling as if the whole city prayed with one throat. Priests came too — some sent by their bishops, some carried by zeal — and Bogdan stood among them as if he had always been master. He gave them duties, assigned their chants, bent their rites toward his flame.

Illarion no longer lay in the nave. Yelka had yielded to the crush of pilgrims and moved him to a chamber behind, set apart from the press. Lord Kozlov himself had ordered the old father's quarters repaired and dressed as best they could be — fresh linen hung, reed mats laid down, every comfort pressed forward, as if each stitch might wash away the shame that the prince had nearly died in his province. He doubled the guard, and Viktor and Andrei at last allowed themselves rest, though one of them stood watch at every hour. Illarion's breath was still shallow, his skin still grey, but none of that mattered. The fire had touched him once — that was enough.

Word of miracle began to spread. A fevered child brought to the steps, cured by a drop of oil and a prayer. A soldier's wound closed in a night after Bogdan's blessing. A woman's barren womb quickened after kneeling at the altar. Rumours, all of them, but spoken in tones that dared no contradiction.

And if the prince's fire drew them, so too did the druid. Yelka walked the square with wolf and raven at her heel and on her shoulder, and the people made way. Some spat, some crossed themselves, but all kept their distance, as if beasts and woman alike were bound to an older law. Between Bogdan's altar and her craft, Ironholt had become more than a garrison. It had become a shrine.

The square had once been houses. Burned rafters, black stone, all cleared down to hard earth. We turned it into ground for the Discipline — space enough for shields and spears to move in time. Morning and night the rhythm held: boys and soldiers sweating in ranks, voices calling the count, dust rising with each step.

And each day more gathered at the edges.

Men from Ironholt's broken garrison, still raw with grief. Townsfolk with nothing left but their arms. Strangers wandering south, saying the mire was war behind them.

Even the Brack captives—forty-four taken on the water, thirty-five chained from Ironholt's fall—watched with hunger in their eyes.

Almost daily one of them stepped forward when the forms ended. "Otets," they called. "Otets. Let us move with you."

I gave them nothing. "No. Your oaths are elsewhere. Mine is to keep you bound."

They bowed, but the word still followed me: *Otets.*

That evening by the fire, Markov leaned close. "You should let them move."

I spat in the dust. "Prisoners don't need training."

He grinned, low and sly. "They don't need steel. Just movement. Keeps them where you can see them. And if we're honest, Yarik, the army needs more bodies. Garrison's thin, refugees look to drift whichever way the wind blows. Better they drift to you than back to the rebels."

I gave him a look.

He shrugged. "Think on it. They already believe. You heard them—*Otets.* Their belief may be the sharpest weapon you'll ever hold. Rebels bleed each time one of their own kneels in your square instead of theirs. You don't want to be an image? Too late. You are. Better to wear it than let them dress you in worse."

"I'm not an image. I'm a man. A man with too many burdens already."

Markov's grin thinned, leaving only the knife beneath. "Exactly. And that is why you're the perfect image. Truth in armour is rarer than any relic. They've seen saints in gold, princes in fire. Let them see you — scarred, heavy, unwilling. That's what will hold them."

He fetched the armour Illarion had given me from the Burning Cross. The set I had shoved away when the siege ended, the set I had never asked for. Markov laid it out piece by piece, as if fire itself had charged him with the rite.

The plate was cold against my skin, weight pressing down with every strap. Each buckle fastened was another oath I had not chosen. He hung Pryaz at my side — the black steel colder than iron had any right to be. The cloak he swung across my shoulders still stank faintly of smoke, as if Illarion's fire clung in its weave.

He fussed as ever, pretending carelessness, but his hands were steady. When he stepped back, I did not see myself in their eyes — I saw Illarion's making, worn on my body.

Mikhail and Sava were watching. No grin, no jape. Only nods, sharp and sure, as if some hollow had been filled and the company was whole again.

I let it stand. Not because I wanted it. Not because I bent to the crown that marked it. But because the armour was on me now, and all eyes were watching, and silence was its own kind of oath.

And still Yelka's words tolled in my skull: *listen to the fool.* But I wondered if she had set this snare herself, letting Markov's tongue lead me into armour I had never wanted to wear.

I found him upright when I entered. Not in the nave, not in the square where men whispered his name like a prayer or a curse, but in his chamber—standing by the cot as if the very sight of it had grown hateful.

His eyes went to my chest first, taking in the gleam of steel. "You wear the plate."

"Markov's doing," I said, the weight foreign across my shoulders. "The men need to see their commander armoured. They need to believe."

"I hear our numbers grow." His voice slurred; the scar pulled his mouth into something like a perpetual sneer. "How many?"

"At least three hundred. More each day—locals, captives turned loyal, garrison men, farmers' sons chasing rumour. They come with whatever steel they can drag out of barns, and we arm those who prove worthy."

His lips twitched—not a smile, more its ghost. "And they follow you." There was challenge in it, testing if I now stood above him.

"No." I did not soften it. When he was ready, they would be his men. I had never wanted their oath. "They follow Christ and Crown, as you commanded. I only take the words."

He studied me with those fever-bright eyes. The silence stretched until he turned away, dismissing my words without need to voice his disbelief.

A cracked mirror leaned against the wall—relic of the old father's quarters, its silver backing spotted with age like a diseased lung. Illarion stood before it, fingers trembling as they touched his ruined face. One cheek carved by the healer's knife, red and angry. The other hollowed by fever until he looked a skull in flesh. His lips split and bloodless. And beneath it all, the old sickness lingered still, written into him like a curse.

His gaze hardened as he stared at his reflection until the glass itself seemed to recoil from what it showed.

I thought him a frightful ruin — half destroyed, fit more for shroud than banner. Yet I had seen the men's faces when word spread he lived. Fear, yes, but more than fear. Reverence. Men will follow a scarred champion who has walked through hell's mouth and returned breathing. He was no longer the golden prince of court-songs, but terror crowned with righteousness cuts deeper than beauty ever could.

"I had a vision as I woke." His voice, flat as stone.

He said no more, and the silence pressed like lead.

"The Sea's Tooth," I offered. "Yelka knows something of it. Where it lies, perhaps what guards it. She speaks in riddles wrapped in mist."

Illarion's breath came harsh and laboured. "And her price?"

"To join the quest. To stand at your side when we sail for it."

He turned then, and I saw something flicker behind his eyes — calculation, perhaps, or merely exhaustion. "She and Bogdan?"

"Like fire and flood," I said. "Each would see the other drowned. But she saved you when the fever cut deepest. Bogdan alone would not have pulled you back."

His eyes narrowed. "What does she truly want?"

I thought of the queen with her webs of whispered words and purchased loyalties. Of Bogdan with his holy fire and his certainty that God's will flowed through his hands alone. Of every grasping hand that sought to shape the prince's path, to bend his destiny to their own design. Each claimed to serve, but in the end, all served themselves.

All I said was: "I don't know."

That was the only truth left to me.

Dusk settled over Ironholt like ash from a funeral pyre. From the palisade I looked down on the square we had carved from ruin—our one triumph wrested from fire and loss. Rank on rank the men gathered, shields clashing in rhythm, spears lifted like a forest of iron teeth, bodies moving as one. Some bore steel torn from the dead, others only empty hands made hard by hunger, but still they moved—southern forms fused with northern drills, each sequence ending in a shout that rolled like thunder against walls too long acquainted with silence.

Mikhail had taken my place in the line, drilling the sword-and-shield, voice cracked but sure. I no longer moved among them. Markov called it stewardship, but the truth was plainer: I was raised to the wall, set apart, set above. Commander by need, not by oath.

I wore the plate Illarion had given me at Drownbank, Pryaz at my side. The weight sat heavy, not mine by choosing, but the men needed to see it. They needed to believe.

The training had run long. Sweat shone in the last light, copper-red against dust and stone. Their voices should have warmed me. Instead a coldness sat in my chest—the sense of standing at a cliff's edge, fog below, the fall unseen.

Then the church doors opened.

Every head turned. The Discipline faltered, rhythm breaking like surf on stone.

Illarion stepped out.

Not the fever-twisted wreck we had carried through the keep's blood. Not the near-dead prince bound to linen and whispered prayers. He had risen remade. His cloak swept behind him, a belt bright with bronze at his waist, boots striking hard against the cobbles. His face was shattered still—scar carved deep, lips pulled into a half-sneer by fever's cruelty—but the ruin only sharpened him. Once the golden prince of song, he had become something else: a figure wrought of pain and purpose, terrible and certain.

Yelka followed, wolf at her heel, raven black against her shoulder. Her eyes were dark, unreadable—but I thought I saw a flicker there, not awe but recognition, as if Illarion's ruin matched something she had long carried in herself. The wolf pressed close as if to tether her; the raven croaked once, flat and harsh, and it sounded less like blessing than witness. Whatever she saw in him, she bound herself to it, though to what end I could not name.

Bogdan came too, lips moving in prayer, his bearing like a priest leading a relic through the streets.

The crowd pulled back in awe and fear, leaving Illarion a clear road. Even the boldest shrank aside, as if a living judgment walked among them.

At the edge I saw Markov, his grin gone. He was not watching Illarion at all, but Yelka. No daze in his face now, no boyish hunger—only something taut and troubled, as if he saw a shape in her the rest of us had missed.

He came to the palisade. To me.

The Discipline fell silent, hundreds of eyes fixed.

Illarion stopped before me. For a moment neither of us moved. The air between us was heavy with all that had passed—his hatred, his threats, my refusals. I had never bent the knee to him. My loyalty had been to his father, Mstislav, King of the Broken Isles. Yet here he stood, not dead, cracked but unbroken, burning with a fire of his own making. And I, who had refused him, found myself bound to his cause all the same.

Morwen croaked from Yelka's shoulder, sharp as iron on stone. Some crossed themselves at the sound, others flinched, as if the omen turned awe to fear.

He stretched out his hand.

I stared at it. A prince's hand, scarred and trembling, but steady. It was not brotherhood he offered, nor forgiveness. It was recognition—that our fates had twined, and neither of us could break free.

I took it.

Then he turned and looked down at his army.

I stood back, released from command, though not released from duty. Duty never ends.

Their shout broke like a storm, rolled the square, shook the palisade.

But in that moment I looked to sea. At the harbour mouth, dark hulls slid in—oars cutting black water in steady rhythm. Three ships, silent in the dusk.

Chapter XLII: Danger Walked in His Shadow

The first ships nosed into harbour to shouts from the Driftlight boys — *Grey Gull, Saltwind* — names they knew like kin. But the third bore no Driftlight mark. Its sail was black wool, patched white, and at its masthead flared the King's Hand — white, stark, fingers outspread. Above the keep, Illarion's Burning Crown already flew. Two banners, two masters, clawing the same sky. I had not seen their like share wind since Mstislav died. It was a sign. Whether of reckoning or ruin, I could not yet say.

Illarion's men crowded the quay, faces tight, shoulders squared as he strode ahead. They followed without command, drawn to him as iron to fire.

Down the gangplank came Ivan. His eyes found Borislav at once. The boy stood in studded leather, axe at his hip, close behind his prince like a shadow. His chin was high, his lip still split from drills, but his hands trembled at his sides.

Ivan's arms lifted as though to seize him — crush him to chest, claim him back. He stopped a step short, catching himself before he could shame his son before prince and men alike. Borislav flinched, half reaching, then stiffened, eyes flicking to Illarion. Waiting for his liege's measure before daring to act.

So they stood — father with arms fallen, son with fists clenched, neither able to bridge the space. Pride and fear bound them tighter than any embrace could. The moment sagged with love unspent, thick as smoke.

I watched it, and felt the bite of recognition. Once I had stood like Borislav, chained to another man's gaze, waiting to be named worthy or cast aside. Oaths had bound me then. Oaths bound the boy now. Perhaps his father's silence was the cruelest chain of all.

And through that hush, another stepped onto the quay.

Not a soldier, not a lord. A cloak of brown wool, plain but well-cut, hem frayed from hard miles. A silver clasp held it shut, though the cloth dragged heavy on one side where hidden weight pulled. Boots polished against the sea-filth marked a man who refused corruption. One hand showed the scar of old loss — two fingers gone at the knuckle, the kind of wound that teaches caution every time it grips.

He did not push. He did not shout. Yet the quay opened before him. A murmur stilled as he passed, and one veteran's hand strayed unconsciously to his hilt. Even the boys of the Discipline, straight-backed, eyes alight with zeal, hushed as if a priest had entered. His face was weathered as oak, his eyes quick and dark, empty of warmth. He looked nothing more than a man in a travel cloak, and yet danger walked in his shadow.

Dragomir. The Queen's shadow. Her hand in the dark, the man who moved fates by inches. He had not come south for battle. He had come for judgment. And now he stood in Ironholt, watching crown and fire contest the same sky.

He took everything in as he stepped clear of the gangplank. Illarion's ruined face, proud and terrible, fire burning in his eyes though fever had hollowed him. The plate on his shoulders too bright for his gaunt frame. My chestplate and Pryaz at my side, the men's eyes sliding between us as though neither prince nor wolf stood higher. Bogdan, black-robed, already gathered to as if fire itself had anointed him.

Yelka with her wolf pressed close, her raven circling high — Dragomir's gaze lingered, weighing her as if he could not decide whether she was healer, heretic, or something worse. Lord Kozlov, sweating thanks that Illarion still drew breath. Guards stiff at their posts. The Discipline, silent, waiting. Even Markov, who tried to smile, but the man's eyes passed over him and left him pale.

It was like he read the whole of our history in a glance, without needing the tale.

Grendel's hackles rose, a low growl rumbling in his throat. Overhead Morwen croaked, harsh and flat, cutting the air like a blade. The quay stilled at the sound.

His eyes came back to Illarion. "Your face," he said, soft as sand on stone. "The scar suits you. May not the Queen, however."

Then his ruined hand shifted at his side. "We need to speak. You, Prince. And you, Wolf." His gaze cut to me like a weight laid on the table. Then, without turning, to the others: "The rest may follow, if they choose. I will not bar them."

No one mistook it for invitation. It was command, quiet as surf closing over stone.

Chapter XLIII: The Queen's Shadow

Lord Kozlov had emptied and given up his best chambers for Dragomir. That was saying little. The common room smelled of resin and damp wool, the walls hung with faded tapestries of stags and rivers gone grey with mildew. The table was oak, scarred and uneven, spread with a few brass lamps whose light made the shadows lurch. A fur rug covered the floor, but moths had chewed the edges. It was the best he had to offer.

Ten men held the corridor beyond Kozlov's door; not a parade, but a measured presence Dragomir could call in a breath.

Dragomir made the room his as if by right. He needed no gilt; presence was his veneer—he folded the moth-chewed rug and the mildewed tapestries into a stage. When he spoke the poor chamber listened.

He sat at the head, cloak draped loose, ruined hand resting on the wood. The hand drew the eye despite all attempts to avoid it—two fingers sheared off at the knuckle, the stumps puckered and pale, the remaining digits scarred white as birch bark. Rumours swirled about how he'd lost them. Some said torture in Strayhorn dungeons. Others whispered of a blade trap meant for another, taken deliberately to preserve a more valuable life. Dragomir himself had never spoken of it, which only sharpened the speculation. Now those remaining digits drummed a slow rhythm on the scarred oak, patient as a hunter waiting for prey to step into the snare.

Illarion took the chair opposite, scar gleaming, finery muted beneath lamplight. His head was high and his eyes flashed warning, but tension coiled in the set of his shoulders, the too-careful placement of his hands.

I did not sit. My bad leg throbbed, but I would not put myself on the same level as prince and shadow both. To sit would have been to claim equality, or at least permission. Neither was mine. So I stood behind Illarion's chair, weight shifting off the wound, my hand near Pryaz's hilt. Not from any illusion that I might strike Dragomir, but from habit. Some reflexes die hard.

Markov leaned near the wall, arms crossed, jaw working as if chewing bitter roots. His eyes darted between the spymaster and the door, measuring distances like a man planning retreat.

Bogdan stood with the righteous bearing of a man convinced that divine will aligned with his own opinions. His bone charms hung heavy in his fingers, but his knuckles were white where he gripped them.

Yelka stood unbowed. Without wolf or raven she seemed smaller, more a girl with herb-stains on her fingers than a witch out of the mire. And yet I felt them still—the wolf's weight at her heel, the raven's eye in the dark. She carried them even here, though no beast had followed her in. Her dark hair hung long and braided around her shoulders, and her clothes—peat-dyed wool with reed-thread charms at the cuffs, bone toggles and a pouch of dried roots at her belt—marked her as an outsider. Yet she met Dragomir's gaze without flinching, as if she'd stared down far worse than the Queen's spymaster in the deep forests around Ravenholt.

Dragomir's gaze rested on her first, cataloguing, measuring. His eyes were the pale grey of winter ice, and they missed nothing—not the herb stains on her fingernails, not the faint resin smear at her wrist, not the way she held herself apart from the rest of us.

When he spoke, his voice carried the flat certainty of a man who had already signed the warrant and come only to read it aloud.

"Chernoknizhnika." His mouth barely moved, but the word turned every head toward her. Sorceress of the black book. Necromancer. For a heartbeat I thought even the lamps dimmed. But she did not flinch. She wore the accusation like someone used to being burned in rumour long before any pyre was lit.

Yelka's eyes did not shift. "No. Some might say znakharka. But names are smoke, and smoke hides more than it shows."

"And what is your purpose here?"

"My purpose is my own. But this much I will say. The prince walks a line sharp as glass. Tip too far, and ash will take more than him."

The word ash made Illarion's eyes flick to Bogdan, his jaw knot once. Dragomir caught the movement, filed it away with the thousand other small details that made him so dangerous.

Bogdan seized the pause, voice sharp as a lash. "She weaves dark magic. Hear her tongue — already she speaks of ash as if judgment were hers to give. Even her familiar is death's omen. How can such a one be allowed to stand here?" His fervour was real, but desperation edged his words. He needed an enemy. "She consorts with beasts and spirits. By the Grey Hand's law, she should be put to flame."

"She is mine." Illarion's voice cut the chamber like steel on flint. His eyes locked with Dragomir's, and for the first time I saw the deeper game: he did not cling to her only for defiance, but because he believed she held the map he needed. She was more than healer—she was compass.

The silence stretched.

Markov's eyes stayed on Yelka, not with hunger but with something tighter, as if he sensed a blade hidden in her calm.

Bogdan's face flushed red above his robes, but he said nothing more.

Dragomir only blinked, eyes sliding back to the table. But I caught the slight tightening around them, the minute pause before his next words. The spymaster was recalculating. And his eyes went once more to Yelka, not long, but long enough. He did not know what piece she was on the board, and men like him feared what they could not name. His ruined hand tapped once, twice. Then his voice came, scrape of steel on whetstone.

"The prince's campaigns have been a disaster."

The words fell into silence like stones into still water, each ripple spreading wider.

"Men wasted on charges that served neither God nor gain. A fleet broken. Stormhold burned and abandoned to rot." His pale eyes swept the room. "The Crown's men die like wheat before the scythe, and the realm bleeds for your pride."

I felt each charge like a physical blow. My shoulders hunched despite my efforts to stand straight. We had failed. All of us.

Dragomir's gaze fixed on Markov first. "Your flirtation with Brack rites cost more than wounded pride. The Volkhva Kharna's death—" He let the name hang like smoke. "—and the uprisings that followed. How many villages smoulder while you gather excuses?"

Markov's jaw worked soundlessly. His hands pressed flat against the wall, knuckles white. "It wasn't—I couldn't have known—"

"Ignorance is no shield."

Next came Bogdan. The prophet straightened, but sweat beaded his brow despite the room's chill.

"You feed madness to men who march," Dragomir said. "Your rites kindle courage that leaves soldiers naked to the spear. The Crown will not shelter those who burn their own faithful."

Bogdan's mouth opened and closed. Righteousness warred with fear in his face. "I serve the faith," he managed, but the words came out hollow.

"You serve yourself."

Bogdan clutched his bones tighter, but said nothing more. In the lamplight, he looked older, smaller—a man whose certainties had crumbled beneath him.

Finally, Dragomir turned to Illarion.

"And you, Prince. You claimed the relic as if legend could be sewn to flesh. You lost ships, spent lives, raised banners that should never have flown." He leaned forward, pale eyes boring into Illarion's scarred face. "The Crown indulged a prince who mistakes arrogance for destiny."

For a long moment Illarion said nothing. Then, slowly, he smiled. The lamplight caught in his eyes and made them coals, and the fire behind them was worse than the wound.

"If I am not the Crown's hand," he said, "then where is the King?"

The words struck like a torch in dry straw. Dragomir's ruined fingers stilled on the table.

Illarion's eyes burned hotter, words striking like blows. "Does he sail the Southern Strait? Does he march the Mirefast to end rebellion? Or does he rot in Velgrad, locked beneath the Queen's key?"

The silence that followed was heavier than any answer. Dragomir's ruined fingers stilled on the table. He did not deny it, and that refusal was admission enough.

Illarion leaned forward, voice dropping low. "We both know his mind wanders lost paths. The Queen hides it behind ceremony, but a throne cannot remain empty. I am his blood, his heir. The crown comes to me by right. It will not be held by deception."

Treason, yes—but also truth. Dragomir's silence stretched like a drawn bowstring.

"If you claim the Crown while the King lives," the spymaster said at last, "you will be named usurper. The law keeps a short rope, even for princes."

Illarion rose, chair scraping across the floor. "The law?" His laugh was bitter, cutting through the chamber's stillness. "You speak of law while we prop up shadows and whispers. How long can a kingdom live on the fiction that its king still rules?" His voice hardened. "I will decide where I go, not the Queen, and never you. I am not the man you remember, spymaster. Press me further, and you will learn how changed I am."

They faced each other across the scarred table—fire and frost—and I thought the realm might break between them.

Then Dragomir smiled. A terrible expression, cold and sharp as winter steel.

He reached inside his cloak and drew out a small packet, black wax gleaming in the lamplight. The Queen's seal pressed into the surface like a brand. He placed it on the table between them with deliberate care.

"Her Majesty's orders. The relic surrendered. The prince returned to Velgrad. By choice or in chains—the preference is yours."

The packet lay between them like a coiled serpent. His ruined hand lingered, jaw tight. He had his orders and would see them carried—but I was not sure he believed them just. This was not the Crown entire, but the Queen's want made law: not vengeance, only the preservation of a son she still called child. The insult cut sharper than steel. Illarion stiffened; he felt it too. Dragomir set the packet down with the ease of a man performing obedience, yet that small tightening at his jaw read like a private question—did he believe the command, or only weigh how far Illarion would bend beneath it?

Dragomir rose, cloak settling like wings. "We leave at dawn," he said. His eyes slid past Illarion and fixed on me. "The Queen's command is plain: bring the relic. Bring the prince. In chains if need be. You will see it done, Yaroslav."

The words cut deeper than any blade. My oaths clashed inside me—Vezhena's command, Illarion's fire, my own vow to end him if rot claimed him. Duty against duty, each pulling until I felt hollowed, split.

At the threshold, Dragomir paused without turning.

"Oh, and Prince Illarion? Your father specifically asked to see you. I believe he wishes to measure what remains of the son he named heir."

The door shut with a soft click, and we were left staring at the black wax seal like a curse upon the table. I felt its weight. The seal was command. The seal was chains. And me—I was the hand sworn to fasten them.

Chapter XLIV: The Map of Blood and Wine

The door closed on Dragomir's cloak. Silence clung to the chamber.

Ilarion stood at the table, hand trembling as he reached for the pitcher. He tried to pour steady; the stream broke, black wine spilling over his wrist. He drank as if the tremor were nothing, but the cup rattled against his teeth and wine ran down his chin, staining his tunic like fresh blood.

For a heartbeat he froze, humiliated. Then he hurled the cup to the floor. Clay burst in shards at his feet. His breath tore out ragged, hot as a forge. He snatched the pitcher and flung it into the wall; it shattered with a hollow crack and wine bled down the tapestry in dark streaks—blood poured over a saint.

"Chains," he spat, chest heaving. "They would drag me like a thief. Me!" His laugh split open—no mirth, only threat. "I will never be bound."

Bogdan leaned close, fingers drumming slow, the sound a dirge. "Do not bend," he said, low and sure. "The shadow hides in parchment and in skirts. He counts names and measures deeds. Let him count ashes, then. His chamber could burn. Accidents come in the night. Who would mourn such a man? Better ash than leash."

He tapped the oak with two fingers, soft and certain. He did not merely counsel; he was shaping the moment—a silence stretched into command, a fear turned into loyalty.

Illarion's hands were still flecked with clay and wine. He said, low and tight, "To kill him here would be folly. They would say I fled judgment. No. Let him crawl back to Velgrad with his tale — and I will follow. I will stand in the capital itself. Let my father see what fire he begot."

Markov let out a dry rasp, almost a laugh, but it died in his throat. He pushed a hand through his hair as if to shake the thought loose. "You speak as if murder were prayer, Bogdan. Set a man's bed alight and the world will call it treason, not miracle. Dragomir dies — King or no King, it's not just leash, it's gallows. For all of us."

Illarion wheeled on him, the ruined side of his face a mask of fury. "You will never speak of what you heard tonight. Never." His voice cracked like a whip, hot with wine and threat.

Markov's hands came up, empty, palms outward. The grin he offered was paper-thin. "I'm no fool. My tongue's not that loose. You think I'd go whispering that the King rots in his chamber? That I'd hang myself for the pleasure?" He swallowed, colour gone from his face. "Not I. But saints save us, if it's true… it changes everything."

He moved on me like a tide — sudden, all motion. Illarion strode up the table, breath hot, wine still dark on his sleeve, and planted himself so close our noses almost met. For a pulse he was furnace and fever; then something colder slid down his spine. His hand went to the hilt, not yet drawn, but the motion read as promise.

"Volkolak," he said, slow and close, breath hot as peat-smoke. "Where does your loyalty lie? Would you follow his orders — chain me like a cur if I will not bow?"

The question slid under my ribs like a knife. The oaths lived there, stacked and cold: the Crown's call, the hand I once swore to hold, Mstislav's table and the old vow that would not unmake itself. My mouth went dry; the salt of those promises rose in my throat like brine.

I chose my words as one lays stones for a bridge. "My loyalty is to the Crown." Each syllable set down to bear weight.

For a single breath his eyes went black, a pit of hurt and hunger that promised no return. In that hollow I saw what he could do — the quick, clean end that would let me sleep under cold earth with my oath unbroken. It was the simplest answer: let him kill me and be done.

He read nothing of that dark thought. When I added, low, "Not to the Queen, not to her spymaster," the line cut him open in a different way. Understanding — slow, sour — crept across his face. His fingers loosened on the hilt. He turned away, but the shadow over his shoulder was not eased.

"Do not make me choose," I added, softer, because a command was not the same as an oath and because some things you must not be asked to name.

Truly, could I even bind him? Near four hundred men moved in morning and evening discipline. Half of them brackfolk. What would they do if Illarion refused the Queen's order? their loyalty was not to the King or the realm, but to the prince of fire.

Illarion paced the length of the chamber, steps ragged, sleeves dripping wine. He wheeled suddenly on Yelka. "The relic," he snarled. "Where is it? You play at healer, at seer — well, speak. Where have you hidden it?"

Her face did not shift. "It is not hidden. It waits. When flame meets fang, it will show itself. Fire chooses its bearer."

Bogdan cut into the silence, his voice a knife of scripture. "Witch's riddles. Poison in a prince's ear. The relics are God's command — greater than king or throne. You are chosen, Prince. Do not crawl to Velgrad."

Yelka did not flinch. "Then let fire answer him," she said, quiet as water through reeds.

The room pressed in on me. Practicalities needled like briars under skin. "Soroka do not have enough ships to carry your host. Four hulls cannot bear four hundred men, let alone the crews to sail them. He means to strip you bare, Prince. To leave you with a chain in your hands and nothing behind it."

Illarion's face shuttered, folding in on itself like a sail furled before storm. He stood still, then spoke with a voice that was small and terrible. "I will not abandon my men."

Markov's tone cut dry across the silence. "An army of Brackfolk without a master drifts quick. Some will run. Most will return to the rebels. Better a cause that feeds them than waiting for scraps."

Illarion's eyes flared, not only with rage but something older, heavier. "If I go, they go. I will not leave them to rot." His gaze fixed on me, sharp as if he could pin me to the oak itself. "You are bound by oath. So am I. And my oath, whatever that snake in wool mutters, is to the men of the realm — to their sons, even Brack sons — and to the fate of Mirefast."

The words rang strange from his lips — not the boast of a fevered prince, but the first flicker of something larger. He spoke of the realm, yet it was himself he cast in its fire.

Markov's hands moved, quick and nervous, like a tailor stitching torn cloth. "Then here's a path." He stepped into the lamplight, dipped a finger in the spill, and drew on the oak with wine for ink. "Here's Ironholt. Your four ships — Soroka takes them to Driftlight. With luck, Dragomir sails with her. Out of your sight, out of your camp."

He dragged a red line north. "The Crown sent ten hulls, five hundred men. Add Ivan's levy and you've got two fists. One's clearing rebels from the high provinces — Crowholt, Greenfen, Saint's Watch." He marked each with a blot of red. "The other marches from Driftlight east and south, sweeping Saltcross clean. That's why Ironholt swells — the rabble driven here, fleeing the fires."

Another line, thicker now, slashed just above. "But the heart of it sits north in the mire proper, and at Bogreach." He tapped the blot hard, as if nailing it down. "The Crown means to drive them there, crush them between the two fists."

Illarion's voice was low, suspicious. "So?"

"So," Markov said, "you march north with your host. You join the Crown's fist, serve their cause. To Dragomir it looks like obedience. To the men, it's victory. You bleed the rebels, stand in the law, and buy time." He leaned closer, grin crooked, eyes sharp. "Then, when you reach Driftlight, you take more hulls — five, maybe more. Enough to carry your whole force. From there you sail east to Velgrad, with your host behind you, not broken on the leash."

He sat back, the map of blood and wine glistening on the oak. "Not treason. Not surrender. Just time bought in the Queen's name, until you choose your own."

Bogdan's voice carried a new edge—zeal sharpened on the whetstone of calculation. "If we march north and link with the Crown's host—if we stand at Bogreach as if to hold it for the King—then the relic's road remains open. The Crown will need us. We walk within the law, yet still bear the flame."

Yelka's face did not change. "You turn the world by the choice you show," she said, flat as water. "Go north, if you would know whether the land names you saviour—or reckoner."

Illarion paced, back and forth, the decision burning across his ruined features. Rage bent toward cunning; the boy's fury reheated into strategy. He spat on the floor and grinned like a man who had found a sword hidden in straw. "Five ships," he said, as if daring the word itself. "We ask. We march. We make ourselves necessary. We do not go meek to Velgrad to be shackled. But—" His eyes locked on mine. "You must not hand me to their leashes. Will you march north for the Crown's war—or bow to Dragomir's command?"

My mouth was dry. My oath to the Crown lay on one wrist like iron; the unspoken seal to the prince pressed on the other. I heard Dragomir's silence, the Queen's inevitable reach. And beneath them both, older still, the weight of a hand on my shoulder, jeweled and heavy, trembling but unbroken. The king's hand. Mstislav's voice, thick with wine and grief, had once called me son when his true son he would not name. I had sworn then—not to crown nor relic, but to the man himself. To keep some ember of him alive when rot gnawed his flesh and devils whispered from the fire. That oath had never loosened, though the world tried to bury it.

The relic, the march, the fire—these were all madness. Yet in that madness I smelled a crack of hope: that by chasing flame into the mire, I might still drive back the dark hand that tugged my lord toward the pyre. Impossible, yes. But love for a dying king had always been impossible. That was my true chain, and it pulled me north.

"North," I said at last. "We march to Bogreach. We aid the Crown's banners."

Illarion's ruined face split in a smile that belonged to no boy, no son — only to a man who had decided the world itself must bend. Not joy. Coronation carved out of ruin.

Chapter XLV: The Measure Taken

Ironholt's quay held the night's chill; dew filmed the planks and turned boot-soles slick. Men moved like shadows between coils of line and tar buckets, quiet in the way soldiers are when a day is about to be decided for them. Above the harbour wall the town lifted, all stump towers and wet stone and a few pale banners stuck to their poles, heavy with mist. Somewhere beyond those walls, Illarion's voice carried—sometimes a barked order, sometimes the sharp of a horn. From the town came the rasp of saws, the ring of hammers, the groan of wagons shoved into line. Somewhere a horn sounded, short and sharp, and men shifted to it. That was the answer.

Dragomir stood where quay met water steps, cloak hem beading with dew. He faced the drums, not me. The ruined hand drew the eye—two fingers gone at the knuckle, the scars white as chalk, as if even his grip on the world had broken short. The other hand rested in his cloak, calm enough, yet the whole of him seemed like a man trying to gather threads that slipped through his grasp no matter how tightly he drew them.

Markov took my shoulder once, light as a bird's foot, and then fell in a pace to my right. He had slept little and hid it well. A grin flickered and was gone.

He did not turn at first. He listened. I followed his gaze to the high lane that ran along the inner wall. Men moved there like a tide, in files that caught and flowed. Banners changed hands. A young voice cracked trying to carry a command, failed, and tried again. The drums did not change.

"Not garrison," Dragomir said, almost to himself. His voice was sand over stone. "He means to march them north."

He turned then. His eyes came to me first, then to Markov, and settled again on me as if he had decided the order once and would stick to it.

"The queen's orders were clear," he said. "Bring him to Velgrad."

"Aye." My voice sounded like a fist closed too long.

"And yet the drums."

I had nothing to say to that that would not be a lie. I kept my jaw shut until it ached.

Markov stepped into the silence like a man warming hands at another's fire. "He obeys," he said, voice light. "North is Velgrad, is it not? His ranks swell — four hundred now — and not enough ships to carry them. At Driftlight there will be. And in the way sits Bogreach. Rebels to crush, mire to clear. When the Crown strikes, he will strike with it. One road, one duty."

Dragomir's eyes moved to him. Not surprised. Weighed, then set aside. "You take words to market like coin, Markov."

"I do," Markov answered. "And I can tell a counterfeit when I hear one. None on our tongues today."

"The relic." Dragomir did not bother with steps between. "Give it to me."

I felt heat in the memory of it, even in the cold air. Bone that burned. A saint's arm that had taught me what judgment feels like when it chooses a man and refuses him.

Markov answered before the flame behind my ribs found my voice. "It's a charm. He carries it like boys carry luck-stones. Let him carry it. It steadies his hand. You don't think saint-bones will nurse a mad king to reason. Neither do I."

Dragomir's jaw shifted, not quite anger, not quite concession — something filed away where no one could read it. "Bogdan binds him in lies — fire and blood dressed as gospel. He plays at sainthood, yet what he preaches is far more dangerous. Strip him of that prophet, and perhaps there is a prince left to rule. Perhaps."

"Yes," I said. One word is harder than many. "I would have him gone if I had the power. But I do not. Nor, it seems, do you. He clings to the prince with the queen's own blessing. Only her hand could cut him loose."

Markov's grin flickered and vanished. "We don't need the queen's hand. By luck or fate, we have another. The healer — Yelka. She bites him like a vixen, and he bleeds. She saved the prince when Bogdan would have drowned him in smoke and ash. She hates him. That hate may yet keep the prince ours."

"So you trade a madman for a madwoman." Dragomir's tone did not bother to rise. "One straight line of ruin for another that curves."

"Which one of us is straight?" Markov asked, as if it were a joke. "Lock him in Velgrad, and he'll rot like a rope in a well. Leave him here, he burns, but other men light off him. You can govern rot. You cannot lead it. Tell me your choice as a steward of a kingdom that will outlive the queen by — " He looked deliberately toward the sea, counting gulls. "By fewer months than you care to whisper."

"Do not speculate where you cannot count," Dragomir said.

His eyes came back to me. "That banner of his."

"Kingdoms have many banners," Markov said smoothly, before I could spend breath on it. "Every army marches under a dozen. His is colour, not treason. The Burning Crown frightens rebels; fright and stories are cheaper than iron. Would you forbid a scarecrow because it wears a crown of straw?"

"His loyalty is to himself," Dragomir said. It was not a question.

"Wrong," I said. The word came harder than I meant, and his eyes fixed on me, not angry — only whetting the blade of his attention.

"There is more to him," I went on, hearing it as if someone else spoke. "Yes, he is proud. Vain. Yet driven. And whatever it is that drives him, he's stronger than I believed. He struck the rebels when they rose, and he held the king's peace when no one else would. There may be…" I stopped, tasting the word before I could spit it. "…something in him yet. Not a king, perhaps. Not yet."

Dragomir's pale eyes narrowed. "That is more than I've ever heard you say in one breath. You believe in him?"

I let the silence pull tight, then gave it a word. "I'd like to."

He tucked the answer away without a flicker, as if storing it for some ledger I would never see. Above us the racket shifted — cart wheels braced, oars dragged across stone, orders shouted and answered. Men were learning how they would move, not yet moving.

"He shames the Crown with his losses." Not a question. A charge laid bare.

Markov's shrug was almost gentle. "Loss shames a man only if no one believes why he fell. They believe in him. That is a harder thing to win than a battle. The truth of his gift or curse—it doesn't matter. He's a beacon. Even if it's foxfire, men will walk toward it. He'll learn. He'll spend men slower. He has to."

"You are asking me to write a different report," Dragomir said, evenly. "From the one I came to write. You can feel the wet in the wind, and call it dry, and think me fooled. I am not."

"I'm asking you to write the whole of it," Markov said. "Not only the tally of ships and graves. Count the hearts that turned to him. Count the men who would not bend for you, but bent for him. Leave that out, and your report is the lie."

A gull screamed. I let my eyes fall to the water; easier than meeting Dragomir's face when he read men like numbers on a ledger. The tide pressed slow against the quay steps. Somewhere inland a laugh rose and broke off, embarrassed. Pryaz dragged at my hip, colder than steel should be.

Dragomir held the silence a long while—long enough I thought we'd been dismissed. When he spoke again, his words had changed shape.

"Protect him," he said. "Whether you like him or not. Whether he earns it or not. If he lives… there are roads still unopened. If he dies—" He looked past me, past the harbour, as if the line of the horizon carried figures written on it. "If he dies, the realm falls faster than you think."

Markov's mouth tightened. He said nothing to that. Good. There are places words do not help.

Dragomir let the silence breathe, then filled it with what we had not asked for and would need.

"I have no eyes in Bogreach," he said. "No ears. The bogs close. There are paths that open for one man and drown another. The ones I sent did not return. The ones who did, did not speak plainly. They stank of peat and said little and laughed at their own empty hands."

"The rebels," Markov said, too cheerful. "They like it when the king is deaf."

"There is something more than men there," Dragomir said, and the way he set the words down made even the gulls hold a beat of quiet. "Not saints. Not devils. Not the old oaths you pretend not to know. Something else. And a weapon. Fire that eats everything. That burns even water. Does not go out when you drown it."

He watched our faces. Markov's grin left. My hand clenched without meaning to; I felt sweat in my palm though the night was cold. Fire that drowned water—that was no weapon a soldier could meet with steel.

"This is not the only fracture in the realm," Dragomir said, voice low, as if tired of being the man who knows things first. "Its timing is unwanted. In the north, Grey Isle rises. The king's breath is shorter than a prayer. You will hear it called rumour. It is not rumour. It is the shape of the months ahead."

We watched the water again because there was nowhere else for our eyes to go.

"I will report to the queen," Dragomir went on. "What I saw. What I did not see. That the prince hides behind his town, raises drums, and plays at being king in a hall that is not his. That you, Yaroslav, stand between oath and rebellion and do not move your feet, because you know there is no ground to step to that will bear you. That Markov runs his tongue like a blade and cuts the air into shapes men can swallow."

Markov bowed once, serious for a single breath.

Dragomir's ruined hand lifted, palm open, as if he could weigh the drums with it. "March north. Sail. Do what you will. The road ends in the same place—unless one of you can change where it leads. If the prince lives, there will be a rope to take hold of when the queen's hand lets go. If he dies, when that rope snaps, you will learn what falling feels like in a kingdom."

He turned at last. His cloak caught the wind and snapped once like a flag. He walked the quay without haste, down to the waiting skiff. Oarsmen held their breath as he stepped in, and they pulled hard for the black-sailed warship that bore the King's Hand — white and stark against damp wool.

The ship took him aboard without cheer, the banner lifting stiff in the morning breeze. Above the keep, Illarion's Burning Crown still flew. Two masters, two signs, clawing the same sky. Dragomir did not look back. He did not need to. He had seen what he came to see: a town answering drums that were not the Crown's, a soldier with a closed mouth, a jester who could count.

Markov's breath came out slow. "He's not wrong," he said. "About any of it."

"Aye," I said.

Markov gave a short laugh. "Strange, isn't it? He walks off empty-handed. No relic, no prince, not even a token show of loyalty. Lets us go without paying a coin. I don't trust men who take nothing when they could take all."

"He didn't take nothing," I said. The words came heavier than I meant. "He took what he wanted. Our measure. Our lies. Our truths. That's coin enough for now. We'll pay the rest in the mire, against rebels and fire, lashed to a prince half-mad with zeal. We'll pay when the Queen reads his words and weighs her fury. And when we stand in Velgrad, we'll pay again. One debt, many tolls. None of them merciful."

He had come with orders to take and claim, and left with neither prince nor relic. The Queen might gnash her teeth, but Dragomir never left empty-handed. His greatest weapon was not steel but knowing—he had tallied us already, weighing use against danger, asset against liability.

What had he written? A prince daring a banner not his own, willing to cleave the world apart if it would not bend. A prophet who cloaked command in prayer, binding men with chains of fire and faith. A rat sly enough to live where stronger men drowned. An old hound, scarred and mean, who might still bite if pointed right—and who had not yet earned the mercy of putting down. Even Yelka: named chernoknizhnika—perhaps only to test what she would yield, perhaps marked as a piece still waiting on the board.

That was Dragomir's gift: to turn men into sums. To strip away what they swore and write only what they were worth. And the worst of it was this—he was rarely wrong. I told myself I was a soldier, that I served the Crown, that all I had done was necessity. He saw only an old killer, teeth dulled but still expected to bite when commanded. Perhaps that was all I had ever been.

Out on the grey the King's Hand shoved off, black wool snapping, the white hand on its masthead stark as a promise. The oars ate the water in even strokes; the ship slid free and took Dragomir with it, a wedge of purpose moving away from our quay. Behind us the work rose again — wheels creaked, axes rang, a line of voices counted loads onto a raft. Not march yet, but the shape of one being built.

Markov swallowed hard, his face pale as morning mist. "Saints' wounds," he breathed. "What have I helped set in motion?"

"We've made our choice," I said. "Now to live with it."

We took the harbour stairs up, boots ringing dull in the damp. The sounds kept time for us — iron struck, wood groaned, men shouted to one another — not the Crown's order, only the will of a man who had decided the world should bend, and set hands to make it so. Inside, oaths lay like knives crossed over my heart—each step north would drive them deeper.

Chapter XLVI: The Gate of Oaths

Day turned on day. Illarion's order at dusk was the seed; we watered it in sweat.

Ironholt became a forge. Smiths hammered heads to fit spear-shafts, re-riveted armour split in Ashenbay's salt. A wheelwright coaxed an axle back into round. Peat-cliffs were cut for carts, bakers sealed loaves in oilcloth, cooks boiled meat until the fat cleared. Nothing left to waste. The city, broken by fire, bent itself into order, and all that labour moved to one end: the march north.

And still, each morning and evening, the swelling ranks of the Discipline moved through their forms. Illarion had named them Holy Fire. Markov broke them into files and fives. But the men called them only *the Discipline*. Already they called themselves that too — as if name and body and step had become one. Their rhythm filled the square where houses had once stood, burned rafters cleared down to hard earth. Shields locked, spear-butts struck, breath rose in white plumes. Their steps struck like a drumbeat that carried farther than drill.

I stood at their head, Illarion beside me, measuring his host. His bandage showed white in the mist, but his eye was bright. He had come back from the grave, and he meant to make it pay.

And he noticed the Brack moving within the ranks, but without weapons. The collared worked through the sequences Markov had allowed them: bare hands, bare feet, bodies cutting and closing like oars on black water. Captives still chained at night, yet they moved with fervour, as if the forms were prayer.

"Who are they?" Illarion asked.

"The captives," I said. "Forty-four from the sea, thirty from Ironholt. They asked to move. I let them. Without steel."

"Why without?"

"One slit a guard's throat with a nail," I said. "I hanged him. He still hangs there." I pointed above, where crows worked the corpse.

Illarion's gaze lingered. "Good."

Mikhail's count rolled across the square; the Brack finished their sequence and stood open-handed.

"Arm them," Illarion said.

"No."

His head turned, smile small as bone. "No?"

"Put steel in a foe's hand, and you set the edge at your own throat," I said.

"They swore to Christ and to me."

"Words are wind. A man can kneel at an altar and rise with murder still in him."

A pause held between us. Illarion's eye weighed me, then the captives. Into that silence a voice carried—steady, not loud:

"Anointed."

One man stepped forward— scarred from the collar, face hollow yet unbroken. He knelt, head to the earth. Illarion watched him as one watches a dog, curious whether it will bite.

"Speak."

"I am Kazek. Bound, but I speak for more than myself. Many here have no love for the rebels. Hunger pressed us, chains drove us. Now we see truth: the Anointed, and the Wolf Otets."

Murmurs rippled. I felt the word strike me like a thrown stone.

Kazek lifted his chin. "The Otets speaks true. Christ is far, nailed to His cross. If you would take our oath, let us swear the oath no Brack would break. A third oath, the truest. Let us swear to Saint Zorian — the Watcher — He Who Stands at the Threshold."

The name moved them. Shoulders tensed; breath caught. Even townsfolk flinched as if an old bone had been dug from the earth. Some crossed themselves; a priest muttered hurried prayer. The name was not safe to speak, yet it lived under their tongues still.

Illarion's brow arched. "Explain."

Kazek met his eye. "Before your priests, he was Zoryan, Keeper of the Threshold. Reed to river, house to road, flesh to death. He weighs. No man lies to a threshold — he passes, or not. Your priests made him saint and set him by the nave door. But we know him. He is the same. Swear us there, Prince, at a gate. Let the Watcher weigh us. If we lie, let Him shut us out."

Illarion smiled, not at Kazek but at the neatness of the hinge. "A gate," he said. "We will have a gate."

At dusk they knelt at Ironholt's northern gate, where charred beams had been raised into an arch. Seventy-four Brack bent to the earth. Torches flared. The townsfolk crowded close; soldiers pressed in, uneasy. The raven wheeled black above the smoke.

Kazek was the first. He touched the beam, blackened wood beneath his palm. He swore in his tongue and in ours: to Illarion, the Anointed; to me, though I had never claimed that title; and to Saint Zorian, who stood at thresholds unseen. One by one they followed, voice after voice, vow after vow. Some spoke steady, some shook, some whispered—but all crossed beneath the beam as if passing from one life to another.

Illarion named each man as he rose. His voice did not falter. Kazek, Drazhan, Miro, Stanek—he spoke them back into being as if they had always been his. Each name fell like a benediction, and I saw how their eyes lit when he spoke them. To a Brack, a man who calls your name is more than lord—he becomes keeper of your soul, the one you follow beyond sense or survival.

They swore to Illarion, the Anointed, and to me whom they called Otets though I was no man's father. They swore in the name of Saint Zorian, but I heard the older name beneath it—Zoryan, the Threshold-Keeper, the god who guards the passage between worlds. Old oaths die hard in the blood.

I should have felt triumph. Seventy-four swords sworn to our cause, men who would hold where others broke. We needed them. God knows we needed them. Yet watching Illarion speak their names, watching belief kindle in faces that had been empty hours before, I felt something colder than triumph.

I had seen this before. Men raised up not for what they were, but for what desperate people needed them to be. The Brack looked at Illarion as if the Saint himself had descended, as if his word could unbind death itself. And Illarion—he did not refuse their faith. He took it, wore it, fed on it. Perhaps he even believed it himself by now.

Such belief can lift a man higher than any throne. It can also make monsters of the faithful and corpses of the anointed. The question was not whether Illarion would fall—all men fall. The question was how many he would drag down with him, and whether I would be the one who placed the rope in his hands.

Chapter XLVII: The Burning Crown Marches

Illarion set his army in order. Its size belied its strength—near four hundred souls if one were generous, though half were farmers who still blistered from their first march. What he lacked in steel he clothed in fire.

At the head stood Illarion himself, scarred face lit as if by coals within, no longer only prince but commander. His counsellors flanked him: Bogdan in black robes, his scripture smouldering on the tongue, and Yelka with her wolf and raven, herbs in her pouch and judgment in her gaze. Between them they looked a trinity—altar, prophecy, and fate—but Yelka's eyes gave no sign she claimed such place. She stood apart even at his side, wolf at heel, raven overhead, as if her oath was to something older.

Beneath that strange trinity came me. General, though the word tasted foreign. My task was to hold the line when zeal frayed, to make sure the army fought like soldiers and not dreamers.

The sotniki were now Mikhail, sword and shield, a hundred under him, steadier than most. Sava, bowmen, eighty thin-eyed and quick-handed, each with a quiver patched twice over. Borislav, elevated again for his valour, and because the men loved him, sworn to axes, eighty men who looked at him as if his youth were proof of their own. And then Zdravko, Stormgrave-born, hardened in Illarion's cruellest drills and bloodied in battles that left more corpses than survivors. Cruel, vicious, but not reckless—he never ran into danger, only made certain others did. Illarion gave him a hundred spears.

To Markov, Illarion gave the scouts—trusting his cunning and fear of being found. Twenty knives and quick feet. He sent them out before sun and after it: once to pace the ridges, once to ride the bog's edge. They came back with hands peat-brown, eyes hollow, muttering of half-drowned causeways and water that drank horses whole. Deadwater lay black to the north, watching, as if daring men to trust its shore.

Illarion named a new banner-bearer—Velemir, a tall lad from Saltcross, chosen more for his reach than his years, but steady enough to hold the Burning Crown aloft.

Among the files were thirty druzhinniki from Velgrad and Stormhold, what remained of real soldiers. Forty-five Driftlight boys, no longer farm-sons but blooded on Ironholt's walls. Seventy-four oath-sworn Brack, collars gone, iron traded for oath. And two hundred and fifty more—raw recruits from town and country, men who had seen fire on the prince's brow and believed.

It was not an army fit for crowns. It was an army for pyres.

Each night Ironholt grew quieter under the same busy sounds: a hammer far off, a scolded curse, a drumline beaten again and again until the mallet fit a man's palm like a second heart. The rhythm was not yet summons but memory, so that even in sleep their breath fell to the beat.

Illarion stood among it, gaunt frame hung with a cloak too fine for war, face a ruin lit by fever's fire. Beside him Borislav bore the banner, straight-backed, jaw clenched to keep the tremor from showing. He had taken his place again, not as boy but as bearer.

Lord Kozlov made his show before the march. He had begged a place in Illarion's shadow, and when the hour came, he led out a horse sleek as could be bred in this mire. Its mane was combed, hooves oiled, saddle cinched with too much care.

"Take it, my prince," he said, loud enough for the square to hear. "So you will not forget who gave it, when songs are sung."

Illarion's ruined mouth drew a smile that was not mockery but something near kindness. He mounted smooth despite the tremor, cloak falling about him like judgment. "I will not forget," he said, and Kozlov's shoulders sagged as though the words had already minted him into history.

Illarion turned then to the garrison captain, the man still bandaged from Ashenbay's fires, armour patched with wire. "You will march with us," Illarion said, and it was not question.

The captain shook his head. "My oath is to Ironholt. These walls are bled thin already. If I go, there will be nothing left but ash and old men."

Illarion held his gaze for a long breath, then nodded once. "Then keep what is yours. Guard it well." No curse, no threat. Only dismissal. That too was judgment.

Ivan came, shoulders wrapped in furs, silver torque biting at his neck. He faced his son—Borislav, sotnik now, eighty axemen behind him, the very weapon Ivan once made his name with. One glance, heavy as a blow, passed between them. Borislav's lips parted as if to speak, then shut again. The words did not come, but Ivan did not look away. Something between them eased, not healed but unknotted enough that it might hold.

Soroka stood apart on the quay, cloak drawn against the morning chill. She did not beg to come; her place was with the Grey Hand and the fleet. Illarion gave her orders to hold Driftlight's harbour until his return. She saluted, no flourish, only iron steadiness. When she looked to me, I found myself wishing she marched with us. Ships had keels and beams that did not waver. Men, less so.

At dusk, before the march, Markov and I were summoned. The Burning Crown was lowered in silence, its canvas cover drawn tight. Together we lifted the reliquary from its place—iron box seared black by the heat within, heavy as guilt. Illarion watched, face carved from fire and ruin; Bogdan muttered scripture, each word thin as a chain. We set it in a wagon already laden with pitch and spears. Canvas was thrown over, ropes knotted twice. To any eye it was another cart of war-stores. Only we four knew different. Bogdan climbed to ride beside it, hands folded as if the reins themselves were prayer. Illarion would not be parted from him, and through them the fire remained at the heart of the march.

At last, all was ready. The gates opened, the drums thundered, and Ironholt spilled its heart. Banners caught the morning light, wagons rattled, and the sound of boots on stone rolled like surf. Spirits rose with the beat. Men laughed too loud, their talk thick with boasts. They clutched bread and smoked fish as if the world itself had bent to provision them.

Markov's twenty knives went first, slipping through reeds and ridges, shadows against the bog.

We marched north on the Mireway, rank on rank.

At the head rode Illarion, gaunt frame in the saddle, face a ruin lit by fire within. Beside him Velemir bore the Burning Crown upright, the banner-guard tight around him.

Yelka kept her own distance, the wolf loping silent at her heel, the raven wheeling high above, a shadow against the pale sun.

Behind them, Mikhail's hundred swords, shields striking thighs in rhythm, steady as iron.

Borislav's axemen next, eighty young and fierce, their prince's squire at their front, jaw clenched as if to prove youth could be an oath.

Then Zdravko's spears, a hundred cruel and hard from drills and battles that had spared few. They marched without haste, as if danger were theirs to give, not meet.

Sava's bowmen followed—eighty lean-eyed, quivers patched and twice-mended, steps light, hands always on the string.

The weight of the host pressed after: wagons groaning under spears, kegs of pitch, salted meat, water casks, and spare timber, guarded by freedmen and druzhinniki who had marched too many roads already.

Among them walked Kazek, no rank but always near the prince's wagon. He guarded nothing that mattered, yet men began to mark his place, muttering that a Brack had found favour at last. Each time Illarion glanced back, Kazek dropped to one knee in the mud, striking his chest with a fist. Others copied him, awkward at first, then certain, until the gesture spread like fire through dry reeds.

One wagon bore more than stores. Beneath canvas and rope lay the reliquary, heavy and seared black, its fire hidden from the men. Bogdan rode at its side, black robes stiff with salt, lips moving ceaselessly. Men thought he prayed for the march, and maybe he did. But I felt him speaking to the relic as if it answered.

A few bowmen lingered as rear-guard, to cut pursuit or drive stragglers forward.

Four hundred souls if one were generous, though the count of real soldiers was less. Still, they moved to one beat, breath and shield and wheel, as if the forge of Ironholt had hammered them into a single shape.

By dusk we reached Ravenholt. The gates were thrown wide; folk lined the road, whispering into their hands at the sight of Illarion's scarred face. Yet none turned away. Awe is a kind of silence, and they gave him that in full. Bread was offered, beer poured, shoulders clapped as though we were champions returned.

The men drank deep of it. They were fed, admired, unbloodied. And I thought to myself: this is how armies believe—when food is warm, when cheers drown doubt, when the fighting lies still at a distance. Tomorrow the road would narrow, the forest would press close, and belief would have to hold without bread or praise. But for this one night, they felt themselves immortal.

Chapter XLVIII: Into the Witherholt

We left Ravenholt to cheers and bells, but before long the road bent downward, and the sound of water reached us. Foam showed between the trees—swift, black, white where it struck stone. Owl Creek. No bird called from its banks, and the name alone made men mutter.

Just beyond the bend stood a hut on a knoll above Owl Creek, herbs drying from the eaves, smoke pale against the trees. To the column it was nothing—just another cottage on the Mireway. But we remembered.

It was here we had come with Illarion half-dead, Bogdan's rites spent, the governor's fear driving us north. Here the raven had marked us, the wolf had measured us, and Yelka had stepped into our path with eyes older than her face. She had not chosen him then, nor coin, nor oaths—only the fire itself. And in that choice she had bound her road to ours.

Markov grinned as the men filed past. "Saints, we thought it might be rebels lying in wait behind that door. Came up ready for blades, whispers of Brack knives in the dark. What we found was worse—a girl with eyes older than her years. We thought to bargain for a poultice. Instead we wagered our necks."

Kazek, marching near, pressed his fist to his chest. "The Wolf Otets chose rightly then," he said, not to Markov but to me, and several Brack behind him nodded. Yelka's eyes flicked to me at the word, unreadable, as if she weighed whether it bound me more than I knew.

Yelka's mouth curved, quick as a knife. "You thought you chose. But fate does not ask frightened men their leave."

The wolf bounded ahead, tail high, pressing nose to the gate. The raven stooped low, croaking sharp, then wheeled to perch on the roof as if it had returned home. Yelka paused with her hand on the fence, but only for a breath. Then she stepped back into the march, the beasts flowing with her as if they had never left.

I called aside. "War lies ahead. You could remain here. Safe. Tending your plants, your beasts. Leave fire and blood to us."

Her gaze found mine, steady, unflinching. "My place is not mine to choose, Wolf. You of all men should know that." and then quieter, "The path is set. To turn aside now would be the truer death."

<hr>

Past Owl Creek the Mireway narrowed, and the Witherholt received us. The forest was older than memory — spruce black as spears, aspen and pine woven tight so no light reached the ground. Moss bled water at every step, and the air hung heavy with resin.

No bird called. No wind stirred. Yet the men swore shapes moved beyond the line of march, slow and deliberate, keeping pace. Armies move by rhythm — drums, breath, cadence of step. Here the rhythm broke. The forest set its own measure, older than kings. The first day had belonged to the men. The second belonged to the trees.

By nightfall we were swallowed whole. The Witherholt pressed close, spruce and pine knotting the sky, aspen leaves whispering though no wind moved. Roots twisted like ribs beneath the moss, and every step felt measured by eyes we could not see. Men muttered of shapes moving beyond the march.

We made camp where the Mireway widened to a dry shoulder. Fires smoked thin in the damp air. Armour steamed, boots stank, men stank worse. No one laughed now. Among the Brack captives only Kazek seemed untroubled. He set the count for their small file, voice harsh but steady, and they moved through the barehanded forms while the rest of the army muttered of shapes in the trees. Men watched him sidelong, half in distrust, half in envy of his certainty.

Bogdan set his mass in the open, black robes stark against the firelight. His voice rolled smooth and low, but the trees took it and flung it back, so each phrase echoed as if spoken from behind us. Some crossed themselves twice. Others would not look into the dark.

Markov dropped beside me, unlacing his boots with a groan. "Gods curse these roads. My feet are blistered raw. The whole army reeks like a midden, and somehow I've ended up marching to war. Me. A trader of knives and lies, not a banner-man."

I looked at him. "So don't be a hero. Stay alive. That's enough."

He tried a grin, half-hearted. "And if war asks more than that?"

"Then let someone else answer."

Illarion summoned us at dusk: myself, Markov, Bogdan, and Yelka.

We had halted deep in the Witherholt, where the trees leaned close and the ground sucked at boots. The army camped a bowshot off, their fires dim through the reeds. Only Viktor and Andrei kept near, at the edge of hearing. A wagon sat behind us, covered in canvas, the relic's weight inside it. Men thought it carried pitch and spears. They were not wrong. They simply did not know what else it bore.

Markov and I came first. The prince sat in the firelight, gaunt frame wrapped in cloak, face ruined but set hard. His eyes no longer wandered with fever. Shadows clung, but strength returned.

Bogdan followed, beads in hand, robe's hem wet with mire. His eyes glowed as if the fire already obeyed him.

Last came Yelka. Grendel padded at her side, yellow eyes catching flame, teeth bared whenever Bogdan drew near. Morwen dropped from a branch to her shoulder, wings brushing her hair, glassy eyes fixed on Illarion as though weighing him for burial.

Bogdan spat. "This work suffers no witchcraft."

Illarion's scarred mouth curled, not in smile but in command. "The wolf knows the fen, the raven knows the sky. She commands both, and she holds secrets I need. She stays."

Grendel's hackles rose, silent but ready, as if to mark the decision. Morwen only croaked once, low and harsh. Bogdan's lips tightened, but he bent his head.

Illarion looked to me. "Krovin. You say she knows of the relic."

"She learned."

Markov did not even feign shame. "My heart spoke. She tricked me with beauty." He grinned, but when he thought no one watched, the mask slipped. His face was measured, wary — seeing her now as something colder than charm.

Yelka's eyes never left Illarion. "He told me what I already knew. Fire tells its own truths, if you know how to watch."

"Demon-fire," Bogdan hissed.

"Or truths your saints fear," she answered.

Illarion lifted his hand, and the silence was sharp. "The relic. The bones of Saint Ilyin. They lie hidden in the mire. Gather them, and the saint will be whole again — and whole, will grant power. Power even to grant life itself."

Bogdan's eyes flared. "The fire of God — as on Sinai!"

Yelka's answer came cool as water. "And as at Gomorrah. Fire heals, yes. But more often it devours." She held his gaze until his beads clicked harder in his fist. Grendel pressed closer to her leg.

Illarion turned to her. "What do you know?"

She stood very still.

She stood still, the raven shifting on her shoulder. It croaked once, harsh. She tilted her head, eyes narrowing. "Hush, Morwen." The bird stilled, but its eyes stayed fixed on Bogdan.

Bogdan's hiss between his teeth was all venom.

When Yelka spoke, her voice carried the weight of something passed down in whispers, mother to daughter, smoke to smoke.

Yelka stood very still. When she spoke, her voice was low, words falling like reeds snapped one by one.

"Fire was the first gift. The hearth. The healing flame. But there was another fire—carried in bone. It burned without end. No water quenched it. No earth smothered it. My mother's mother called it poison."

The wolf lay close at her, steady as stone.

"She told me they bound it. Sealed it in urns. Cast them into the black mire where no light could follow. Swore it must never rise again."

She paused, as if with words unsaid. Then, after a breath, continued.

"Yet greed is patient. Some drew them back. They found visions—storms, commands, fates. The fire ate them hollow. Left their lungs like ash. Cursed, outcast, untouchable. But conquest makes use of all it finds. In the breaking, they rose again. Outcasts became covenant."

Her fingers tightened on her staff.

"They call themselves Fire Volkhvy. Their elder—Vrasida—binds them with blood and flame. They are not whispers. They are the rebellion's heart. They would see the mire burn, and any who refused them." Her hand tightened on her staff, knuckles white, but she gave no reason why the words seemed to wound her more than the rest of us.

Morwen shifted, wings rustling, glass eyes catching the firelight.

Her words left a hush. Even Bogdan's tongue stilled.

Illarion's hand trembled, though from sickness or hunger I could not tell. The firelight carved hollows in his ruined face, so the scars seemed less flesh than molten seams, as if what burned inside him might yet break through. "I saw it," he rasped. "As I lay dying. A fang—black stone, rimed with ice. Do you know it?"

"The Black Fang," Yelka said. "It is their mark. Cut into talismans. A sign."

"No," Illarion snapped, fierce, desperate. "Not a sign. A place. I saw it."

Yelka's gaze dropped, shadowed. "The Bogreach holds many secrets. Some say the Fire Volkhvy keep their flame there. A place where the land rises sharp, like a tooth from black water. The Fang. Rumours speak of fire that will not drown, burning even on the mire. It is the heart of the rebellion, and of their power. If the vision is true, then your path is set. Destiny waits in the Bogreach."

Illarion dismissed us. Yelka left with her beasts, the wolf brushing her leg, the raven launching skyward with a cry that rasped like iron.

I watched them go. The wagon sat heavy in the dark, the relic chained within. Fire waited in the mire, unquenchable. Whether it would raise us or ruin us, I could not say. I only knew my oath would drag me to meet it.

Chapter XLIX: Stone Bridge

Two days we marched in the Witherholt, and it had no end. Roots clawed our path, water stank of rot, and the men's boots grew heavy with black muck until each step landed like a grave shovelled shut. Salt pork turned slick in its own fat; moss-strained water tasted of rust. The boys of Driftlight muttered old prayers against reed-spirits. The freedmen spat into the mire, swearing it kept their lungs clear.

By the second day the forest itself began to sicken. The ground sagged, bleeding into pools. Trees stood farther apart, their crowns ragged against a darkening sky. Wind shifted wet and cold, salt riding its edge as though the sea had pushed its tongue inland. The air bit at us like knives left in ice. Men slowed without meaning to. They knew this land swallowed armies.

Toward dusk the world broke open. The Witherholt spat us out onto its edge, and what lay before was no longer forest but mire. Water spread black and wide between roots. Reed-mats drifted like broken rafts. The sun sank low, but its light was dimmed, swallowed by haze that thickened to the north.

Then we saw it: a river wide as judgment, black as poison, sliding slow as oil. The stench of it struck first—peat, sulphur, something older. Its surface bore no ripple, no bird, nothing living. It stretched from east to west as far as sight, a moat of foul water drawn before the Bogreach as if the land itself wanted no trespasser.

Across it rose stone: a bridge, broad and ancient, ribbed with lichen, its arch humped like the spine of some drowned beast. The stone was dark, almost green-black, slick with years of rot. It was the only crossing. Looking on it, men drew breath as though they had seen salvation. I felt only dread. It was no gift. It was a threshold. Cross, and you might never return.

Kazek fell to one knee at the bridgehead and pressed his forehead to the stone, as if the Watcher weighed him anew. He rose with mud on his brow and shouted that the Gate had opened for the Anointed. The captives behind him copied, half in zeal, half in fear of being left outside. Men who might have fled pressed forward instead, eager not to be shut out by whatever power Kazek claimed had judged them.

Markov's scouts waited on the far bank. Their faces told the tale before their tongues moved. The Bogreach burned.

Not a hearth-fire, not village flame, but swathes of mire aflame. Smoke rose in black pillars, thick as storm-clouds, blotting half the northern sky. Even across the water we smelled the stench — peat and flesh smouldering together.

Illarion stood at the bridge's crest, the last sun striking his ruined face. He did not flinch. Bogdan's beads clicked sharp as bones under a knife. Yelka stood with her wolf pressed close, her raven circling above. The bird croaked once, harsh and slow, and men shivered as if judged. She did not flinch, only watched the smoke with an expression I could not read — healer weighing sickness, or witch marking omen.

I gripped Pryaz, its steel colder than water. We had come to strike — but fire had already struck first.

Illarion would not risk the army penned on the southern side, where one torch could cut us off with the river at our backs. So we marched over — stone beneath our feet, black poison sliding below, the reeds whispering like teeth in the wind.

The north bank was worse. Mud sucked at boots, gnats swarmed in choking clouds. The ground gave no echo when struck—only a thump like flesh. We raised camp on a strip of firmer earth where bridge met land. No fires. Only hooded pitch-lamps, their glow pressed low.

The men muttered. The Brackfolk worst of all. They spat charms into the muck, whispering of Bogreach men who drank flame and breathed it back as judgment, of trees that lured wanderers with voices sweet as kin before crushing them in roots, of black shapes that slipped under water and pulled a man down without ripple or cry. And more than once I heard the same curse, muttered in Driftlight's tongue: the Fang has opened its mouth.

Boys who had sworn oaths in Driftlight now swore new ones: never to sleep until we had left the Bogreach behind. And still the mire glowed. Not with flame we could see, but with a dull ochre shimmer behind the smoke, as though embers smouldered under the water itself. The air stank scorched though no fire touched our eyes.

Few slept. I walked the lines until my legs ached, watching boys twitch at every rustle, freedmen clutch axes like charms, even the druzhinniki glancing back at the bridge as though it might vanish by morning.

I found Markov sitting on a coil of rope, knife point idly scratching a knot. No grin on him. His eyes tracked the raven circling high against the stars, then dropped quick when he saw me.

"You're quiet," I said.

"Not quiet." He shook his head. "Just… less fool than I was."

I raised a brow. He gave a short laugh with no humour in it.

"When she came, I was blind. A fool, aye. Foreign, beautiful, strong, dangerous—so sure of herself. I was drawn like a moth to a flame." His hand tightened on the knife. "But there's more to it, Yarik. I think maybe she cast a spell on me."

"You're a man, Markov. She's a woman. That's no witchcraft—just you trying to impress her."

He shook his head hard. "No. You remember when she chose me to help her? All the time I spent at her side—fetching, boiling, holding—and then what happens? I told her about the relic. Saints, the secrets I've kept, Yarik. The things I've swallowed that would've bought my weight in gold. And then I meet one girl, and I spill the truth?"

I waited.

His voice dropped. "She saw me for what I am—weak. Easy to twist. She isn't what she says, Yarik. Not healer. Not znakharka. No village-witch either. At first I thought she might be Volkhva. But no. She's something darker."

Dragomir's word rose in my mind—chernoknizhnika. Black-book reader.

Almost as if he read my thought, Markov went on, "If she wanted the prince dead, she's had a dozen chances. But she keeps him alive. She keeps him listening. And now he hears her almost as much as Bogdan. How is that even possible?

He believes every mad word that priest spits, and still — still she has him."

I told him he was imagining shadows, but in my heart I wasn't sure.

Markov leaned close, voice harsh. "No, Yarik. I'm telling you — she manipulates him. She maneuvers him. Maybe all of us. Remember when she told him to march north? He followed. There's something coming, and I don't like it."

Above, the raven croaked once, harsh. Markov flinched and set his jaw. "I don't trust her beauty anymore. That was the bait. Now I want to know the hook — and whether the men will see it before it's in their throats."

I listened. His words had teeth, sharper than his jokes.

I thought of telling Illarion. Dragging him from his fever and watching him laugh it away. But he would not listen. We had no proof — only a worry, and the night's teeth in us. Still, I felt it in my bones. She could not be trusted. Her intentions would show themselves in time; if she was fire, she would burn us by degrees, as fire does.

Until then there was only one thing to do: forward. Hold. Keep the line. Nothing else buys breath.

I laid a hand on his shoulder. "Maybes don't make blades. I don't kill on whispers. If she lights us and men burn, name her. Say the word — I'll do it. Proof, not panic."

It was a long night. And when dawn came, none of us were rested — only raw, as if the mire had already set its hook in us, and the battle ahead was only the line drawing tight.

Chapter L: Through Fire and Water

We went in single file, three hundred men wound through the mire. Markov led with his scouts, pale reeds parting before them, icy water lapping at their thighs. Illarion and I followed, and behind us the line shivered forward one by one—shields strapped, heads bowed, breath steaming in the cold.

The mire showed no mercy. Each step was weight and doubt. The paths were narrow, half-submerged, black earth crusted thin over water that sucked and bit. Stray too far and you sank. I had told them—no armour, no helms, no weight beyond shields. Some listened. Others did not. Fear makes men cling to steel, even when steel kills faster than the enemy. Those who bore it tired first, legs heavy, boots dragging. One stumbled and the mire swallowed him to the waist before they hauled him out. He limped on, broken. The file stepped around him, and he was lost behind us.

Scouts waded on either flank, water to their hips, faces taut with every ripple. They carried no torches, only knives and short pikes. If the Volkhvy had watchers here, they would see us only as a shadow smearing through the reeds. That was Illarion's command—no sound, no light, no mail. Surprise was the only shield left to us.

The cold bit deeper the farther we pressed. Breath came in clouds. The sun was gone, the sky lowered to smoke. The mire smelled of sulphur, rot, and old iron. Every so often the path vanished beneath water, and we had to step down blind, boots sinking into mud, water slapping our bellies before the boards rose again. Men cursed low, or prayed. Some spat charms against spirits. Others muttered the

Fang's name, as if the land itself had opened its mouth to swallow us.

We had no punts, no rafts. The wagons stayed behind under heavy guard—axes mostly, Illarion's order. They were to cut trees and shape poles, build rafts against our return. If we took the temple ahead, we would send for them. If not, the supplies were lost anyway. Better to risk men than lose both men and meat to the water. Yelka waited with them, Grendel pressed close. Morwen did not. The raven lifted from the wagon-rail as we went and shadowed the column—black against the smoke, slow-winged, keeping to our dead ground. Men flinched when her shadow crossed their faces and then pretended they hadn't.

I remembered Mstislav's campaign through these same swamps, and the men who had laughed at warnings. One gone in a sinkhole, another dragged under with no ripple, armour shining for an instant before black water shut above him. I remembered the temples too—stilts rising from the mire like black teeth, archers braced above. You could not cut their legs—the wood was too hard, peat-cured and old as stone. The only hope was shields locked tight, a rush up their ramps, or surprise before the arrows found you.

Illarion knew it. He said nothing as we marched, but his scars gleamed faint in the smoke-light, his ruined face hard. Not the reckless prince who once stood bare-headed on the sea trusting in saints. This one counted cost in silence, and his silence weighed more than any speech.

The file moved. Three hundred men, strung through the black water like a rope ready to break. I gripped Pryaz at my hip, its weight a reminder. Black steel, colder than the water around it.

The line dragged forward, boots sucking, shields scraping, breath harsh in the fog. The cold thickened until it felt like the air itself bit us. Fog pressed down from the smoke-stained sky, closing sight to a few yards. Men vanished in front of me and reappeared as grey shadows, no more substance than ghosts.

The mire grew louder. Not the men—most held their tongues—but the land itself. Reeds hissed in shifting gusts. Birds called once, sharp and strange, and were answered by another farther off. Not the same note. A signal. The scouts stiffened. Markov muttered something sharp, eyes flicking to the raven's shadow above. "Her bird's voice in their throats," I thought I heard, but the mist swallowed the rest.

Markov raised a hand without turning. "Something's wrong," he muttered, voice nearly lost in the mist. I pointed forward. There was no turning back.

The water deepened. What had lapped at boots now licked thighs, then hips. Shields dragged. Men cursed as they tried to lift them high. The path dipped unseen, then rose again only in places. Many waded off its edge without knowing, chest-deep in the cold black. Panic rippled through the line like a shiver.

Then the fog shifted.

The reeds thinned. The water opened wide. For a breath the file faltered—no cover, no shadows, nothing but the black spread before us. Out of it rose the temple, its stilts like sharpened stakes, its body crouched high above the mire. Narrow ramps coiled up its legs. Shadows moved along its edge, vague through the smoke, but we knew. Archers. Watchers. Death waiting.

Illarion lifted his hand, and the men began to spread, breaking single file to fan toward the stilts. Water surged to their chests, icy, pulling breath from mouths. Shields lifted overhead, dripping and heavy.

Then it came.

A sound like the world tearing open—deep, grinding, shrieking as though the mire itself screamed. One, then another, then a chorus. Catapults? No. Something older, worse. A thunder of jars launched into the dark. They shattered in mid-air and on water, bursting into sheets of flame.

Fire that burned on water.

It roared across the mire, orange and green, oil-fed, unquenchable. The air howled with heat and smoke. Men shrieked as it caught their shields, their cloaks, their hair. The black water itself burned, reflecting back the light until the fog became a chamber of flame.

The Fire Volkhvy had waited. And now they struck.

The fire fell on us like judgment, and men broke like kindling. Some fled back into our line, shields wreathed in flames that clung like living things, eating through leather and flesh alike. Others pressed forward through the shallows, wading chest-deep while the water around them turned to liquid fire. Their faces seared in the glow, eyes wide and white, mouths open in screams the flames devoured.

The temple loomed above us—a fortress of death perched on rotting stilts. Its dock led straight to the first storey, a killing floor boxed in by slits. Above, a second platform jutted out into the smoke, where urn-bearers moved with their jars. Arrows hissed from the low windows, urns arced from the heights, and the mire burned red below.

An arrow punched through young Luka's throat with a wet crack. He was barely seventeen, beard still soft. The shaft jutted from his neck like an obscene finger as he toppled backward, blood frothing from his mouth to mix with the burning water. The flames spread from his corpse in hungry tongues.

"Forward, you dogs!" Illarion bellowed from the open water, his scarred face a mask of red-lit fury. For a heartbeat he stood like a corpse lit by fire, but I saw death reaching for him — three arrows arcing down like striking hawks.

I lunged and caught him by the shoulder, hauling him flat behind a sodden clump of reeds. He thrashed like an ox in pain, every muscle a promise of hurt. "You would have me crawl like a cur?" he spat, flecks of blood and salt on my cheek.

"I'd keep you breathing." My hand clamped the meat of his arm. Arrows thunked into the mud where he'd stood. "You die here, the kingdom dies with you."

His eyes burned with more than reflected flame, but his hand stayed from the hilt.

The east approach was a slaughter-plain of timber and rot. Men climbed the ramp in single files and were unmade. Clay jars burst, fire spilling like curses given form. Planks glowed red, flesh charred, boots slid in the slick. Bodies heaped so high the living had to climb them like a wall of dead. The screams braided into one endless note.

On the first storey, bowmen leaned from their slits, arrows hissing down into the press. Men went to their knees, pinned before flame touched them. Above, the urn-bearers ruled. Robes dark, arms scarred, they cast their fire into water, wood, and flesh alike.

Sava's bowmen answered from the mire. Their shafts arced through smoke, knocked men from the galleries. Sometimes they found the higher perch and brought an urn-bearer down, shattering with his load. But for each that fell, another rose, chanting louder than the arrows' hiss. They bought heartbeats, nothing more.

We slithered deeper into the marsh — twenty souls still mad enough to follow. Viktor and Andrei, silent as stone. Borislav burned beside me, fever-bright, half a dozen axemen already stinking of pyre. Mikhail kept his six hard swords close, discipline our only raft against the flood.

My limp dragged at me, each step a knife in the joint. No glory in it. Just a refusal to stop. Stand still and die.

The path twisted and failed. Through the reeds I saw them — shapes uncoiling from the temple's far side. Not common villagers, but the Fire Volkhvy: women robed in red-dark cloth, oil-jars cradled to their breasts like relics. With them moved their Otets — broad-shouldered men who flowed like water, skin dark with tattoos, hair bound for war, serpent blades strapped to their backs.

One Volkhva lifted her arms; the others began a harsh, low singing to the mire as they boarded. They did not flee like broken prey. They withdrew with the calm of those who know they will strike again.

At their head rode the heart of their power — a brazier of black iron, blue-white flames licking inside its bowl despite the damp. A woman with white hair held it to her breast as she stepped into the lead punt; her sisters closed around her in a ring. That fire was no common thing. It writhed like a living serpent, and the air above it shimmered with heat that should not have survived this sodden place.

They were already lost to us. Illarion's eyes flashed to the brazier—fierce as hunger and recognition both—but we could not chase. We were hemmed in by arrow and flame.

Watching them pole away into the mist, I saw our path. The front ramp was a slaughter-plain, arrows and urns waiting. But the coven's dock still jutted empty into the water on the far side. I pointed toward it and down—we would go beneath, through the dark water.

We slid into the freezing mire. The water was black as grave-water, cold as iron, dragging breath from our lungs. But it hid us from the archers above and offered a passage beneath their burning rain.

I pushed forward under the surface, lungs on fire, tasting mud and blood and things I did not want to name. My groping hand struck timber—the dock's algae-slick support beams. Above them, broad steps climbed toward the temple's belly. The back way in, unguarded now that the coven's guardians had fled with their precious flame.

Here, in the wake of their retreat, lay our chance to gut the temple from within.

We hauled out like drowned men, leather streaming, teeth rattling. Arrows hissed but we were under their arc now, too close.

Borislav pressed my shoulder, axe flashing. Illarion rose beside us, shield high, scarred face lit with fury hotter than the jars above. Together we drove up the blood-slick stairs.

My hand found Pryaz. The blade came free, black and thin as frost. It caught the firelight but gave nothing back. A spear glanced my shield; Pryaz split a throat as if it had been waiting.

The first line broke like reeds — boys with hollow cheeks and shaking spears. Behind them stood the true teeth: men with serpent blades slick with poison, their flesh carved with the Black Fang.

The dock ground and screamed under the press. Blood slicked the boards, ran in rivulets that swallowed footing. More of our people clawed up behind, screaming as arrows found gaps in mail.

Inside was worse. A maze of beams and nests. Arrows loosed at arm's length punched through shields. Spears shot from holes sudden as snakes, splitting throats, taking eyes. One found me. The point bit my side; fury burst from my mouth. Pryaz struck timber, bit deep, came back dripping. The air was thick enough to chew — pitch smoke, incense, blood. Spears cracked like bones. Knives slid between ribs. Men grappled like beasts.

Borislav pushed too far. His axe swung wide; a serpent blade slid under his ribs. He staggered, choking, and his axemen roared, dragging at his arms, trying to pull him back. I should have been faster. I should have been closer. Ivan had set me to guard him, and I reached for the boy as if my arm alone could turn back the cut, as if a vow could bind flesh against steel. But my hand found only his shoulder, already slick, already slipping away.

He sagged into the wall, spitting red. His eyes found mine — still fever-bright, still burning with fire he could not quench. His lips worked as though to form a word — father, prince, or nothing I could name. No sound came, only blood. Then his head fell, and the banner of Driftlight was gone from the world.

Andrei kept to Illarion's flank. A spear meant for the prince punched through his back. He collapsed into Viktor's arms, blood spilling over his chest. Viktor shoved him aside and Illarion surged on untouched.

A boy rushed me — couldn't have been more than fifteen, all elbows and desperate courage. His blade came up in a wild swing. I caught his wrist, turned it, felt the bones snap. My pommel caved in his temple and he dropped like a stone, blood pooling around his head. He twitched once, then lay still.

We carved deeper. Above, the second storey thundered with the fire-throwers. Jars shattered, liquid fire spread. Beams cracked like breaking teeth. Smoke rolled so thick it blinded. Men coughed blood, stumbled weeping, and still fought.

A rebel ran past, hair ablaze, swinging a broken spear. Mikhail's shield broke him down. Three of his men hacked until nothing moved. Then a jar struck Mikhail himself. Fire ate his mail, skin blistered, his scream cut short. He fell thrashing. The stink of him burned into my clothes.

"Up!" Illarion roared, his voice raw with smoke. "The stairs!"

We forced the steps, climbing over bodies. Five Otets barred the landing, serpent blades weaving in smoke, faces carved with the Fang. One lunged for my throat. Pryaz met him. Poison nicked my cheek, burning hot, but my steel slid under his ribs and ended him.

Illarion broke another — blades singing, then one buried in an eye. Death took him twitching.

At last we reached the Volkhvy platform. Ten women in black stood among their jars, arms scarred and painted with ash. We cut into them through smoke and heat. Pryaz drank robes, flesh, screams alike. The Black Fang carved on them was finished in blood by my hand. There was no triumph in it. Only the work.

"Take them alive!" Illarion shouted, desperation raw.

Too late.

One seized an urn, shrieking words I could not know, and dashed it to the floor.

Flame took them whole. The platform roared white, then black, the sound like a mountain breaking. Heat struck harder than steel. Timber burst, nails screamed loose. The air itself turned to fire.

Something lifted me — blast, hands, I could not tell. The floor gave way.

The blast stole sound as well as sight. For a moment I heard nothing but a long, rushing silence, as if the mire itself had exhaled. Then smoke closed over me like a hand. Screams, mine or theirs, blurred. The world rolled black and red. Pryaz slipped from my grasp and was gone.

When my eyes opened, the temple was behind me. Fire climbed the stilts rung by rung, beams cracking as they gave. Black smoke poured upward in choking columns, rolling over itself, thick as tar, blotting sky and sun alike. The air was poison — pitch, flesh, oil — each breath a wound in the lungs. Even the reeds bent from it, their green shriveling to ash. The marsh itself burned — water turned to judgment, bubbling, spitting fire back into the sky.

I was in the muck, dragged through reeds, my body tossed in another's grip. Illarion's ruined face loomed above, eyes red with flame. His hands were iron on my collar, hauling me clear of the ruin.

I remembered Yelka's tale — fire bound in bones, hunger without end. Not life, but a face that devours it. She had named it, and here it was, loosed before us.

Through the smoke came a sound — a raven's cry, long and cracked, or only the timber screaming. Black wings, or just the dark rolling over me. Healer stayed behind, but her shadow had followed. I could not tell. Then the dark took me.

Chapter LI: Through Ruin, Forward

I drifted in and out of waking, each return a cruelty.

I woke under weight — the press of bodies. Flesh slick with blood leaned heavy on me. The stench of pitch, ash, and burned hair filled my mouth. A knee ground my ribs. Beside my ear, a man's rattle sounded like drowning through mud. The planks beneath us groaned, black water slapping hollow against the hull as men hauled us inch by inch.

We were heaped like firewood, half-living and half-lost, dragged behind a rope line. No oars, no order. Just shoulders raw with strain, boots slipping on mud that might as well have been blood. They cursed and pulled, teeth clenched, hauling us back toward the bridge.

Above, reeds bent like mourners, smoke streaming east where the temple had stood. I tried to lift my head, failed. The world was weight and heat, the stink of char and ruin.

The temple had burned with all inside it — rebels and our own, locked together until fire judged them both. Near a hundred gone in the space between one breath and the next. Spears, axemen, swords, bows. Recruits who had scarcely learned to march, veterans who had. Fire devoured them without care. Their names ended in smoke. The Brackfolk suffered worst. Half their number cut down in the blaze, the rest burned raw. I saw Kazek, skin blackened where flame had kissed him, hair scorched to the scalp. Yet his lips moved still, whispering "the Anointed" as if each syllable were breath enough.

Only a few punts survived the wreck — patched planks, scorched timbers that would always stink of failure. Fifteen, twenty bodies dragged back, the rest left where flames and mire would finish the work. I was among the carried. Beside me men coughed once, twice, and fell still. By the time the boats scraped the bridge, half of what was hauled was already stiffening. Some lasted only until their boots touched planks, then dropped.

I watched them slip and could not tell if I envied them.

Illarion stripped in the open air and let them work while men gathered to stare. They could not look away — not from the ruin fire had carved into him, but from what endured. The right side of his face, his arm, his ribs — all blackened and raw, blistered flesh risen like islands from a sea of char. His tunic hung stiff with soot, heavy as a corpse.

Yelka knelt first, her hands steady with cloth and salve. She cleaned the burns, bound the rawest places, her voice low as she told him where to breathe. Yet her gaze was not on wounds alone. She watched him as if she knew the path already, and feared what might happen if he failed to walk it.

Bogdan stood above her shoulder, murmuring prayers, tracing the sign of flame across the ruined skin. His beads clicked once, then stilled, his voice the thread that held steady.

For a moment they did not fight. Healer and priest bent together over the same body, her herbs and his invocations working side by side. Neither yielded, neither broke.

Illarion endured them both. He did not weep, nor curse. He drank water with careful hands that shook badly enough to spill half down his scorched chest. When her fingers pressed deepest wounds, a low keen escaped him, and Bogdan's words wove through it like rope through water. Twice his head sagged as if sleep or faint would claim him, but he forced it back upright.

"I saw it," Illarion rasped, voice rough as ash. His eyes were fever-bright, fixed not on us but on the north. "The brazier. The same flame I dreamed. It waits."

Bogdan's face sharpened, joy and dread bound in one. "Yes. God's fire kept for you. Not lost, but waiting. Destiny itself." His words fell like chains, tightening with every syllable.

Yelka's green eyes did not flinch from the thought of flame. Yet the way they lingered, steady and unblinking, seemed less fire than mire — dangerous, patient, hungry. It was as if the bog itself looked through her, marking a path for him long before this night, and only waiting for ruin to drive him onto it.

The men watched and felt both fear and fire rise in them. His face was a ruin, his body a map of burns, yet heat seemed to shimmer from him as though he had carried the blaze back out — and meant to follow it.

We boiled the last grain into thin gruel that tasted of ash. Meat was torn small as coin, hoarded like prayers. To eat felt like theft from the dead, but it steadied the hands.

Sleep came in fits. Men woke choking, hands reaching for weapons that were gone, names on their lips that no one answered. Yelka moved among them like winter's midwife, binding wounds of flesh and spirit. Grendel pressed close at her side, a black shadow with eyes like coals, his presence a reminder that breath still clung. Above, Morwen circled slow, glass-bright eyes catching every shiver of weakness, the bird's harsh cry marking who would not last the night.

Where Yelka could not save, she kept men from dying in madness. Sometimes she sang — old cradle songs bent into burial hymns, rough promises that death was only another kind of sleep. But when she turned away, her mouth set hard, as if each loss cut deeper into a wound that had never closed. Her wolf steadied the living, her raven measured the dying.

Bogdan tended those who slipped beyond her reach. He wrapped them in scorched cloth that had once borne banners, naming saints and drowned spirits in the same breath. His voice made the reed-smoke seem like incense, though the air stank of char and blood. The men bowed because there was nothing else to offer. Some wept. Others stood hollow-eyed, their grief too dry for tears.

The axemen finished their work, cutting peat-black logs, lashing rafts. Their faces were hollow, their grief sharper than frost. Borislav's fall hung over them all — the boy struck down with a serpent-blade under his ribs until blood drowned his mouth. Promise wasted.

But my grief was not theirs. They mourned a leader, bright and young, cut down too soon. I mourned what Ivan must face. No father should bury a son. Yet war makes fathers gravediggers, again and again. Boys take up axe and banner thinking war will make them men. It does not. It makes killers, and corpses, and leaves the living with nothing but silence to carry home.

When I closed my eyes, I saw Ivan's face in Driftlight — waiting for a son who would not return. I had no word that could carry that weight. No song could make it less bitter.

The rafts they built were crude platforms, tar-lashed, pitched to leak. They shoved them into the black channels, testing weight with poles. These would bear spears, food, the wounded who might still learn to walk.

Markov argued low to me and any who would listen: "No path leads through this mire. None. A fool's errand to push north here. We go around, link with the Crown host at Saltcross—there's sense in that." Even some veterans muttered agreement. Zdravko spat but did not counter. Sense said turn aside. Zeal said forward.

Rumours whispered like omens. Some said the Crown's host had been broken at Saltcross, banners trampled into mud. Others swore Velgrad's spears had cut through Bogreach and were grinding the rebels to dust. Men spoke soft, afraid the mire itself might choose which tale to make true.

At dusk Illarion climbed the gallery of nailed planks. His cloak hung in scorched tatters, face a ruin, eyes fever-bright. He looked north where smoke still rose, as if he saw through it to what waited. "I saw the brazier," he rasped. "The bones slipping from the temple. Not lost—waiting. We will not go around. We go through. Rafts at first light."

The word fell like a blade. Men bent their heads and finished their lashings. Rafts meant water, fog, ambush, fire—but no one spoke against him.

I lived. That was all. My side bound, my skin mottled with burn-spots that itched like rot, but breath still in me.

A shadow dropped beside me with a flask. Markov. Unblooded, unburned, not a scratch on him — not even singed hair or mud-caked boots to prove he'd been anywhere near the fight. He didn't grin or mutter some sly word, didn't make excuses or spin tales of narrow escapes. He just pressed the water to my cracked lips.

I drank, choking on both the water and something sharper — the taste of knowing good men had died while Markov lived by crouching low. When I looked back at him, his jaw was set hard, carved into lines I'd never seen before. He hated it — hated that he'd survived by keeping his head down while braver men rushed into fire. Shame weighed on him heavier than steel.

And still, I was glad. Glad he breathed, glad to see his face among all the ones I would never see again. Better his shame than his silence. Better his guilt than another grave.

He glanced about, checked no one was watching, then slid something from beneath his cloak. My breath caught. Pryaz — Illarion's black steel, its edge still sharp as judgment despite the flames.

"How—?" My voice cracked like a boy's.

He shook his head once, sharp as a blade-cut. "It found me."

Later, when the worst of the wounded were counted, he told me the rest. He'd been crouched in the reeds, pressed flat against the mud while the temple burned, when something hissed through the air and buried itself a finger's breadth from his ear. Pryaz — flung from the blast that had torn it out of my hands. He'd wrenched it free with hands that shook so violently he near dropped it back into the mud.

"It near killed me to touch it," he admitted, showing the faint burns across his palms. "Like it knew what I was. What I hadn't done."

I stared at him, amazed despite myself. If there was a saint of luck, Markov had become his reluctant priest. Yet looking at his hollow eyes, I wondered if this fortune wasn't its own damnation — to live when heroes fell, to carry their weapons when you'd never earned the right.

The blade lay by my side, heavy as accusation, cold as old blood. I didn't know if it had sought him, or if it had refused to let me free of my unspoken oath.

At dawn the reliquary was brought out. It could not be hidden any longer. Illarion would not be parted from it, so it was lashed onto the stoutest raft. Four men bore it to the water, their shoulders bowed, faces turned away as though to keep from breathing what it carried. Bogdan hovered close, whispering prayers as if the air itself might strike him.

The chest was iron-bound oak, black with age. Saints' names and spiral wards scarred its bands, gouged deep as if they had been fought over, not carved. The wood looked dry, but never cold, as though it carried its own warmth. Sometimes, when the river damp touched the iron, it gave a faint tick, like cooling steel. That sound was enough to make hands flinch toward knives or crosses.

Men gave it names in whispers: witch-box, fire's coffin, judgment in wood. A few asked what it was, but no one who mattered gave answer. Rumour did the rest. Some swore it was a sword, sharper than any forged. Others said a shield, proof against any blow so long as the box was kept close. One tale called it the heart of the Awakened One, stolen from the depths; another that Illarion could not be killed while the chest remained unbroken. No tale held for long. The box itself unmade certainty.

They spat when they passed it, or prayed, or stared too long. Even Bogdan, who bent near with moving lips, would draw back sharp when the bands gave their sudden tick, as if jaws had snapped shut on him.

Yelka did not flinch. Her gaze held the chest as though she had been waiting for it all her life, though whether in dread or in hunger I could not say. For a moment I thought of Markov's words in the Witherholt—that she had steered us north not for healing, but for some darker covenant. A bargain with the fire-priests, perhaps, or worse, a design to see prince and relic swallowed whole by the mire. She stood silent, but silence is its own kind of oath. And I could not read hers.

Two hundred and eighty men stood when the count was taken — what remained from nearly four hundred. Captains lived; some units were halved. Scouts cut to less than ten. Loss enough to gut an army, yet still Illarion bound them in fire.

Kazek limped among the ranks, skin seared, hair scorched to the scalp, but belief carried him where flesh failed. "Anointed!" he shouted, voice torn raw, fist striking his chest. At first only a handful answered, hoarse and uncertain. Then others took it up, louder, until the sound rolled like a drumbeat over the wounded and the ash.

Illarion watched. In the ruin of his mouth I thought I saw triumph — not for survival, not even for victory, but for the fire that burned now in voices not his own.

The worst-wounded were set on wagons with what little guard could be spared, to be hauled back south toward Ironholt if the road held. The rest took poles in hand.

I looked back once as smoke still coiled from the temple's stilts. Somewhere in that ash lay the bones of a hundred who had marched beside us. We who moved on were named survivors. I was not sure it was mercy. And when I caught Yelka's green eyes across the camp—wrong-coloured, glimmering like the mire's own hunger—I wondered if she already knew which of us would endure, and which had only been carried this far to feed some purpose yet unspoken.

Chapter LII: Into the Black Reach

We pushed north into the Bogreach. Twenty crude rafts, two salvaged punts, and two hundred eighty men — or what remained of men after fire had taken its due. The water here was older than the channels we had known, hungrier. It pulled at our poles like grasping fingers, black as old blood beneath a starless sky. The current fought with malice, as though the mire itself resented trespass.

Progress was measured in yards, not miles. Each stroke bought with aching shoulders and curses. Reed-walls rose like the ribs of some long-dead beast, funneling us into passages that shifted when no one watched. The air stank of rot and drowned leaves, centuries fermenting in black water. Not earth, not water — something between. Even prayer felt swallowed.

Markov's scouts went first because someone had to. Some swam the choke-channels where rafts could not pass, knives clenched in blue lips, eyes just above a surface that might hide anything. They returned shaking like fever victims, muttering of coils thicker than a man's thigh sliding unseen beneath them. Markov himself forced it once, then afterward sat silent on the raft's edge, rocking, refusing another plunge. For a man who joked at death, silence was worse.

Some of the boys could not swim at all. Farm lads who had known no more water than a millpond. When the punts filled, lots had to be drawn. Youth flung into black water that seemed eager to claim them.

"Kick, or the bog takes you," I told one.

"What if I can't?" he whispered.

"Then you learn now."

He did. Some didn't.

Losses came quiet and constant. Stepan's throat swelled fat around a dart before we could cut it out. Gavril vanished with a splash so sudden I thought I had imagined it. A freedman lay shivering as his leg blackened to the knee, and I had to hold him still while Bogdan prayed him under.

Then fire from the unseen—clay jars hurled out of fog, some sputtering smoke, others blossoming sudden storms. *Witchfire*, the men called it, green tongues that crackled even on water. Not many, but enough to gnaw nerves. Small terrors, each one a wound in spirit. Whispers said Vrasida herself had breathed the jars alight, that her fire could not drown.

Illarion stood staring into the haze, hand resting on the reliquary's iron edge as if he could drink strength from it, though I saw his knees tremble under the scorched cloak.

Bogdan bent near him whispering fire into prayer.

Night stripped the marrow from us. Frost glazed reeds like brittle glass, lips split, gloves stiffened. Men hollowed by hunger simply stopped fighting and slipped under, drawn to stillness.

The rebels owned the water. A hiss of arrows, the whisper of a dart, then nothing but ripples closing. A raft set adrift carried only corpses with throats opened like second mouths. We struck back at reeds and silence. The mire showed us whose side it served.

Once, a voice called Zdravko's name from the fog—his mother's, sweet as spring water. Men stiffened, some even swayed toward it. Zdravko spat into the mire and lifted his spear.

"Dead don't call me," he growled. "Only cowards answer."

Then came laughter—high, thin, reeds rattling with no wind. At dawn we found a ring of pale mushrooms glowing on the bank where he would have stepped. The Brackfolk muttered of the Leshy, lord of drowned forests, wearing voices of the dead to lure the living. One man whistled nervously, and the sound came back thick, wrong. He clapped a hand over his mouth, trembling. Even Bogdan crossed himself, though he tried to hide it. Yelka alone moved untroubled, stepping from raft to bank with her wolf at her side. Men turned their eyes away — whether in awe or fear I could not tell.

The rebels pressed close, then slid away before steel could answer. Only Sava's bowmen gave reply, loosing blind into reeds, and sometimes a cry told us their shafts had found flesh. We prized each silence that followed, for it meant arrows had not been wasted.

Twice they overreached. Our men hauled one down, hacked him apart, his serpent blade clattering free. Another died the same, throat cut before he could vanish beneath the black. But for each corpse we left floating, half a dozen of ours sank choking. Their blades dripped poison; even a scratch blackened veins before dawn.

Each raft gone made the rest seem heavier, as though death climbed aboard with us. Some muttered the witch led us wrong, deeper into graves. Others slipped into reeds, hiding beneath muck, letting leeches chew them rather than face darts from shadows.

We were no longer soldiers—just prey crouching low enough to escape notice.

Chapter LIII: Two Hundred

The Bogreach killed as much by cold as by tooth. Frost lay in the reeds at dawn, glazing each stalk in brittle glass. Gloves stiffened, lips split, breath hung white. Some men stopped struggling and slipped under, lured by the stillness of black water.

The land itself struck against us. Stone outcroppings jutted from the mire like bones, slick with moss, their roots clawed raw by current. Cliffs split the treeline, slate veined white like scars. More than once a raft smashed on hidden rock, pitching men into a hunger that did not give them back.

At sunset we glimpsed a solitary hill rising from drowned forest—a fang of stone, black against the sky. Men whispered, Illarion swore, and the word *Fang* took on a weight heavier than prayer. His burned hand traced his scars as if scripture.

"I saw it burn in the fire," he whispered. "It waits."

The only one untouched was Yelka. Her steps barely sank the peat, her balance never broke. Once I saw her walk where water should have swallowed her, Grendel pacing at her side, Morwen wheeling above. She moved as if following a map none of us could see. When pressed, she only said, "There are paths. I know them." She named no stone, no tree. Men muttered behind her back — witch or saint, guide or betrayer. None dared ask aloud.

Markov scouted with Dmitri and Feliks through a reed-choked channel. Only he came back—mud-slick, bleeding, knife wet with more than water. He stumbled onto the raft and sat hard, staring at his hands.

"Where are they?" I asked.

"I…" His jaw worked like he was chewing leather. "The water… it does things to a man's head."

"What things?"

"Dmitri started laughing. Wouldn't stop. Then he—" Markov's voice cracked. "He came at me with his knife. Said I was rotting, that he saw worms under my skin. Feliks tried to hold him, and Dmitri cut his throat."

The raft creaked under us.

"I had to," Markov said at last. "He kept coming. Even when I stuck him, he kept laughing."

After that, Markov was not the same. When Illarion ordered him forward again, he sat rocking on the raft, hands knotted in his hair, knife clutched but useless.

Bogdan's voice bound fear into faith. He crouched beside the reliquary as if guarding a king's corpse, whispering saints of flame, arms spread in every ambush. His words turned terror into command: that fire would spare the strong and claim the weak. Men bent to it, not because they believed, but because they had nothing else to hold.

Illarion's ruined hands traced his scars as if reading holy lines in flesh. "The weak are claimed," he said. "The fire keeps the rest."

Some men bent to the words, as though terror itself had been hammered into command.

"Where is it?" Illarion demanded again and again, voice like rusted chains, eyes scouring the mist. "The Black Fang rises above the mire. I saw it — fire marked it for me. Where is it?" Sometimes his gaze wavered, unfocused, as if he saw nothing but flame behind his lids. Other times his voice rang sharp enough to cut, and men flinched as though the question itself might strike them. Others bent their heads, too hollow to care.

When another raft slipped its lashings and shattered on a stone spit, Illarion turned on Yelka.

"Are you leading us — or drowning us?"

She glanced north, not at him. "Debts are paid there," she said. Nothing more.

Her tone carried no proof. For the first time, I saw doubt in his eyes — not of fire, but of her.

With every loss, whispers thickened. The witch was not guiding us forward at all, but back upon our own tracks. Each step a bargain with the Leshy, each mile a tithe of our blood.

By the time we dragged the rafts onto a spit of half-frozen peat that second night, nearly two score men were gone — killed, drowned, poisoned, vanished. I counted each face I would never see again until the numbers blurred. We had begun with two hundred eighty. Now we were closer to two hundred.

Worse waited.

Chapter LIV: The Drowned

We found a rise no larger than a barge, roots and mud lifted a little above the mire. No fire. Night pressed black as pitch, alive with small noises — things moving unseen in the reeds, water sucking at its own skin. Men huddled close, blades loose in hand, as if steel might give warmth. I lay on mud cold as iron and stared at clouded stars that felt farther than they had ever been, pitiless in their cold. Around us the Bogreach shifted and whispered, patient as hunger.

Markov pressed near, shoulders hunched, eyes wide. His knife trembled in his fist, but not from cold. "She's leading us to hell, Yarik," he muttered. "Hell in watery graves. The water's in my head. We're all going mad, one by one."

I did not answer. In the Bogreach, madness was only another way to drown.

Silence followed — not absence, but listening. Every man waiting, ears straining. The reeds hissed with a faint wind. Something splashed far off, too heavy for bird or fish.

A man struck flint to steel. Sparks spat once, twice.

"No light," Illarion rasped. "No fire."

Still the clicking went on, desperate, faster. Sparks leapt, caught.

Radoslav rose with a burning branch, eyes wild, teeth bared like a beast cornered. The flame shook as badly as his grip. Men shrank, whispering prayers. Illarion cursed, but the mire had already answered.

Shapes dragged through mud beyond the firelight, circling. The torch fell, hissing in the muck like a throat drowning. Hands clawed up—grey, slick, clothed in reed-rot. Faces empty of breath yet clinging with hunger, eyes wide through slime. One by one, they rose.

"Saint's mercy," someone gasped.

Radoslav gave no cry. The mire opened under him, arms seizing. Only bubbles remained. Danko tried to laugh—"It's only shadows, only—" His laugh drowned as hands dragged him under.

Illarion seized the torch, fire flaring across his scarred face. His ruined arm shook but he would not lower it. "Hold the line! Spears forward!"

Torchlight jagged in my eyes, showing too much — empty sockets that still stared, teeth grinning through rot. Spears struck home, but the bodies clung, pulling weapons into muck. Zdravko stamped, heel crunching through a sodden skull. "Don't give ground! Let them drown again!" Sava's bowmen loosed blind into dark. Milorad roared once before the mire folded over him.

Markov stood frozen, knife hanging like dead weight, eyes fixed on Yelka—wolf pressed close, raven croaking overhead—as if begging her to deny it. "She's walking us into graves," he whispered. Not fear, but the hollow certainty of a man already broken. I saw Dmitri's laugh in his ears, and shame twist his mouth as if he knew he would break the same way.

Bogdan raised his arms beside the reliquary, beads clicking, voice rolling above screams: "Fire is judgment! Fire alone burns rot!" He named saints and spirits both, damning them alike, and some men struck not at drowned alone but at their own terror, eager to prove themselves unclaimed. The torch's light gleamed off the reliquary's iron, and eyes clung to it as if it were shield and altar both.

Grendel tore free into the press, jaws breaking bone with no blood. Morwen wheeled overhead, her cry tearing through the din like iron on stone.

I fought with Pryaz, black edge carving through necks and arms. They fell, but falling meant nothing—the mire swallowed and raised them anew. My legs sank deeper, breath ragged, only the edge in my hands keeping me from being dragged under.

Viktor fought at Illarion's side, shield high, spear punching down again and again. His hoarse voice called men to rally round the prince.

Still, the mire fed. Men went under in silence, some screaming, some without a sound. I lost track of how many. Dozens, perhaps more. Faces I knew a moment before were gone when I turned back. When at last the shapes slackened and the water stilled, our line was ragged as torn netting.

Silence followed, broken only by panting and the hiss of torches. Illarion swayed but did not fall. Zdravko's jaw clenched like iron. Sava's hand trembled. Markov's blade shook. Yelka stood untouched, raven's wings folded, her eyes unreadable. Men looked at her with fear as much as hope, as if she had called the drowned as easily as she had escaped them.

I cannot swear whether they were flesh, trick, or something between. I only know the mire fed, and we were the meat it chose.

Chapter LV: They Drowned Her

Morning came without warmth.

The water around the mound had skinned over — a thin, brittle crust of ice that cracked if you leaned on it. Frost needled the reeds. Light crawled up from the east as if ashamed to show what it had found.

Bodies lay where they had fallen: some half-frozen on the rise, some drifting in the shallows, some gone altogether. A headless torso hung snagged on a root, red ice feathering the wound. Arms were hacked free of their owners. Faces I knew had gone pale as wax; eyes clouded like river-stones. The black water bore them away like offerings to whatever hungry thing ruled this place.

We huddled in the middle of our shrinking island — fewer than a hundred now. A score clutched wounds that would fester before noon. Another score sat hollow-eyed and slack. The rest were bones in rags, waiting for the mire to finish what war had begun.

Prince Illarion sagged where he sat, hands open, eyes shut. The rags hung on him too large, as if the fever had taken the meat and left only the shape. He tried once to lift the reliquary, fingers scrabbling at its iron clasps, but strength failed him. He folded back as a man does when there is no more to give. The fire that had driven men into his shadow since Stormgrave Isle — the thing that made boys follow him into pyres and crags — had burned itself out.

Then the murmurs turned. Not against him. Against her.

They looked at Yelka. She crouched at the circle's edge, wolf at her hip, raven hunched on her shoulder like a scrap of living shadow. Men with cracked lips and salt-white faces fixed on her with eyes that had gone wolfish. They blamed her silence, her otherness, the way death seemed to slip past her while it took the rest of us.

"Witch," someone hissed.

The word spread through the survivors like fever. Hunger needs a shape to bite. We had trusted her to read the hidden channels; now, with brothers floating face-down, the men needed something to bleed for what they had lost.

Even Kazek, who had limped through fire with zeal in his mouth, stared at her now with something like hatred. The burns had taken half his hair and seared his flesh, but not his faith in the prince. Faith in her, though—that was gone. He struck his chest once and rasped, "The Watcher weighed us, and she gave us to death." Others took his cry, twisting it darker, until the words *death-servant* and *Chernoknizhnika* hissed from their throats.

Bogdan gave their rage its scripture. "The old ways demand blood for passage. Cast her to the water, and the bog will release us."

His voice held the cadence of liturgy, though no holy book I knew ever named the slaughter of women as cleansing. But these men were past books. They were only mouths and knives.

The circle closed.

I felt it then—the tearing under the ribs, the thing that comes when fear and hunger rots the line between man and beast. The same black mouth that had opened in me in the Mirefast years back, when Dobrava met her dark end. We had been too long in the swamps then—breathing rot and fear, burying friends in unmarked graves, and something in me had grinned and licked its lips. I became *Volkolak* in those reeds, the beast who enjoyed cruelty and a woman's screaming. I knew that beast well. Too well. He has followed me since, and not just in name.

She would die; the mire would taste blood. Hunger does not ask mercy.

When she backed toward the water, trapped between the mob and the bog, I stepped between them.

I could not have said why. Perhaps a deeper habit — not honour, not bravery, but whatever remained of the man who could tell necessary death from the death that eats you whole.

"They aren't men anymore," I told her.

My voice came out strange to my own ears, like a borrowed thing that still remembered mercy.

"Run."

She did not move. Her breath smoked in the cold. The wolf pressed closer, hackles up; the raven watched with eyes like black jewels. There was no swagger now — only a small, raw thing that made my chest hurt.

"Please." It came out as if someone had to drag a rope through mud. "Please — don't let it end like this."

She swallowed and kept looking at me as if I might answer with a map or a promise.

"They drowned her." The words were torn out of her like a scab ripped free. Saying them hurt; the memory flared and cut, and that hurt had been the heat she'd tended all these years, a tinder she fed to keep moving. "They held my mother under the black pool because she would not bow to their rites. I swore on her body to burn their mountain to ash. I believed — spirit's teeth, I believed — that if I lived I could make them pay."

Her hands trembled once, then steadied like a woman setting a last net. She turned toward Illarion. "When you came I thought you'd be the hammer. I thought you'd take me to the Black Fang and I'd finish it." Her voice split. "But now—now we die here and they live. I swore on my mother's grave, and I will die for nothing."

She leaned so close I could see the white of her eyes fraying at the edge. "Let me finish it. If you will not—then kill me clean and quick. I cannot—" the word broke—"I cannot be left to bleed for an oath that ends as empty as smoke."

The mob closed in: teeth, breath, the small cruelties hunger teaches. The stink of it was worse than blood — not rage, but the sour want of men who longed to see pain shared. Bogdan raised both hands as if to bless the slaughter. His eyes gleamed as if her death might prove his own prophecy true.

Then Illarion stood.

There was no blaze in him. No trumpet or rapture. He rose as a man does who has slept long and dreamt of ash: slow, a little wobbled, shoulders bowed under a weight no one else could see. For a long moment he simply stood, swaying as the cold took him.

When he looked at us his face had no triumph. Something colder moved behind his eyes, not zeal but a precise, hard decision.

"She speaks truth," he said. His voice was small and flat, and it carried across the water like a bell rolled into winter. "Her enemy is our enemy. The Fire Coven burns children and calls it holy. If she seeks their ruin, she is no betrayer."

The mob faltered, not from faith but because a prince's word still cut through the last of men's chaos. Bogdan pushed forward, righteous fury in his throat. "My lord, she has led us to ruin. The bog takes us because —"

"The bog takes us because we are weak," Illarion said. There was none of the old roar, just this: a fact laid down. "Because I have been weak. Because I hoped for half-measures and bargains."

He turned to the iron-bound chest we had hauled with us through every sunk thing and every starved night. Its oak was dark with old blood and newer frost. When he spoke again it was like the setting of a stone.

"Open it. Use the relic."

Bogdan recoiled as if struck. "Not yet! The hand is but a part. We must gather the bones — the saint's shards — else the power will burn through us. One piece will not suffice; it will eat what it can and leave us empty." His eyes were wide — not with faith, but with fear. For once the priest looked less like a prophet than a man staring at his own grave.

"Then we burn," Illarion said, and there was no heat in the words, only decision. "We take what it gives. We use it up. After that, we push on to the Black Fang and finish what we came to do."

He did argue. He did not ask for assent. He gave the order as a man states the time of day.

The men drew back from Yelka, not out of belief in his mercy but because when command falls from empty hands it still shapes what people will do. The silence after a thing like that is an animal thing — heavy, listening.

Bogdan's hands shook as he reached for the clasps. Around us the bog lay patient as stone, as if it had been waiting centuries for men to come and feed it with their fires and their foolishness.

I watched Yelka's face. The raven shifted and settled; the wolf pressed its nose to her hand and whined — a small, keen sound that said, in its way, whether she would go willingly or be taken. She looked at me then, and in that look there was no plea left for saving. Only the shape of her oath, burning like a coal in a cold fist.

Chapter LVI: Smoke for a Crown

We bore the reliquary to the rise of roots where the ground held firm. Yelka stayed by the shore, leaning on Grendel, Morwen fluttering to a branch as if he wanted a clearer view.

The chest sat quiet. Ashwood blackened by fire, bound in iron carved with saints' names and spiral wards of restraint. Warm to the touch, though the morning air bit cold.

Bogdan bent over it, whispering as he worked the locks, voice steady, almost tender:

"*Sanctus Ilyin, lux in tenebris.* Fire that judges. Fire that endures."

The latches screamed. Steam rose. He opened the lid.

Inside lay stone polished black, holding a bed of ash. Not dead, not cold. Warm, shifting faintly as though it breathed. The men murmured—some craned forward, some drew back.

Bogdan plunged his arms into the ash. When he rose he held bone: long, heavy, blackened yet whole. A forearm, charred to cinder, still burning at the seams. The fire did not consume.

Gasps broke. No prayer yet—only disbelief. Then he drew another, ember-glow in its bulb. Each relic smoked but did not crumble.

Kazek bent low, whispering of judgment fire, then cried aloud: "Anointed! The Awakened One foretold!" His voice cracked but carried. The Brack answered first, hunger in it.

Illarion stood before them, scars lit as though prophecy itself had carved him. Disbelief turned to worship, awe to terror, until even those with no Brack blood bent their knees with the rest.

Bogdan lifted the bones high. Ash rained like black snow. His chant rose, voice swelling though it cracked once — not fear, but awe, as though he too doubted flesh could bear such fire.

"Lux aeterna, ignis aeternus. Fire that burns the rot. Fire that crowns the chosen."

The men dropped to their knees — not commanded, only overcome. Even I felt the ground pull me. Illarion bent until his brow touched earth, scars lit as though smouldering within. When the glow touched him he shuddered, teeth clenched, as if the fire scalded him from the inside.

The fog thinned, as if the reliquary's breath drove it back. Pale light speared through reeds, striking the water until it gleamed like a mirror of flame.

Bogdan circled Illarion three times, bones aloft, voice breaking into shout:

"Ecce princeps! Ecce ignis! Ecce iudicium!"

When he lowered the bones, smoke seemed to cling about Illarion's head like a crown. Then it was gone.

Illarion raised his face. His voice came raw, cracked, but steady: "North."

Not a cheer, but poles striking water answered him. Rafts pushed forward. Even those still trembling from last night's drowned attack bent their shoulders, as if fire had lashed them onward.

I followed, but my heart stayed behind with the ash. I had seen men kneel before fire before, and it had never ended in mercy.

The mire opened. Trees pulled back. And there at last, as the last shreds of mist lifted, the Black Fang showed itself: a hill of stone blacker than night, jagged and cruel, lifting from the swamp like a tooth meant to bite the sky.

Chapter LVII: The Black Fang

The Black Fang rose out of blacker water. At distance it was a tooth in the marsh; up close it was a cliff, slick with old salt and moss, streaked where rain ran like ash. The nearer we came the larger it grew, shouldering the horizon aside until there was only stone, and the curl of steps cut up its flank like a scar.

We poled in under silence. Sava's archers knelt two to a punt, bows low, eyes narrow. A small dock jutted from the stone—planks tar-black, cleats iron. Two sentries stood there with serpent-blades on their hips and staves in hand, hooded in grey. One of them turned, mouth opening to call.

Sava hissed, *Loose.*

Two reeds of sound. Two bodies toppled without a word.

Less than a hundred of us made the landing. Planks creaked. Poles thudded. Markov was first to shore, shoulders hunched, knives twitching, eyes darting. I followed with Pryaz and my shield, my bad leg already complaining at the step onto rock. Illarion came last—one long sword, one short, their edges split-forged, both ready. His body was a column of scars and stubbornness. Behind him, Bogdan touched the reliquary—ash-box heavy with burning bone—with two fingers and crossed himself with the same hand, as if he thought the sign of God and the ash-box were kin.

The stair cut up the Fang in a slow spiral. Landings broke the climb—wedges of stone, low shrines, doors set into the mountain where huts had been carved from rock. The wind off the water tasted of iron. Above, Morwen wheeled, her shadow crossing us like another's thought.

We went in twos. Zdravko took the right file with his axemen; Sava with the bowmen on the left; Illarion and Viktor just ahead of me, the prince keeping both blades loose at his thighs, Viktor's shield overlapping his. Markov clung to the wall, fingers skittering over stone, counting doorways with the twitchy caution of a thief who never trusted locks.

Yelka came behind, staff in hand, knife at hip, Grendel pressed to her knee.

Four men bore the reliquary up the stone, backs bent, veins black with strain. Others pressed close as if its weight might spill onto them, guarding with their shoulders, stealing strength from the nearness. Bogdan walked beside, whispering to it as though it drew breath. Kazek bent close behind him, lips moving in a Brack prayer of judgment fire, his eyes never leaving the ash-box.

The first landing held a shrine with bone lamps, a low lintel, a door ajar. The men inside had ash on their faces and the slack look of those who trusted a bell to guard their sleep. Markov went with two scouts—Olen, narrow-eyed and restless, and Turo, who never spoke above a mutter. He twitched along the wall, not brave—just too mean to die.

A breath, a slip, the door opened. A muffled cry. When they came out again all three were standing, though Olen's knife dripped and Turo's mutter was gone to silence. Markov had blood streaked up his arm and across his cheek, as if he had wrestled in it. He spat, wiped his face with the back of his hand, and pinched the lamp shut like a man crushing a beetle. No alarm.

We crept low and reached the next landing. A hut with a slit window, a second door, a man at each. Sava's archers feathered one through the slit and took the other in the throat as he turned to raise a horn. Zdravko caught the horn before it fell and set it down as if it were a child. We went by like wolves moving through a fold.

At the third, the door stuck. Viktor shouldered it and the hinges sang. The woman within was old and quick. Her hand found a rope and yanked before Markov's knife found her throat. Bronze thundered the alarm up the Fang. The bell's voice kept ringing in the stone long after her body stopped.

"Up," Illarion said. His voice was smoke.

We climbed into war.

Chapter LVIII: The Pinnacle of Fire

They met us on the stair where only two could stand abreast. Otets with serpent-blades and hands bare, no shields—men trained to be still until the strike, their whole lives pared to blade and bone. Volkhvy with jars and staves, the jars stoppered with pitch and sealed in red. The first rank came fast. Sava's bows answered—clean, ruthless—and the narrow way filled with men already dead. Then the quivers emptied. Sava cast one aside with a curse and drew a short sword as if he meant to use it better than the bow.

The jars came. One shattered on the wall above and spilled a ribbon of fire that crawled down the stone, licking where there was no oil. Witchfire. The heat blistered skin under mail.

We fought like men stuck in a throat. The Otets gave no shout, no wasted cut—only stillness, then the flash of a hand or blade. There was no flanking, no clever way. Just step and kill, step again. Bodies went over the edge with small sounds that ended quickly. Some of them burned as they fell; those left a streak in the air like a writing no one would read.

My limp made the narrow turn mean. Each rise set a spike under the knee. The shield helped me climb; it also made me a wall. I caught blades on its rim, smashed knuckles and teeth, cut low with Pryaz, turned, cut high, felt the wrist-shiver of steel meeting bone. Blood made the steps slick. Men slipped and did not rise.

Illarion was a flame that refused to gutter. His long blade worked clean and his short struck like a snake; when one jammed in ribs he changed hands without looking and stepped into the next man. He bled from three shallow cuts and one deep one along the ribs. Viktor's shield lived next to him, the spear punching over it to make more space than the stair wanted to give.

"Prince!" someone shouted—the sort of prayer that wears the clothes of a name. A stave cracked against Viktor's helm and he sagged, then surged again, eyes red with sweat. He blocked two, took a third in the side, and drove his spear clean through a man's mouth. He did not look down at the shaft quivering in that face. He did not have time.

Yelka moved when she had to and when we made the room. She was not made for that stair. None of us were, but she least. A jar burst two landings above and a spray of burning liquid kissed her shoulder; cloth caught and Grendel threw himself against her side, teeth snapping at flame, tearing fabric, dragging it away. She cut the smoulder with her bare palm, face tight and pale, and kept climbing with blood beginning to run from the hand.

Markov disappeared twice. When I saw him, his mouth was set in a thin line and a smear of black showed where a stave had broken against his ribs. He moved quieter after that. I saw him once under a fallen man, and then the fallen man jerked and would not rise again. When he came up, his knife was red to the hilt.

A jar landed at Zdravko's boots and burst up his legs. He did not scream the way most men do. He snarled, dragged an Otets into the blast, hugged him until the other stopped, then hurled both fire and corpse away. He killed two more before a third jar struck his chest and stuck like a curse. He tore it free with both hands and flung it. His throw saved us. It cost him everything. His beard burned like a saint's candle. He laughed once before another blade punched him to his knees with the sound of a dropped shield.

Above, the bell had become a chant. Voices layered until they were one sound. We pushed up under it. Somewhere behind me I heard Kazek's rasp, half-chant and half-sob, calling the fire judgment and crying that prophecy walked in blood up the stair. His voice clung like smoke, and men pressed harder as if belief itself shoved their backs. An Otets went down near him, blade clattering across the step. Kazek snatched it up like a starving man grabs bread. The curved steel looked wrong in his hands until he began to use it. He hacked, every stroke a prayer through broken teeth. Half his face burned away, but he did not fall. I feared what he might become if he lived.

My bad leg went from pain to wood. A blade slipped under the rim of my shield and bit into my thigh. Fire flared through me and the stair wavered. Grey closed in, then black, and then it opened like a door.

I have been wolf and man, but neither name fits what comes through that door. Not rage — rage is blind. This was blood boiling to joy, marrow singing, death embraced. The volkolak rose and I did not resist. It tore through me, made my arms stronger than bone should bear. No man could climb that stair and live. The beast climbed it laughing.

I drove the shield rim into a face and felt teeth go. Pryaz cut low and stayed low — hamstring, calf, heel. A stave broke against the boss; I took the rest of the wood and put it through the throat that owned it. A man tried to speak to me — his mouth moved, words lost beneath the roaring — and I had no language to give him. Only work. When the world returned, there were fewer of us and fewer of them, and the steps were red, and we were still climbing.

We came out onto the pinnacle.

The top of the Fang was no larger than a hall floor. Wind from three sides, a waist-high wall of stone along the lip, a brazier in the centre crouched on iron legs like an animal. Fire lived in it—coals and bones together, the heat wrong, the colour wrong, a steady, hateful burn. A ring of Volkhvy stood between brazier and sky—twenty, maybe fewer; some old, some girls not old enough to be called women. Around them thirty Otets held a broken line with serpent-blades whispering death—more than we had left to give. Vrasida stood out like a thorn—white hair, seamed face, eyes like banked coals. The heat from the brazier made the air waver around her as if she were a mirage.

"End it," Illarion said. There was nothing left of prayer in his voice. Only command.

The first rush broke on us and we broke it. Viktor took the point with the last of what he had, shield high, spear like a nailed oath. An Otets slid in low, serpent-blade flicking while his other hand clawed for Illarion's wrist. Viktor shouldered him wide and took the blade that wanted the prince. It went deep under the mail and he made a noise like a cart axle when it cracks. He did not fall. He held the wall, bleeding into his boot.

Sava's sword-work was quick and mean until a spearhead found the gap above his collar, sliding deep. He went backwards three steps and would have gone over if one of his men had not caught him. He swore, laughed, swore again, and tried to stand. The laugh was a bad sound. He sat and fought from his seat and cut a man who thought a seated archer was meat.

Zdravko was not there. The space where he should have been had fire in it and no man.

Markov came out of shadow behind the Volkhvy line. His blade slipped under a robe and made a soft wet sound and a softer one after. He did not see the stave that found his ribs; it broke there with a crack that sounded like winter. He went down to a knee, stabbed up blind, and found something vital.

Bogdan's voice rose behind us as the reliquary reached the pinnacle — "*Lux in tenebris, ignis iudicans*" — and then he was there, reliquary hand on the lid, other hand raised. An Otets came in low — fast and precise — and drove his serpent-blade up beneath Bogdan's ribs while his free hand slammed the prophet's arm aside. Even as Bogdan staggered, another stepped in from the flank, two thrusts between the shoulders, each clean as practice The prophet folded, his hand raised as if he tried to bless us with his last breath.

Yelka reached the circle — dragged forward by our press whether she willed it or no — and nearly died there. An Otets used the flat of his blade to knock her staff aside and drew back for the thrust that ends a story. Grendel hit him mid-step, mouth on the man's throat, teeth in the artery. Both went down hard. The Otets' blade found Grendel's ribs; the point slid in between them and the shaft buried to the fletching. Grendel kept his teeth and shook until the man stopped and then tried to stand and could not. He looked at Yelka while his life was running. She put a hand to his head and spoke a word that had nothing to do with saints and everything to do with love. He died with his ears flat and his eyes clear.

There is no clean way to say how we finished it. We were too few for anything clean, they too desperate for mercy. The Volkhvy had jars but no space to throw; the jars became suicide then, women clutching them to their chests and lunging as if the nearness of death were a sacrament. We cut those who came, and some still burst, and flame took friend and enemy without choosing. The Otets came in waves, and each wave was fewer than the last.

Vrasida stood at the brazier and sang. I did not know the words, only the shape of them—old, hard. She reached in and lifted bone that burned but did not consume, and the fire ran along that bone like a snake on a branch. She meant to end us in one stroke, burn the Fang, burn us, burn the marsh, burn the sky. Illarion saw her see it.

He went through three men like cloth. The short blade found a throat and stayed; the long took a wrist. He kicked a jar back into the legs that bore it, and the legs went away. Smoke cleared, and he reached Vrasida. She swung the burning bone like a mace. He let it miss him by the width of a prayer and drove steel into her belly. She folded around the blade but did not fall. She bit through her own tongue to finish the word. He cut her throat, and the word ended there. Her hand clawed for the brazier as she fell. Burning bones spilled in an arc, making a ring of fire around them.

Someone was shouting my name. I turned on the shout. An Otets had his blade under Viktor's arm. I hit him with my shield as if the shield were a hammer and felt something give in him that would not mend. Viktor sagged. I grabbed him by the harness and propped him against the brazier's stone, and he smiled at me with blood on his teeth, the good smile men make when they know the cost.

"Keep him standing," Illarion said without looking. His voice was thinner now.

We kept him standing until the last of the line broke. It broke like wet bark—slow, string by string—and then all at once. The few who ran found the reliquary guard. One made it to the stair and found Sava waiting, sitting there like a snare.

The wind took the smoke sideways and the sky came back in pieces. Morwen sat the brazier's rim like a judge, beak black with wet. Her eyes were hammered glass. Around her the dead lay with their mouths open to the same cold air, and there was no difference in it for any of them.

Bogdan lay at the edge of the circle in a shine of his own blood. He was full of holes like a sieve. A man bent to close his eyes and could not, because Bogdan's eyes would not stay shut.

Sava breathed, barely. Zdravko did not. Markov was propped against the wall with an arm across his ribs and a grin that fooled no one.

Yelka laid Grendel down where there was no fire and set his head on her lap. Her hand was bound in her own torn sleeve, blood soaking through, face a pale thing lit by the brazier's wrong light. She did not cry. Morwen watched her from the stone rim, black beak wet, eyes like hammered glass—a ferryman without oar or coin, ushering the wolf's spirit across whatever river waits for beasts, if they have souls at all.

Illarion stood by the brazier with both blades down, their points in the ash. He looked like a man who had gone past pain into whatever is beyond it. The burn along his ribs smiled blackly through torn mail. His breath made a small smoke in the cold wind. He looked at the bones in the fire the way a thirsty man looks at a river.

"We have it," someone said. I do not know who. It was the kind of sentence men say to make the world make sense.

She lifted her eyes then. Grendel's weight was still across her knees, but her gaze was no longer on him. It climbed the firelight, found Illarion. For this cause she had given her wolf, and thought the price paid. Yet something in her face shifted, as if she had woken to see the cost was only beginning.

I looked down the stair we had climbed. It was a red line coiled around the Fang, bodies like dropped torches along it, some still smouldering. I looked at the brazier, and the bone that would not burn away, and at the priest who would not close his eyes, and at the wolf that would never rise again.

We had won the Fang. The flame still lived.

I wiped blood from Pryaz and could not tell whose it was. My arms still trembled with the beast's strength, though my mind was my own again.

I have called it curse, called it sin. On the Fang it was necessity — we would not have lived without it. This is what I tell myself: that the beast saved us, that there was no other way. Perhaps this is true. Perhaps I only need it to be true.

This was victory's cost. Not only the blood we spilled, but what we became to spill it. The Volkolak does not bargain. It only hungers.

And I fed it.

One day I will let it in and it will not leave. I know this the way I know winter comes. Perhaps that day is already past, and I am only telling myself I am still the one who chooses.

Chapter LIX: The Prophet Who Would Not Die

He should have died.

Steel under the ribs, punching through mail into the soft places beneath. Steel through the back, between the shoulder blades, seeking the spine. The prophet folded with both wounds spilling him like a burst wineskin, and I thought we had lost him in the same breath we lost half our line. I have seen men cleaved, burned, drowned — none ever rose from wounds that left so much blood on stone.

But when I looked again, Bogdan still moved.

He lay there drowning in his own breath, chest hitching though the holes should have collapsed his lungs. Blood frothed pink at his lips, air that had no business reaching his mouth. His eyes rolled white, then snapped back, fever-bright, staring at something none of us could see. He tried to speak — wet noises at first — and then a whisper:

"Lux... in tenebris. Ignis... indicants."

The men who heard it stepped back. Blood in the throat steals speech first, yet his voice carried pure.

Illarion dropped beside him like a man struck. He tore his cloak into strips, teeth ripping seams, knotting cloth around wounds that should have emptied a man in heartbeats. His face was a boy's again — smeared with gore, eyes wild with fury that God might claim His prophet before the work was done. He pressed the makeshift bandages hard against Bogdan's side and back, blood soaking through faster than he could bind, yet somehow less than before.

"The bleeding slows," someone whispered. "Look—it slows."

Whether from pressure or providence, the red flow had eased to seepage. Bogdan's breathing settled into rhythm, though each rise of his chest caught and held longer than nature allowed.

"Search everything," Illarion commanded, voice cracking like a prayer offered up as ransom. "Tear their halls apart. Cloth, herbs, wine—anything that might keep breath in him."

The men scattered through the ruined chambers, desperate to return with something, anything to explain why a dying man still drew air. They brought torn robes, clay jars of bitter powders, wine gone sour in broken amphorae. Illarion mixed them with the blind faith of a man drowning in deeper waters than he could fathom.

When he lifted Bogdan's head to pour wine between his lips, the prophet's eyes opened. Not the clouded stare of the dying, but sharp and knowing, as if he had been listening to conversations in another room.

"My prince," he whispered, voice clear though his lungs should have been drowning. "The fire... endures."

Then he closed his eyes and slept like a man at peace, chest rising and falling in steady measure.

Silence followed, heavy as stones. Some of the men crossed themselves. Others touched iron or muttered charms their grandmothers had taught them. A few simply stared, pale with the kind of fear that wears the mask of wonder.

"Saints preserve us," someone breathed. "He should be cold."

But Bogdan slept warm beside the scattered bones of our enemies, breath misting in the mountain air like any living man's. By morning, when we changed the bandages, the wounds had stopped weeping entirely. The holes were still there—dark and deep—but sealed somehow, as if his flesh had remembered older lessons about holding together.

Illarion stayed with him through the night, one hand on the prophet's shoulder, whispering prayers that sounded more like negotiations. His face shone with something between gratitude and terror, the look of a man who had asked for a miracle and received something he wasn't sure he understood.

And Bogdan breathed—regular as tide—sleeping beside death, but not claimed by it.

Near four hundred had set out from Ironholt when the leaves were still green and men still believed in clean victories. Now only fifty stood on the pinnacle, breathing smoke and counting ghosts. Any who were not veterans before had become veterans in the truest sense—scarred not just by blade and fire, but by the weight of watching good men die for inches of stone. They were zealots now to Illarion's cause, not from faith but from the terrible knowledge that comes when you have paid too much to quit. Fire was burned into their marrow, and they would carry it until their own bones crumbled to ash.

We saved who we could, and ended when ending was kinder. There is an art to mercy no priest teaches—knowing when a man's eyes have already turned inward, when the breath rattles like dice in a cup, when the pain has eaten through to the soul. A blade between ribs when the healer shook her head. A cup of wine thick with bitter herbs. A hand on the shoulder while the light faded. When the pain is taken from dying, most die well. Some even smiled. Those are the ones hardest to forget.

Sava lived, after a fashion. The serpent-blade that kissed him just above the collar left more than a scar. The poison twisted his neck and shoulder into a ruin of knotted muscle and dead flesh, and it crawled into his mind as well. His wit turned jagged. He laughed at what was not funny, asked for blood when we offered water, and drank both with the same relish. When he spoke of the battle, his eyes lit like a child's at feast-time. "Did you see how they burned?" he would ask, giggling. "Like candles. Like beautiful candles." We kept him, because he had earned it, but we watched him always. Some wounds never heal, and some men never come back from the places pain takes them.

Kazek lived, though he left half his sight on the Fang. A shard from a bursting jar had scored across his face, burning the socket to ruin. The lid sealed over red flesh, and where his eye had been there was only a hollow that wept long after the wound closed. When we carried him down, he said the fire had judged him and left what it pleased. He spat blood with the words, and swore he would serve until both eyes were ash.

Viktor lived, though the gods alone knew why. We laid him beside the spilled brazier where the heat shone on his pale face like false sunlight. Blood seeped through his bandages, his breath shallow as a bird's. Illarion knelt there, voice raw from smoke, promising anything—gold, land, salvation itself—if only Viktor would stay.

Viktor listened with the patience of a man who had already made his peace, then smiled that grim smile that had carried him through a dozen fights. "Three things, my prince," he whispered. "A soft maiden with gentle hands, more guards for you than one man can count, and a prince wise enough to refuse God's anointing when it comes wrapped in chains."

He chuckled at Illarion's silence, a sound like wind through autumn leaves. "The first for me, the second for you, the third for the kingdom. Promise me that much, and I'll rest easy."

Then he shut his eyes. His chest still rose and fell, like a tide that could not decide whether to stay or go. He was still breathing when I last looked, still fighting whatever war waits behind closed lids when a man stands on the threshold.

The rest—their names have become ash. Stepan who sang in the line. Gavril who could make anyone laugh. Young Pavel who always spoke of the beauty of the girl he would marry. The freedman whose leg turned black. The boys who learned to swim in black water, and the men who drowned teaching them. Each name a weight, each face a debt carried down from the mountain.

Fifty of us walked away from the Black Fang. In the arithmetic of war, that was what mattered. Fifty witnesses to what fire could do when fed the right fuel. Fifty men who had stared into the throat of darkness and come back with embers still burning in their souls.

Whether that made us blessed or cursed, I could not say. But I knew this: once a man has swallowed fire, it is never gone. It smoulders in the marrow, waiting for breath.

Whether that made us blessed or cursed, I could not say.

Chapter LX: The Reliquary and the Crown

We laid the bones together at last.

The left leg of Saint Ilyin, blackened but whole, gathered from the fallen brazier and picked from the ground where it had scattered. Splinter by splinter we had gathered it—char still clinging, marrow long gone, yet the thing still warm to the touch. Illarion himself bent to fit the pieces, his hands trembling as though each fragment cut him deeper than any blade. Bogdan guided him, lips moving in what might have been prayers or blasphemy—I could not tell.

When the leg lay complete, they lowered it into the reliquary beside the arm. Ash closed over them both, but not silence.

The chest *breathed*. No other word for it. Heat rose like the draw of a forge, and the seams flared red where iron should have stayed dark. Men pressed closer, not driven back but drawn in like moths to flame. Their faces burned ruddy in the glow, eyes wide and unblinking. Some crossed themselves with trembling hands. Others only stared, as if waiting to be weighed and found wanting.

Even at the edge of the circle, I felt the warmth reach me. This was not the comfort of hearth or summer sun. This was a fire that had no business offering solace—only consumption. The men swayed nearer as if drunk on its heat.

Illarion did more than sway. He leaned over the chest until the glow caught his scars and made them blaze like fresh brands. His eyes closed, and for a moment I thought the fire was pouring into him, filling some hollow place. His throat worked like a man drinking deep from a well.

Bogdan lifted his arms toward the light.

"The flame is unquenched," he declared, his voice carrying over the crackling air. "The saint is not broken. Fire judges. Fire endures."

The reliquary answered with its own voice. Ash shifted and whispered. The bones gleamed along their seams as if still burning, though no smoke rose. Unquenchable fire without fuel, bone that should have been cinder yet had outlasted stone and steel and the years that ground both to dust.

I watched the light dance in Illarion's eyes and wondered what it was he thought he was drinking from that sacred flame.

When the fire dimmed to ember-glow, men turned to plunder. The Black Fang yielded its treasures as any fortress does once its walls fall silent.

We found coin first—sacks heavy with sols, stamped with the faces of forgotten kings and dead saints. Some were so ancient their features had worn smooth as river stones. Jewels followed in glittering profusion: rings that still clung to finger-bones, amulets carved from jet and amber, pearls large as a child's teeth. We stacked the wealth by the shore until the rafts groaned under their weight. All of it Illarion's by right of conquest, though the men handled each piece like children at their first market day.

Then came the holy things. Not tokens of the saints, nor the king's blessed relics—these belonged to the old Brack faith.

Gold icons hammered into serpent-shapes, their eyes gleaming with inlaid gems. Chalices chased with patterns of reed and wave, their surfaces green with age. Altar-cloths stiff with salt and old blood, worked with threads that caught the light strangely. Relics stolen from drowned temples when the Otets turned against their own kin to preserve the ancient rites.

Men argued over them—should they melt the gold for practical coin, or bear them as trophies? Bogdan wanted them burned as heathen blasphemy. Yelka would keep them for their craft and beauty. I wanted no part in deciding which gods still breathed power into their metal.

Weapons lay scattered throughout the stronghold—serpent-blades wrapped careful in oilcloth, horn bows strung with sinew, spears standing in neat racks. Armour too: scale shirts that rippled like fish skin, half-helms crested with bronze, mail shirts red with rust but still sound. Men stripped the dead without ceremony and chose what fit, trading leather for reed-work, iron for carved bone.

Illarion himself chose nothing from the heaps. He only walked among his men like a lord surveying stores already counted and spent.

But food and water proved greater treasures than gold or steel. Barrels of smoked fish, sides of salted bog-deer, casks of ale that had aged in darkness. Springs cut deep into living rock, their water cold and sweet as mountain streams. Men cheered louder for these necessities than for any jeweled crown.

Some cheered too greedily, thinking opportunity meant licence. A boy was caught with a silver chain knotted beneath his shirt. He did not weep when they dragged him before Illarion's judgment seat. He bent his back to the oak without protest, took his beating with clenched teeth, and stood bloody but unbowed when the last blow fell.

Illarion's voice rang over him clear as struck iron.

"All belongs to me by right of war," he said, his words carrying to every ear. "And from my hand each of you will receive your rightful share. No theft. No cheating. Fire judges our hearts. A fair hand binds us stronger than chains."

The boy nodded through split lips and was lifted back among his brothers. None shunned him afterward—a man who owns his punishment walks clean again.

Not all were so clumsy in their greed. Markov drifted through the heaps of treasure with his hands clasped behind his back, eyes sharp as a hawk's, face blank as fresh snow. If he lined his cloak with hidden pockets, no eye caught him. He would never be taken—discretion was his particular gift, and he wielded it like other men wielded blades.

Such vast wealth we had won. Illarion claimed it all by ancient right, and in that claiming bound his men tighter to him than any sworn oath could have done.

Chapter LXI: Through Glass, Clear

Markov found them, of course. He always did. If there was a knife hidden in a boot or a coin stitched beneath a hem, it would be his fingers that prised it free. This time it was a chest of long brass tubes, each capped with glass and swaddled careful in oil-cloth. He staggered up from the store-room with one under each arm, grinning as though he'd unearthed the bones of some forgotten saint.

"Spyglass," he said, still breathless from his climb. "Or looking-glass, or peeper—whatever name pleases you. Used right, you can count the lice on a gull's head from half a mile off." He squinted through the wrong end, cursed colourfully, then flipped it with practiced ease. "Saints preserve me, the thing actually works."

He carried his prizes to the heights of the Fang, where wind-carved stone offered the best vantage. We climbed after him, boots slipping on steps slick with moss and years of spray, until the mire spread beneath us like some drowned and forgotten kingdom. I had thought the Bogreach endless—a black sea of reeds and twisting channels that swallowed horizon whole. But through that circle of worked glass, the world sharpened to impossible clarity. Distant trees sprouted individual leaves, water revealed the silver flash of fish beneath its surface, and smoke rose thin as thread from fires no naked eye should have reached.

Men swore under their breath, as if sight itself had turned to witchcraft.

Markov steadied the longest glass against a tooth of weathered rock, his usual grin fading. When he spoke, his voice had gone flat as hammered metal. "That's not mist rising. Those are campfires."

Illarion took the glass from him with hands that still trembled—though the relic's warmth had bled some colour back into his gaunt cheeks. He set the brass tube to his eye and stood motionless longer than any of us could have managed. When he finally lowered it, the red of his scars seemed to catch and hold the morning light.

"Crown banners," he said, his words carrying clearly in the still air. "Black cross on red field—Saint's Watch cohort. And there, to the east..." He pointed with one scarred finger. "Ivan's colours with the leaping stag of Greenfen. The queen has sent both her hounds."

"Who commands?" I asked.

He raised the glass again, studying the distant camp with the patience of a hunter. Then came that thin smile of his, the one that never warmed his eyes. "General Kravchenko. The careful one. He never spends men when time and hunger will serve as well. See there—he has the rebels penned in their temple, no more than two miles north of where we stand. He'll starve them until they beg for the mercy of fire."

The men around us murmured—some relief, some worry. To glimpse the Crown's host after so long drifting masterless in these channels was like sighting land through storm-spray. Hope and terror walked hand in hand.

Illarion turned from his vigil, the reliquary crouched at his feet like some iron hound, ash-heat still breathing from its sealed seams. "We will not stumble blind into his camp like masterless brigands. Kravchenko must know the Fang has fallen, that heaven's fire has rendered judgment here. Two men will carry word north."

None moved at first. He let the silence stretch, his gaze sweeping over faces made hard by marsh-fighting. At last two stepped forward—Olek, from Velgrad, broad-shouldered and steady, and Sreten, a reed-thin archer from Driftlight.

Bogdan blessed them in the sacred fire's name, touching each weathered brow with fingers that carried heat leaked from the chest. Some blessing, some brand—I could not say which.

They broke their fast first on real provisions—wheat bread still soft, smoked fish that flaked white and sweet, even dried berries from the Fang's hoarded stores. It was the first meal in weeks that did not taste of rot and desperation. Some said it was merely good food after long hunger. Others swore low that it was the relic's grace that set true strength flowing back into their limbs.

When they had eaten their fill, the two messengers wrapped themselves in dark cloaks, checked the edge on knives and the strength of cords, then headed down to the docks. We watched from the stone heights until morning mist swallowed them whole, leaving only ripples to mark their passage.

Illarion stood long after they had vanished, the spyglass still gripped in one hand, his eyes fixed on those distant northern fires that marked the Crown's camp.

"Now Kravchenko will know," he said at last, his voice carrying strange satisfaction. "Not merely that we survived this place. That *fire* survives. That heaven's judgment burns on, whatever earthly powers may decree."

The words hung in the marsh air like smoke from some offering neither wholly blessed nor wholly damned.

Chapter LXII: Where Fire Leads

Yelka moved like one already half-spent, her strength poured out like water from a broken vessel. Her emerald eyes still burned with that wrong light, but without Grendel's weight at her side they seemed sharper, hungrier—like the mire itself staring through her. Her shoulder was raw where witchfire had kissed flesh, blistered and weeping. Her hands were bloodied from smothering cloth that had burned through leather and bone anyway. She had saved who she could—carried water to the dying, bound wounds with strips torn from her own cloak, cut away scorched flesh with trembling fingers that never ceased their work. Yet she walked as though all her vigor had drained away and nothing remained to fill the hollow places. Grendel was gone, and with him that bright weight of shared life that had carried her through the worst nights. Only Morwen remained now, circling above or perched black and watchful on the stone, her eyes harder and colder than winter glass.

I found her on the highest ledge of the Fang, gazing out over the endless marsh. She did not turn when my boots scraped close, though I made no effort at silence.

"You won your vengeance," I said, though the words felt blunt, too small for the smoke-thick air between us. "Your mother can rest now."

She raised her arm, and Morwen lit upon it, talons cutting her skin. She fed the raven scraps of meat, and I did not ask whose flesh it was.

Her voice came hoarse, frayed by fire and grief. "I thought my oath ended with the Fire Coven. But look around us.

Every chain, every torch, every banner — they are all born of the same fire."

The raven croaked, black wings beating against the wind, and she did not look away.

"My vision was too small, Volkolak," she said. "Shadowed by my pain. We have torn the heart from this place, and for that I am glad. But Morwen shows me the sickness is deeper. The raven does not circle Mirefast alone — she marks the whole kingdom, from altar to high hall, from drowned reeds to Velgrad itself. The poison runs in every vein."

She drew a breath, as if steadying herself for a future half seen, and none of it good.

"My mother may rest. But I cannot. Not while the rot breathes in every oath, even from the throne itself."

I thought then of the king — Mstislav, crowned yet hollow, a man gnawed from within until only madness sat the throne. We had burned the Fang, but his rot ruled still, seeping through crown and court alike. Yelka's emerald eyes were fixed on that sickness now, their brightness turned uncanny against the soot upon her face.

With Grendel gone, it was the raven's wings that steadied her, black pinions carrying her gaze beyond Mirefast, beyond Driftlight, beyond the reach of any of us. Her vengeance had been for her mother. What she sought now was judgment for a kingdom. And I knew: whatever course Illarion set, her path would not turn aside.

Illarion joined us then, his step dragging, his breath ragged, but his presence filling the ledge. Smoke had marked him worse than any blade, yet he stood straight, fire clinging to his eyes, hard and bright as a forge.

"You saved them," he said at last, voice clear in the thin air. "You saved me as well."

She bowed her head—not in deference, but in bone-deep weariness that bent her shoulders like a yoke. For a moment the green of her eyes dulled, as though even that unnatural fire guttered without the wolf to share its weight.

"I would have you travel with us," he went on, each word measured. "Not merely as healer, though your skill honours any company. But as one who has walked through fire and come out unbroken. As one of us—bound by more than convenience."

Morwen shifted on her perch, black claws scraping stone, and croaked once—a sound like judgment given.

Yelka lifted her face, the soot masking her features until only her emerald eyes caught the light. Her words came steady and sure, without hesitation: "Yes. You made your choice in Ironholt's shadow and bound me then, though I did not understand it. We travel now in currents I cannot name—toward fire and ice, tooth and crown. My place is with you, for good or ill, until this path reaches its end."

Illarion's smile was both wound and crown, terrible and beautiful together. "Bogdan will curse me for it."

"Then let him curse," she said, her voice bearing the first hint of steel since the battle's end. "I have been cursed by better men, and survived them all."

Above us, the raven spread her wings against the smoke-stained sky, feathers catching what little light remained—seal or benediction, I could not tell.

Illarion turned from her without answer, his eyes drawn past the ledge to the ruin below.

Illarion's gaze swept the ruin. The temple stood gutted but unbroken, black stones veined with soot, carved saints coughing smoke. He turned to his captains. "Leave no shrine standing," he said. Quiet, absolute. Every man heard it. None spoke against.

I felt the shape of the order more clearly than any shouted command. A message must be sent — something to make the country count the cost before it chose to rise. Perhaps if the rebels saw what becomes of a shrine, they would lay down arms. Better a few hanged than a field of graves.

Torches lifted. Oil spat black upon the stones. The wind shifted and the fire leapt as if eager to obey. The timbers roared, stained glass burst, and the air filled with the stink of pitch and prayer alike. Illarion stood until the roof fell in, the light painting his scarred face gold and red. "The Fang was their altar," he said. "Now it is our warning."

The fire did the speaking.

We descended together, the three of us and the raven, down stone steps slick with spray and years. Below, the men were loading the last of the boats. The reliquary sat wrapped in its iron shroud, still breathing warmth into the air, still drawing eyes like lodestone draws iron. Some crossed themselves when they looked on it. Others only stared, as if waiting for judgment to fall.

The boats rode heavy in the water — coin and steel, sacred bone and bitter plunder all lashed together. Markov checked the knots with the care of a man who knew one loose rope could send fortunes to the bottom. Bogdan stood apart, his face turned north where Crown banners still burned, his lips moving in prayer or curse.

"Where do we make for?" I asked Illarion.

He gazed across the channels where the mist was lifting, revealing silver paths winding between the reeds. "North first, to Kravchenko. The Crown must see what we carry and what was burned here. From there, east to Driftlight. Ivan will have word of his son." His hand strayed toward the reliquary, then fell back. "After that… we will see."

Illarion's gaze moved between us, then to the reliquary's iron shell. Heat shimmered from it, the air trembling like breath before a prayer.

Bogdan's voice cut through the morning mist, steady as a priest at altar. "Fire judges."

Yelka inclined her head, the raven shifting on her shoulder, its claws rasping against leather. "Fire endures," she said softly.

Illarion's gaze swept from one to the other, then to where the boats waited heavy with spoils and bone. His own words came last, measured and absolute. "Then we follow where fire leads."

Markov gave a short laugh, sharp as a knife drawn in the dark. "Aye. And may the saints forgive us — fire's got a habit of leading men straight into graves."

No one answered him. The poles bit deep, the boats slid forward, and the marsh closed over what we had burned.

By the time we pushed from the quay, the Fang was burning behind us. The blaze climbed higher than the tower ever had, a column of black smoke spearing the morning sky. Even through the fog it could be seen for miles—the mark of judgment, or warning, depending who watched.

The boats moved heavy but sure, riding low beneath their burden. Morwen launched into the grey sky, her cry echoing off the ruin before she wheeled north, a black speck against the smoke.

We carried the saint's bones like thieves with stolen gold—men who had killed in holy places and claimed heaven's mandate. Illarion spoke of fire leading us, but I wondered if we were not simply following our own hunger, calling it destiny because that was easier than calling it choice.

The queen's summons waited ahead. Soroka and the *Burning Crown* moored in Driftlight's harbour, waiting to bear relics and prince north to Velgrad. But would Illarion honour that pact? Or spurn it, keeping fire and bone for himself, hungering to raise a kingdom out of ash?

The channels slipped behind, silver paths dwindling to mist. I thought of Dragomir's warning—the rope he named, lifeline or noose. Was Illarion rising toward a crown, or falling into fire? Strip him of Bogdan's gospel and perhaps there was still a prince to rule. But with the reliquary at his breast, each step he took seemed heavier, harder to turn aside.

We are all bound by our beasts, and by blood. Yelka sought judgment for a rotting kingdom, and judgment had already blackened her hands. Bogdan sought God's approval, and each prayer he spoke was written in ash. Illarion reached for a crown of fire, and it had already half consumed him.

And I—I sought nothing, for I had long since stopped believing I deserved to seek anything at all. Yet the beast still stirred in my blood, quieter now but never sleeping. Each time I loosed it, I called it necessity. But necessity is a door that opens only one way, and I had walked through it too many times to remember how it felt to keep it shut.

Destiny or choice, I could not say. The dark waters bore us north, and we told ourselves we steered the boats. Yet it seemed to me the current was stronger than any of us.

North, then. To what end?

Not peace — that was never promised us.

Only fire.

Appendices

Named Characters

The Core Company

- **Yaroslav Krovin** — Called *the Volkolak*

- **Prince Illarion** — Scarred heir to the northern throne, bearer of Saint Ilyin's fire

- **Markov Zaytsev** — trickster and survivor

- **Bogdan** — Priest and prophet of fire

- **Yelka** — Healer, with her wolf **Grendel** and raven **Morwen**.

The Crown and Its Instruments

- **King Mstislav** — Conqueror of the Isles

- **Queen Vezhena** — Cold architect of the realm's will

- **Dragomir** — The queen's spymaster

- **General Kravchenko**

Mirefast: Thanes, Governors, and Priests

- **Ivan the Broad** — Thane of Blackreef Fief (Mirefast)

- **Borislav** — Ivan's son

- **Lord Kozlov** — Governor of Blackmere province, seat of Ironholt.

- **Father Anatol** — Priest of Driftlight.

- **Marcus** — An old surgeon

The Brackfolk: Saints, Rebels, and Seers

- **Rogdai the Tidecaller** — Legendary Brack king from the age before conquest *(historical)*.

- **Dobrava**— Revered Volkhva burned after the fall *(historical)*.

- **Vrasida** — Elder Volkhva of the Fire Coven, keeper of the Drowned Flame.

- **Radalya** — Leader among the Brackfolk.

- **Kazimir** — Otets.

- **Kharna**— Volkhva.

The Army of the Burning Crown

- **Viktor, Andrei** — Illarion's personal guard

- **Mikhail the Butcher, Sava One-Eye, Petyr, Radovan, Krill, Zdravko** — Sotniki

- **Kendric, Veynar** — Desyatniki

- **Kazek** – prisoner who pledged devout fealty to Illarion

- **Velemir** — Banner-bearer

- **Luka, Stepan, Gavril, Danko, Milorad, Radoslav, Pavel, Olek, Feliks, Dmitri, Olen, Turo, Sreten** — Soldiers

- **Tomek** — A tall boy in Illarion's ranks.

The Fleet

- **Captain Soroka** — Commander of *The Burning Crown*, Illarion's warship.

- **Vedek** — Merchant captain of a *Zubatka*.

- **Tomas Krull** — Ship's *medicus*.

Ghosts and Absences

- **Anya** — Yaroslav's wife (*deceased*).

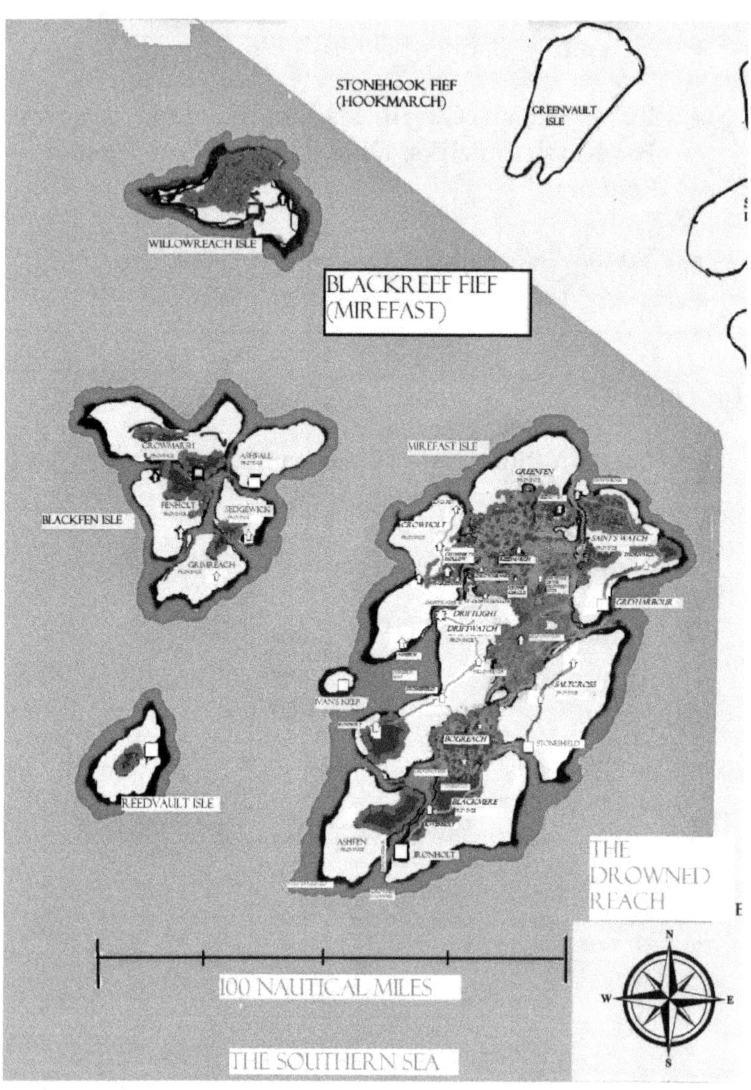
STONEHOOK FIEF
(HOOKMARCH)
GREENVAULT ISLE
WILLOWREACH ISLE
BLACKREEF FIEF
(MIREFAST)
CROWMARSH
ASHFALL
FENHOLT
SEDGEWICK
BLACKFEN ISLE
GRIMREACH
MIREFAST ISLE
GREENFEN
CROWHOLT
SAINTS WATCH
GREYHARBOUR
DRIFTLIGHT
DRIFTWATCH
SALTCROSS
IVAN'S KEEP
BOGREACH
STONEHELD
REEDVAULT ISLE
BLACKMERE
ASHFEN
IRONHOLT
THE DROWNED REACH
100 NAUTICAL MILES
THE SOUTHERN SEA
N
W
E
S

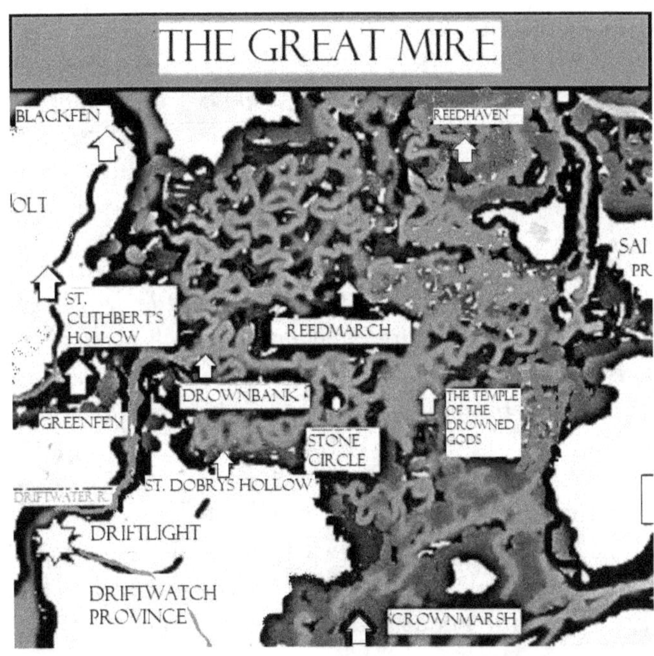

THE GREAT MIRE
BLACKFEN
REEDHAVEN
OLT
SAI
PR
ST.
CUTHBERT'S
HOLLOW
REEDMARCH
DROWNBANK
THE TEMPLE
OF THE
DROWNED
GODS
GREENFEN
STONE
CIRCLE
DRIFTWATER R.
ST. DOBRY'S HOLLOW
DRIFTLIGHT
DRIFTWATCH
PROVINCE
CROWNMARSH

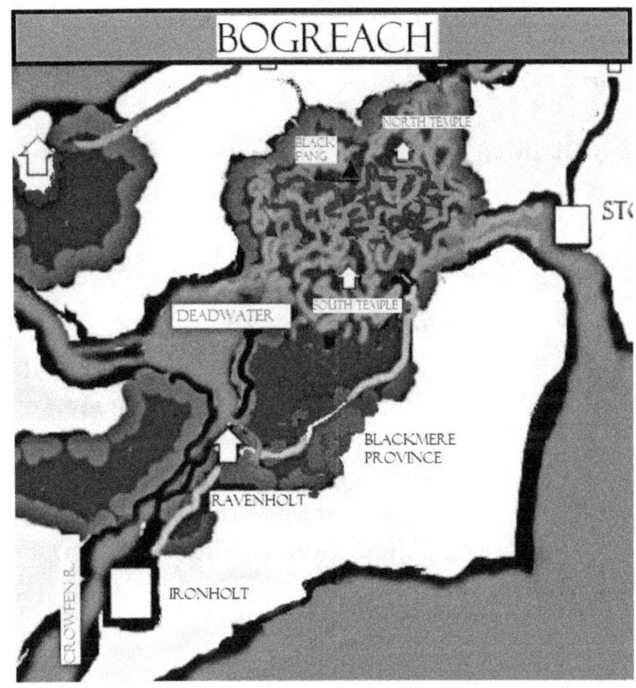

BOGREACH
NORTH TEMPLE
BLACK
FANG
ST
DEADWATER
SOUTH TEMPLE
BLACKMERE
PROVINCE
RAVENHOLT
CROWFEN R.
IRONHOLT

Encyclopaedia Brackica

A Treatise on the Post-Conquest Weapons and Armour of the Mirefast Brackfolk

---

"It is a mistake, often fatal, to mistake simplicity for weakness. The Brackfolk, who for centuries fought with little iron and less honour, have shown a talent for shaping the tools of survival into weapons of uncommon cunning. Conquest scattered their armies and drowned their temples, but the reeds have a way of growing back."

A brief historical framing of how Brack martial culture transformed after the conquest: tools into weapons, ritual objects repurposed, northern iron scavenged and reshaped, and how guerrilla needs shaped their arsenal.

I. Blades of the Mire

Serpent-Blades

The serpent-blade is the signature weapon of the Brackfolk Otets — a single-edged sabre with a flowing forward curve, broader near the tip to bite through reed and sinew alike. Its weight favours chopping strokes and short, brutal arcs, not the measured thrusts of northern swords. The grip is long, wrapped in river-leather, with a flared pommel for leverage and a simple guard to turn aside hooks. simple guard to turn aside hooks.

Otets scabbard these blades across the back rather than at the hip, an adaptation born of marsh fighting where reeds catch and footing falters. Drawn over the shoulder, the weapon clears without hindrance, ready for the sudden, low slashes that mark Brack style. Etched wave-spirals along the spine recall the marsh-serpent itself, and among the Otets each blade carries lineage — heirloom, oath, or curse. In northern hands the weapon feels ungainly; in the mire, wielded with both hands or one, it is as natural as a fishing spear.

Bog Knives and Reed-Cutters

The humble tools of the mire — knives for cutting peat, gutting fish, trimming reed — became weapons out of necessity rather than design. Short-bladed and broad, they lack the elegance of the serpent-blade but compensate with brutal practicality. In the close quarters of a stilt-village alley or reed-thick ambush channel, a knife that can split bone with a single backhand stroke is more valuable than any duelling sword.

Most are forged from scavenged iron, some little more than reshaped tools with new grips bound in seal-hide. Yet the Brack wield them with deadly skill. They strike low and often, seeking the femoral artery, the gut, or the armpit — any place where even a man in mail must bleed. Entire bands of marsh-fighters have been known to arm themselves with nothing more than these knives, using speed and the cover of the land to close distance before a northerner can bring his heavier blade to bear.

Hooked Knives ("Crookfangs")

If the serpent-blade is the weapon of the Otets warrior, the crookfang is the tool of the assassin and the ambusher. Its defining feature — a recurved tip not unlike a boar-snare hook — allows the wielder to catch a limb, shield-rim, or weapon haft and wrench it aside. In skilled hands it can pull a mailed man from a horse or drag a shield down to expose the throat.

Crookfangs are most often seen in the hands of Brack scouts and marsh-fighters who fight without formation or heraldry. They strike from punts, low in the water, pulling men overboard before finishing them in the mud. It is a dishonourable weapon by northern standards — but in the flooded channels of Mirefast, where footing is treacherous and the first blow decides all, dishonour is a luxury the Brack cannot afford.

Bone and Jade Ritual Blades

Though rare on the battlefield, ritual blades carved from bone or jade glass retain deep symbolic weight among the Brackfolk. Volkhvy priests use them for sacrifice, oath-binding, and other rites; yet in times of desperation they have been turned against northern throats. Lacking the durability of iron, they are brittle and often single-use, but their edges can be keen as a surgeon's scalpel.

What these weapons lack in battlefield utility they make up for in the terror they inspire. Prisoners executed with bone knives are said to carry their killers' curses into the afterlife — a superstition that has unsettled even hardened Crown soldiers. For this reason alone, Volkhvy warbands sometimes carry them into battle, less as practical weapons than as instruments of fear.

II. Bows and Projectiles

Reed Bows

The reed bow is a weapon of adaptation — born of scarcity, refined by centuries of marsh fighting. Too poor in iron and timber to rival the great northern yew bows, the Brackfolk learned to make their bows from what the land would yield: layers of river-reed and willow laminated with fish glue, backed with sinew stripped from seal or stag. The result is a short, light bow rarely exceeding four feet in length, quick to draw and quicker to loose.

Its range is unimpressive by northern standards — a hundred paces at most, and with limited penetrative power against heavy mail — but within the cramped confines of the mire it is a deadly tool. From the cover of a reed-bed or a low punt, Brack archers can rain a half-dozen shafts in the time a northern longbowman looses two. They aim not to kill outright but to cripple: the face, the forearm, the unarmoured thigh. Once wounded, a man floundering in knee-deep water is as good as dead.

Some reed bows are further adapted with bone or horn tips to resist moisture warping, and the finest are reinforced with narrow plates of bog-iron riveted into the grip. Such refinements remain rare and prized, often reserved for scouts or temple guards.

Bone-Tip Arrows

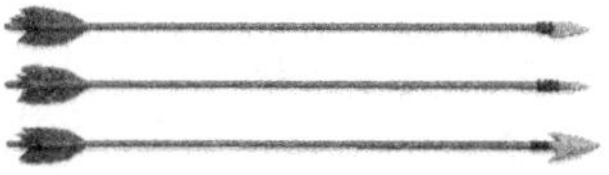

The scarcity of metal that defines Brack warfare has produced an astonishing array of alternative projectiles. Bone-tipped arrows remain the most common — carved from the ribs of boar or stag, fire-hardened, and fletched with marsh-fowl feathers. They are light, cheap, and easy to make in large numbers. Against plate they are useless, but few northern soldiers wade into the mire in full harness; against leather or bare flesh they tear deep and leave ragged wounds that fester quickly in the damp.

The Brack make extensive use of *drag arrows*, their barbs carved backward to resist extraction. Soldiers struck by these often die not from blood loss but from infection or drowning as they struggle to pull free. Reports from the early years of the conquest describe volleys of such arrows loosed not at the front line but at the retreating wounded — a deliberate tactic to fill the shallows with dying men and stall an advance.

Barbed Swarm Darts

Lighter than arrows and deadly at shorter ranges, the so-called *swarm darts* are thrown by hand or hurled from reed-slings in dense volleys. Barely a foot in length and tipped with carved bone or crude bog-iron, they are not meant to kill individually but to overwhelm. A well-timed swarm can shred a formation's exposed faces and forearms in the space of a breath.

The darts' true menace lies in what coats them. Brack fighters smear the tips with mire-rot — a stagnant slime of decayed plant and animal matter — or with the bile of marsh-serpents, both of which fester into lethal infections if not swiftly treated. Northern physicians recommend immediate cauterization or amputation, but in the confusion of a marsh ambush, few have that luxury. Even when they do not kill, the fear of them often breaks discipline faster than steel.

III. Throwing Weapons and Ambush Tools

Marsh Javelins ("Water-Spears")

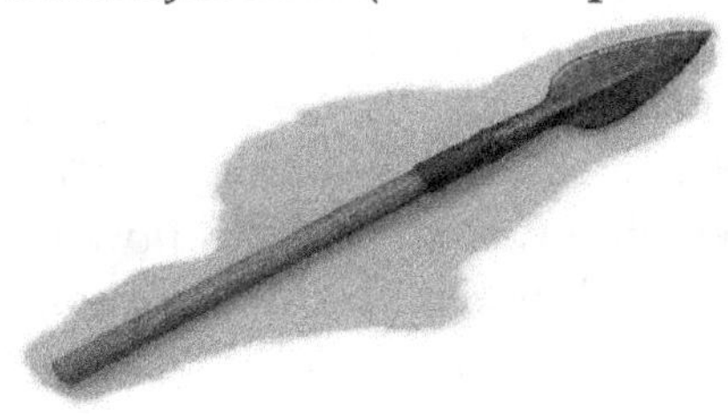

The so-called *water-spears* are the simplest of Brack missile weapons — short, heavy javelins balanced for overhand throws from punts or shallow footing. Their broad, leaf-shaped heads are designed less to pierce plate than to drive deep through leather, seal-hide, or flesh, and the added weight helps them punch through wet reed screens or the wicker sides of northern river craft.

At close range, a skilled thrower can hurl a water-spear with enough force to unseat a man from horseback or punch through a rower's ribs. The Brack favour ambushes launched from cover — a dozen spears arcing out of the reeds before vanishing back into silence. Northerners unaccustomed to such tactics often mistake the javelins for crude peasant arms. They learn too late that a man floundering with a shaft through his thigh is as effective at halting an advance as a dead one.

Hooked Casting Blades ("Gaffs")

Unique to the mire are the hooked throwing knives known as *gaffs*, crescent-shaped blades with recurved points that snag in whatever they strike. Too light to kill outright, they serve instead to maim and unbalance. A gaff in the calf drops a man into the mud. One in the rigging tangles a sail. One hooked into a shield rim can wrench it from a soldier's grasp at the worst possible moment.

The Brack throw them not singly but in clusters, each carried in a reed-woven bandolier across the chest. A dozen knives loosed in a heartbeat create chaos: men stumble, lines falter, shields drop. Veteran Crown marines now fix greaves and vambraces more tightly than before, knowing that a single hooked blade can pull them off their feet — and in the mire, to fall is often to drown.

Eel-Forks

Adapted from the fishing tools that feed the reed-villages, the eel-fork is a wickedly effective close-range weapon. It consists of a short haft tipped with three or four prongs, each barbed backward like a fish-hook. Originally used to spear eels or pull tangled nets from the water, it was turned on invaders during the first years of resistance and has remained a staple of Brack ambush craft ever since.

The fork's true strength lies not in killing but in control. A thrust into a horse's flank brings the beast down thrashing; a jab at a man's knee or ankle pins him in place long enough for a knife or dart to finish the work. Against cavalry, eel-forks have proven especially deadly. More than one northern charge into the shallows has ended in disaster when horses, screaming and speared, threw their riders into the mire to be dragged under.

Tethered Hooks

Perhaps the crudest of Brack ambush tools, the tethered hook is also among the most feared. It is nothing more than a length of rope or rawhide attached to a heavy iron hook, yet in marsh fighting its uses are many. From punts, Brack fighters cast them into the rigging of ships to foul oars or tear sails. From the reeds, they drag northern soldiers from decks or horses into the sucking mud.

There is a certain ritual to their use. Two men will often cast together: one to hook a shield rim or pauldron, the other to yank hard and topple the target. Once in the water, the same hook that felled the foe becomes the tool that drowns him, pulling him deeper until the mire swallows him whole. Northern manuals now warn captains never to linger near reed-banks or low punts, yet even forewarned, few are prepared when the hooks fly.

IV. Fire and Alchemy

Witchfire Urns

Of all the weapons forged in the drowned lands, none has inspired such terror — nor demanded such respect — as the witchfire. Known in northern records as *ignis insatiabilis* ("the fire that cannot be quenched"), this alchemical compound is both the most terrible invention of the Brack resistance and the one most poorly understood by Crown scholars. It is a substance that burns upon water, clings to flesh, and devours wood, leather, and steel alike until nothing remains but ash and smoke.

The witchfire is contained and deployed in clay or bronze urns, sealed with wax and pitch to prevent premature ignition. The mixture itself is believed to be composed of rendered animal fat, peat-oil, and saltpeter, thickened with tar drawn from the deep bogs. Yet there is more to it than mere craft: captured urns have shown subtle signs of ritual preparation — inscribed spirals and serpent sigils carved into the clay, fragments of bone or ash sealed within — suggesting that the Brack regard witchfire not as a weapon alone but as a sacred force. Among Volkhvy covens, it is said that *the fire remembers,* and that to wield it without proper rites is to invite ruin.

On the battlefield, witchfire has changed the nature of war in Mirefast. Urns are hurled from punts into the hulls of northern ships, where they burst and spill their burning contents across planks and water alike. Once lit, the fire cannot be doused by water; attempts to smother it with sand or wet hides often fail, as the substance clings and spreads like oil. Reed-beds set alight by witchfire burn until the bog itself turns to smoke, and ships struck by it are all but doomed unless their crews cast themselves into the water — where many drown before the flames relent.

Mire-Poisons and Toxins.

Beyond witchfire the Brack wield quieter alchemy: poisons smeared on barbed arrows, reed-shafts and short blades. The commonest, nicknamed **mire-rot**, is a mash of bog-berries, marsh-fungus and serpent gall. It rarely kills swiftly; instead wounds fester, fever spreads, and the victim's cries rot discipline as surely as the flesh. A sharper mix, the **ash-acid**, is brewed from peat ash, vinegar, nettles and shellfish. It burns tissues, hastens blood-poisoning, and turns even shallow cuts crippling.

Preparation is half-craft, half-rite. Volkhvy covens grind and ferment in secrecy, sealing jars with bone or smoke so each batch bears the weight of oath and curse. Northern surgeons advise cauterization or amputation, but the damp undo such remedies. Thus a Brack arrow, even blunted, can be as decisive as steel: wounds that will not close, men who cannot march, and armies undone by the mire itself.

V. Armour of the Drowned

Seal-Hide Coats

True to the land that shaped them, Brack armour is not the armour of knights or kings. It is built not to impress in courts or endure a siege-wall but to survive in mud, water, and silence. The most common defence of a Brack fighter is the seal-hide coat: overlapping layers of tanned hide cut thin for flexibility, treated with fish-oil and wax to resist water. It clings close to the body and moves easily with the fighter's stride, allowing a man to wade, swim, or vanish into reed and shadow without the weight that would drag a northerner down.

Seal-hide will not turn a broadsword nor stop a spear thrust — it is armour of evasion, not defiance. Yet it dulls the bite of darts and bone-tips, blunts slashing blows, and, perhaps most crucially, it does not rot or seize when soaked. Crown soldiers who mocked such "skins" as peasant rags soon learned the folly of marching in heavy mail that pulled them under with every misstep. Many a drowned knight was found still chained to his own hauberk, while the Brack around him slipped through the channels like eels.

Bone-Bound Breastplates

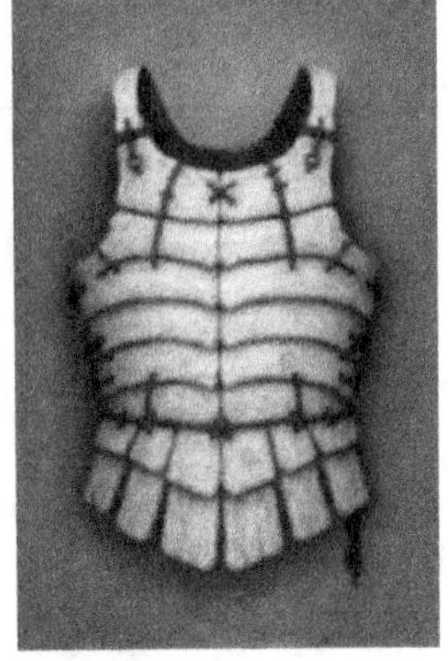

While rare, some Brack warriors — often temple guardians or chieftains of resistance bands — wear heavier defences known as bone-bound breastplates. These are constructed from the shoulder and rib bones of great beasts, boiled and scraped clean, then bound together with waxed cord and set upon a backing of hide. Though primitive in appearance, they are surprisingly resilient: a well-made breastplate can deflect glancing sword-strokes and even resist the thrust of a narrow spear-head.

Their true value, however, is not purely defensive. Bone has deep ritual resonance in Brack belief, and armour made from the remains of the drowned or the slain is said to carry their strength. Crown scholars scoff at such superstition, but it is notable that men wearing these breastplates fight with a ferocity disproportionate to their number, as if convinced that the dead themselves fight alongside them. More than one northern patrol has broken against a handful of such warriors who refused to yield even when pierced through.

Hybrid Harnesses

The long decades since the conquest have produced a final, telling adaptation: the hybrid harness. These piecemeal suits combine scavenged elements of northern armour — pauldrons, greaves, gorgets — with traditional Brack construction. A lamellar vest of bog-iron plates might be stitched over seal-hide, or a salvaged steel pauldron strapped to a reed-woven cuirass. Such harnesses rarely match and never gleam, but they testify to the Brack talent for salvage and repurposing.

These composite armours offer slightly improved protection without sacrificing mobility, though they remain far lighter than the panoplies favoured by Velgrad knights. The Brack show little interest in adopting shields or helms of northern design; both hinder their agility in the mire and prove more liability than asset in water. Even their hybrid armour speaks to the same principle that shapes all Brack war-craft: what cannot endure the swamp is left behind. Only what bends and adapts survives.

Final Remarks

It is tempting to dismiss the armour of the drowned folk as crude — to measure it against the forged plate and linked mail of the north and find it wanting. Yet such judgment betrays a failure to understand the land itself. Mirefast swallows weight and punishes rigidity. It rewards speed, silence, and resilience over splendour. In that world, the Brack have created defences that are not merely armour but *adaptations* — armour shaped by water as much as by war. In the end, their greatest protection is not what they wear but how they fight: unseen, unburdened, and gone before the weight of northern steel can drag them down.

Ordered Timeline of Conquest of the Isles

(Winters Before the Common Era)

27th Winter — Grey Isle Fief
Formerly the **Gvazdari of Boarcliff Kingdom**. First to be broken, its stone fastness shattered by northern steel.

25th Winter — Sealwatch Fief
Formerly the **Straitborn of Straitsward Kingdom**. Subjugated after bitter fighting along the channels, the straits bound by Crown garrisons.

22nd Winter — Stonehook Fief
Formerly the **Stonehook Builders of Hookmarch Kingdom**. Yielded without war, its masons trading sovereignty for survival.

16th Winter — Blackreef Fief
Formerly the **Brackfolk of Mirefast Kingdom**. Conquered only after years of attrition, its drowned temples silenced but not forgotten.

10th Winter — Strayhorn Fief
Formerly the **Voryani of Hornlands Kingdom**. Fell when its horse-lords were broken in the snow.

5th Winter — Stormgrave Fief
Formerly the **Survivors of Stormward Kingdom**. Conquered after storm and famine left its fleets ruined.

1st Winter — Splitfang Fief
Formerly the **Fangborn of Fanghold Kingdom**. Last to fall; its fang-spire blackened, its oath torn in blood.

Part I: The Folkloric Beasts

Leshy

The *Leshy* is the forest spirit of Slavic myth, guardian of beasts and trees, often appearing as a tall man with grass and bark for hair, whose voice mimics familiar sounds to lure wanderers astray. He is a trickster and a keeper both: hunters would make offerings to avoid being led in circles. In the novel, the Leshy is not shown directly, only whispered about in Bogreach, where soldiers fear laughter and doubled paths. This reflects the folkloric role of Leshy as a presence felt rather than seen, the embodiment of forest law.

Marsh-Cat / Morskoi Kot

Slavic folklore includes tales of uncanny cats tied to water and marshes, sometimes linked to the *domovoi* (house spirit) or as omens of death. The term *morskoi kot* literally means "sea-cat" and in older folklore could refer to seals or large predatory creatures glimpsed at rivers' mouths. In *The Drowned Oath*, the Marsh-Cat is a black predator haunting the reeds. It functions as an omen more than an enemy, recalling how in Slavic superstition cats — especially black ones — mark boundaries between the living and the dead.

Morskoi Zmey

The *zmey* (dragon or serpent) is a familiar figure across Slavic myth, often depicted as a many-headed dragon fought by saints or heroes. In East Slavic tradition, *Morskoi Zmey* literally means "Sea Serpent," a creature of the deep waters. Unlike Western dragons, zmeyi are less associated with hoarding gold and more with elemental force — fire, storm, or flood. In *The Drowned Oath*, the Morskoi Zmey appears not as a visible dragon but as a presence summoned by blood offering in Mirefast. This adaptation emphasizes the folkloric belief that waters are appeased with sacrifice and that blood poured into a river can stir powers beneath.

Rusalka

The *Rusalka* is one of the most famous Slavic female spirits. Originally linked to fertility and water, by the 19th century she became associated with the souls of drowned young women, often suicides or betrayed brides. They lure men into the water with beauty, laughter, or song, then drown them. In *The Drowned Oath*, Rusalki are never directly seen, but soldiers hear women's laughter in the reeds, and men vanish into mist when they follow the voices. This alludes to the folkloric danger of temptation and the fear of women's spirits bound to water.

Strigoi

The *strigoi* are revenants of Romanian and Slavic lore — restless dead who rise from graves to sap vitality, or living men cursed to wander in half-life. They are precursors to later vampire traditions. Folklore describes them as thin, pale, with open eyes, lying in coffins as though alive. In *The Drowned Oath*, Illarion is likened to a strigoi when he lies with eyes open, fevered and unresponsive, more corpse than prince. The comparison roots his condition in dread: whether he is living, dead, or something caught between.

Vodyanoi / The Drowned

The *Vodyanoi* is among the most enduring figures in Slavic water-myth. He is a male water spirit, usually imagined as a naked old man with a frog's face and greenish beard, dwelling in rivers, lakes, and ponds. He drowns men, particularly millers and fishermen who cross him. Over time the figure broadened: in Russian and Ukrainian villages, *utoplenniki* ("the drowned ones") were said to rise as his servants. The Drowned of *The Drowned Oath* draw on this latter tradition — not the frog-faced lord, but the drowned dead animated in his service, bloated and grasping, embodiments of death by water.

Volkolak

The Slavic *volkolak* (literally "wolf-pelt") is the analogue of the werewolf, though older and broader in meaning. In some regions it meant a shapeshifter who donned wolf skin; in others, it referred to men cursed to become wolves for a set number of years, or even to the lunar eclipse (when the "wolf" devoured the sun or moon). In the narrative, Yaroslav calls himself Volkolak not because he changes shape, but to claim the deeper folkloric truth: he is a man who has become beast in deed and in spirit, feared by Brackfolk as much as wolves were feared in field and forest.

Part II: The People of Rite and Order

Chernoknizhnika

The term *chernoknizhnik* (plural *chernoknizhniki*) comes from Russian folk speech and literally means "black-book man." It was used in the late medieval and early modern period to describe a sorcerer or wizard thought to own a *chernaya kniga* — a "black book" of spells, charms, and forbidden prayers. In Orthodox polemic, this was a label of heresy, sometimes attached to village cunning-men who practiced forbidden rites alongside Christian ritual. The figure blends fear of literacy (books as sources of hidden power) with fear of illicit knowledge.

In *The Drowned Oath*, the Chernoknizhnika are imagined as Brackfolk adepts of forbidden scripture, fusing drowned memory with corrupted fragments of saints' texts. They represent the terror of knowledge turned against orthodoxy, sorcery by way of scripture. Historically the name is real, but their organized role in the Mirefast setting is fictional — a dramatization of how heresy and book-magic were feared in the Slavic world.

Otets

The word *Otets* simply means "father" in Slavic languages, and in Orthodox practice it is the common address for a priest. It is not in itself a mythological term. In the historical record, *otets* designates a spiritual father, confessor, or elder, without any martial meaning.

In the novels, the Brackfolk *Otets* are re-imagined as the martial half of their religious tradition — ascetic father-teachers who not only preached but also trained children in sacred forms of endurance and combat. This is an invention rather than a piece of folklore, but it draws plausibility from the wider Slavic and Byzantine world, where monks sometimes fought, and where discipline of the body and discipline of the soul were linked.

By giving them this name, the story binds priesthood to paternal authority and endurance. Where the Volkhvy embody vision and sorcery, the Otets stand for memory and law, their "forms" passed from father to child as both prayer and weapon.

Volkhvy

The *Volkhvy* (singular *volkhv*) are drawn from authentic Slavic history. In Old East Slavic the term means "magus" or "sorcerer," and medieval chronicles describe them as the pagan priests and seers of Kievan Rus'. They presided over sacrifices, interpreted omens, and were believed to command storms or prophecy fates. When Christianity spread, the volkhvy led uprisings in defense of the old gods, which is why Orthodox scribes condemned them as deceivers and rebels.

In *The Drowned Oath*, the Brackfolk Volkhvy preserve this role as guardians of ancient rites. They are not harmless keepers of memory but dangerous in both vision and deed. The Fire Volkhvy in particular, led by Vrasida, draw on the darker folklore of conjurers who could call flame or ruin crops. Thus the novels amplify a historical figure into a mythic order: part priest, part sorcerer, part revolutionary.

Znakharka

The word *znakharka* (feminine; *znakhar'* masculine) means literally "knower" or "one who knows." In Slavic folk culture, it refers to a village healer, wise-woman, or herbalist — sometimes trusted, sometimes feared. Znakharki were midwives, bone-setters, gatherers of herbs, and preservers of charms. Orthodox authorities often tolerated them if their cures were practical, but condemned them when they slipped into incantation or folk ritual.

In *The Drowned Oath*, Yelka is explicitly named *znakharka*, and the title signals her ambiguous standing. To the Brackfolk she is healer, seer, and intermediary with beasts; to northerners she is perilously close to witch. This tension reflects the historic ambivalence: the znakharka was indispensable in peasant life yet always half-suspect, straddling the border of medicine and sorcery.

Sotnik / Sotniki

The term *sotnik* (literally "hundred-man") is historical, drawn from medieval Slavic military organization. A *sotnya* was a unit of roughly one hundred soldiers, and the *sotnik* its commander. Records from Kievan Rus' and later Cossack hosts preserve the role: a middle-ranking officer responsible for discipline, provisions, and battle-plan execution.

In *The Drowned Oath*, the sotnik is the field officer who "owns the plan and the blame." His authority is weighty, his failures visible. Readers may think of a company commander: accountable for the lives of his hundred and for the shape of the fight itself.

Druzhinnik / Druzhinniki

The word *druzhina* means "retinue" or "band," and in medieval Rus' it referred to the armed household of a prince. A *druzhinnik* was thus a sworn retainer, a professional warrior who pledged loyalty to his lord in return for pay, gifts, and status. Chroniclers describe them as the hardened core of early Slavic armies: experienced fighters who could both advise and command.

In *The Drowned Oath*, the druzhinniki are the oath-bound veterans who steady a wavering line. They represent the continuity of professional soldiery: not peasants pressed into levy but men trained by years at a prince's side, carrying both scars and authority.

Desyatnik / Desyatniki

From the word *desyat* ("ten"), the *desyatnik* was the leader of a small file or section, usually ten men. Historical sources show the term in Rus' tax and military records, where the *desyatnik* supervised not only men in arms but also households grouped in tens for levy and tribute. In war, he was the lowest officer, closer to his men than to the princes above.

In *The Drowned Oath*, the desyatnik is the sergeant of the line. He drills the boys, counts heads, and enforces the orders of the sotnik. His authority is personal, immediate, and often resented, for he is the one who must make boys into soldiers under the eyes of their kin.

Danilo

Patron of: Warriors, brave deaths

Symbol: Dented helm

Lore: Once a boy-soldier who fell defending a retreat, Danilo was raised to sainthood by the survivors he saved. His helm, caved in by a war-hammer, is preserved in Velgrad's crypt. Warriors invoke him not for victory, but for a worthy death — no shame, no surrender. His rites are grave and spare: a thumb pressed to the brow, a name spoken only once.

Dobrina

Patron of: Healing, birth, practical mercy

Symbol: Crossroads

Lore: Midwife and wanderer, Dobrina carried herbs in a bone cup and walked barefoot between plague villages. Her death came nursing strangers. Crossroads are marked with her sign — a woven thread or a jar of fennel seeds — where choices must be made. She is called upon in childbirth, pestilence, and grief's wake.

Dobroslav

Patron of: Farming, rural endurance

Symbol: A hand scattering grain

Lore: During the seven-year famine, Dobroslav refused to eat until every child in his village had been fed. His fields alone bore fruit — a miracle or curse, no one knows. Raiders slew him planting spring barley. Each spring, the first seed is cast in his name. His cult remains strongest along the western isles, where soil is poor and hunger constant.

Dobry

Patron of: Bridges, crossings, safe passage

Symbol: Rope or planks bound with nails

Lore: Said to have been a ferryman who carried refugees across the marsh-channels until raiders drowned him with stones. His shrines are built at fords and bridges, marked with ropes and nails hammered into posts. Travelers whisper his name before crossing water or thresholds, seeking safe passage.

Ilyin

Patron of: Fire, judgement, martyrdom

Symbol: Teeth, bones

Lore: Burned alive beneath the old cathedral, Ilyin was said to rise again in flame, screaming warnings that came true. His relics blacken wood but do not burn. Fire-walkers and fanatics claim his blessing. Others call him the Burned One — no longer martyr, but omen. His symbol is feared on storm-prayers, carved with blood into shipbeams.

Kosma

Patron of: Justice, lawful vengeance, judgement

Symbol: Chain, fetters

Lore: Judge and penitent, Kosma was chained to the altar until he named every man he'd wronged — and forgave each name aloud. Salt lines are laid in his name to ward deceit; night vigils kept with iron and silence. His cult is strict and somber: no candles, no indulgence. Only truth, weight, and waiting.

Mikhail

Patron of: Soldiers, captains, guardianship

Symbol: Sword raised upright

Lore: Once a captain who stood alone at the breach until dawn, his men slain around him. He fell when the sun rose, but his stand bought victory. In his name, swords are lifted point-upward before a march, never downward. His cult is strong among officers who must guard lives with their own.

Mikula

Patron of: Oaths

Symbol: Cairn

Lore: When called to raise arms against kin, Mikula laid down his sword, knelt upon the threshold, and was slain by his own cousin. They say he died smiling, bound to his vow.

His cairn is kept by those who swear hard oaths — stones laid in silence, blood or salt between them. To break such a vow is to call his curse.

Ognevara

Patron of: Flame, torches, light in darkness

Symbol: Torch or brazier

Lore: Once a marsh-spirit who carried fire between villages, feared as both guide and destroyer. After the conquest, she became Saint Ognevara, and her torch a holy sign. Church rituals incorporate Brack traditions of reeds bound and lit in her name to guard children from drowning. She is also invoked when light must be carried through storm or battle.

Olexa

Patron of: War

Symbol: Red-marked weapons

Lore: Banner-bearer of the last stand at Narven Gate, Olexa bled from five wounds but did not fall. Her banner, red with blood, rallied the broken host. Her symbol is daubed in red ash on spear-points before battle. Warriors say her ghost walks behind those who hold the line. Never a leader — always the one who stayed.

Petron

Patron of: Messengers, omens, words carried

Symbol: Raven feather, sealed letter

Lore: The Brack speak of a dusk-spirit that takes the shape of a raven, bearing warnings across marsh and sky. Feathers left on doorsteps were taken as its touch — news of death, or reprieve. After conquest the church renamed it Saint Petron, a hermit who carried letters in the plague years and died on the road with his last message still bound to his wrist. They teach that a raven finished his task, pecking at a door until the letter was read. To the faithful, Petron is patron of runners, sailors, and all who trust their lives to words delivered. To the Brack, the raven is still what it was: omen first, messenger second.

Radegund

Patron of: Perseverance, endurance in suffering, widows, towns under trial

Symbol: Ice, snow-marked lintels

Lore: Wife of a convert, Radegund walked forty miles through blizzard to halt the wrongful execution of her husband. She arrived too late — he was already slain — and collapsed, frozen at the scaffold. Yet her endurance through storm, guided only by faith, was taken as miracle. Her martyrdom inspired conversion, and churches bear her name where winters bite hardest. She is invoked when endurance is demanded: widows keeping hearths, towns besieged, the sick holding out against cold nights.

Stepan

Patron of: Endurance, long suffering

Symbol: Blood

Lore: Stepan was dragged behind an oxcart through the tidepools of Dunlev before he spoke a single complaint. His blood marked each hollow in the stone. In his name, penitents walk barefoot through salt shallows, bearing no burden but pain. He is not prayed to, only endured. His grace lies in silence.

Vira

Patron of: Hearth, widows, home

Symbol: Key

Lore: Vira was a widow who gave her door's key to every refugee who passed, until nothing remained. They found her starved but smiling, holding a child she'd hidden from raiders. Her image stands at thresholds — carved from bone or wood, tucked into lintels. In her name, salt and ash are placed at windows when the sea winds rise.

Yarila

Patron of: Drowned, exile, fog

Symbol: Driftwood, black shells

Lore: Some say Yarila was never a man, only a name murmured by those lost at sea. Others claim she was a mother whose child was taken by the tide — and she followed. Lanterns are lit in her name when ships depart, placed in hollowed driftwood and set adrift. She answers not prayers, but grief. Her voice is the foghorn no one hears until too late.

Yevstafiy

Patron of: Drowned, sailors

Symbol: Driftwood cross

Lore: A sailor who bound himself to his mast as the storm claimed his ship, Yevstafiy was found days later — dead, but unbroken. In his name, driftwood crosses are set afloat with candles when a ship is lost. His blessing is endurance, not rescue. Sailors say he walks the deeps, dragging drowned men home.

Zorian

Patron of: Watcher, thresholds, oaths

Symbol: Charred wood, iron nails

Lore: Once Zoryan, god of the liminal path, he stood where one thing ended and another began: hearth to road, river to sea, life to death. The priests of Velgrad made him saint, setting his image above nave doors, a stern figure with hand outstretched to weigh the truth of those who passed. Brack still whisper the older name. For them, no man lies at a threshold: he speaks truly, or he is cast out. Oaths sworn at a gate are said to bind tighter than blood, for Zorian hears. His tokens are charred beams and iron nails — remnants of what bars or opens a way. To swear falsely at the Watcher's gate is to bar yourself from every other.

Author's Note

I began writing *The Saint's Reckoning* when I embraced my own voice. I am not young, and I have always told stories — but now I tell old man stories. With age the tales change. They are no longer about *what will I become?* or *boy meets girl*. I have become. I found my wife, my work, raised children. I have built many things and broken many things.

We have gods and myths and epics because most of us are not heroes, yet something in us strains toward greatness. And sometimes we do achieve greatness — though rarely because we set out to be great, but because we work and strive, love and protect, bleed and weep. No one gets away unscathed. In the midst of all that, with luck, we leave something behind for others to speak of when we are gone. The beauty of life lies in both its joy and its suffering — for together they forge the tales we leave behind.

The stories that matter do more than entertain. They speak a truth. Yaroslav Krovin, my *volkolak*, speaks that truth for me — or rather, I speak through him about the things that endure: the oaths that matter, even if we are drowned for keeping them.

Thank you for reading *The Drowned Oath*. I plan for three more books in the series. Then, with luck, we will find out what happens when Saint Ilyin is assembled — or perhaps discover that the bones never mattered at all.

If you are interested in finding out more about me and my novels, please visit www.harwoodjones.com and leave a comment. I'd love to hear from you.

— Troy

Books in the Saint's Reckoning Series

Book One: The Oathbearer, A Prophecy of Flame

Book Two: The Drowned Oath

www.ingramcontent.com/pod-product-compliance
Lightning Source LLC
Chambersburg PA
CBHW070731120726
47910CB00001B/57